"Forg[otten]...
first con[cern]...
you from...

She im[patiently waved this away.] "You left your hirelings to die."

The elf lifted one shoulder in a dismissive shrug. "They are human."

"I am half human," Arilyn retorted.

"You are also half dead," Elaith pointed out.

Drow

Candlelight shimmered down the sword's rune-carved length and winked with ominous golden light along its double edge. Liriel's dagger, which was long and keen and coated with drow sleeping poison for good measure, seemed woefully inadequate beside it. The wisest course would probably be to toss a fireball and settle the damages with the innkeeper later. It'd be messy, but there was something to be said for a quick resolution in such matters.

Demon

"Since you know something of my history with mortals, you are no doubt aware that I breed only twin-born sons. They will look alike, but one will favor his sire. You won't know *which* one, of course. We are tossing the dice, you and I, with much riding on the outcome."

This was the moment Renwick had dreaded. Was it possible to lie to a demon? Could Yamarral hear the nervous quickening of his heart, smell the stench of falsehood in his sweat?

Novels by Elaine Cunningham

Songs & Swords

Book I
ELFSHADOW

Book II
ELFSONG

Book III
SILVER SHADOWS

Book IV
THORNHOLD

Book V
THE DREAM SPHERES

Book VI
RECLAMATION
March 2008

Starlight & Shadows

Book I
DAUGHTER OF THE DROW

Book II
TANGLED WEBS

Book III
WINDWALKER

EVERMEET: ISLAND OF THE ELVES

CITY OF SPLENDORS: A WATERDEEP NOVEL
(with Ed Greenwood)

T70437

THE BEST OF THE
REALMS
Book III

The Stories of
Elaine Cunningham

Edited by
Philip Athans and Erin Evans

WHITE PLAINS HIGH SCHOOL
MEDIA CENTER

THE BEST OF THE REALMS
Book III

The Stories of Elain Cunningham

©2007 Wizards of the Coast, Inc.

All characters in this book are fictitious. Any resemblance to actual persons, living or dead, is purely coincidental.

This book is protected under the copyright laws of the United States of America. Any reproduction or unauthorized use of the material or artwork contained herein is prohibited without the express written permission of Wizards of the Coast, Inc.

Published by Wizards of the Coast, Inc. FORGOTTEN REALMS, WIZARDS OF THE COAST, and their respective logos are trademarks of Wizards of the Coast, Inc., in the U.S.A. and other countries.

Printed in the U.S.A.

The sale of this book without its cover has not been authorized by the publisher. If you purchased this book without a cover, you should be aware that neither the author nor the publisher has received payment for this "stripped book."

Cover art by Wayne England
First Printing: May 2007

9 8 7 6 5 4 3 2 1

ISBN: 978-0-7869-4288-6
620-95954740-001-EN

U.S., CANADA,	EUROPEAN HEADQUARTERS
ASIA, PACIFIC, & LATIN AMERICA	Hasbro UK Ltd
Wizards of the Coast, Inc.	Caswell Way
P.O. Box 707	Newport, Gwent NP9 0YH
Renton, WA 98057-0707	GREAT BRITAIN
+1-800-324-6496	Save this address for your records.

Visit our web site at www.wizards.com

CONTENTS

THE KNIGHTS OF SAMULAR 1

THE BARGAIN 41

ELMINSTER'S JEST 73

THE MORE THINGS CHANGE 77

THE DIRECT APPROACH 95

SECRETS OF BLOOD,
    SPIRITS OF THE SEA 121

THE GREAT HUNT 153

SPEAKING WITH THE DEAD 173

STOLEN DREAMS 207

FIRE IS FIRE 229

POSSESSIONS 251

A LITTLE KNOWLEDGE 279

GAMES OF CHANCE 303

TRIBUTE 323

ANSWERED PRAYERS 329

Published for the first time in this volume.

THE KNIGHTS OF SAMULAR

You always learn something interesting at fantasy conventions. One year I found out there was an ongoing audition for the last book in the Harper series. This was originally planned as a series of stand-alone novels, but things quickly became unwieldy as books bred sequels, trilogies, and sub-series, and occasionally crossed over to link with other trilogies or series. Any product tree drawn under those circumstances would probably end up looking like something a toddler whipped up with an Etch-a-Sketch. So the plan was made to end the series with a "pivot book" that would introduce characters and plot threads to be developed through future books and game products.

It didn't work out that way. Editorial direction shifted, and Thornhold, *which was written to be that pivot book with all kinds of loose threads for other authors to pick up and develop, was published as the last Harpers book. Period. Readers were justifiably confused. I chalked it up to a learning experience, vowed never to write another book that was quite so open-ended, and resigned myself to leaving a lot of unanswered questions.*

Then, rather unexpectedly, I got the opportunity to revisit some of the Thornhold *characters in* Reclamation, *the sixth and final book in the Songs & Swords series. Another door opened when Peter Archer suggested that I write a follow-up to* Thornhold *for the new short story for this anthology.*

This story endeavors to tie up a few of those loose threads and to shed some light on the more puzzling aspects of the novel. It doesn't revisit all the characters or answer all the questions, but it puts several of the threads on a path toward resolution.

THE KNIGHTS OF SAMULAR

*17 Flamerule, the Year of the
Enchanted Trail (925 DR)
Griffenwing Keep, a mountain fortress
near Ascalhorn*

The demon was not at all what Renwick Caradoon had expected.

Massive bat wings, scales the color of molten lava, terror and evil incarnate—the grimoire had hinted darkly of such things. Renwick, given his admittedly small talent for magic, would have been content with a whiff of brimstone and a tentacle or two. To his surprise, the creature standing in a circle of painstakingly drawn symbols looked more like a mildly disgruntled scholar than an agent of evil.

"Have I the honor of addressing the great incubus Yamarral, Lord of Chaos and Carnality?" Renwick inquired cautiously.

In response, the demon held up the book he'd

been perusing, displaying the scene vividly painted on night-black parchment. The illustration was *moving*, and a glance at the writhing figures was all the answer Renwick required.

"You cannot summon a demon without speaking his true name," Yamarral observed as he tucked the book into his plain brown tunic. "Do you doubt the laws of magic, or is this your notion of polite conversation?"

Common enough words, and the clipped cadence indicated a very human state of annoyance, but ah, the voice! Music lurked in those deep, rounded tones, and the accent, both charming and elusive, seemed strangely enhanced by the demon's nondescript human appearance. Renwick had heard it said that men were seduced by their eyes and women by their ears. By that measure, innocent and impressionable little Nimra was all but damned.

No, Renwick told himself sternly. Nimra was descended from the Guardians of Ascalhorn. She was a true scion of her illustrious forebears, and a paladin's daughter. She had grown up at her grandsire's knee, her eyes shining with wonder as Maerstar spun tales of magical treasures the Caradoon family had collected for generations. The old bard had staggered out of the ruins of Ascalhorn with a single precious book, but his stories of the family legacy had set Nimra's soul aflame. Renwick had trained her for the coming task. She was resolved to see it through; she would survive with her virtue intact.

"I wish to strike a bargain," Renwick began.

Yamarral smirked. "And what boon do you offer me, little wizard? Perhaps you would teach me the art of patience? Clearly you have learned it well; while you labored over the summoning spell, Selûne's crescent belly swelled with light three times, and three times did she give birth to moondark."

Actually, Renwick had been working toward this moment for much longer than three months. Only through long, difficult striving could he cast spells other wizards tossed about with ease. Summoning demons was a tricky business for anyone, and he was justly proud of this accomplishment. Still, the demon's mockery stung.

Renwick reached for the framed miniature on a nearby table and thrust it toward Yamarral's sneering face. "Save your insults for those who wish you ill, and save your pretty words for *this*."

"This" was Nimra, a slender, doe-eyed beauty in the first bloom of maidenhood. Thick braids of glossy brown hair framed a sweet, sun-browned face, and her simple green gown bared her arms and clung to budding curves. The little smile curving her lips gave her the look of a dryad caught in the midst of some small mischief. The portrait was a true and skillfully rendered likeness, and it had the desired effect.

Dark hunger flared in the demon's eyes. For one soul-staining moment, Renwick glimpsed the true nature of the summoned creature. He managed with difficulty to suppress a shudder.

"My brother's daughter, the child of his dissolute youth," he said. To his relief, his voice did not shake too badly. "My brother is the paladin Samular Caradoon. His duties often take him far from home, so the girl looks to me for direction. She wishes to learn Mystra's Art. I have promised to find her a suitable teacher."

"Ah." Yamarral nodded sagely. "And you would release me into your world so that I might . . . *school* her, in exchange for magic that would set your thoughts in proper order and place the mastery of magic within your grasp."

As summaries went, the demon's was flawless.

Renwick simply did not see things as other men did. To his eyes, symbols turned this way and that upon the page, rearranging themselves into unintelligible patterns that required long study to decrypt. His mind demanded that certain runes be written in certain colored inks or they would be perceived as something altogether different. There was nothing wrong with his memory, but his spells, once learned, were still unreliable, for he was likely to invert words and gestures. None of these troubles, however, lessened his ambition or dimmed his conviction that he was destined for great things. The notion of gaining mastery over his malady through a demon's magic pained him, as did the role he must play to convince Yamarral that he was a "worthy" ally, but some paths toward the greater good must needs pass through dark and dangerous places.

"A fair exchange, for you will not soon tire of the girl," Renwick promised. "She is as quick-witted as she is fair. Under your tutelage, she could become a wizard of great power. Through her, your dominion over these parts would be assured for many years to come."

"This has possibilities," Yamarral admitted. "And what form would your payment take?"

"A blood token."

The demon's brows flew upward. "Long years have passed since a mortal bound himself and his bloodline to my service! I had thought this knowledge lost since before the Ilythiiri took to tunneling into the dirt like badgers and calling themselves drow. But since you know something of my history, I assume you also know what befell those who treated with me?"

"Of course."

"Of course," Yamarral echoed with mock gravity. "And you hope to avoid this . . . *how*?"

"I am twin-born."

For long moments, demon and wizard regarded each other in silence. "Either you are not quite the fool you appear," Yamarral said softly, "or your folly exceeds all boundaries previously known to me."

A frisson of unease ran up Renwick's spine, but he

refused to entertain doubt. Some mystical force bound the twin-born, inclining them toward a shared purpose. This was common knowledge; the demon assumed, as Renwick had intended him to, that Renwick meant to transfer any ill effects of this magic, as well as the legacy of demonic bondage, to Samular and his descendents. But Renwick had made long study of the twin-born tie and was confident in his knowledge of its strengths and weaknesses. If any man could stretch them in ways never before tested, it was he.

He cleared his throat. "You will have the traditional safeguards, naturally. Our bargain is void if you are returned to the Abyss by me or any other. I will possess whatever magic our bargain yields until the day you return to the Abyss, but any new spells or magical devices I might wish to create in the future will require either your consent, or the will of your blood-bound servants."

"By which you mean the paladin's pretty daughter and the demonspawn I intend to get on her." Yamarral lifted one brow, and his lascivious smile turned sly. "Since you know something of my history with mortals, you are no doubt aware that I breed only twin-born sons. They will look alike, but one will favor his sire. You won't know *which* one, of course. We are tossing the dice, you and I, with much riding on the outcome."

This was the moment Renwick had dreaded. Was it possible to lie to a demon? Could Yamarral hear the nervous quickening of his heart, smell the stench of falsehood in his sweat?

Renwick fashioned a smirk and set it firmly upon his lips. "Where it is written that the blood token must be held by only one heir at a time? And is it not possible that kinsmen, as well as descendents, could be bound by the blood-token pledge? Why could I not share the burden *and* the benefits with two others of my blood?"

Yamarral thought it over. "The thing has never been

done, but I see no reason why it could not be as you say."

"Then let the token reside in three parts. I will claim one third of the token and derive from it the power I need for my daily work. The three parts, wielded with the agreement of three blood-bound, must unite to realize the token's full power. We will also divide among us the consequences of that power." Renwick shrugged. "Hardly the legacy the good paladin might desire, but no doubt his faith will sustain him through the dark times ahead."

Yamarral laughed delightedly. "You surprise me, Renwick Caradoon! I did not expect such vile treachery, and I mean that as a compliment."

"Taken as such," Renwick lied. He set Nimra's portrait down and picked up the ready parchment and quill. "Now, shall we discuss the particulars?"

29 Mirtul, the Year of the Banner (1368 DR)
Waterdeep

To a man whose height could be measured by a single hand-span, even a paladin's library was a dark and dangerous place.

Algorind stood at the edge of the writing table, glumly measuring the drop to the thick Calishite carpet. Six, perhaps seven times his current height. He could jump, but not without injury. And to what purpose? Where would he go, and how could he defend himself against the dangers his new size brought? The mouse that had scavenged a few stray crumbs from the floor before disappearing into the paneled wall was, relatively speaking, the size of a dire wolf.

Algorind has been left on the table earlier that afternoon to await the arrival of his host—or perhaps more accurately, his jailor. To occupy the time, he'd studied his surroundings with eyes that measured familiar things in new and often disturbing fashion.

Tapestries covered the walls with scenes from famous battles, woven in realistic hues of red and bronze. Whenever a draft rippled these hangings, the depicted figures seemed to quiver with impatience, as if eager to resume their slaughter. Twin gargoyles crouched atop the marble fireplace, demonic statues so skillfully carved that Algorind half expected to hear the sudden snap of unfurling bat wings. He was not much given to grim flights of fancy, but given his current size, everything in the luxurious study was monstrous in scale, and therefore slightly ominous.

The grim aspects, however, were less disturbing to Algorind than the opulence. The table on which he stood was fashioned from a single plank of Halruaan bilboa. That rare and costly wood also paneled the walls, frequently in exquisitely carved scenes. Leather-bound tomes filled tall bookshelves. A painting depicting the rollicking afterlife to be found in Tempus's fest hall covered the high ceiling. The silver drinking bowl on the table smelled of sugared wine and was big enough for Algorind to bathe in. The dainty spoon next to it, even though it was large enough to serve Algorind as a credible spade, looked ill suited to a warrior's hand. Algorind, raised and trained by the Knights of Samular in the austere fortress known as Summit Hill, found such riches puzzling and unseemly.

But who was he, of all men, to judge?

On impulse, Algorind knelt beside the spoon and peered into its polished silver bowl. He was slowly returning to his natural size, but did his disgrace leave a lingering stain? Was it written upon his countenance for all men to read?

His reflection stared somberly back, a miniature version of his former self, slightly distorted by the curve of the spoon but still the face he'd seen mirrored in the polished metal of his lost sword: a man not yet twenty years of age, with a steady, blue-eyed gaze and close-cropped hair nearly as curly and fair as a lamb's fleece. He was broad and strong from years of training and stern discipline, clad as simply as any farm lad. Out of respect, Algorind had set aside the pure white tabard bearing the Order's symbol: the scales of Tyr's justice, balanced upon the hammer of his judgment.

Tyr's judgment.

A new thought struck Algorind, one strange and powerful enough to rock him back on his heels. By Tyr's grace, even a fledgling paladin could learn the truth of a man's nature—including, perhaps, his own?

Algorind had never sought to weigh his own heart. He was not even sure this was possible! The Knights of Samular were a military order, not a monastic one. Action, not introspection, was the business of Summit Hall.

The need to know swept away all reservations. Algorind bowed his head in fervent, silent supplication. As he prayed, a sense of peace and quiet joy settled over him, as palpable as incense in a cloister. The troubling events of the last tenday faded into insignificance. Tyr was with him still.

As Algorind sank deeper into the healing calm, a strange image flooded his mind. Stunted fields brooded beneath a dark and lowering sky. Briars and noxious weeds grew in profusion, slowing choking out the last few wholesome plants. Brackish water collected in dips and hollows, and black-winged scavenger birds circled overhead in patient silence, awaiting their own grim harvest.

The vision jolted Algorind from his devotions. As he leaped to his feet, an enormous hand—a warrior's hand, gnarled with age and seamed with the scars of many battles—closed around him.

The young man instinctively reached for his sword but found only the mockery of an empty scabbard. Defenseless, he was jerked off the table and swept up to a great height.

A moment passed before he made sense of the huge, craggy visage before him. He was staring into the bright blue eyes of Sir Gareth Cormaeril, one of the greatest paladins of living memory.

"You were invoking Tyr."

The old knight's voice smote Algorind's ears like peals of thunder, like the judgment of Tyr Himself. Algorind's first impulse was to confide all to the great paladin—the unorthodox prayer, the disturbing vision that followed. But some instinct Algorind did not know he possessed urged him to keep his own council.

"I was praying," he admitted. The suspicion on Sir Gareth's face, magnified past the possibility of subtlety, required more, so he added, "I am deeply troubled by my recent failings."

Algorind's stern conscience rebelled at this evasion, but Sir Gareth seemed satisfied. He lowered Algorind to the table, then pulled up a deep chair and seated himself so that they were still eye to eye.

"You will have need of the god's counsel, and mine as well, if you hope for a favorable decision from the masters of Summit Hall," he said briskly. "We have much to discuss before your hearing, and scant time to prepare."

Puzzlement furrowed Algorind's brow. *Preparing* for a trial? What strange notion was this? The truth was told and judgment was passed; what more could there be?

"I trust in Tyr's justice."

Sir Gareth inclined his head piously, leaving Algorind to marvel at the flicker of impatience on the old knight's face.

"So do we all, but your trial touches upon great matters, things that concern the deeper mysteries of the Knights of Samular. You will be allowed to answer the charges brought against you, but some things, for the sake of the Order, must remain unsaid."

"But surely nothing is secret from Master Laharin!"

"The master of Summit Hall will not be the only man at the counsel table. Harper representatives will be present, as will witnesses from among the common folk."

Algorind nodded reluctantly. "What would you have me say?"

"Your task was to deliver Cara Doon, a child of Samular's bloodline, to the protection of the Order. To that end, you brought her to Waterdeep. She was stolen away by a Harper known as Bronwyn, who is sister to the child's father—a priest of Cyric who calls himself Dag Zoreth. The child was spirited away to Thornhold, a fortress of the Order, recently taken in battle by Dag Zoreth and held by Bronwyn and her dwarf allies."

The young man's confusion grew as he listened to this partial recitation of fact. "Bronwyn said she rescued the child from a south-bound slave ship."

"What of it? She is a Harper, one who meddles in the affairs of her betters! She is a treasure hunter who despoils the crypts of the ancient dead. She does business with the Zhentarim, and she handed one of the rings of Samular over to Dag Zoreth. She professes no god, at least not openly. She is a light-skirt who has known many men and wed none. By any measure I know, the woman is not to be trusted."

"That may be so," Algorind said carefully, for he had seen enough of Bronwyn to suspect that the truths Sir Gareth spoke did not tell the whole tale of the woman, "but the fifty dwarves she freed from the slave ship will claim otherwise."

Sir Gareth's smile was grim. "We cannot keep the Harper wench from speaking at your trial. The dwarves, however, may find themselves otherwise occupied."

A chill ran down Algorind's spine. Was it his imagination, or did those words hold an ominous ring?

He forced himself to listen respectfully as Sir Gareth

outlined the points Algorind should cover and those he should avoid. At last the old knight nodded, satisfied with the young man's recitation of carefully selected facts.

"All will be well, my son," he said warmly. "I am certain you will be restored to your place in Summit Hall. I will speak for you. Nay, more than that—I will sponsor you on a new paladin quest!"

This was a generous offer, but Algorind's sense of unease deepened. The proper response would be to draw his sword and offer it in fealty. For the first time, Algorind did not regret his empty scabbard.

Fortunately, Sir Gareth did not seem to require a response. He removed Algorind from the writing table to "suitable quarters"—a large birdcage, outfitted with a folded linen towel for a cot and an acorn cap for a chamber pot. A snuffbox served as a table, and on it was a thimble-full of ale and thick slivers of cheese and bread. The cage sat upon a small, round table, one that was even higher off the floor than the writing table.

Algorind eyed his new quarters with dismay. "Sir, am I a prisoner?"

"The cage is for your protection, nothing more. Given your size, it seemed prudent. I'll leave the door open, if you like, and you can close it if need arises."

"May I have my sword? The Harper who brought me here said he would give it to you."

Sir Gareth plucked a long silver pin from his tabard, a gleaming broadsword, in perfect miniature. He regarded it for a moment, his gaze shifting between the weapon and the young man.

"You have grown somewhat. The sword has not. But I suppose it will serve as a table knife."

The knight dropped the tiny weapon through the bars of the cage, so that it fell onto the folded linen "cot."

And with that, the vaguely uneasy feelings Algorind had experienced since entering Sir Gareth's home took sharp, disturbing focus. Surely no true paladin would treat a sword dedicated to Tyr with such casual disregard!

It all made sense now: the vision of corrupted fields, the carefully tailored story that left out any mention of Sir Gareth's part in the tale of little Cara Doon, even the lavishly appointed home. Sir Gareth had long served as treasurer for the Knights of Samular. Every paladin of the order paid tithes, and all of those funds flowed through Gareth's hands. No wonder the Harper who'd brought Algorind here had had such difficulty finding Sir Gareth's home. Algorind had assumed the clerics of Tyr's temple were merely protecting the old knight's privacy, but now that he considered their responses, it seemed more likely that they themselves didn't know. And small wonder Gareth kept them away—they would not be pleased to learn how their tithes were put to use.

Algorind schooled his face to a calm he did not feel and stood quietly through Sir Gareth's parting advice. He listened as the door to the library was closed and locked, his host's footsteps echoed down the hall. Once the outer door thudded shut, Algorind set to work unraveling long threads from the loosely woven linen and plaiting them into a makeshift rope.

He worked quickly, anxious to finish before Sir Gareth returned. When he judged the length sufficient, he tied one end of the rope to the bars of his cage and tossed the rest off the table. He lowered himself to the floor, and then used his dagger-sized sword to cut off a length of rope. This he coiled and tucked through his belt.

Tracking was a skill all future Knights of Samular learned in boyhood, but Algorind had never expected to track a mouse across a Calishite carpet. It was surprisingly easy; the signs of the creature's passage were as visible to Algorind's eye as those a deer might leave in the belly-high grass of a meadow. He followed the trail to a small knothole in the wood panel, one made nearly invisible by the grain of the wood and shadows cast by nearby furnishings.

Algorind crawled through the knothole and lowered himself carefully into a thick layer of dust, wood shavings, scraps of plaster, and other detritus. The clutter inside the wall was dimly visible in the light that filtered down from an opening high overhead. This was a huge relief to Algorind, for he had expected to grope his way through total darkness in search of an exit.

Even so, the way *out* was also a very long way *up*. The young paladin took a deep breath and began to climb.

Hours passed as he pulled himself toward the light, finding handholds in the rough wood and plaster. His fingers bled and the muscles in his shoulders sang with pain, but he dared not slow his pace. Day was swiftly giving way to darkness, and the bit of sky visible through the opening under the eaves was turning a dusky purple.

Finally a ledge appeared just above Algorind. He pulled himself up and rolled onto a broad, flat board.

Standing was pure pleasure. He took a moment to stretch out sore muscles before venturing out onto the roof. As he flung his arms out wide, his fingers brushed against soft fur.

Algorind leaped away, drawing his weapon as he spun back toward the unknown creature.

His first response was, oddly enough, surprise; he'd never considered that demons might have fur.

Soulless black eyes regarded him from the center of hideous brown face, one so malformed that only when the fanged mouth opened did Algorind realize the creature was hanging upside down.

A keening scream burst from the "demon." Immediately the air was full of the thunder of wings and a chorus of hellish, high-pitched shrieks.

Never had Algorind heard such a sound. It reverberated against the inside of his skull, grating against bone like the talons of a dragon hatchling trying to claw free of its egg.

The board beneath his feet seemed to spin and tilt. He dropped to his knees for fear of falling, hands clasped to his ears. Blood trickled through his fingers, and the pain in his head soared beyond any he'd ever known, worse than that of being trapped in Bronwyn's siege tower and shrunk smaller than the bat he'd just disturbed.

And not just one bat—a vast colony of them, roosting in the attic of Sir Gareth's house. For what seemed a very long time they swept past him, their wings buffeting him as they darted out into the gathering night, shrieking all the while.

When at last they were gone, Algorind struggled to his feet and waited for the worst of the dizziness to pass. A high-pitched ringing was the only sound he could hear. That troubled him, but he would deal with it later. As soon as he could walk, he made his way to the opening.

The city of Waterdeep spread out before him, in all its splendor and squalor. Fine city gardens and ornate fences fronted the buildings in Sir Gareth's neighborhood; urchins picked through discarded crates for scraps of food in the narrow alleys behind. The twilight sky glowed like liquid sapphires, and streetlamps winked into life as lamplighters hurried along the streets, racing against swift-coming night. Algorind could see the leisurely swing of bells in the high tower of a nearby temple. No sound reached him. Except for the ringing in his ears, the city was eerily silent.

He eased through the opening, testing his weight on the narrow ledge beyond. The roof, which was tiled in blue slate, rose in a steep angle.

About five feet away from Algorind's perch, a drain pipe carried rain water to the street below. It appeared to be fashioned of segments of pipe, short enough for him to employ his rope and move from one to the next. But at his current size, five feet might as well be a thousand, and the slate ledge between Algorind and the drainpipe had worn away.

He studied the roof. Several tiles had crumbled or fallen away altogether, and moss and lichen grew in the dirt that settled over the passage of years. A ribbon of moss started just above his perch, growing upward and then meandering across the roof. If he could climb just a couple of feet up the roof, he could make his way across to the drainpipe.

Algorind tugged at a handful of moss and found it surprisingly stable. He began to climb, and for many moments the effort absorbed his entire concentration. Too late, he sensed a disturbance in the air above him and looked up into wide yellow eyes and reaching talons.

Faster than thought, the owl snatched him up and winged away.

Algorind reached for his sword, but immediately realized the folly of attacking his captor in mid-flight. Sooner or later, the owl would find a perch and Algorind would do whatever he could to defend himself. He settled himself as best he could and got a grip on the owl's talons, which were as hard and dry as the roots of a great tree.

Despite the gravity of his situation, Algorind started to enjoy the sensation of flight, the rush of night wind. The world spread out before him, city streets reduced to ribbons and great buildings no grander than a child's blocks. Beyond the city walls lay the lush darkness of meadow and farmlands, and beyond that, who could tell? Anything was possible. Even the stars looked like tiny silver apples, ripe for plucking.

Never had Algorind known such exhilaration, such wild joy! He threw back his head and let out a great shout of laughter. He would likely die this night, but now, at this moment, he was *flying!* By Tyr's Hammer, whatever came after would be a small price to pay!

27 Tarsakh, the Year of the Red Rain (927 DR)
Griffenwing Keep

Everything had gone wrong. Horribly, incomprehensibly wrong.

Renwick had been so certain Samular would applaud his plan to recover artifacts long entrusted to the Caradoon family. Of that large and noble clan, only their father had survived. Renwick was certain he and his brothers could recover or duplicate those lost treasures. To what other task should the three living Caradoon men dedicate themselves, if not this?

But Renwick's attempts bind a demon to this cause had torn open a rift between him and Samular. Their twin-born affection was all but sundered by the death of Amphail, their older brother, who *had* been willing to bear one of the three rings and hold another for his firstborn son. And Nimra—

Nimra. The very thought of her nearly broke Renwick's heart. Nothing else in his whole misbegotten scheme had gone so terrible awry.

It didn't take the demon long to realize that Renwick had deliberately misled him, that he had intended all along for the three rings to go to the three Caradoon brothers, all of them dedicated to the service of Tyr. But by then, it hardly mattered. The ancient spell Renwick had taught Nimra, one that promised an innocent could bind a demon to her will in the service of good, had failed.

In a cruel twist of irony, Nimra had fulfilled all of Renwick's false promises to Yamarral, and more. Amphail had died with Nimra's dark magic coursing through his veins, Nimra's dagger at his throat. With his death, two of the rings passed to Nimra's twin-born sons. And upon Nimra's death—*may Tyr forgive him that grim necessity!*—control of those rings passed to Renwick, their guardian.

The weight of so much magic had burned years from

Renwick's life in a matter of months, turning his hair prematurely white and etching deep furrows in his face. No one mistook him for Samular's twin now; indeed, most people thought him the eldest of the three Caradoon brothers. He had ceased correcting them, for what was that to him? All that mattered was setting right what had gone so wrong.

Renwick stole a sidelong glance at the man who walked at his side. His companion was tall, dark-haired, and bearded. His age was impossible to tell; he walked with the easy stride of youth, but his eyes held the weight of centuries.

At the moment, those eyes were fixed upon the fortress ahead. Griffenwing Keep was ancient; Caradoon ancestors had built it upon the site of an even earlier stronghold. The original earthwork mounds were still visible around the wall of grey stone. Towers loomed above the tall outer wall. The overall aspect was craggy and rough, as if the mountain had taken this form of its own choice. The gardens surrounding the wall, however, showed the touch of Art. Some dark whimsy caused the fountains to run red and filled the garden with blood red flowers. This was Nimra's work, a symbol of what she had become in two short years. To Renwick's eye, the garden was more disturbing than a monster-infested moat.

"I am grateful for your assistance in this matter," he told his companion.

The wizard sometimes known as Khelben Arunsun responded with a curt nod. "You did well to send for me. Ascalhorn is trouble enough. How did demons come to command this stronghold?"

"A prideful wizard, a summoning gone awry," Renwick said, genuine sorrow and regret painting his tones. "But before her death, my niece gave me the means to banish the demon."

Khelben gave him a searching look, and Renwick felt

the subtle tug of truth-test magic. It slid off him easily; few spells recognized a lie fashioned by placing two truths next to each other. Let Khelben think Nimra was the prideful wizard who had summoned the demon. It was better so.

Renwick slipped one hand into the bag at his belt, stroking one of the tiny hands hidden within—another grim necessity, for the blood token required the rings to be *worn* by three of Samular's blood. Still pink and perfect, the little fingers curled and flexed in the grasping movements common to healthy babes. His young wards lay at Caradoon Keep, where they would sleep peacefully until his return, knowing neither pain nor loss. He was not, after all, a cruel man.

Deals with demons were notoriously tricky, but a canny wizard could find his own out-gates. The blood token required the rings to be *worn* by three of Samular's blood, and wielded by combined will. Yamarral had neglected to specify that "blood" and "will" had to come from the same individuals. *Combined will* was necessary, of course, and the infants had no opinions of their own. Fortunately, Khelben Arunsun had no shortage in that regard.

Renwick surreptitiously slipped the rings from the two tiny, living thumbs. The rings expanded in his grasp to fit his much-larger fingers. With a flourish, he presented the trio to Khelben.

The wizard glanced at the rings and raised his gaze to Renwick's face. He looked unimpressed, even slightly impatient.

Piqued, Renwick snapped, "These are more powerful than you could know! United, the three rings form a rare and mighty artifact known as a blood token."

"The demon has offspring?" Khelben demanded. Understanding swept over his faced, followed by a mixture of sorrow and revulsion. "So that is the measure of Nimra Caradoon's alliance with this demon."

Renwick silently cursed himself for this lapse. But

how could he have known Khelben would be familiar with magic so ancient and obscure? It had been vigorously suppressed; there were perhaps five written references yet in existence, and Renwick owned three of them.

He quickly gathered himself. "Then you know I hold the means to banish this demon. I am heir to Nimra's folly and guardian of her sons, but I lack the magical strength to accomplish the banishment alone. Bind your will to mine with the spell I will teach you, and thus will all be done."

The wizard asked Renwick many pointed questions. Fortunately, his knowledge of blood tokens was not as complete as Renwick had feared. When at last Khelben was satisfied with the carefully prepared half-truths, he turned his attention to the spell. This he learned with demoralizing speed and ease.

Their shared casting was more successful than Renwick had dared hope. The entire keep, including the blood red gardens, simply faded away.

For a long moment Khelben stared in stunned silence at the mountain meadow. He turned to Renwick, and whatever he saw in the younger wizard's face seemed to deliver a second blow. Khelben steadied himself against an oak and took a long breath. "The rings you used in the casting. What else can they do?"

"Why do you ask? Was this day's work not enough for you?"

Temper blazed in Khelben's eyes. Before Renwick could respond, the wizard seized him by the cloak, lifted him off his feet, and slammed him against the tree.

"There were *people* in that keep, you lying orc-whelp!" he roared. "A blood token would have dispelled the demon, nothing more. Tell me where you found those three rings, and the nature of their power!"

Renwick summoned a smile and a lie. "What they were meant to be, I do not know." He couldn't resist adding, "What use I have made of them . . . you will not know."

Khelben released him and stepped back, his face set with grim purpose. "You know you cannot stand against me in spell battle."

"I do not intend to." Renwick lifted both hands to show that the rings had disappeared from his fingers. "The rings, and a partial knowledge of the power they wield, are in the hands of an adversary you cannot defeat."

The disbelief on Khelben Arunsun's face was priceless. Renwick had heard tell the wizard was elf-blooded. Khelben didn't particularly resemble his elven forebears in physical matters, but apparently he was as convinced of his own superiority as any high elf noble.

"You do not ask me of whom I speak. Pride forbids it, I suppose," Renwick observed. "I will tell you nonetheless. Samular will hold the rings, as will his descendants after him."

"The paladin?"

"Samular is not just any paladin. He is destined for legend. With my help, of course."

Khelben nodded slowly as he came to understand just how far out of reach the rings had been placed.

"A paladin's way is righteous and good," Renwick said, finding an unexpected pleasure in rubbing salt into the wizard's wounds. "If you do not stand with him, many men will assume you stand against him."

"That may be so, but that much power cannot be easily contained," Khelben warned. "You will not be able to keep the rings secret forever. Some day they will fall into other hands, and be used for other purposes."

Renwick smiled. "Then it is in your best interest to make certain this does not occur. After all, you helped send nearly two hundred innocent souls to an unknown fate. Once the tale begins to be told, who knows where it will end?"

Khelben did not react well to threats—or perhaps he resented the implication that his conscience could be silenced. He lunged at Renwick, eyes blazing with wrath. This time Renwick was ready for him. He dropped a portable hole onto the ground and stepped into it.

The mountain wind rose to a wail as Renwick swept along the magic pathway. He emerged safely inside the grey fastness of Caradoon Keep, and not a moment too soon. The shouts of the guards and hostlers in the keep's courtyard announced his brother's eminent return.

Renwick gathered up his robes and took the stairs two at a time. If he hurried, he'd have just enough time to reassemble Nimra's babies before their grandsire arrived.

29 Mirtul, the Year of the Banner (1368 DR)
Waterdeep

A sharp, staccato tapping dragged Danilo Thann's attention from his studies. He glanced up from a particularly thick, dusty tome and noted the shadows playing against one of the multi-paned windows placed high on the opposite wall. He shaped a cantrip with a quick, one-handed gesture. The latch opened and the window swung inward. A silver owl swooped in, dropped its burden on Danilo's desk, and flapped up to perch on a high shelf.

Danilo was not particularly surprised to note the identity of his small visitor. Algorind had been a thorn in Bronwyn's side, and therefore his own, for the better part of a month. Since no reasonable man would expect the paladin's nature to change along with his size, Danilo had set up certain safeguards against Algorind's escape.

"Thank you, Vichart," Danilo said, addressing the owl before turning to the rather windblown Algorind. "And you, sir; did you tire so quickly of Sir Gareth's hospitality?"

The tiny paladin shook his head and pointed to his ears.

Upon closer scrutiny, Danilo noted the faint smear of blood on the young man's neck and in his pale hair.

"Can't hear me, eh? No fear, I've a healing potion hereabouts that should turn the page on that chapter."

Danilo unlocked a drawer, rummaged, and withdrew a small glass vial. He eyed Algorind and considered the dosage. Perhaps just a drop ... No, there was no telling how much would cure and how much would kill.

"I suppose there's no help for it," he murmured as he reached for a book covered with dark green leather. "I'll have to put you back to rights. A waste of magic, in my opinion, but there it is. Fortunately for you, I've done little but study the history of your order since this business began. The size-changing magic of the siege tower was not particularly complex. Devising a spell to reverse it was surprisingly simple."

Devising it might have been an easy matter, but judging from the set of Algorind's jaw and the beads of sweat on his too-white forehead, his rapid return to normal size was far from painless. When he regained his former height, Danilo handed over the vial and pantomimed drinking.

After a moment's hesitation, the young man did as he was bid. Color flooded back into his face, and he rolled his shoulders like a man who'd just put down a great burden.

"The ringing is gone." His face brightened. "I can hear myself speak!"

"Well, there's a down side to everything, isn't there?"

Algorind nodded absently. "You restored me."

"Yes, and imagine my surprise! I was actually trying to shrink a goblet down to your former size, for hospitality's sake."

The young man continued to regard him, his expression uncomprehending. Danilo sighed.

"That was a small jest. Very small, apparently."

Algorind inclined his head in a small bow. "I am grateful for the restoration." A surprisingly boyish grin lit his face. "And for the flight, as well!"

"Really? I was about to apologize for that. Owls are so seldom a preferred mode of conveyance. Will you have wine?"

"Thank you. I am very thirsty."

Danilo walked over to his serving cabinet. He poured a small measure of wine into a large goblet and added chilled water and a spoonful of sugar. A child's drink, but it would be more appropriate to Algorind's thirst, and, Danilo suspected, to his experience.

The young man nodded his thanks and took a polite sip. His face brightened. "It is more pleasant than I expected, and far more refreshing."

"Drink as much as you need," Danilo instructed. "It's mostly water, and will do you no harm."

Once Algorind had emptied his goblet and another like it, Danilo indicated a chair. "We have much to talk about, so much I hardly know where to begin."

The paladin took a seat and turned a puzzled expression upon his host, who was pouring himself a goblet of unwatered wine. "What is a light-skirt?"

Danilo let out of a burst of startled laughter. He set down the decanter and leaned back against the serving cupboard. "Not exactly how I expected to begin, but very well, let's start there. It's a rather prim way to insult a woman's virtue by insinuating that her skirts, being light, are easily lifted."

"Oh."

He noted the crimson creeping into Algorind's face. "May I ask where you heard that term?"

"Sir Gareth said it of Bronwyn."

Danilo's smile disappeared. "Indeed," he said coldly. "Since we're exchanging gossip like a couple of fishwives, why don't you tell me what else Sir Gareth had to say?"

"He said that Bronwyn does business with the Zhentarim."

That was true, but it was hardly common knowledge. Danilo shrugged lightly. "No doubt he referred to her brother, the priest Dag Zoreth."

Algorind shook his head adamantly. "No, Sir Gareth mentioned this priest, but as a separate matter."

The intensity of the young man's manner was beginning to make sense to Danilo. So were a great many other things, and all of these insights suggested that he had vastly misjudged the young paladin.

He settled into his chair before responding to Algorind's unasked question. "You're quite right—those are two separate issues. Bronwyn does indeed have dealings with the Zhentarim. Or more precisely, she *did*. Now that rumors of her Harper alliance are being bruited about by the good men of your order, I imagine several people of Zhentish persuasion are busily disposing of the treasures and forgetting the information she sold them. But other than the people involved in these business dealings, only Bronwyn, her gnome assistant, the archmage of Waterdeep, and I know of her Zhent contacts, and I can guarantee you that Sir Gareth did not receive this information from any of us. Make of that what you will."

A sorrowful sigh escaped the paladin and his shoulders slumped as if under a heavy weight. "It is as I feared, then." He glanced up at Danilo, his expression rueful. "It must be difficult for you to believe a man such as Gareth Cormaeril could be in league with the Zhentarim."

"Actually, it doesn't task my powers of imagination."

The young man's gaze sharpened. "Forgive me if I misspeak, but you don't seem to hold paladins in high regard."

Danilo shrugged. "I'm not an admirer of your order, that much is true, but that opinion doesn't indicate a general disregard for the religious life. As you know, my uncle, Khelben Arunsun, has long been at odds with Samular's knights."

"I am not aware of that history."

The Harper choked on a sip of wine. He carefully set the goblet down. "How is that possible? Their disagreement is central to the order's reason for existence."

"Perhaps the order exists for other purposes, as well," Algorind suggested.

"Perhaps? Do you mean to tell me you have devoted your life to a cause you do not understand?"

Algorind returned his gaze without faltering. "My life is dedicated to Tyr's service. I understand that well enough."

"If you were merely a paladin of Tyr, I would agree with you, but you are allied with the Knights of Samular, a military order with a particular mission."

He reached for a large blue gem lying amidst a heap of books and scrolls. "This is a *kiiri,* an elven memory stone. The elf who carried it was a bard and a scribe. He left it as an aid to those who wished to study his work. He was present at the taking of the fortress Thornhold by Samular Caradoon, your order's founder. Would you like to see that event through the eyes of the bard who witnessed it?"

"Such a thing is possible?" Algorind marveled.

Taking the question for assent, Danilo went to a large cupboard and removed from it a metal stand, an ornate device that looked a bit like a sundial. He placed it near Algorind's chair and then fitted the *kiiri* into an impression in the flat surface. A round mirrored glass fitted into the frame above it.

"Look into the glass," he instructed. "You will see and hear everything the bard witnessed. After the first few moments, you might forget you are not actually present."

Algorind leaned forward, his face avid with curiosity. As the ancient scene played out, the Harper watched the shifting emotions on the younger man's face with something akin to pity. Danilo had delved into the *kiiri's* storehouses and found the memories disturbing, but the reality behind the Knights of Samular was sure to have a far more profound effect on the young paladin.

When at last the vision faded away, Algorind sat back in his chair. His heart raced as if *he* had been among the followers of the great Samular, fighting to oust a warlord from his fortress. And the Fenrisbane—or Kezefbane, as the order's scholars would have it—the size-shifting siege tower that had featured in Algorind's recent humiliation, had been a mighty weapon used for the glory of Tyr. And yet....

There had been something profoundly wrong with the Kezefbane. Evil clung to it like mist rising from a swamp. Apparently Algorind had not been the only one to sense this. The twin-born grandsons of Samular, identical unbearded lads clad in the white and blue of Tyr's sworn warriors, wore identical expressions of horror as they regarded the white-haired, white-cloaked wizard who commanded the siege tower.

What might have come of that, Algorind would never know. An arrow shot by one of Thornhold's defenders brought down the wizard. And while Samular's followers swarmed over the walls, the wizard died in the arms of his paladin brother. There could be no mistaking the resemblance, though Samular was broader and his brown hair was untouched by age, and the paladin had wept as he referred to the wizard as his twin, his other-self.

Strange. None of the stories Algorind had learned at Summit Hall mentioned Samular as twin-born, or spoke of his wizard brother. Of Wurthar and Dorlion, the twin-born paladins who built the Holy Order of the Knights of Samular, he had heard much. Tales of their mighty exploits and virtuous lives had been the mainstay of his early training.

He lifted his gaze to the Harper's watchful, sympathetic face. "Tell me of Samular's brother."

"That's Renwick Caradoon." Danilo quickly told the story he'd been piecing together.

"It would appear," he concluded, "that Renwick tricked Khelben Arunsun—a wizard who is commonly thought to be the current archmage's ancestor—into helping him banish the demon Yamarral, along with the inhabitants of an entire keep, to a small plane, one from which the demon cannot escape of his own power. The conditions of the original blood token agreement probably stated that Renwick's power would continue until the demon was returned to the Abyss. By banishing him, Renwick made sure this couldn't happen. Rather clever, keeping a demon exile by his own magic."

Algorind shook his head sadly. "All those people sacrificed to one man's ambition! I suppose it is a blessing Renwick Caradoon died before those ambitions could be fully realized."

In response, Danilo handed over an ancient book, which was opened to a sketch of a tall, round tower. "That is Caradoon Keep, which Renwick used as his lair during his life, and to which he retreated after death."

"But how could he retreat after he—"

Danilo cut him off with a gesture of one hand. "Turn the page."

The paladin did so, and immediately recoiled in surprise. The old tower now stood just outside a vast fortress of sand-colored stone. He knew this place very well, for he had been raised and trained there.

"Have you never wondered why that tower was outside the walls of Summit Hall?" the Harper asked softly.

Algorind nodded. "The masters said only that it contained a great and powerful magic that the Knights of Samular must safeguard. Renwick Caradoon?"

"I'm afraid so. Renwick intended to hold his power for a

very long time, either as a living man or a lich. I thought at first that Samular imprisoned him, but have come to suspect that Renwick imposed exile upon himself as a means of penance."

"And the Knights of Samular distrust Khelben Arunsun, Waterdeep's archmage, because his ancestor and namesake took unwitting part in Renwick's plan?"

A fleeting smile touched the Harper's lips. "Let's just say my esteemed uncle is more than capable of making his own enemies."

"Indeed. There is much distrust between the Harpers and my order."

"And with good reason. The Kezefbane was only one of the magical items Renwick created or recovered from Ascalhorn. To this day, men seek those items—and not all of them belong to your order. In fact, there is a secret society in Amn dedicated to this purpose. Under Khelben's direction, the Harpers have been opposing them for years. Since the society and your order share certain goals, the Harpers' efforts sometimes conflict with the activities of Samular's knights, especially where the bloodline of Samular is concerned. For obvious reasons, the society in Amn has an interest in Samular's descendents. It is my belief that Bronwyn was bound there when she was stolen as a child."

A disturbing possibility occurred to Algorind. "And Cara Doon, as well? Bronwyn's niece?"

"Most likely. Cara is going to be particularly attractive to these people. Not only does she possess one of the rings of Samular, but she has prodigious magical talent. Her mother was Ashemmi, an elf with enormous ambitions, a black heart, and the morals of a cat. In fact, I would not be surprised to learn she was recruited to seduce Dag Zoreth in hope of breeding a magically gifted child of Samular's bloodline."

"That is . . . monstrous," Algorind whispered. "And Sir

Gareth traffics with these people? How could he keep such evil hidden for so long?"

"I can think of several reasons," Danilo observed, "foremost among them Sir Gareth's fame. People, even paladins, usually see what they expect to see. Consider also the wound that withered his arm and ended his active career. Well-mannered people avert their eyes from lamed men so as not to appear indelicate. Every Dock Ward pickpocket knows this trick, and some use it to good effect, for good folk are disinclined to gawk at people who have obviously suffered some injury."

"Men who rise above their disabilities are admired, and Sir Gareth continued his work on behalf of the order, working as a treasurer," added Algorind.

"And that, too, has helped him, for such work is mostly solitary, and kept him from day to day contact with the men of his order. Familiarity might have dulled the sheen of his reputation and allowed men to see how dark his soul had become."

"There is much wisdom in your words," Algorind conceded. He looked up at Danilo, his expression uncertain. "What should I do now, sir? I seek your council."

That seemed to amuse the Harper. "Shall I list the reasons why you shouldn't? In the interest of saving time, why don't you tell me what *you* think must be done."

"My order needs to know about Sir Gareth."

"Indeed," he said slowly. "It is possible that his façade will shatter when it is closely examined. But it is also possible that he has been magically protected from such inquiry. Did you pray for insight into his nature?"

"No, sir; it was my own heart I sought to know. I caught a glimpse of Sir Gareth's, almost like something seen from the corner of my eye."

"Interesting. But it might be difficult to persuade your elders to try this method, or convince them that what you saw was the truth of Sir Gareth."

"Then what should we do?"

Danilo considered this. "If Sir Gareth put Cara on that south-bound ship, there will be records somewhere. As luck would have it, I have friends in low places. In time, I should be able to gather enough information to support your accusations. But a witness would be better."

"But what good man has been witness to Sir Gareth's misdeeds?"

"That's the problem, isn't it?" Danilo mused. He shook himself and sent his guest a rueful smile. "I have been remiss. You are hurt and in need of healing."

Algorind frowned. "You restored my size and my hearing."

"Yes, but the healing potion I gave you was specific to that hurt. Your hands are nearly raw."

Danilo rummaged among his collection of potions and took out a tear-shaped bottle filled with dark fluid in which swam tiny motes of light. He regarded it for a long moment before handing it over. "This should solve the problem."

The young paladin nodded his thanks and tipped back the bottle. A feeling of wonder suffused him as he regarded his unblemished hands. "They were healed almost before I swallowed. Even the old scars are gone!"

"It's an unusually powerful potion," Danilo said evenly as he reached for the empty vial. "Now, about Sir Gareth . . ."

Yes, what *about* Sir Gareth? To Algorind's surprise, he was no longer certain *what* to think of the old knight. His doubts and fears, so firmly held just moments before, felt as insubstantial as wisps of morning fog.

"Sir Gareth is a hero of our order," he mused. "If the vision I saw was truly a glimpse of Sir Gareth's heart—and I am no longer so certain that it was—perhaps the darkness described the pain from his wounds, or perhaps he is suffering through a time of discouragement. If he had given himself over to evil, if he had truly done the things you suspect, surely my elders would have known!"

"I'm not surprised you think so," Danilo said, idly turning over the empty potion vial in his hand. "And what do you intend to do next?"

"I will go whithersoever Tyr and you deem fit to send me."

Again the Harper laughed, but it seemed to Algorind that the sound lacked any real mirth.

"Tyr and me, is it? Now *there* are two vintages I never expected to see in a single goblet!" He abruptly sobered, looking more serious than Algorind would have thought possible. "For the nonce, forget about my opinion. Forget about the Order. What do *you* think you should do?"

After a moment's consideration, Algorind said, "I would warn the dwarves of Thornhold. Sir Gareth mentioned that they might be prevented from speaking at Summit Hall."

"Indeed. Did he say how, or by whom?"

"He did not. But no doubt Sir Gareth has knowledge he did not see fit to share with me."

"No doubt," the Harper murmured. "If a dwarf's got something on his mind and the desire to share it, he's not easily silenced, but I'll send word to Bronwyn at Thornhold." Danilo lifted one brow. "Unless you prefer to go yourself?"

"I would like nothing better, as I would beg her pardon and little Cara's for wrongs unwittingly done. And yet," he added wonderingly, "I feel compelled to return to Sir Gareth. It may be that he will need an aide in the years to come, someone he can trust to help him with all of his many duties."

The Harper's smile seemed a bit sad. "I thought you might feel that way."

The silver owl chose that moment to flap over to the window and out into the night. Algorind watched it go, a wistful smile on his face.

"If you're to aid Sir Gareth, you'll need a horse and a new sword," the Harper observed. "I know a fine sword smith who doesn't mind doing business at this hour. As for a mount, well, it just so happens that I have friends at the Pegasus aerie."

Algorind was on his feet at once. "A winged horse would consent to carry me?"

"They're less particular than you might have heard," Danilo said in a droll tone. "Before we leave, there is one question my study was unable to answer. Of the twin knights, Wurthar and Dorlion, which inherited his sire's dark nature?"

"It matters not at all," Algorind said, marveling at the truth of his own words. "The light of Tyr's grace shines equally upon all men. What we are, we chose to become. What we do, we choose to do."

Danilo nodded, but his gray eyes looked troubled. "So you are not dismayed to learn the founders of your order were demon-spawned? You will hold nothing against Bronwyn and Cara, who share this heritage?"

"As long as neither of them shrinks me again," Algorind said fervently, "I will be content."

☙ ☙ ☙ ☙ ☙

Later that night, Danilo let himself back into his townhouse with a muttered spell and an impatient wave of one hand. He was too tired and dispirited to be bothered with keys.

His commendable halfling steward had left a lamp burning in the entrance hall, but the study beyond was deep in shadows. Even so, he could make out the outline of a tall, broad-shouldered man seated near the softly glowing embers of the hearth fire.

"You should bolster your wards," instructed a deep voice, slightly burred with the accent he occasionally neglected to hide. "As you have just demonstrated, they are far too easy to breach."

With a sigh, Danilo entered the room and flopped down into a chair opposite Waterdeep's archmage. "I thought you might drop by. No doubt the smell of magical meddling drew you like strong cheese does mice."

"You seem heavy of heart," the great wizard observed. He held up the empty vial, the second potion Danilo had given the young paladin. "It is no small thing, to magically control a man's will."

"No small thing?" Danilo echoed incredulously. "It's wrong. It's *evil*. It's no better than rape!"

"And yet . . . "

"And yet," Danilo echoed softly. He rubbed his hands over his face and sent Khelben a rueful look. "I have condemned you for far less. In truth, I have judged you harshly over the years."

"That is what young men do."

They sat together in silence, sharing the solitude that comes from great power and difficult choices. At long last, Danilo asked, "Can any good come of this night's work?"

"No man can see all possible outcomes," Khelben said, "and on the whole, this is a good thing. The multiplicity of possible truths would drive one mad. So can too much power. And since there is nothing you fear so much as madness, you have fought against me these many years, shying away from realizing your full magical potential and rejecting any suggestion that you might be my successor at Blackstaff Tower."

Danilo stared at him. "I didn't think you knew."

"You might be surprised how well I understand you," Khelben said. He nodded to the untidy pile of books and scrolls on Danilo's study table. "You have a wizard's talent, a bard's passion for history, and a sense of duty that demands you employ both in service to others. This is your path, and it is good and right that you follow it."

Moved beyond words, Danilo merely nodded his thanks.

Khelben cleared his throat. "So you will be leaving for Tethyr soon?"

"Yes, before the tenday's end, and I will not be going alone. My lady Arilyn has rights to redress; Elaith Craulnober has people to kill." Danilo shrugged. "Business as usual, only this time my ill-assorted elven friends find themselves in rare accord."

"Indeed! Should I be relieved to hear that, or worried?"

"A little of both, I daresay."

Khelben chuckled and rose to leave, which brought Danilo politely to his feet. The archmage regarded the younger man for a long moment.

"Mystra's blessing upon you, son."

Danilo smiled at him. "I won't be gone forever—a few years at most. To a man of your long years, that's a mere eye blink. I'll see you upon my return."

A strange expression crossed the archmage's face, a flicker of emotion, quickly mastered. Khelben lifted a hand in farewell and disappeared into mist.

❦ ❦ ❦ ❦ ❦

6 Eleint, the Year of Lightning Storms (1374 DR)
Summit Hall

Laharin Goldbeard, the Master of Summit Hall, studied the papers spread out before him. His face paled as he read the bills of lading and shipping records linking Sir Gareth to the Zhentarim and, worse, to the Collectors Guild, the wicked treasure-hunters of Amn whose collective purpose was an evil twin to that of the Knights of Samular. Finally he fingered the scrying ring that, moments before, had revealed the face of Dag Zoreth, a priest of Cyric and member of the Zhentarim, who had impatiently answered "Sir Gareth" in a manner suggesting long acquaintance.

The paladin glanced up at one of the tall, fair-haired men standing before him. "How is it, Algorind, that you spent more than five years gathering this information? I won't deny that you've done a great service to the order, but subterfuge is difficult for a paladin whose heart is true."

"But not impossible," interjected his companion, a well-dressed nobleman a few years older than Algorind. "I placed him under a magical compulsion that caused him to set his doubts aside until such time as he had collected proof your order could not ignore. I coerced his will to this purpose."

Laharin regarded the man sternly. "You freely admit to this?"

"I do," Danilo Thann said evenly; "furthermore, I would take upon myself any blame that might fall upon Algorind, and I submit myself to your judgment."

"You do not fall under our jurisdiction."

"Nevertheless."

The master nodded and turned to the elderly man seated nearby, an armored guard standing on either side. "What say you to these accusations, Sir Gareth?"

"Papers can be forged and well you know it!" Gareth said sternly. "A wizard who would force another man's will could easily create an illusion such as the device before you. And Lord Thann was once a Harper, kinsman to Khelben Arunsun—and as such, an enemy to our order."

Laharin listened gravely, then turned to Algorind. "What response would you give to this?"

"Sir Gareth has spoken long about the faults of other men." The young paladin glanced at Danilo Thann. "But it seems to me that a good man will own his errors. I would consider warily any man who does not."

"Well said." Laharin rose and addressed the old knight. "Sir Gareth, in view of your long service to the Knights of Samular, and in concern for the reputation of our order, you will not stand a public trial, but go into quiet confinement."

Gareth looked relieved. "The sentence is just. Whatever might have come of my past actions, I never had any intention of doing evil."

"Neither did Renwick Caradoon. I trust you will find his company instructive."

Sir Gareth paled. "Sure you don't mean—"

"As you yourself observed, the sentence is just." Laharin glanced at the guards. "Take him to the Founder's Keep."

To his credit, Sir Gareth left without protest, carrying himself with the dignity that recalled his heroic youth. Once the room was cleared of armed paladins, Laharin sank bank into his chair and wearily regarded the two young men standing before him.

"What penance would you place upon yourself, Algorind? Lest you judge too harshly, let me remind you that this man has offered to take your punishment upon himself."

The young paladin did not need to consider. "Let me serve the Knights of Samular by seeking out the artifacts Renwick Caradoon created or recovered from Ascalhorn, and return them safely to the order."

"I see," Laharin said slowly. His gaze flicked to the small, brown-haired woman sitting quietly in the corner. "And you could do this work better than the Collectors Guild? You could retrieve from Amn those devices these villains have already claimed?"

"Not alone, sir." Algorind's face flushed, but he held the master's eyes. "Bronwyn Caradoon knows the work of collecting antiquities. She speaks the languages of Amn and other southern lands, and she has had dealings with some of the men in the Guild."

"And you, Bronwyn? Would you share this task?"

The woman rose, her pretty face set in determined lines. "Those whoresons killed my family to get to me.

They kidnapped my niece Cara once and they've made three more attempts since. Give me a quill and tell me where to sign up."

A smile spread across the Laharin's face. "A fitting task for a daughter of Samular! Welcome home, child. And you, Lord Thann; are you content to let Algorind take the full consequences of this penance on this own shoulders?"

Something in his tone brought bought a look of alert inquiry to the young noble's face. He glanced from Bronwyn to Algorind, and understanding dawned. Since Bronwyn had no kinsman present, Laharin was granting Danilo, her friend and sponsor, the honor of giving consent to the proposed partnership. Danilo noted how the mismatched pair stood together, hands joined in common purpose . . . and watched as their hands slid apart, slowly. Reluctantly. He turned back to Laharin with a wry, knowing smile.

"I daresay this 'penance' will repay Algorind's debt in full, as well as fees and penalties beyond the dreams of the greediest moneylender."

"I knew Bronwyn's mother," the master observed, his eyes twinkling, "and the memory of that acquaintance, while fond, does nothing to contradict your observation. Your lady is Arilyn Moonblade, the half-elf Harper?"

"Yes."

Laharin nodded, a wry smile on his bearded face. "That suffices, as well."

Algorind listened to this exchange with obvious puzzlement. "I don't understand."

The master of Summit Hall and the nobleman exchanged a look of rare and total accord. "You will," they said in unison.

*Originally published in Realms of Valor
Edited by James Lowder, February 1993*

THE BARGAIN

This story takes place shortly after the events of Elfshadow, my first FORGOTTEN REALMS *book. It was also my first published short story, and it sets the tone for many tales to come in at least one aspect—irony. You'll find a lot of that in these pages.*

Arilyn Moonblade, a half-elf fighter and Harper agent, has just been cleared of suspicion in the case of the Harper Assassin. She has nearly shed her much-hated nickname—again, "the Harper assassin," this time as **a grim honorific recognizing the fact that people she fought usually ended up dead.** *She and Danilo* **Thann,** *a nobleman from a wealthy merchant family of Waterdeep, are sent to Tethyr on a mission for* **the Harpers,** *a mission that requires Arilyn to—wait for it—infiltrate the assassins' guild.*

Some half-elves just can't buy a break.

THE BARGAIN

The one thing Arilyn Moonblade hated above all else was being followed.

"But how do you know someone's trailing you?" demanded Arilyn's companion, a nattily attired nobleman who picked his way delicately along the littered docks of Port Kir. "If you haven't actually seen or heard anything suspicious, how can you be so sure?"

With a frustrated sigh, Arilyn tucked a handful of her dark curls behind one pointed ear. How could she explain to Danilo Thann something that, to her, was both art and instinct? She just knew. There was a silent rhythm to stalking, a rhythm known only to the best hunters and rangers—and assassins.

"A wizard can sniff out magic," she said slowly, absently waving away an overeager merchant attempting to spray her with jasmine perfume. "And I believe a paladin can often sense when evil is near."

"Ah." Danilo's gray eyes warmed with understanding as he studied the distracted half-elf at his side. "I take it that patience, for lack of a better word, has an aura of its own."

Arilyn smiled without humor. "Something like that."

"Has this been going on long?"

She shrugged. "Since Imnescar."

"Since—" The nobleman broke off abruptly, then let out a long hiss of exasperation. "Arilyn, my dear, someone's been stalking us through two kingdoms, and you don't see fit to mention it? Never came up in conversation, is that it?"

"This is the first time we've been alone," Arilyn said, a trifle defensively.

Danilo glanced pointedly around the teeming marketplace. Beyond the docks the Sea of Swords gleamed silver in the waning light, the horizon touched with the last faint pink of sunset. Most of the merchants were busily folding their bright silk tents and rolling up the mats that had displayed pottery, crafts, and exotic produce. The crowds had not diminished, but evening shoppers generally had goods of a different nature in mind.

"We're alone, you say? How odd," Danilo mused. "I've often been alone with beautiful women, and things were never quite so hectic and noisy. Not initially, at any rate."

"You know what I mean," the half-elf said curtly. For many days, she'd had little opportunity to speak to Danilo in private. They'd arranged to travel with a merchant caravan en route from the northern trade city of Waterdeep to Calimport, its counterpart in the South. Merchants were the only northerners welcome in parts of Tethyr, and, swept along on the tide of commerce, Arilyn and Danilo had moved unquestioned through the southern lands.

Today they were to begin their true mission.

Arilyn and Danilo had been sent by the Harpers—the self-appointed guardians of freedom and justice in Faerûn—to bring a warning to Tethyr's ruling pasha. This was not an easy task, for Pasha Balik wanted nothing to do with "meddling northern barbarians." Repeatedly he'd refused Harper messengers or missives, and attempts to gain the ear of someone in his inner circle had also proved futile. Danilo had been charged with finding or creating a back door into the pasha's court; Arilyn's task was to keep the young nobleman alive during the process. Knowing Danilo as she did, Arilyn felt that her mission was sufficiently challenging without the aggravation of an extra shadow.

Even so, the half-elf had developed a certain grudging respect for her pursuer. Tracking a merchant caravan along the major north-south trade road was no test of skill; avoiding detection for so long was another matter. No other member of the company had realized they were being stalked, not even the powerful Harper mage at her side.

Arilyn cast a sidelong glance at Danilo, who was idly whistling the melody of an off-color ballad. Few who knew the young man might guess that he was either Harper or wizard. Danilo Thann was known as a dandy, an amateur mage whose spells comically misfired, a foppish dilettante with amusing pretensions toward bardhood. His self-satisfied smirk and extravagant attire bespoke wealth, ease, and privilege. In truth, Danilo cultivated that image. Prominently displayed on the amethyst silk of his jacket was the crest of a noble merchant family of the Northlands. His billowing trousers were tucked into impractical suede boots, and the voluminous sleeves of his silk shirt were embroidered with tiny runes in gold and violet threads. The nobleman's garments were loose and flowing, cut to mask his lean, powerful build, just as the sparkle of jewels on his sword's hilt distracted the eye from its keen and well-used edge. Danilo's facade made him an effective Harper agent, but it annoyed the Nine Hells out of Arilyn.

"It's getting late," she said abruptly. "Let's find a quiet place to plan our next move. Some food wouldn't hurt, either."

The nobleman's face lit up at the suggestion. "I know the very spot. Local color, and all that." He took Arilyn's arm and led her down a maze of alleys to a low wooden building that possessed all the charm of an abandoned warehouse.

"Local color, just as promised," Danilo said with enthusiasm as he swung open the door. He removed his plumed hat and tucked it under one arm, then patted his blond hair carefully into place as he beamed down at her. "Isn't this splendid?"

"This" was a tavern of sorts, a vast sprawling taproom that was anything but splendid. If the room were thoroughly swept and aired, it might qualify as squalid.

The taproom was crowded with tables and booths, most of them filled. It was a local haunt, judging from the swarthy faces and the distinctive blue-purple robes of Tethyr's natives. The crowd comprised men of all ages and social classes. *Only* men, Arilyn noted, though a row of doors lining the north wall of the taproom suggested that women were not entirely absent from the establishment.

Danilo ushered Arilyn into the room. The patrons nearest the door studied the new arrivals, their faces betraying a mixture of interest and hostility. At one table, however, three well-dressed locals eyed Arilyn with speculation and began to argue.

"Ah, Lord Thann!" proclaimed a nasal voice. Arilyn turned to see a squat, dark-robed man waddling toward them, his pudgy hands outstretched in welcome.

Danilo greeted the innkeeper by name, inquired after the health of his wives and children, and requested his customary table. The man ushered them to a corner table—which was already occupied—and dismissed the lesser patrons with a few curt words in the local dialect. Beaming widely, the innkeeper wiped the table with the sleeve of his robe, promised them a wine fit for Pasha Balik himself, and hurried off.

"Is there one tavern in the world where you're a stranger?" Arilyn asked with a touch of asperity.

Danilo pursed his lips and considered the matter. Before he could speak, a blue-robed man approached their table.

"I am the servant of Akim Nadir," the man told Danilo, and he gestured toward one of the three men Arilyn had noted earlier. "My master wishes to purchase your woman."

Danilo placed a restraining hand on Arilyn's arm. "Let me handle this," he said. Turning to the servant, he asked, "How much does your master offer?"

"Twenty gold."

"Danilo, this is no time for foolishness—"

"I quite agree," Danilo broke in. He reached across the table and patted her sword hand as if consoling her. "You're worth several times that amount, I should say."

"Let go of my wrist and get rid of this man," she said through clenched teeth.

"And miss a chance to hone my bargaining skills?"

"Twenty-five?" the servant suggested.

Danilo shook his head, his face alight with mischief. "Eyes that shame the desert sky," he noted in a wheedling tone.

"Thirty gold. No more."

"Look at her," Danilo persisted, deftly swiveling in his chair to move his shins beyond the reach of the half-elf's booted feet. "Have you ever seen such skin? Moonlight upon pearls! A hundred gold would be a bargain."

"Perhaps fifty," the servant allowed. "Has she any special talents?"

"Well, she's rather good with that sword of hers," Danilo

said thoughtfully, "though I doubt that's what you had in mind."

"That's it." Arilyn jerked her hand free of Danilo's grasp. Rising to her feet, she glared down at the servant. "Take your business elsewhere."

The man blinked, not comprehending. A woman unveiled in such a place was surely for sale. "To whom should I make an offer?" he asked, his eyes darting about the room.

Arilyn drew her sword. "Talk to this."

Light glinted off the ancient moonblade, pooling in the elven runes carved down its length. The man's black eyes widened and he stepped backward so abruptly that he stumbled over the hem of his robe. The matter settled to her satisfaction, Arilyn sheathed her sword and resumed her seat.

Danilo shook his head. "Your bartering technique could use a little work."

"Didn't it occur to you that he was serious?" Arilyn demanded, stabbing a finger in the direction of the retreating servant. "The saying here is 'Barter met is bargain sealed.' What would you have done if he'd met your price?"

"I'd've asked him to throw a couple of camels into the deal."

"Cam—" Arilyn broke off, dropping her head forward. "All right, I'll play: why camels?"

"For my mother, of course. The redoubtable Lady Cassandra bid me acquire something interesting for her stables," Danilo replied mildly.

Arilyn fought against laughter, but the mental image of the elegant Waterdhavian noblewoman astride a camel was too much for her.

"You really ought to laugh more often. It becomes you. Ah, thank you," Danilo said as the innkeeper appeared at their table with two large goblets. The nobleman sipped at his wine and praised it extravagantly.

"The grapes are grown on my own lands," the innkeeper

said modestly. "I'm honored that you are pleased."

"More than pleased," Danilo said. "My family deals in fine wines, you know. Perhaps if I were to join your guild, I could carry your wine—and your fame—to the North."

The innkeeper's smile faded abruptly. "I would like that very much, Lord Thann, but I doubt it will be possible. You will excuse me." He bowed quickly and scurried away.

"What was all that about?" Arilyn asked warily.

Danilo picked a bit of cork out of his wine. "You may have noticed that this establishment is not the sort of place I usually frequent. It is, however, a meeting place for guildmasters. Didn't you see the sign outside? The Guilded Dagger? Terrible pun, but there you have it."

"Yes? So?"

"The guilds control every aspect of trade in Tethyr, which makes them rather influential. If Pasha Balik refuses to give the Harpers an audience, perhaps he'd listen to a representative from one of the local guilds." Danilo took another sip of wine. "Namely, me."

Arilyn choked on her wine and set down her goblet with a thunk. "Danilo, the guilds are plotting to overthrow Pasha Balik. We're here to warn him, not join the other side."

"Guild membership would give me access to the pasha's court," Danilo argued. "Moreover, as a guild insider, I could find evidence that would force Balik to listen to us."

It wasn't a bad plan, but Arilyn was in no mood to be generous. "Which guild would you join? The procurers?" she asked in an acid tone.

"Now, there's a thought," Danilo said with a grin. "Come now, Arilyn. Don't tell me you're upset over a little harmless bartering. My asking price was too low—is that it?"

"It's not easy to get into the guilds here," the half-elf said, ignoring his teasing. "Membership is passed down from father to son, or earned through apprenticeship. You could buy your way in, I suppose, but these people are more

The Best of the Realms • 49

likely to be impressed by a clever bargain than by a pile of gold and jewels. Do you have a plan?"

"Not yet," Danilo admitted. "I'll think of something, though."

"Another thing." Arilyn leaned in closer and spoke with quiet urgency. "If the guilds learn you're a Harper, they'll assume you're here to meddle—"

"A reasonable assumption," he broke in.

"And you'll be as good as dead. I say keep away from them."

"Guild rule was attempted once in Waterdeep," Danilo reminded her, his voice suddenly serious. "It was, to put it mildly, a disaster. Pasha Balik might have his faults, but he's the strongest leader in Tethyr and the best hedge against political chaos in the area. If I have to go through the guilds to get the pasha's ear, I'll do it."

As Arilyn nodded reluctant agreement to Danilo's plan, a grim possibility occurred to her. Perhaps guilds allied against Balik—which would include the powerful Assassins Guild—had already discovered their Harper identity. That would explain the mysterious pursuer and his skill at stalking; southern assassins were peerless killers trained at a secret college known as the School of Stealth. It also meant that the Guilded Dagger was the most dangerous spot in Port Kir for them to be lingering over a glass of wine.

"Let's get out of here," she murmured, and quickly explained her fears. The nobleman was silent for a moment, then reached across the table and covered one of her hands with his.

"Arilyn, we're not known as Harpers. If someone is indeed watching you, it's undoubtedly due to your unfortunate reputation as—"

"Point taken," interrupted the half-elf quietly.

Although she had worked for the Harpers for years, she had just recently joined their ranks and few who knew of her would suspect her affiliation. She was known as a sword-for-hire. Given the political unrest in the area, the sudden appearance of a known assassin would be cause for concern. Any number of beleaguered rulers might want her watched.

Danilo gave her hand a quick, sympathetic squeeze and then nodded toward the entrance. "Who do you suppose that man is?"

Grateful for the change of subject, Arilyn glanced at the front door in time to see the innkeeper fold himself into a deep bow. The recipient of this courtesy was a lone man whose dark purple robes were drawn close against the sudden chill of the night. Light glinted off a golden ring on his outstretched hand.

"I wouldn't know. Does it matter?" she asked.

"It might. Look where he's being seated."

The half-elf watched as the newcomer was escorted to the taproom's finest curtained booth. Just before the innkeeper drew the gaudy drapes, Arilyn caught sight of the newcomer's face. He was a beardless lad, probably no more than fourteen or fifteen, and he returned Arilyn's scrutiny with intensity remarkable for a boy his age.

"Here we go again," Danilo observed calmly. Arilyn followed the line of his gaze and immediately forgot about the youth. An enormous bearded man approached their table, his black mustache twisted with a sneer of challenge.

"You wish to barter with your sword, eh?" taunted the man. He drew a scimitar and leered down at Arilyn. "Let us make a bargain, elf woman."

"You know the ordinances, Farig!" the innkeeper scolded, rushing up to the table. He flapped his hands at the brute as if he were shooing chickens. "Outside, outside."

As Arilyn rose from the table, she murmured to Danilo, "You're the one who likes to barter. Do you want to take this one?"

The Best of the Realms • 51

Danilo brightened. "In a manner of speaking, yes. You handle the sword end of the deal, though." The nobleman removed a large gold-and-amethyst ring from his finger and held it aloft. "I'll wager this that the elfwoman wins," he said loudly. There was a rumble of laughter, and soon a small crowd circled Danilo's table, arguing odds and laying bets.

The half-elf suppressed a smile as she followed the tavern bully out into the street. She knew what Danilo would bet against his ring and her skill: full guild membership.

The Guilded Dagger emptied as its patrons followed the combatants outside. Arilyn noted that the strange, intense lad was among the crowd. To her eyes, he looked troubled and oddly disappointed.

But other, more pressing matters demanded her attention, so Arilyn turned back to her opponent. Drawing her sword, she held it before her in a defensive stance. If at all possible, she wouldn't harm more than the man's pride.

The big man shrugged off his outer robe, baring massive arms and a thick torso gone soft around the middle. "What price does your sword require?" he asked, clearly enjoying himself. "Do I let it draw first blood?" The crowd laughed at his jest.

"Offer the sword a new scabbard and get on with it, Farig!" one man called. "Why tire the elfwoman in battle?"

The answering chorus of bawdy laughter abruptly faded when the fighters crossed swords. For several moments Arilyn simply parried the blows, giving Danilo the chance to raise the stakes on his wager. It proved to be good strategy; before long a sheen of perspiration glistened on the man's dark skin, and his breathing grew labored. When his confident sneer wavered and disappeared, a murmur began to ripple through the crowd.

The game forgotten, Farig put his full strength behind each slash of the scimitar. The bloodlust in his eyes proclaimed that Arilyn was no longer a prize to be won, but an enemy who must die. With a fierce yell, the southerner delivered a backhanded blow, striking Arilyn's forearm with the dull edge of the scimitar. The force of the blow jarred her to the bone and knocked her sword from her numbed hand. Farig shouted again, this time in triumph, as he raised the scimitar aloft for a final strike.

The half-elf ducked and rolled clear of the descending blade. Drawing a dagger from her boot, she threw herself upward. Her knife drove hard under her opponent's ribs and found his heart. Arilyn felt more than heard the faint metallic click as her steel met another blade. With a puzzled frown, she yanked her knife free. The huge man fell face forward into the street.

From the corner of her eye, Arilyn noted that Danilo had become the center of an arguing, gesticulating crowd. Unnoticed by the tavern patrons, Arilyn stooped over Farig's body. As she had suspected, a knife protruded from between his third and fourth ribs. She pulled it out, and her eyes widened. Carved on the handle was a curving Calishite rune. Arilyn had seen the symbol before. It was a badge of pride, carved into each weapon owned by an assassin trained at the School of Stealth. And as she turned the knife over, she found many smaller markings scored into the handle, one for each person the knife's owner had killed.

Arilyn tucked the weapon away in her boot, and her eyes scanned the dark streets. Although there was no sign of her mysterious "rescuer," she could sense that he was near. Determined to catch him, Arilyn hurried to Danilo's side and grabbed his arm.

"Let's go."

"Soon," he said in a smug tone. "I'm bartering for guild membership. Given time, I might even get them to throw in those camels for Lady Cassandra."

"Now," she insisted, giving him a sharp tug.

His lazy smile never faltered as he shook his head and peeled her fingers from his arm. Holding her hand in both of his own, he kissed her palm then briefly rested it against his heart. The courtly gesture was a pointed one; through the fabric of the dandy's jacket, Arilyn felt the outline of his concealed Harper pin.

"Remember why we're here," he murmured.

By the time Danilo had been sworn into the Wine Merchants Guild of Tethyr and had brought several rounds of drinks for his fellow businessmen, a frustrated Arilyn had discarded any thought of pursuing the mysterious man who had stalked her, then tried to save her. Not until the Guilded Dagger's last patron staggered out into the night did she have the chance to tell her story. Danilo agreed that they should try to catch her pursuer with as much discretion as possible, to avoid compromising their larger task. The best way to do that, assuming the skilled tracker would still be on Arilyn's trail, would be to draw him away from the crowds of Port Kir.

The Harpers quickly retraced their steps to the camp their caravan had made on the city's outskirts. They made their excuses to the caravan leader, claimed their horses, and set off south through the Forest of Tethir.

The night was dark, and the pale sliver of moon did little to dispel the deep gloom of the forest trail. Even though the road was wide enough to allow merchant wagons to pass, ancient trees met overhead in a thick canopy. On either side of the trail grew a tangle of vines and underbrush. Merchant caravans usually braved the Forest of Tethir only by day, to avoid the bandits and wild beasts that prowled the forest after nightfall. Knowing this, the Harpers rode without speaking and kept alert for the smallest signs of danger.

Daybreak was near when the half-elf finally caught sight of her pursuer. Feeling secure behind his leafy screen, the assassin had ventured close enough for Arilyn to get a look at him.

A human might not have seen him at all, but the half-elf's keen night vision perceived the well-hidden horse and rider. The assassin was lithe and slender, and even in the saddle gave the impression of proud, almost regal bearing. His stallion—Amnian, by the looks of him—seemed to share his rider's haughtiness as he moved on cloth-wrapped hooves through the shadowy forest. The man was wrapped in a dark cloak, so there was no telling what weapons he carried, save for the long throwing knife he had clenched in one hand.

The knife puzzled Arilyn. Why would this man try to save her at the tavern, only to attack her now? Determined to snare the elusive stranger and get some answers, she reached into a saddlebag and withdrew a small throwing knife attached to a coil of unbreakable spider-silk thread. At one end of the thin rope was a small noose; this she slipped over the pommel of her saddle. A quick tug secured the rope.

The tethered knife at the ready, Arilyn unpacked a small, round iron disk no bigger than the palm of her hand. After adjusting the tiny shield's strap over her left hand, she hefted the small throwing knife to remind her muscles of its weight and balance. Her movements were so small and unobtrusive that even Danilo did not note her preparations.

From the corner of her eye, Arilyn saw her pursuer slip down from his horse. Bent low, he crept silently toward her through the thick, night-shrouded underbrush. When only a thin strip of foliage separated him from the path, he straightened to his full height and readied his own blade for the attack.

The assassin's throw went wide, spinning toward the flank of Danilo's horse. Arilyn flung out her left hand, and the knife glanced harmlessly off the tiny shield in her palm. In the same instant, she hurled her own blade. It whizzed toward its target, the thin cord streaming after

The Best of the Realms • 55

it. The half-elf's keen ears heard the silken whisper of the uncoiling thread, the rustle of leaves parted by the missile, and then nothing.

"I say! What's going—"

Danilo's startled outburst was cut short by the fierce expression on his companion's face. Arilyn motioned for the nobleman to stay put, then swung down from her horse.

The half-elf was certain her knife had hit its target, yet her victim had not cried out. Considering the weapon she'd used, that was strange indeed. The knife was cunningly designed so that the tip would spread upon impact into four barbed prongs. The resulting wound was shallow, but it was painful and exceedingly messy. Nearly impossible to withdraw, the knife was an effective way to stop and snare someone at close range.

Arilyn silently parted the curtain of vines and took a look at her attacker. He stood in a small clearing, his back toward her. His head was turned in profile as he tugged at the weapon embedded in his hip. From the wound's location, Arilyn could guess why his throw had gone wide; he must have spun around too far on his follow-through. He'd have to learn not to do that, if he intended to hit anything.

As Arilyn watched, the assassin abandoned his attempt to withdraw the pronged blade. Drawing a small hunting knife, he began sawing frantically at the spider-silk cord. Her gaze shifted upward to his face, and she recoiled in surprise. Her captive was the lad she'd seen back at the tavern.

The boy had the deep black eyes, prominent hooked nose, and swarthy skin common to natives of neighboring Calimshan. Since leaving the Gilded Dagger, he'd discarded his robes. Now he was clad in loose-fitting silk garments of a dull, indeterminate color, clothes that struck Arilyn as being a uniform of sorts. If the young assassin was a student at the School of Stealth, his skillful stalking and his stoic acceptance of pain would be a credit to his masters. His aim could use work, though.

Arilyn slipped silently into the small clearing. Moving directly behind the boy, she tapped him on the shoulder. Startled, he whirled toward her, dropping the knife in his surprise. A flick of Arilyn's booted foot sent the weapon flying into the underbrush. Shock claimed the boy's face for only an instant, then his young features firmed into a grim mask and he raised his fists to do battle against the armed half elf.

Something almost like admiration stirred in Arilyn's heart. Apparently she'd snared a small hawk.

"Do you have a name?" she asked

Her question took the boy by surprise. "Hasheth," he answered, before he could think the better of it.

"That blade has to come out," she said. Even in the faint moonlight, she could see Hasheth blanch. A sympathetic smile curved her lips. "It's not as bad as you'd think. A hidden device on the handle releases the barbs, and they fold up as the knife withdraws. There is no more pain than any other shallow wound would cause." She paused and raised one eyebrow. "They do teach you to withstand pain at the School of Stealth?"

"Of course," he responded indignantly.

So she was right about the boy—he was a student assassin.

"If you want that knife out, you'll have to turn around."

"No man turns his back on an enemy," Hasheth proclaimed.

"Really." Arilyn folded her arms. "In that case you'd better prepare to walk back to the School of Stealth. You'll never sit on a horse with a knife in your—"

"Enough!" The lad silenced her with an imperious gesture. Pride and pain fought for dominance of his dark face. Finally he turned, averting his eyes. "Quickly," he muttered from between gritted teeth. "I have not all night to waste."

"Have a few other assassinations lined up, do you?" Danilo asked cheerfully as he strode into the clearing.

"Didn't I tell you to wait?" Arilyn asked.

"Sorry," Danilo responded without a touch of repentance. "I would have died of curiosity, and cheated this lad out of his fee. Let's have a look at your would-be assassin, shall we?" The nobleman drew a bit of flint from the bag that hung at his waist and muttered an arcane phrase. His spell was rewarded with a flash of light, and a small campfire appeared in the clearing's center.

"I say, that must have stung," Danilo said as he eyed the boy's messy wound.

Hasheth's black eyes swept over the nobleman's silken attire and expression of prissy dismay. The lad sniffed and he turned aside, dismissing Danilo as one unworthy of notice or comment.

"The knife?" he reminded Arilyn.

The half-elf selected a slender pick from the small tool pouch at her belt. She slid it into a hidden opening on the knife's elaborate handle. When she heard the tiny click, she pulled the blade free. The boy's only response was a quick intake of breath.

Danilo made an exaggerated show of sympathy, then took a vial from his leather bag and handed it to the boy. "A healing potion," the nobleman explained in response to Hasheth's suspicious glare.

"I have no use for your barbarian sorcery," the would-be assassin said with contempt.

"Ordinarily I'd consider that a mark in your favor," Arilyn told the boy. She eyed him sternly and ordered him to drink up. After one final suspicious glance at Danilo, the young assassin complied. The bleeding slowed, and color began to return to his face.

Arilyn folded her arms across her chest. "You've been

following me since Imnescar. Why?"

"I do not know what you're talking about."

She drew the assassin's blade from her boot and held it out. "Maybe you'd like to explain why you killed that thug at the tavern."

"You speak nonsense," Hasheth said with scorn. "That is the knife I threw at you just now."

"No, it isn't," Danilo said, producing an identical knife from the bag at his waist. "I picked up your knife before I strolled over. By the way, have you any idea how close you came to skewering my horse?"

Arilyn took the knife from the mage and studied the blades. Both were carved with the School of Stealth's mark, but the weapons differed subtly in weight and balance. She flipped the knives over. The one that had killed the tavern fighter was scored with dozens of small carvings, while Hasheth's was smooth and unblemished. If the unmarked knife told a true story, the young assassin had not killed before.

The half-elf looked up at Danilo. "There are two assassins."

"Only two? Given the fees you charge for your services as a bodyguard, I would expect no fewer than seven."

She ignored him and turned to Hasheth. "Where's your partner?"

"I have none," he said. "If you met another assassin this night, what of it? Assassins are common enough around taverns."

"But knives like this are not," Arilyn persisted. "Someone from the School of Stealth wanted to keep me alive back at the tavern. Why?"

"That I cannot tell you, but I owe him a debt," Hasheth said bluntly. "If you had died at the hands of that drunken oaf, I would have been cheated of my sand-hue sash."

Danilo noted the flash of pain in Arilyn's eyes. She'd worked long and hard to rise above her dark past, only to be confronted with it time and time again. In Tethyr, members of the Assassins Guild advertised their skills with different colored sashes. To advance in rank, one had to stalk and slay an assassin of the next level. Now would-be assassins were challenging her for the right to lay claim to her dark reputation.

The Harper clasped his hands behind his back, a casual stance that disguised his nearly overwhelming impulse to throttle the lad with the sand-hue sash he coveted.

"No offense, Hasheth, but did it ever occur to you that you might have skipped over a few levels here?"

"That is absurd," Hasheth said haughtily. "The school's masters would not dare mock me in that manner."

"They wouldn't dare, eh?" A reflective look crossed Arilyn's face. "Where do you hail from, Hasheth?"

"My home is in Zazesspur, if that is what you mean."

"But you have the look of a Calishite," she noted. "Perhaps your mother was from Calimport?"

"Is this a state dinner, that we make polite conversation?" Hasheth demanded. "I am your prisoner. Kill me if you will, but don't trouble me with your woman's chatter."

"Charming lad," Danilo murmured. "Nice of him to suggest such an attractive option. Can we take him up on it?"

Arilyn shook her head. "We'll take him back to Zazesspur. Sorry, Hasheth, but you'll have to find some other way to earn your sash."

"A wise man knows when the battle is lost," the boy agreed.

Danilo regarded their captive warily, noting the sly twist to his lips and the smooth insincerity of his tone. His gaze shifted back to Arilyn. Her lovely face was inscrutable, but she was obviously up to something.

"Marvelous," he muttered, just loud enough for Arilyn's elven ears to pick up. "I've always wanted a pet adder."

She sent him a sidelong glance. "We need to keep riding. We'll be out of the forest and into the Starspire

60 • Elaine Cunningham

Mountains soon. That road is best traveled in the early morning hours."

Hasheth nodded. "The mountain pass is a wasteland as hot and barren as any desert. In the heat of day your northern skin would peel like that of a molting snake," he said with relish.

"Charming lad," Danilo repeated.

"Still, he's got a point," Arilyn commented. "The sun will rise within the hour. If we press on we should get through the pass before highsun."

The dandy sighed deeply. "Can't we at least stop here long enough for some breakfast? I'll cook."

Arilyn agreed reluctantly, and the trio settled down around Danilo's fire. The nobleman began to rummage in his bag, drawing forth a small cookpot, a tightly covered dish of salted fish, a package of dried mushrooms, a package of herbs, a large silver flask of water, and another containing a dry cooking wine. Hasheth watched, his mouth agape, as each item appeared from the small sack.

"It's magic," Danilo explained as he deftly combined the ingredients. "The bag holds much more than appearances would indicate."

The young assassin quickly masked his astonishment. "No porcelain? No linens, no candelabra? You have adapted well to the rigors of travel, I see," he noted with keen sarcasm.

"I try to keep a civilized touch," Danilo said. "Under the circumstances, that might not be easy."

Arilyn caught the underlying warning in her companion's voice. "Do you still have any of that goldleaf tea, Dan?"

Hasheth brightened. "I would be happy to prepare it. No northerner has the ability to brew a decent cup."

"Who could refuse such a gracious offer?" Danilo rummaged in his bag again, found an oddly shaped covered pot and a package of tea leaves, then tossed them to the boy. Hasheth took up the water flask and busied himself with the task.

When the tea was ready, Hasheth filled Arilyn's mug and handed it to her with a courtly bow. Then, almost as an afterthought, he poured another cup for Danilo. Before sipping, Arilyn inhaled deeply, and her sharp elven senses picked up a foreign note in the fragrant steam. She caught Danilo's eye, glanced down at his mug, and gave a subtle shake of her head. The mage raised his eyebrows and painted an "I told you so" smirk on his countenance.

"Would you be offended if I didn't drink first?" she asked Hasheth.

"Of course not. Only the prudent live to old age," the lad replied graciously. He reached for her cup, offering, "I myself shall taste it for you."

The half-elf had anticipated that response, and the faint gleam in Hasheth's eyes confirmed her suspicions. Without doubt, he had an immunity to whatever poison he'd slipped into the tea. It was a common trick in an assassin's repertoire.

"I would not dishonor you with such a task," Arilyn said with grave formality. "Actually, I'd thought of feeding the tea to your horse."

Hasheth's smug expression melted into the slack frustration of defeat, and he pounded the ground with balled fists. "Why have the gods sent you to torment me?"

The half-elf waited until the boy's rage was spent. "Why would your masters want you dead, Hasheth?"

"Apart from the obvious reasons, of course," Danilo added.

Hasheth turned furious eyes on his captors. "Can you not hear? My masters decreed that you must die, elfwoman. Then I can advance to the next sash level."

"Let's step into reality for a moment, shall we?" Danilo suggested. "Our home is many days to the north. Didn't it occur to you that an assassin whose reputation had traveled so far might prove a bit of a handful to someone your age?"

Before the young man could respond, Arilyn broke in. "How old do you think I am?"

Hasheth blinked, clearly puzzled by her question. His eyes traveled over her delicate features, curly raven hair, and slender form. "Three-and-twenty rains," he guessed.

Arilyn shook her head. "Try three-and-forty."

"It is not possible," Hasheth protested, his brow furrowed in disbelief. "You are young and most beautiful."

She brushed back her thick curls to display pointed ears. "I'm a half-elf, remember? I'll probably outlive your grandchildren. When I started sword training, your mother was no doubt an infant. How old was she when she came to your father's harem?"

"Fourteen," he answered absently.

"For as many years as you and your mother have lived, I've been a hired warrior. I fought for the Alliance in the war against the Tuigan barbarians. I have earned a place of honor among the Harpers. Knowing this, do you still think you were sent to fight an equal?"

Arilyn softened her harsh words with a smile. "In a few years, this may change. You have much talent, Hasheth, and one day we may well meet on an even field. But that day has not yet come." She paused, and her expression hardened. "No one uses me or my sword against my will. I don't intend to be the instrument of your death, despite your masters' best-laid plans."

"You lie," Hasheth said, but his face betrayed a touch of uncertainty.

"Someone wants you dead," Arilyn repeated. "That's easy enough to prove. Since I won't take the job, it will go to another."

Hasheth stared at her for a long moment. "I will think about your words."

The three travelers turned their attention to Danilo's fragrant stew. Hasheth scorned the offer of a spoon, instead using pieces of flat, hard travel bread to scoop up bits of fish and mushrooms. The lad ate hungrily, but with a nimble delicacy that struck Danilo as oddly familiar. He resolved to mention his suspicious to Arilyn as soon they could speak privately.

After their meal, at Danilo's insistence, Arilyn tied a length of rope around Hasheth's ankle and secured the end to her own saddle. The boy submitted to the indignity calmly, and not until they left the forest behind them did he speak to her again.

"I have heard of the Harpers," Hasheth stated casually, but his tone clearly implied that he had heard nothing good. He wheeled his horse aside and placed as much distance between himself and his captors as the tether rope allowed.

Danilo reined his horse close to the half-elf's mare. "Mind if I borrow your bow? I've never had an urge to shoot someone before, so I don't have one of my own."

Arilyn smirked. "I can see the temptation, but try to resist."

"Why? You'd be surprised how much time I save by giving in to temptation immediately."

"Ease off, Dan. He's just a boy."

"Perhaps so, but he is not your average student assassin. Noblemen in Tethyr seldom use forks or spoons. It's supposed to be uncouth. Another of the pasha's notions about northern barbarities, I believe. Then there's the matter of that horse he's riding. I'm an excellent judge of horseflesh, and I can assure that only the very wealthy could afford such a mount. And have you noticed the boy's ring?"

"I was wondering when you'd get around to that ring," Arilyn murmured. "So Hasheth has money."

"He's clearly both noble and wealthy, but he disdains

such things in others. He positively despises what he sees in me—"

"For that he needs a reason?"

Danilo reached over and took Arilyn's chin between his fingers, turning her face to his. "You're enjoying this far too much," he observed.

"Get used to Hasheth, Dan," she said as she eased her horse away. "He's our contact at Pasha Balik's court."

Danilo squinted at the sun, which had crested the top of the Starspire Mountains. Already it glared at them like an angry red eye. "My dear, I'm afraid this desert heat is addling you."

"Why? You've concluded that Hasheth is noble. He names Zazesspur as his home, but his face is that of a Calishite. Pasha Balik's palace is in Zazesspur. The pasha is a native of Tethyr, but he's known to stock his harem with the women of the South. Hasheth admitted to being born in a harem, and very few men in Zazesspur keep harems. And does his dislike of northerners remind you of someone?"

"All right, it's possible that he's the pasha's son," Danilo conceded. "Possible. We can't be sure."

"We could ask him."

"I like it," Danilo mused. "Simple, direct. The youngster likes to talk, so it just might work." He cupped his hands to his mouth and called out, "Tell me, Hasheth, how does Pasha Balik feel about having an assassin in the family?"

"Your father would disown *you* sooner than mine would me," the boy responded curtly. "Better an assassin than a fool."

Arilyn chuckled. "That answer your question?"

"It'll do. But what makes you think that Hasheth will work with us?"

"He will if we can convince him his life is in danger."

The nobleman's face suffused with unholy glee. "I can think of several ways to accomplish that feat."

"Don't bother. The second assassin will strike soon. He has to, if they plan to blame Hasheth's death on a northern barbarian."

"Ah." Danilo drew in a long breath. "I think I've got it. Hasheth's masters send him after you, fully expecting you to kill him. It was a chance to be rid of him and remain guiltless. And knowing how Pasha Balik feels about 'northern barbarians,' they're probably expecting Hasheth's death to put the old boy right over the edge."

"That's my guess," Arilyn agreed. "His son's death might prompt Balik to limit trade with the North—making the people of Tethyr turn against him. The way would be clear for the guild alliance to make its move."

"Devious," the nobleman muttered. "And the other assassin—the one who's been following us since Imnescar—was supposed to make certain you and Hasheth met up, I suppose."

"Probably. If I don't kill Hasheth, he will. You can bet I'll still be blamed, though."

Danilo was silent for a long moment. "So what do we do now?"

"We keep Hasheth alive."

As the three travelers rode deeper into the pass, the day grew oppressively hot and the landscape more barren and forbidding. Heat rose in wavering lines from the sand and from the scattered clusters of rock. The only signs of life were the colonies of lizards sunning themselves on rocky ledges. The creatures seemed to be everywhere, and Danilo marveled that anything could enjoy the punishing heat.

"Look at that large rock formation," the half-elf said quietly. The pass narrowed up ahead, with a flat ledge to the left side of the trail and a huge, jagged pile of boulders blocking escape to the right.

"Is our assassin lying in wait there?" the nobleman asked.

"Could you choose a better place? Once I move, you keep an eye on Hasheth."

They rode until they were almost level with the rock. Suddenly Arilyn threw herself from her horse, tugging violently at the line that bound their young captive. Caught unaware, Hasheth fell heavily to the rocky ground.

Arilyn was back up in a heartbeat, moonblade in hand, rushing toward something Danilo had yet to see. A tall, dark-bearded man sprang up from behind the rocks, a pair of scimitars flashing in the sunlight. Danilo noted that the attacker's dark, close-fitting attire was identical to the garments worn by Hasheth.

The young assassin staggered painfully to his feet, cursing the rocky trail and the woman who had caused his fall. As he watched the battle raging before him, fierce joy filled his heart. The accursed woman would die, and at the hands of a brother assassin! Hasheth's eyes narrowed at that thought, and he stooped to pick up a shard of stone, wedge-shaped and sharp. Perhaps this was a gods-granted chance to fulfill the duty assigned him....

"I wouldn't recommend it," said a voice edged with steel. A blade bit into the base of Hasheth's neck. "Turn around slowly."

Hasheth did as he was bid, silently cursing himself for being bested by the barbarian peacock. He'd forgotten about Danilo, so accustomed had he become to ignoring the fool.

"Look over at the rock ledge," the northerner ordered, lowering his blade until it was level with the young man's heart. "It could change your outlook considerably."

Puzzled, Hasheth looked—and recoiled from the sight before him. All but one of the sun-loving lizards had fled. The lone remaining creature writhed and twisted, impaled by a slender, familiar knife. The blade, which was deeply wedged in a rocky crevice, flashed in the bright sunlight as the lizard flopped about. The creature gave one final, consulsive shudder and lay still.

Only moments before, Hasheth had been directly between the dead reptile and the former hiding place of his "brother assassin."

"Arilyn cut that a bit close, wouldn't you say?" Danilo observed in his irritating drawl.

"The elfwoman spoke the truth," Hasheth said softly. He turned and met Danilo Thann's eyes squarely. "Return my knife," he commanded. "She spoke truth, and she saved my life. I would come to her aid."

The nobleman chuckled and lowered his sword. "Not if you value your skin, you won't." He motioned toward the ledge. "Have a seat. This shouldn't take long."

"But—"

"Sit."

Absorbed in the battle before him, Hasheth could only nod. He clambered onto the rock, barely registering the dead lizard beside him, or the northerner's comic grimaces as he fastidiously removed the creature.

Arilyn Moonblade fought like no other Hasheth had seen. She held her ancient sword with both hands, yet her strike was as quick as a desert snake. Easily she engaged both of the Calishite's flashing scimitars. Within moments the man fell backward, clutching at his slashed throat.

The half-elf stooped and cleaned her sword in the sand. Like one asleep, Hasheth slid from the rocky ledge and drifted forward, his eyes fixed in horrified fascination on the dead man.

Danilo came to stand beside Arilyn. "I'd wager my entire gem collection that the boy had never seen death close at hand—until now, that is."

"He's lived a sheltered life," Arilyn responded softly. "Few men die in a harem."

"And those who do, die happy."

Oblivious to the Harpers' conversation, Hasheth

dropped to his knees beside the body. His hands reached toward the man's outer shirt, hesitated, then parted the dark folds. A quilted sash of pale silver silk girded the dead man's undertunic. Hasheth looked up at Arilyn.

"This man wore a shadow sash," he whispered, "and you killed him with ease."

The half-elf pushed a handful of black curls off her damp forehead and shrugged. "He was better at stealth than at honest combat."

"Even so, the gray sash marks its wearer as an assassin of the highest rank and skill," the lad said quietly, never taking his eyes from the corpse.

"Oh-oh," Danilo murmured, suddenly realizing what was coming.

Hasheth drew in a steadying breath and quickly unknotted the sash, tugging it free of the dead man's body. He rose and presented it to Arilyn with grave formality. "This belt and rank are now yours."

Arilyn eyed the proffered sash and swallowed hard. "What am I supposed to do with it?"

"Wear it with pride," Hasheth responded earnestly. "The sash will bring you much respect in these lands, and many offers from men of wealth and power. The shadow sash also grants you entrance into the Assassins Guild, and even a position in the ruling body of the School of Stealth, should you desire it."

"Two guilds," Danilo said softly. "Between the Assassins Guild and the Wine Merchants Guild, we could surely get the information we need."

Arilyn glanced at Danilo's sympathetic face and gave a curt nod of agreement. She gingerly plucked the sash from Hasheth's outstretched hands and tied it quickly around her waist.

"I was not ready to listen to your words," Hasheth said, an apology in his tones. "Will you now tell me what brings the Harpers to our lands?"

"We would like Pasha Balik to remain in power," Danilo began.

The young man smiled. "Already you have my interest. That is my wish as well."

Hasheth listened politely as Danilo spoke, but the boy's face darkened with shock and outrage as the mage related the guilds' plot against the pasha. He sat in silence for many moments after the story had ended.

"What's wrong, Hasheth?" Arilyn prodded.

The young man shifted uneasily. "Clearly I must withdraw from the School of Stealth if I wish to stay alive, but doing so would be regarded as a failure. The guild would not hesitate to spread false tales of my cowardice, which would bring great dishonor to me and to my father. This is more than a matter of pride," Hasheth added quietly. "I wish to aid my father, but will he regard the words of a man without honor?"

"You might be able to leave the School of Stealth without dishonor," Danilo said thoughtfully.

"I do not see how," the boy replied, his face glum.

The nobleman grinned. "Barter much, Hasheth?"

"That is generally a task for merchants and servants, but I am familiar with its principles. One begins by suggesting an impossibly high price, which is countered by an equally absurd low figure. Eventually both parties settle somewhere in the middle."

"Precisely," Danilo said. "This is what you do: you and a servant will take this man's body to the assassins' guildhall. If I understand the rules, his death earns not only the sash rank, but guild membership and a position at the School of Stealth. Demand all three. That's the high bid."

"But I did not kill him," Hasheth protested.

"This is barter, remember? What place does honesty have in making a bargain?"

A touch of humor lit the boy's eyes. "Go on."

70 • Elaine Cunningham

"The guildmasters will counter with a low bid, perhaps offer to pay you this man's bloodprice. You merely sneer and toy with that priceless scarab of yours," Danilo suggested, casting a covetous glance at the boy's ring. "Then, after a suitable pause, you suggest that you might be willing to give up the position at the School of Stealth."

"The guildmasters won't be satisfied with that," Hasheth protested. "It is true that they will not willingly make a man of my years a master assassin, but if they indeed plot against my father, they cannot allow me into the guild."

"Exactly," Danilo said patiently. "Guild membership is the main issue, and most of their attention will be focused on it. When they release you from your commitment to the School of Stealth, they'll be thinking of you in terms of a potential master assassin, not a failed student."

"Go on," urged Hasheth, a crafty smile lifting the corners of his mouth.

"They'll release you from the school and make a counter-offer. Since they can't have you poking around in guild business, all they can offer is the shadow sash itself. You pretend to think it over, then casually observe that an assassin of such high rank must be allowed into the guild, so that her activities can be monitored and her fees properly tithed. Emphasize 'her' subtly."

"Ahhh." A slow, admiring smile crept across Hasheth's face. "That will befuddle them."

Danilo grinned. "That's right. You'll change the direction of negotiations abruptly, gaining an advantage through surprise. Introduce your 'servant'—that's you, Arilyn—as the woman who overcame the shadow sash. Repeat your demand for rank and guild membership for her—and imply you were speaking for Arilyn all along. Chances are they'll be so relieved to be rid of you that they'll embrace Arilyn. Figuratively speaking, my dear," Danilo assured the half-elf.

"But what of my assignment? I can hardly champion a woman I was ordered to kill," the boy pointed out.

The nobleman raised one eyebrow. "If the guildmasters bring that up, remind them that you were released from the school, and therefore, from any assignments. Barter met is bargain sealed, as they say hereabouts. You'll have gotten the better of them, and they'll probably admire you for it."

Hasheth's delighted laughter rang out over the wasteland. "You think like a southerner: devious and subtle. It would seem that I have misjudged you."

"Everyone does," Arilyn said. "That's why he's such an effective agent."

"Lord Thann is a Harper, as well?" The young man's brow furrowed as he thought this over. "A nobleman can join such a group?"

"Even a pasha's son," Arilyn said with a smile. "In time."

Hasheth nodded thoughtfully. "I might like that."

Danilo folded his arms and smiled broadly. "Then perhaps it is time for you and me to barter. Tell your father all that has happened. Tell him that Arilyn and I will seek proof that the guilds threaten his power. Ask him to hear what we say and judge for himself."

"That is your high bid?" scoffed Hasheth.

"You interrupted me too soon," the nobleman said plaintively. "I was going to ask for that ring of yours, as well."

The boy's dark eyes flashed. "That is absurd! This ring is a mark of royalty. Here is my offer: as you ask, I will deliver your warning to my father. You may not have the ring, but I will be your ears and eyes in Tethyr. From this day, I will pass to the Harpers whatever information reaches the pasha's court."

"Throw in a couple of camels, and you have a deal," Danilo offered.

"Done."

The young man concluded the bargain in such solemn fashion that neither Harper had the heart to explain that Danilo had been joking.

"Congratulations, Danilo," Arilyn murmured, struggling to keep the laughter from her voice. "We've done our duty to the Harpers and you finally got your two camels."

Published for the first time in this volume.

ELMINSTER'S JEST

Mark Twain wasn't much of an opera fan. He once suggested that Wagner's music "was probably better than it sounded." The same could be said of Danilo Thann, who, at least for the first few years of his Harper career, was a far better bard than most people credited him. That's no reflection on the collective musical discernment of the good people of Faerûn, for Danilo deliberately fostered his foppish, dilettante image with silly tavern tales and bawdy ballads. "Elminster's Jest" is a ballad Danilo "taught" to a singing sword, which Elaith Craulnober very reluctantly wielded in the novel Elfsong. *Only part of the ballad appeared in the novel—not because of editorial censorship, but because that's all I included in the story. Here's the whole thing.*

ELMINSTER'S JEST

Attributed to (read, "blamed upon") Danilo Thann

There was a knight who longed to wield a more impressive lance
To carry into battle and to aid him with romance.
A wizard overheard the knight and granted his request.
The noble knight was overjoyed to see how he was blessed.

CHORUS:
Hey there, ho there; a lesson's here for you:
Be careful what you ask for, for your wishes may come true.

The knight went to a party with his weapon thus enhanced.
The lance made dining difficult and tripped him when he danced.
The next day at the tournament he won the jousting meets,
For all who faced his fearsome lance fell laughing from their seats.

CHORUS

The knight espied a lady who admired his staff of oak.
They'd scarce begun their gentle joust before the staff had broke.
The knight sought out the wizard, who replied when brought to task,
"Your wish bespoke how long it was, and not how long 't'would last."

CHORUS

Repeat Chorus if possible, run if necessary. . . .

Originally published in Realms of Infamy
Edited by James Lowder, December 1994

THE MORE THINGS CHANGE

There's quite a bit of distance between Evermeet, the island realm of Queen Amlaruil, and the Branch Davidian compound in Waco, Texas, but this story started in both places. After the debacle at Waco, I got to thinking about the fragility of an unexamined, all-encompassing world view. Some of the people who died in that fire came from a religious background very like my own. I've seen what can happen to people who were raised to think of their philosophy as Sole Truth, accept without question the "package deal" it presented. All too often, a single crack in this paradigm can bring the whole edifice down like a crystal castle. Strangely enough, many people who experience a break of this nature tend to seize upon the next all-encompassing package that comes along. And there doesn't have to be a religion on either end of the process: some people break free of super-controlling parents only to join a cult, kibbutz, or a corporation that demands eighty-hour work weeks. If the only life you know involves functioning within a strictly defined set of rules and mores, finding your own way isn't easy.

This is not the sort of thing easily translated to fiction—unless, perhaps, you're talking about elves and magic swords.

Elaith Craulnober excelled in the role of elflord of Evermeet, but when his expectations were confounded, his opinion of himself and his understanding of his place in the world shattered. He utterly abandoned the life he knew and the values he held. But the more things change, the more they stay the same; he threw himself with equal fervor into the next role that came along. The distance between elflord and crime lord is shorter than it might appear. Many years passed before Elaith began to understand the dangers inherent in the unexamined life. When he entrusted the training of his daughter Azariah, heir to the Craulnober moonblade, to Arilyn, he gave the half-elf this advice: "Teach her the rules, and then tell her to question them."

THE MORE THINGS CHANGE

Whenever Elaith Craulnober wished to find his future wife, he knew precisely where to look. He knew also what she would be doing. Although he didn't entirely approve, he'd long ago abandoned any notion of taming the fierce elven lass.

The young elflord hurried through the palace gardens and down a path that took him deep into Evermeet's royal forest. He made his way to a grassy clearing shaded by a canopy of ancient trees. As sure as sunrise, Princess Amnestria was there, sword in hand and skirts kilted up around her knees. Her blue eyes blazed with concentration as she faced off against the finest swordmaster in the kingdom, and her pale face shone like a damp pearl. With both hands she clung to her practice sword—a long, broad blade that looked far too heavy for her slender strength. Her knuckles were white and her arms shook from the strain of balancing the oversized weapon.

Elaith's jaw firmed. He strode forward into the glen, determined to have a few words with the princess's instructor.

When Amnestria caught sight of the handsome, silver-haired elf, she dropped her sword and flew into his arms like a delighted child. Elaith caught the elfmaiden and swung her off her feet in an exuberant spin, delighting in the playful mood she always invoked in him. Theirs was an arranged marriage, but in this as in all things, Elaith considered himself the most fortunate of elves. He was extremely fond of the princess, and justly proud of the brilliant match.

Even without her royal lineage, Amnestria was remarkable. She possessed rare spirit and fire, and a pragmatic intelligence. Her beauty was not yet in full flower, but already minstrels had begun comparing her to Hanali Celanil, the elven goddess of love. She had blue eyes flecked with gold, and the rarest hair color among moon elves: a deep, vibrant blue-black that poets likened to spun sapphires. Her features were delicately molded, her form exquisite. Amnestria was the very embodiment of moon elven beauty.

Yet something about her often struck Elaith as too ... human. That was the only word for it. Despite her merry nature, the princess displayed the intensity of purpose and singular focus usually associated with that vigorous, short-lived race. Battlecraft was her passion, and she divided her spare time between her swordmaster and the war wizard who tutored her in battle magic.

Remembering the source of his ire, Elaith set Amnestria down and prepared to castigate her swordmaster. The older elf, however, had discreetly slipped out of the clearing and was heading down the forest path, sympathy and nostalgia etched on his angular face.

Amnestria noted his departure and wrinkled her nose. "My teacher is deserting me before I'm ready to stop," she said. "Let's have a match!"

"It is not fitting for the captain of the king's guard to cross swords with a princess," Elaith said in the patient, gentle tone he used rather frequently with the girl.

She dimpled, and her eyes mocked him. "You're just afraid that I'll best you, and then Father will turn your job over to me!"

"The guard exists to protect you, my dear princess, not employ you. No member of the royal house has ever served in the ranks, and you're not likely to change things," he reminded her. "The king has too much regard for tradition."

Amnestria responded with an inelegant snort. "Tell me something I don't know!"

"You misread me, *damia*," Elaith said earnestly, using an elven endearment directed to sweethearts or children. "I meant no disrespect to the king."

"Of course not." Amnestria sighed heavily, but her dancing eyes still teased him. "That would be hoping for too much."

"What do you mean?" His tone was sharper now.

"You're a dear, Elaith, but sometimes I worry for you." She paused, reflecting. "It's the hardest thing to explain."

"Make an attempt," he requested coolly.

"You're always so proper, and you follow the rules as if they were graven in alabaster. You're—" Amnestria broke off, clearly at loss for an explanation. Her slender hands milled in small circles as if she could create an air current strong enough to draw out the right words. "You're . . . you're such an elf."

"Of course, *damia*," he agreed, a little amusement creeping back into his voice. "What else would I be?"

"But don't you ever think about all this?" she persisted with the earnestness of the very young. Her slender hand traced an arc in the direction of the nearby palace, the wondrous moonstone castle that was the very heart of Evermeet. "I've never heard you wonder why, or question, or challenge anything. You just do whatever's expected, and you do it better than anyone else. You're the consummate elf," she repeated. Her natural effervescence asserted itself, and the golden lights in her eyes danced like giddy fireflies. "An elf's elf. The very epitome of elfdom," she elaborated, then bubbled over into giggles.

With another lightening change of mood, the girl snatched up her sword and whirled on her betrothed. "Fight with me!" The words were half request, half demand.

Elaith made her a formal bow. "But Your Highness, is that not what we were doing?" The glint of humor in his amber eyes belied his words, and Amnestria let out another peal of laughter.

"I suppose we are." She struck a pose straight out of an ancient, illustrated tome: sword tip resting on the ground before her, one elegant hand extended. "My lord, let us make peace. You are my silver knight, and I your only love," she said, mimicking the courtly language of elven legend.

Responding in kind, Elaith bent low over her hand and pressed it to his lips. With a sudden flash of insight, he realized that despite her lighthearted game Amnestria spoke simple truth. He loved this child-woman with all his heart. He averted his eyes from her frank gaze, lest he reveal emotions she was not yet ready to comprehend. For Amnestria's sake, he tucked away the pang and the joy of this revelation, hoarding it like a red dragon guards its dearest treasure.

"Why are you practicing an ancient fighting technique?" he asked, turning the conversation to the subject dearest to her heart. "Are you performing in an historical masque for the midsummer entertainments?"

"No! This is swordcraft, not play," she told him in a stern voice.

"Then why?"

Her dimples flashed again. "You've met my great-aunt Thasitalia?"

"Yes," he said flatly. The elfwoman was a free-sword who'd traveled widely, debasing her moonblade by lending her skills to anyone who could offer gold and adventure. The mercenary's tales enthralled Amnestria, and Elaith considered Thasitalia a bad influence on the restless princess. Still, he had to give the elfwoman credit. Moonblades were rare and so powerful that few could wield them. As the last in his family line, Elaith stood to inherit such a blade from his grandsire. He considered this his greatest honor, a mark of his heritage no less cherished than the elven princess he loved.

"Thasitalia made me her blade-heir!" Amnestria announced, holding out both hands to him. "Now we will each have a moonblade. Isn't that marvelous!"

"It is indeed," he said with genuine warmth, taking her hands and giving them a little squeeze.

"We'll need to have scads of children, so we can choose the strongest among them as blade-heirs," she said in a matter-of-fact tone that brought heat to Elaith's cheeks. Seeing this, the maiden rolled her eyes and dropped his hands. She arranged her face in a lugubrious pose and intoned, "It is not seemly to speak of such matters, Your Highness," in a wicked imitation of Elaith's precise, mellifluous tones.

"But anyway," she continued in her own voice, "Thasitalia told me to start practicing with a two-handed grip and a heavy sword. Her moonblade's magic adds unusual speed and power to the strike, and she says that I must develop strength and quick reflexes, or I won't be able to control the sword."

"So you're in training, preparing to inherit a moonblade?"

"Of course. Aren't you?"

Smiling, Elaith touched the shoulder of the white uniform of King Zaor's elite guard. The insignia there proclaimed his rank, and finely wrought pins attested to his expertise in a number of arts and weapons. "All my life I have prepared."

☙ ☙ ☙ ☙ ☙

Directly across the street from Waterdeep's southernmost docks stood a ramshackle barn of a tavern, optimistically named the Tumbled Wench. The tavern was frequented by sailors and dockhands, free-swords in search of adventure, merchant captains, bored local dandies, and bemused travelers from a hundred ports and a dozen races. Local wisdom had it that the Tumbled Wench wove as good a picture of Waterdeep as a visitor was likely to get: a chaotic tapestry of splendor and squalor.

Exotic smoke filled the air with fragrant haze, and business deals mingled with bawdy laughter in cheerful cacophony. Wealthy merchants and noblefolk with a taste for gritty adventure bumped elbows with low-rent escorts and tattered street people. The prospect served the needs and tastes of all: for a few coppers, patrons could eat their fill or drown their miseries. Efficient barmaids bustled about with trenchers of seafood stew and tankards of foaming ale. More expensive libations were available, and the kitchen would roast herb-stuffed fowl to order. The occasional panicked squawk of birds in the back courtyard attested to the freshness of this fare.

Oblivious to the bustle around him, a dazed young elflord sat at the long wooden bar, nursing a single glass of Evereska sparkling cider. His choice of beverage, so unusual in the rough taverns of the Dock Ward, caused more than one patron to smirk and nudge his neighbor.

The snide witticisms were spoken softly, though, for few seasoned fighters offered open challenge to a well-armed elf.

As Elaith sipped at his cider, the vague sickness that had haunted him throughout his long and unaccustomed sea voyage slipped away. His ebbing discomfort made him all the more aware of the aching void that both filled and consumed him. Evermeet had been his life, Amnestria his love, and he had chosen to leave them both.

His meeting with the princess in the forest glade had been their last, but for their farewell. That very night his grandsire's spirit had passed on to Arvanaith, and the Craulnober moonblade had become Elaith's to claim.

Never would Elaith forget the horror of watching the pale light of the moonstone, the magic-bearing gem in the hilt of his inherited sword, fade to the dead, milky whiteness of a blinded eye. The moonblade had rejected him, choosing dormancy over an unworthy heir.

This possibility had never occurred to Elaith. He had felt neither doubt nor fear as he'd unsheathed the sword, although he well knew that many heirs failed to claim a moonblade. Most of these unfortunates had been struck dead by the swords, but if an elf were the last in a family line, the hereditary blade would merely fall dormant. To safeguard the potent artifacts from misuse, the original crafters had endowed the swords with the ability to discern character and motivation. The moonblade apparently sensed some flaw Elaith had yet to discover for himself.

"Your mother uses gray squirrels for currency!"

The cryptic remark, spoken in loud and badly accented Elvish, shattered Elaith's reverie. He spun about on the barstool to face the man who had spoken.

"Are you addressing me?" Elaith asked politely, speaking the widely used trade language referred to as Common.

A nasty grin split the man's bearded face. "I knowed it! The elf ain't deaf, just too good to speak when spoke to."

Belatedly, it occurred to Elaith what the human had been trying to say. The man had delivered a mangled version of an insult, of the sort elven children tossed at each other in fits of pique. More amused than insulted, Elaith studied the human with open curiosity.

The man stood a hand's span over six feet, and he appeared fit and heavily muscled. He wore a uniform of sorts—black leather armor that sported an elaborately tooled crest on the shoulder. Curly brown hair rioted over his shoulders and spilled into an abundant beard, and his face was twisted into a leer of challenge. One meaty hand rested on the grip of a dagger, and his booted feet were planted wide. Yet his bravado was marred by a pair of red-rimmed eyes. The scent of cheap ale rolled off him in pungent waves.

Elaith was not tempted by the challenge. Even if the drunken soldier had possessed the full measure of his wits, there were strict rules against dueling someone of lesser rank.

"I will not fight you. It would not be—" Elaith broke off abruptly, for the word *honorable* no longer seemed to apply to him.

The man sneered, mistaking Elaith's hesitation for cowardice. "You'll fight if I say you will." He kicked the barstool out from under the elf.

Elaith saw the move coming and leapt lightly to his feet. The stool upended with a clatter that echoed through the suddenly silent taproom, and patrons seated by the bar quickly remembered urgent business at the far side of the tavern. The elf was not pleased to be the focus of attention. He resolved to end the matter swiftly.

With a theatrical flourish, the huge drunk pulled his dagger and lunged. Elaith stepped to the left and seized the man's thick wrist with both hands. A slight twist brought the man to his knees. The elf slammed the back of the beefy hand onto the barstool, locking his opponent's arm in an extended position. Then Elaith lifted one booted foot and stomped on the elbow. Bone gave way with a cruel splinter. The man fainted away without uttering a single cry.

Silence reigned in the tavern for only a moment. Another, even larger man stepped forward, clad in the same black leather armor. He nodded at his fallen fellow. "That's my cousin," he growled.

Elaith folded his arms. "My condolences," he said. "Since none of us can choose our kin, I shall not hold this misfortune against you."

"We can choose our friends, though, and you ain't one of mine." The mercenary reached over his shoulder and drew a broadsword from the sheath on his back.

Chairs scraped across the floor as the patrons cleared an impromptu arena in the middle of the taproom with an alacrity that suggested such fights were far from uncommon. The barkeep glanced up, then went back to polishing the pewter mugs.

"Borodin," the man said firmly. "Remember it. That's the name of the man who's gonna kill you." He raised his weapon in challenge.

Elaith reached for his sword, but hesitated when his fingers touched the lifeless moonstone. Borodin marked this hesitation with a derisive snort.

Something snapped within the elf's heart.

Stooping, Elaith pulled the sword from the fallen man's belt. The weapon needed a good oiling and sharpening, for the sword was blunt and the edge visibly pitted. Elaith studied it for a moment, then pointedly raised an eyebrow and met his opponent's glare.

"This should do," he said. His tone conveyed utter contempt for both the weapon and his challenger.

Borodin raised his sword high and brought it down in a sweeping cut. Instead of the satisfying clash of steel on steel, his effort was met with the crack of breaking wood.

He had just enough time to note that his victim was an upended bar stool before his plowed heavily into the bar. Mugs scattered with a mocking clatter.

For good measure, Elaith smacked Borodin's backside with the flat of his borrowed blade. Guffaws echoed throughout the tavern.

Borodin whirled and delivered a backhanded slash. Elaith parried the blow easily. With practiced grace, he spun his blade outward in a lightning-fast circle, flinging Borodin's sword arm wide. In the same moment, he pulled a dagger from his belt and stepped in close. The point of the dagger bit into Borodin's throat.

For a long moment they stood frozen, Elaith's cold amber eyes promising death. Then, with a deft, downward flick, he slashed open the leather lacings on the man's jerkin. He leaped back and tucked his dagger into its sheath. In a gesture of utter contempt, he lowered his sword arm to his side and beckoned for Borodin to attack.

"Ten coppers on the elf!" shouted a gravel-voiced sailor. Other patrons joined in, making wages and laying odds.

The man advanced, his bearded face crimson but set in determination. With his initial rage spent, he fell back into a more disciplined fighting style. At one time, the man had been well trained, but by Elaith's standards, Borodin possessed neither finesse nor imagination.

By honor and custom, he should have ended the matter at once, for his opponent was clearly outmatched. Yet Elaith continued, openly taunting the man with his superior skill. The elf was driven by a cold anger he'd never known he possessed, an icy temper than numbed the pain in his own heart. For the first time since he'd left Evermeet, Elaith could put aside his sense of disgrace and failure. With cruel humor and stunning swordcraft, he played out the fight for the amusement and delight of the rough patrons.

As the minutes ticked by, Borodin's sword arm slowed and his breathing grew labored and raspy. Finally he could take no more. He fell to his knees, and then his forehead met the floor with a resounding thud. Several of his mates came forward and pulled him to his feet. They staggered out into the night with their burden, running a gauntlet of mockery.

A roar of approval and laughter engulfed the tavern, and Elaith found himself in the center of a back-slapping throng. A plump, red-bearded man, also wearing the tooled leather uniform, offered to buy the victorious elf a drink. "After all," he said as he dangled a small leather purse in front of Elaith's face, "you won the money for me! The name's Rix, by the by."

The friendly overture struck Elaith as odd behavior indeed for a man whose comrade had just been bested, but he accepted the offer and followed the man to the far end of the bar. At Rix's signal, the barkeep handed them each a tall, narrow glass filled with a thin liquid as golden as honey.

"What is this?"

"Firewine." The soldier winked and slurped at his drink. "Bottoms up!"

Elaith took an experimental sip. The pale liqueur had none of the subtlety or complexity of elven spirits, but it was nearly as powerful. He drained the glass with dark pleasure; the firewine filled his mouth with a dry, bitter heat. His new companion gaped, then guffawed.

"Never trust a man—or an elf—until you've seen him fight and drink," Rix said cheerfully. "And on both counts, you're surely not to be trusted!"

He craned his neck and shouted at a knot of black-clad fighters near the tavern door. "Xander! Sign up this elf! Tonight, mind you, or the whole lot of us will quit!"

One of the men broke from the group and made his way toward the bar. With a mixture of puzzlement and deep interest, Elaith watched his approach. Xander was a man of middle years, in the prime of his strength. He was slender and tall, with skin the color of polished teak, wavy black hair plaited into a single long braid, and mocking black eyes. He walked with sinuous grace, but Elaith noted a military bearing and air of command. The elf could recognize a leader in any guise, and he rose to his feet in an instinctive gesture of respect.

Xander studied the young elflord for a long moment. "A good recommendation, Rix. Tell Malcolm to give you twice the usual finder's fee. Now, off with you. I need to speak with our new recruit."

The red-bearded mercenary picked up his glass and strolled off, grinning broadly. Xander took the seat Rix had vacated and gestured for Elaith to resume the one beside it.

The bewildered elf sank onto the barstool. "You wish me to join your regiment?"

"Regiment? Oh, that's priceless!" Xander's white teeth flashed in a smile of genuine amusement. He took a gleaming black pipe from a bag at his belt and pressed a bit of pipe weed into the bowl. The barkeep at once held out a lighted brand, his manner clearly deferential. Xander puffed for a moment, then leaned casually against the bar. "I'm the leader of a mercenary band. Treasure hunters."

Elaith nodded slowly. By all reports, the humans of Waterdeep were like so many dragons, hoarding useless wealth and measuring their success by the height and luster of the pile. That had always seemed strange to Elaith. A life of acquisition was entirely foreign to the values that had hitherto ordered his life. As he considered the matter now, however, he found the wonderful simplicity in this system appealing.

"You should have killed Borodin, you know," Xander observed.

Elaith stared. That was the last piece of advice he would have expected, even from this amazing man.

"Although your performance was amusing and your swordsmanship most impressive, you've made yourself an enemy. That was totally unnecessary. As a rule, you ought to eliminate enemies as they occur, not create them and let them linger to trouble you again later."

"I am unfamiliar with such . . . rules."

"They're easy enough to learn. Just do whatever needs doing to get rich and stay alive in the process. Above all, look out for your own interests." Xander took a long draw, then blew a wreath of clove-scented smoke at the elf. "You could do quite well for yourself if you cast your lot in with the Claw."

"You would have me? I disabled two of your men!"

"That you did." The mercenary captain considered Elaith for a time, sipping thoughtfully at his pipe. "With your skills, I can replace two men with one elf—and pocket another share of the treasure myself."

Elaith paused to ponder the unfamiliar logic. "Treasure," he repeated, more to buy time than to signify interest.

"Big treasure. Ever heard of Erlunn?"

"Of course." Erlunn had been one of the great centers of elven culture in the Northlands. The elves had long since moved on, and their civilization had been swallowed by the ancient wood known as the High Forest.

Xander pulled a metal tube from his belt and removed a small roll of parchment. He spread it out and tapped at a spot near the river labled Unicorn Run.

"Rumor has it that, centuries back, the elves buried their dead and all their wealth among the roots of oak trees. Your good friend Borodin—" Xander paused and tossed his head toward the tavern door "—found a stand of ancient oaks surrounding a circle of stones. When he pulled the moss off the foot of the stones, he found these markings. We copied them here on the map, and later paid a priest of Lathander to translate them."

Xander pointed to the runes scrawled along the bottom of the parchment. "According to this, Borodin found a burial site."

Tomb robbing, the elf thought with a touch of horror. His dismay must have shown on his face, for Xander lifted one black eyebrow in inquiry.

But Elaith had no ready answer. The life Xander offered him was as far from the peace and discipline of Evermeet as anything the elf could imagine. No traditions, no rules but expediency, no goals but power and wealth. The elf nodded slowly as the new mode of thinking began to take root in his mind.

"Borodin's an even bigger fool than I took him for. Your hired priest was not much better. These are runes of protection," Elaith said, tapping the curving symbols. "The standing stones and the oak trees are guardians. The actual grave sites would be much deeper in the forest."

"You could find the true site?" Xander asked.

"Possibly. But if I am to join your ranks, I must know more about the life you lead."

"What's to know? Just do what you're told and don't spend much time wondering why."

Elaith recoiled, for the mercenary's advice was an uncanny echo of words Amnestria had spoken in the forest glade. The life that Elaith had lived on Evermeet felt as distant as a forgotten dream, but it seemed that some things remained the same. As Amnestria had so perceptively noted, he could do whatever was expected of him, and do it better than anyone else.

Elaith leaned back in his chair and returned Xander's steady, cynical gaze. "If I am to replace two men, I expect to receive two full shares of the treasure."

An approving smile split the mercenary's dark face. He gestured to the barkeep, who produced two new glasses of firewine. Xander lifted his glass to the elf in a silent salute.

Elaith raised his own glass and tapped it against his new employer's, in a manner he had seen among the fighters. A toast, they called it, a ritual used to seal a pact.

The elf drained the firewine in one long draught. As the golden liquid seared his throat, Elaith willed it to burn away his past, as well.

◈ ◈ ◈ ◈ ◈

Many years passed, and Elaith seldom thought about Evermeet or pondered how vastly his life had changed since he'd left. He could not help but do so now as he faced the two women seated in his lavish study. One was his daughter; the other should have been.

Elaith studied Azariah, his blade-heir and only child. The proper elfmaiden sat with downcast eyes. Her golden hands were demurely folded in her lap. She had been raised on Evermeet as a ward of the royal court, and was everything Elaith once had been. This was her first visit to Waterdeep as an adult, and her first confrontation with her father's dark reputation. Although Azariah tried to hide it, she was also daunted by Arilyn Moonblade, the half-elven woman beside her.

Arilyn waited calmly for Elaith to speak, all the while regarding him with Amnestria's gold-flecked blue eyes. He had known the half-elf for years, and had observed her with a mixture of admiration and longing. Arilyn was a fierce, stubborn woman who had made her mother's moonblade her own. She had inherited Amnestria's beauty and spirit, and a certain wisdom that the elven princess had once tried to share with Elaith. It was this that prompted Elaith to entrust his daughter's training to her.

He had endured much to restore the magic to the family's moonblade. Azariah's heritage, her success, was more important to Elaith than his next breath. Yet as he studied the beautiful elven maiden and reflected on all

The Best of the Realms • 95

the qualities she embodied, he realized that there was not so much difference between his old life and his new. Granted, he had amassed tremendous wealth and a well-earned reputation for treachery and cruel humor. He was feared and envied for his success as a treasure-hunting mercenary, and for the unofficial power he wielded in Waterdeep. Yet the changes were more a matter of style than substance. He did what was expected of him, acted in ways defined by his chosen role. And as Amnestria had noted that afternoon on Evermeet, he did it better than anyone.

Elaith no longer wondered why his moonblade had rejected him, those many years ago.

The elf handed Arilyn a tightly rolled scroll. "This is a history of the Craulnober moonblade—its wielders, its magic. This is what Azariah must know. Teach her the necessary skills, make sure she understands the rules."

Elaith paused, and his amber eyes held the sadness that comes in wisdom's shadow. "Make sure she learns the rules," he repeated softly, "and then, above all, teach her to question them."

Originally published in Realms of Magic
Edited by Brian M. Thomsen and
J. Robert King, December 1995

THE DIRECT APPROACH

If you're a fan of the Chicks in Chainmail *anthologies, you might recall a short story by Esther Friedman entitled "The Broad in the Bronze Bra." This story tickled me, and I decided to take the motif of time-traveling female barbarian and run with it. The resulting tale takes place in the short interval between* Daughter of the Drow *and* Tangled Webs. *At the time Liriel Baenre was hanging out in Undermountain, waiting for a ship that would take her and Fyodor of Rashemen, her berserker companion, on the next leg of their journey. The story's unpublished subtitle is "Girls' Night Out in Skullport," which sums things up rather well.*

THE DIRECT APPROACH

Skullport, an underground city hidden far below the streets and docks of the more respectable port of Waterdeep, was one of the few places on the Sword Coast that offered wary welcome to the drow. Elsewhere, the dark elves' fearsome reputation earned them the sort of reception otherwise reserved for hordes of ravening orcs; in Skullport, a drow's night-black skin merely guaranteed that she could walk into the tavern of her choice and not have to wait for a table.

Dangerous and sordid though it was, Skullport appealed to Liriel Baenre. It boasted all the chaos of her hometown but lacked the inhibiting customs and the ever-vigilant eyes of its priestess rulers. Liriel's stay in the underground port had been brief, but long enough for her to learn that anything could happen in Skullport. And usually did.

Even so, she was not prepared for her midnight visitor, or for the strange manner in which this visitor arrived.

Earlier that evening, Liriel had retired to a comfortable chamber above Guts and Garters, a rough-and-tumble tavern renowned for its dwarf-brewed ale and its bawdy floor show. This was her first quiet evening since entering Skullport, and her first opportunity to study the almost-forgotten rune lore of an ancient barbarian race known as the Rus. Liriel's interest in such magic was passionate and immediate, for in two days she would sail for far-off Ruathym. There lived the descendants of the Rus, and there Liriel would learn whether this rune magic could shape the destiny of a drow.

After several hours of study, she paused and stretched, catlike. The sounds of the tavern floated up to her: the jaunty dance music, the mixture of heckling and huzzahs, the sound of clinking mugs, the occasional brawl—all muted by thick stone to a pleasant murmur. Liriel did not desire to join the festivities, but she enjoyed knowing that excitement was readily available should the spirit move her to partake. Besides, the noise made an agreeable counterpoint to her reading. With a contented sigh, the young drow lit a fresh candle and returned to her book, absently tossing back a stray lock of her long white hair as she bent over the strange runes.

In any setting, dark elves survived only through constant vigilance. Liriel, although deep in her studies, remained alert to possible dangers. When the garish tapestry decorating the far wall shuddered and began to fade away, she responded with a drow's quick reflexes. In a heartbeat, she was on her feet, a dagger in one hand and a small, dangerously glowing sphere in the other.

The wall dissolved into a vortex of shimmering light—a magic portal to some distant place. Liriel's first thought was that her enemies had found her. Her second thought was that her enemies were getting better.

Liriel was no stranger to magical travel, but never had she seen anything like the silent storm raging before her. The colors of a thousand sunsets mingled in the whirling mist, and pinpoints of light spun in it like dizzy stars. One thing was clear: whoever came through that portal would be worth fighting.

A smile of anticipation lit the drow's golden eyes, and every muscle in her slight body tensed for the battle to come.

The portal exploded in eerie silence, hurling multi-colored smoke to every corner of the room. The magical gate disappeared and was replaced by the more mundane tapestry, before which stood a most peculiar warrior.

Liriel blinked, wondering for a moment if a figure had somehow stepped off the tapestry's battle scene. The barbarian standing before her was more like some ancient illustration, brought improbably to life, than a creature of flesh and bone.

The drow stared up—way up—at a human female warrior. The woman was taller than the elven girl by more than a foot and was at least twice as broad. Fat braids of flame-colored hair erupted from beneath a horn-bedizened bronze helm and disappeared into the thick reddish bearskin draped over her shoulders. Apart from these garments and a pair of knee-high, shaggy-furred boots, the warrior was virtually naked. Leather thongs bound weapons to her person and held in place a few strategically placed scraps of metal-studded leather. The woman's skin was pale, her muscles taut, and her curves of the sort usually encountered only in the fantasies of untried youths and libidinous artists. In fact, the warrior's curves, costume, and theatrically grim expression suggested to Liriel that this woman was supposed to be part of someone's evening entertainment. Obviously, she'd missed a turn somewhere on magic's silver pathways.

"Nice entrance," Liriel observed, "but the floor show is in the main tavern."

The barbarian's sky-colored eyes narrowed, and she reached over her shoulder for the hilt of her broadsword. Tossing back her helmed head, she took a long, proud breath—dangerously taxing the strength and expansion capacity of her scant leather garments—and lifted her sword in challenge. Remnants of the luminous smoke writhed around her, adding significantly to the overall effect.

"Behold Vasha the Red, captain of the Hrothgarian guard, hired sword arm of the Red Bear Clan, and eldest daughter of Hanigard, queen of the ice water raiders," the warrior announced in a voice that shook the windowpanes and promised doom.

Liriel got the feeling that this introduction was usually met with groveling surrender, but she wasn't overly impressed by her visitor's credentials. That broadsword, however, was another matter entirely.

Candlelight shimmered down the sword's rune-carved length and winked with ominous golden light along its double edge. Liriel's dagger, which was long and keen and coated with drow sleeping poison for good measure, seemed woefully inadequate beside it. The wisest course would probably be to toss a fireball and settle the damages with the innkeeper later. It'd be messy, but there was something to be said for a quick resolution in such matters.

Liriel hauled back her arm for the throw and let fly. The barbarian used her sword to bat it back, in a movement so cat-quick that Liriel would have applauded, had she not been busy diving behind her writing table.

To the drow's astonishment—and infinite relief—the fireball dissipated with apologetic fizzle. She scrambled to her feet, keeping the table between herself and her visitor.

With a deft swipe, she snuffed the candle, leaving the room in darkness.

But if Liriel's visitor felt herself at disadvantage, she did not show it. A smug little smile lifted the corners of the warrior's mouth. "Foolish runecaster! Your foul magics avail you not against such as Vasha. You cannot escape the justice of the Rus, though you flee through time itself! Return with me for trial, or die now by my hand." The muscles in the barbarian's sword arm twitched eagerly, leaving little doubt as to which option she preferred.

Liriel waved away the threat impatiently. This had possibilities! Magical portals could give transport to distant places, through solid objects, even into other planes. Could they could span the centuries, as well?

"Please tell me you're truly a warrior of the Rus, and not some low-rent courtesan with bad fashion sense."

A scowl creased the woman's brow. Her glacial blue eyes thawed just enough to register uncertainty, and she squinted into the shadows that hid her foe.

"Have I not said? Did you not hear? I am Vasha the Red, daughter of—"

"You said, I heard," Liriel snapped. "But where did you come from? And more important, from *when*?"

"This is the twelfth year of the reign of King Hrothgar. The *last* year of his reign, as well you know! In the dark of the hunter's moon, Hrothgar was slain by your foul magic!"

The drow pondered this announcement. She had been extremely busy of late, but she was fairly certain she hadn't killed anyone by that name. Upon further consideration, she recalled that the adventures of a King Hrothgar were recounted in her book of rune lore. He'd been outwitted by a renegade runecaster of dark and exceptional power. But by Liriel's best calculations, that had happened nearly—

"Two thousand years ago!" she said, regarding the

swordwoman with new respect. "I'll say this much for you: you can hold a grudge with the best!"

Vasha was neither flattered nor amused. "Surrender, runecaster," she bellowed as she hauled her sword high overhead.

Liriel feinted a lunge to her left, and the swordwoman followed with a slashing attack. The mighty blow would have riven Liriel neatly in twain, had it only connected. But the elf dived to the right, rolled twice, and was back on her feet in time to witness most of the sword's descent. It swooped down to slice cleanly through Liriel's rented bed. The coverlet, mattress, ticking—even the roping and wooden slats of the frame—gave way before Vasha's wrath. The bed collapsed in upon itself like a spent puffball mushroom, spewing feathers upward into Vasha's face.

The barbarian reeled back, sneezing violently and repeatedly. Liriel took advantage of this development to cast a spell of holding, effectively freezing Vasha in midsneeze. That done, the drow stalked over to the ruined bed, plucked her book of rune lore out of the drifting feathers, and shook it before the swordwoman's contorted, immobile face.

"This is what led you here, you blazing idiot! This book describes rune magic, of a sort that no one has cast for hundreds of years. You're chasing the wrong wizard!"

Liriel took a long, deep breath to compose her wits and calm her temper. Then she snapped her fingers, and at once the darkness was banished by floating globes of white faerie fire. In the sudden bright light, her delicate, elven face shone like polished ebony. She tucked her abundant white hair behind elegantly pointed ears, then propped her fists on her hips.

"Tell me," the drow purred with silky sarcasm, "do I *look* like a runecaster from the Red Bear Clan?"

Vasha did not offer an opinion, but some of the bloodlust faded from her trapped eyes. Liriel took this as a good sign.

Nevertheless, she pried the sword from the barbarian's hands and hurled it into a far corner before releasing the spell of holding. She had an offer for Vasha, and, in her experience, people tended to bargain much more reasonably when they were unarmed.

☙ ☙ ☙ ☙ ☙

"I tell you, Liriel, daughter of Sosdrielle, daughter of Maleficent, the runecaster is near," insisted Vasha. "The vile Toth, son of Alfgar, misbegotten upon Helda, the goddess of boars, whilst she was in human form—or so Alfgar claims—is in this very city." The barbarian's voice was slightly fuzzy now, and her ruddy face glowed with the combined warmth of the tavern's fires and too much dwarven brew. Still, she spoke with a conviction that rattled the globe on their table's oil lamp.

The drow leaned back in her chair and signaled for another round of drinks. A half-orc servant hastened over with two more foaming mugs. Vasha threw back her head and quaffed her ale without once coming up for air. She slammed the empty mug on the table and ripped out a resounding belch.

Liriel sighed. The swordwoman had a prodigious thirst and an apparently endless capacity for dwarven ale. Although Vasha's tongue loosened a bit with each mug, Liriel feared that the barbarian would drain the tavern's cellars before giving up anything useful.

"Believe me, magical travel can be tricky, and in your case something went wrong," the drow explained yet again, clinging to her patience by her fingernails. "Listen, Vasha: I'll help you get home, but first you must tell me more about your people's magic."

The swordwoman scowled and reached for her companion's untouched mug. "But I am Vasha, daughter of Hanigard—"

Liriel slammed the table with both fists. "I *know* who you are, for the love of Lolth! Just get to the blasted *point!*"

"Some warriors of the Rus know rune magic. My family is not among them," the swordwoman said sullenly. "We spit upon magic, and those who wield it rather than honest weapons. Even the sword I carry, passed down to me upon the glorious death of Hanigard, queen of the ice water raiders—"

"What. About. The sword?" Liriel prompted from between clenched teeth.

"It cleaves through magic, as you have seen. That is all the rune lore I know, or care to know."

The drow lifted both hands to her aching temples. "Let's go over this one more time. Why do you insist that the runecaster you seek is in Skullport? And why did you promise me rune lore, if you have none to give?"

Vasha reached into a boot—the only garment large enough to yield much storage space—and pulled out two objects. One was a small leather-bound book, the other a broken bit of flat stone carved with elaborate markings. Liriel snatched up the book at once and gazed at its creamy vellum pages with something approaching reverence. This was an ancient spellbook, yet the pages were as white and the runes as sharp and clear as if they'd been inscribed yesterday.

"Written by Toth's own thrice-bedamned hand," Vasha said. "The book is yours, in fulfillment of the word of Vasha, daughter of Hanigard, and so forth. According to the runecasters who sent me here, Toth escaped to a distant place of wicked rogues and fell magic, where such as he might walk abroad and attract no more notice than bear droppings in a forest."

"That describes Skullport, all right," Liriel agreed as she tucked the precious book into her bag. "But then, it describes a lot of places."

The barbarian picked up the piece of stone and handed it to Liriel. The fragment was as hot as a live coal; the drow cursed and dropped it. She glared at Vasha and blew on her throbbing fingers.

"The closer the runecaster, the warmer the stone," Vasha explained. "This is a fragment of a time-coin, one of the very excesses that prompted King Hrothgar to censure Toth, to his ultimate sorrow. With this stone, the vile runecaster can travel at will through time."

Liriel reached for the coin shard, the pain in her fingers forgotten. "How does it work?"

Vasha shrugged. "The secret is in the stone coin, and in the runes thereon. How it was done, I know not, and neither do I care. This much I can tell you: Toth left half of the coin in his keep, that he might later return. This shard comes from that half; the rest remains in the judgment hall of the Red Bear Clan. Once I have Toth and the pieces of the coin he carries on his person, I can return with him to my own land and time. When the time-coin is again whole, the lawful runecasters will see it destroyed for once and all."

The drow absorbed this in silence. "If the time-coin's magic remains potent no matter how many times it's divided, Toth could jump from Skullport to yet another time and place, as long as he leaves behind a bit of the coin-half he carries. This could take a while."

Vasha's jaw fell slack as she considered this possibility. "It may be as you say," she allowed, eyeing Liriel thoughtfully. "Perhaps the gods did not err in sending me to you, after all. No honest warrior can walk the twisted pathways of a dark elf's mind, yet such might be the straightest way to a wretch like Toth."

"Don't think I'm not enjoying all this flattery," said Liriel dryly, "but if we're going to find your runaway runecaster before he goes somewhere and some*when* else, we'd better get started."

The barbarian nodded and reached for the remaining

mug. She drained it as she rose to her feet—a quick but unsteady motion that tipped her chair over backward and sent it skidding along the floor. A patron just entering the tavern stepped into its path.

Liriel saw the collision coming but could do nothing to avert disaster. There was barely time to cringe before the chair crashed into a purple-robed illithid. The creature's arms windmilled as it fought to keep its balance, and the four tentacles that formed the lower half of its face flailed about as if seeking a saving hold. There was none, and the illithid went down with an ignominious crash.

A profound silence fell over the tavern as everyone there studiously minded his own business. The illithid scrambled awkwardly to its feet and scuttled over to intercept the barbarian woman, who, heedless of danger, was striding toward the tavern door.

Vasha pulled up just short of the man-shaped creature. Her wintry eyes swept over the illithid, taking in the stooped, misshapen body, the bald lavender head, and the pupilless white eyes and writhing tentacles that defined its hideous face. All this she observed with detached curiosity. But when her gaze fell upon the arcane symbols embroidered upon the creature's robe, her lip curled with disdain.

"Stand aside, runecasting vermin, if you value your life," she ordered, placing a hand on the hilt of her broadsword.

Because drow knew illithids like cheese knows rats, Liriel saw what was coming, and she pushed back from the table with a cry of warning. Too late: the mind flayer let out a blast of mental power that sent Vasha's auburn braids streaming backward. The swordwoman stood helpless— her eyes wide with shock and her powerful muscles locked in place—as the illithid closed in to feed. One purple tentacle snaked upward and flicked aside the woman's horned helmet. In the silence of the tavern, the clatter of bronze hitting the stone floor resounded like a thunderclap.

But the noise was promptly overwhelmed by Vasha's battle shriek. With sheer force of will, the warrior tore herself free from the mind flayer's grasp. Her sword slashed up from its scabbard, lopping off the probing tentacle. The purple appendage went flying in a spray of ichor, and the illithid staggered back, its vacant eyes bulging weirdly.

Not one to be content with mere dismemberment, Vasha leapt at the creature and wrestled it to the floor. She quickly pinned the writhing mind flayer, and, sitting astride its chest, neatly braided the three remaining tentacles.

The utter absurdity of this act jarred the dumbfounded drow into action. Liriel darted over to the barbarian and dragged her off the fallen illithid. She shoved the much larger woman toward the exit, eager to escape before any of the stunned patrons thought to summon what passed for law in Skullport.

At the doorway Liriel paused and glanced back into the still-silent tavern. "She's new in town," the drow announced to the room at large, and then she slipped into the darkness beyond.

☙ ☙ ☙ ☙ ☙

Skullport was located in an L-shaped cavern many feet below sea level and curved around the deeply hidden Sea Caves. Accordingly, it was damp and dark. Much of the cavern's light came from the eerily glowing fungi and lichens on the stone walls and the water-stained wood of the buildings huddled haphazardly together. Some of these glowing fungi were mobile, and viscous globs of the stuff inched along the stone-ledge walkways until they were booted out of the way or squashed underfoot into luminous green puddles. Clouds of mist clung to the lanterns that dotted the narrow, twisting streets with feeble light, and everywhere the air was heavy with the smell of sea salt and the stench of the city. Travelers and merchants of many races—few of which were welcomed in most other cities—sloshed through puddles and streams whose contents were best left unexamined.

With each step, Vasha's fur boots became more bedraggled, her visage more dangerously grim. Yet she strode steadfastly along, clutching the stone coin in her hand and choosing her path by the heat it gave off.

Liriel might have admired the woman's single-minded fervor, except for the fact that it was likely to get them both killed. The drow jogged along behind Vasha, her eyes scanning the crowded streets and dark side passages for dangers the barbarian would not perceive. That was no small challenge, for if Liriel could imagine a person less suited for life in Skullport than Vasha the Red.

The city's multilayered intrigues—although muted by the "safe ground" policy that made trade between enemies possible—were complicated by bizarre magical occurrences, the legacy of the city's founder, one extremely mad wizard. Vasha's rune-carved blade might have been forged to dispel magical attacks, but all magical weapons had limitations, and Liriel had no desire to find out what these might be.

Just then Vasha waded carelessly through a tightly huddled cluster of haggling kobolds. Her passage sent the rat-tailed merchants scattering and allowed the object of their disputation—a comely halfling slave girl—to dart into the dubious safety of a nearby brothel. The cheated kobolds wailed and shook their small fists at the departing barbarian. Vasha spared the goblinlike creatures not so much as a glance, but disappeared into a small dark alley.

Liriel recognized the opening to a tunnel, a particularly dark and dangerous passage that twisted through solid rock on its way to the port. She muttered a curse, tossed a handful of coins to appease the gibbering kobolds, and sprinted off in pursuit.

The drow raced down the tunnel. She rounded a sharp turn at full speed, only to bury her face in the thick fur of Vasha's bearskin cloak.

The collision did not seem to inconvenience the barbarian in the slightest, but Liriel rebounded with a force that sent her staggering backward and deposited her on her backside. From this inelegant position, she had a clear view of the magical phenomenon that had not only given Skullport its name, but had also brought Vasha the Red to an abrupt stop.

Bobbing gently in the air were three disembodied skulls, larger than life—or death, to be more precise—and glowing with faint, rosy light. Liriel had never seen the Skulls, but she'd heard enough tavern talk to know what they were. Remnants of the mad wizard's defenses, the Skulls appeared randomly to give absurd tasks to passersby, or to punish those who disturbed the city's tentative peace. By all accounts, bad things happened to those who heeded them not. And by all appearances, Vasha was in no mood to heed. Her sword was bared, and her muscles knotted in readiness as she took the measure of her new adversary.

The middle member of the weird trio drifted closer to the warrior woman. "Stranger from another time and place, your ways do not belong in these tunnels," it informed Vasha in a dry whisper. Its jaw moved as it spoke, clicking faintly with each word.

"In my land, voices from beyond the grave speak words worth hearing!" proclaimed the warrior. She brought her sword up and gave the floating skull a contemptuous little poke. "Tell me something I don't know, or get you gone!"

"Um, Vasha—" began Liriel, who had a very bad feeling about what was to come. Tavern tales indicated that challenging the Skulls was not a good idea. Indeed, the bony apparition glowed more intensely, and its teeth clattered in apparent agitation.

"For your arrogance, and in punishment for disturbing the rules of safe ground, your assigned tasks will be long and noxious," decreed the Skull. "First, you must capture and groom a thousand bats. Save the loose hairs and spin them with wool into a soft thread, which you will then dye in equal parts black and red. Weave from the thread a small black tapestry emblazoned with a trio of crimson skulls, and hang it in the tavern where you slew the illithid."

Vasha scoffed. "The squid-creature died from so small a wound? Bah!"

"Next, you shall seek out a company of goblins, invite them to a tavern, and serve them meat and drink," the Skull continued.

"Vasha the Red, a serving wench to goblins? I would sooner bed an orc!"

"I was getting to that." There was a peevish cast to the dry voice.

Liriel scrambled to her feet and tugged at the barbarian's fur cloak. "Agree to anything, and let's get out of here!" she whispered urgently. "And by all the gods, don't give that thing ideas!"

"I shall give it somewhat to ponder," promised the swordwoman in a grim tone. "No one, living or dead, gives orders to Vasha the Red!"

With that, Vasha flung back her sword arm—sending Liriel tumbling once again—as she prepared to deal a whole new level of death to the presumptuous Skulls. Her sword slashed forward in a mighty stoke that reduced all three of the floating heads to dust and fragments.

Pieces of bone sprinkled the stone floor with a brittle clatter and a shower of rapidly fading pink sparks. Then, just as quickly, the fragments flew back into the air and reassembled into a single large skull. The apparition hung there for a moment, glowing with intense, furious crimson light, and then winked out of sight.

Liriel leaped to her feet. "Damn and blast it, Vasha, you can't go smashing everything in your path!"

"I don't see why not."

"Oh, you will," the drow muttered, noting the faint glow dawning in the void left by the departed Skulls. She dived for safety just as the glimmer exploded into an enormous whirlwind of rainbow-colored light.

Out of this magic tunnel stepped a ghostly wizard—the apparition of a long-bearded male garbed in the pointed hat and flowing robes of an age long past. Tavern rumors suggested that all wizshades resembled a certain sage currently residing in faraway Shadowdale. As to that, Liriel could not attest, but she could not help noticing that this wraith-wizard's hair, robes, and skin were all of the same vivid emerald shade.

Vasha the Red, meet wizshade. The green.

This bit of dark humor flashed into Liriel's mind and was gone just as quickly. Frantically, she reviewed her current magical arsenal, but the power of the wizshades was reputed to far exceed those of most mortal wizards. Liriel doubted that any of her ready spells would have much effect.

Vasha, naturally, took a more direct approach. The warrior slashed with deadly intent at the green wizard's neck. Her sword whistled through the wizshade without achieving the desired decapitation. Again, on the backswing, the broadsword passed right through the seemingly solid wizard. Neither blow cut so much as a hair of his verdant beard.

The barbarian fell back a step and shot an inquiring glare in Liriel's direction. The drow, however, was just as puzzled. According to tavern lore, magical weapons could inflict real damage upon wizshades. But Vasha's broadsword, which until now had sliced through magic like a knife through butter, had drawn not a single drop of green blood. Worse, the wizshade's emerald-colored fingers had begun an ominous, spellcasting dance.

Suddenly Liriel understood what hadn't happened, and why. The broadsword had been warded to destroy magical attacks; it had no magical powers of its own. But Liriel had weapons that might serve—strange devices steeped in the unique radiation magic of the Underdark.

Liriel snatched a spider-shaped object from a bag at her belt and hurled it at the spell-casting wraith. Her throwing spider whirled between the gesticulating green hands, and its barbed legs bit deep into the wizard's gut. The apparition shrieked, tore the weapon free and flung it aside, and then dived back into the vortex. The whirl of multicolored light sucked in upon itself and disappeared.

Vasha tucked away her sword and regarded Liriel with approval. "You see? Magic cannot stand before honest steel." She stooped to retrieve and examine the throwing spider. "Even when the steel is in so strange a shape," she mused.

The drow decided not to waste time with explanations. She reclaimed her magic weapon from the woman and returned it to her bag. "Let's go," she urged, knowing that the Skulls' orders could not long be ignored. "Either we find your runecaster and get you out of the city by day's end, or you'll be grooming bats for the rest of your natural life!"

"I'd rather bed a satyr," muttered Vasha darkly.

"Well, sure. Who wouldn't?" agreed the drow as she pushed the barbarian firmly along the tunnel.

The swordwoman, who was becoming accustomed to the elf's dark sense of humor, shot a scornful look over her shoulder. But the expression on Liriel's face—at once serious and dreamily speculative—turned Vasha's withering glare into an astonished double take.

"This is indeed a strange place," she marveled.

Liriel nodded her approval. "Well, praise the Dark Lady. You're finally catching on."

◉ ◉ ◉ ◉ ◉

But Vasha the Red's insight proved to be shallow and fleeting. Throughout the rest of that night and most of the following day, the warrior woman met every obstacle with a ready sword and a snarl of contempt. By the time evenfeast hour rolled around, they were no closer to finding the elusive Toth than they'd been at the onset of their quest. On the other hand, Vasha had hacked a sentient jelly into quivering globs, dueled to the death with an ill-mannered ettin, surgically dampened the ardor of several pirates on shore leave, and trimmed the wings from the shoulders of a small but aggressive wyvern, after which she'd advised the creature's dumbfounded wizard master to have the hide tanned and made into a decent pair of boots. In short, only through a mixture of dumb luck and brute strength did she and Liriel survive the day.

When she could bear no more, the drow steered her charge into the Burning Troll. It was a pricey tavern, but the food was good, the halfling servants were prompt, and the patrons could be reasonably sure of an entertaining brawl. As soon as they were seated, Liriel ordered roast fowl and bread, wine, and a bowl of cold water. She plucked the stone coin from Vasha's hand and threw it into the bowl. The hot fragment met the water with a hiss of protest, and then subsided. Liriel wished that the human was half as reasonable.

"Forget about the coin for now. We can't keep running around Skullport, following a piece of rock and killing whomever you please."

"Why not? I've done just so these many hours."

"And we have so much to show for it," Liriel returned with acid sarcasm.

The barbarian could not dispute this failing. "So?"

"This Toth is slippery, even for a wizard. To catch him,

we'll need planning, subtlety, treachery. I know of some people who for the right price . . ."

Her voice trailed off, for it was clear that the swordwoman was no longer listening. Vasha's dangerously narrowed eyes were fixed upon the bowl of water meant to cool the stone fragment. The water was now at a full boil. Steam rose from the roiling surface, and the stone tumbled in the churning water.

The barbarian drew her sword and used it to point toward the tavern door. "Behold Toth, son of Alfgar!"

Liriel beheld. An involuntary smile curved her lips as she did so, for standing just inside the door was Vasha's male counterpart: tall, muscular, flame-haired, and dressed without regard for modesty. On him, the drow noted with approval, less was definitely more. But she wondered, fleetingly, where he carried his spell components.

The runecaster was not at all cowed by the spectacle of an enraged Vasha. He sauntered directly over to their table. With insolent ease, he conjured a third chair and straddled it.

"By what fell magic did you find me?" demanded the warrior. Her face and voice were as fierce as usual, but Liriel suspected that Vasha was both embarrassed and unnerved at being caught off guard. Liriel was none too happy about that, herself. She'd spent the day in Vasha's wake, too busy trying to stay alive to realize that the runecaster had been leading them on a merry chase. He apparently had a devious streak, something that the drow understood very well and should have recognized.

"Greetings, Red Vasha," Toth said amiably. "I heard you were in town and assumed you were looking for me, so I followed the trail of destruction to its source."

"If you are so eager for battle, let it begin," snarled the swordwoman. "I challenge you to a contest of honest steel!"

Toth cast a wry look in Liriel's direction. "Notice she

did not suggest a battle of wits. Our Vasha might be eager, but even she would not enter a fight unarmed."

The insult sent Vasha leaping to her feet. The table upended with a clatter, bringing a faint cheer from the tavern's patrons. So far, the evening had been too quiet for their liking.

The warrior brandished her sword; Toth plucked an identical blade from the empty air. They crossed weapons with a ringing clash, and the fight began.

The combatants were well matched and in grim earnest, and the tavern patrons were not long content to watch and wager. Sme strange force drew them into the mayhem, as surely as bees to clover. Small skirmishes broke out here and there. Those who had blades used them. Others took up lesser weapons, each according to his strength: humans and half-orcs brawled using fists and feet, goblins and hags pelted each other with mugs and bread, mongrelmen lobbed shrieking halfling servants at the ogres, who promptly returned fire with furniture. In moments the entire tavern was engulfed in wild melee.

Liriel edged to the side of the room, skirting the worst of the fighting and occasionally ducking a flying halfling. Despite the natural immunity to magic that was her drow heritage, she could feel the seductive tug of some unknown spell pulling her toward battle. This Toth was good.

But however good he might be, the runecaster underestimated Vasha if he thought that a tavern-wide brawl might distract her. True, the goblins' mug-throwing had showered her repeatedly with ale, and the growing piles of bodies necessitated some extra footwork in the dance of battle, but the swordwoman did not seem to care or even notice. Her face was set in an ecstatic grimace as she slashed and pounded at her long-sought prey. Liriel watched closely, impressed that Toth managed to hold his own against such fury. But then, drow wizards were trained fighters, so Liriel knew that swordplay was no serious deterrent to spellcasting.

Spellcasting was generally frowned upon in this tavern, but the melee thoroughly absorbed the attention of the other patrons. Thus the drow was the only one to see the forgotten wedge of stone rise from a puddle of water on the floor, fly into the runecaster's hand, and meld with the half-circle he held. Only she saw Toth slip the time-coin into his scant loincloth, saw his lips move as he spoke unheard words of magic.

For a moment Liriel eyed the handsome runecaster and wished she'd paid better attention when that halfling pickpocket had tried to teach her the trade. She quickly cast an incantation of her own, then waited confidently for what surely would happen next.

Toth disappeared, as expected.

And with him went the spell of battle-lust. Most of the combatants stopped fighting at once, blinking stupidly as they regarded their upraised fists or drawn blades. One ogre, who had lifted a halfling overhead and hauled him back for the throw, stopped so abruptly that the hapless servant went flying backward as opposed to hurtling into enemy ranks. His shriek, loud and shrill in the sudden lull, indicated that he did not consider this fate an improvement. The halfling crashed feetfirst through the tavern's wooden door and hung there, half in and half out, groaning softly.

The rush toward the halfling-bedecked exit was sudden and general. All who could leave the tavern did so, for participation in fights of this magnitude was usually rewarded with a night in Skullport's dungeons. In mere moments Vasha and Liriel were the only able-bodied persons left in the room.

The barbarian's roar of frustration rattled what little crockery remained. "Coward! Oath breaker! Vile runecasting son of a wild pig!" shrieked Vasha, shaking her sword and dancing with rage.

"You should have seen that coming," the drow said calmly.

"How could I, Vasha the Red, an honest warrior, foresee such treachery? I fought with honor! Here I stand, drenched in the blood of mine enemy—"

"That's ale," Liriel pointed out.

Vasha looked down at her sodden raiment and saw that it was so. This mundane discovery leached a bit of the fight—and a good deal of pride—from the barbarian's eyes. She tucked away her sword, crossed her arms over her mighty bosom, and pouted.

"Blood, ale. It matters only that Toth has escaped to where only our daughters' daughters might find him!"

"Oh, I don't think so," said the drow in a satisfied tone. She held out her palm. Lying in it was a stone coin, whole except for a small wedge.

Wonder lit Vasha's eyes. "That is the time-coin! But how?"

"Typical devious drow tactics. I stole it from Toth, using a simple spell. Sometimes magic is the most direct method, after all."

Vasha conceded with a nod. "Magic has triumphed, strength has failed," she admitted humbly. "But where then is Toth, if he cannot travel through time?"

"A wizard powerful enough to construct a time portal could be almost anywhere," Liriel said. "My guess, though, is that he's somewhere in Skullport. It's exceedingly dangerous to travel to a place never before seen. Also, once he realizes he's missing that coin, he won't go far."

This reasoning brought glowing hope to Vasha's face. "Then we can still hunt him down!"

Liriel lunged at the departing barbarian and seized the edge of her bearskin cloak. "I've another idea, but you must agree to the use of magic."

The swordwoman subsided, bowing her head in resignation. "How can I not? Vasha the Red has failed. I yield to the wisdom of the drow."

Liriel held up the runecaster's book. "This tells how to use the coin. We'll step back in time, to the point just before Toth came into the tavern. And this time, we'll be ready for him."

Vasha agreed. She stood guard while Liriel studied and cast the intricate spell, and she managed to hold on to her temper and her sanity when she found herself once again seated across the table from Liriel in an undamaged tavern. But the sight of a small coin fragment at the bottom of the bowl of water made her swallow hard.

"We have failed! Toth still holds his half of the coin; he can flee!"

"Why should he?" Liriel retorted. She pulled a knife from her boot and used it to fish the stone from the rapidly heating water. "He's coming here looking for us, remember? He doesn't know that I'll lift his half of the coin."

As she spoke, the drow fingered a tiny pocket just inside her sleeve, where she had hidden the nearly whole coin that had traveled back in time with her. She did not understand how this had happened, or have any idea how the coin could exist simultaneously in its past and present forms. But she saw no reason to speak of this, or any harm in keeping silent. As long as Vasha got her runecaster and brought him back to stand trial before the ancient Rus, all would be well.

Vasha still looked puzzled, but she allowed the drow to position her near the tavern door, in plain sight of any who might enter. Liriel took her place nearer the entrance. "Toth will be looking for you, so I've got a better chance at getting in the first blow," the drow explained. "If I miss, feel free to step in."

The barbarian shook her head. "I do not doubt your success. What shall you do—imprison the runecaster in some mysterious dark-elven spell?"

"Something like that," Liriel said absently. She retreated

into herself, seeking the innate magic that flowed through the fey dark elves. Summoning her natural power of levitation, she drifted up to hover high above the doorway's lintel.

This act was easy enough for Liriel, something that all drow of the Underdark could do. But this was not the Underdark, and the spectacle of a floating drow was unusual enough to draw every eye in the tavern. Even Vasha stared, bug-eyed and gaping.

Thus it was that Toth, when he entered the tavern, noted the general bemusement and instinctively followed the line of the patrons' collective gaze. When he looked up, Liriel was ready—not with some spell, for she could not know what magical defenses this powerful runecaster might have. This time the drow took a page from Vasha's book: she used the hilt of her dagger to bashed the poor sod between the eyes.

Down went the mighty Toth. Liriel floated lightly to the floor and crouched beside the fallen runecaster. She patted him down, found his half of the coin, and pressed the smaller fragment to it. The stone pieces joined, flowing together as smoothly as two drops of water.

The drow handed the restored coin to Vasha. "As much as I'd love to keep this, you've got to get home before the Skulls come looking for you."

"My thanks, Liriel, daughter of Sosdrielle, daughter of Maleficent," the barbarian said gravely. "I shall long remember your wisdom, and never again will I disparage the power of magic or the importance of treachery!"

Liriel shrugged. "Just don't get carried away. Although I never thought I'd admit it—especially after the day I've just had—there are times when the best approach is the most direct one. Even if that's a good swift blow."

The swordwoman nodded, pondering these words as if they'd come from an oracle. "Complex indeed is the wisdom of the drow," she marveled. "Though I live a hundred years, never could I fathom it all. And yet," she added, her voice becoming less reverential, "there are some things that even such as I can learn."

Out flashed Vasha's blade once again, and the glittering point pressed hard against the base of Liriel's throat. "The second time-coin," the swordwoman said flatly. "The one you brought back with you. Give it to me."

For a moment Liriel considered trying to bluff. Then, with a sigh, she handed it over. "But how did you know?"

Vasha smiled thinly. "You wished to learn about the Rus. What better, more direct way than to travel back through time yourself? Since you gave up the coin so easily, I knew that there must be another." With that, she shouldered the unconscious runecaster, held up one of the identical time-coins, and spoke the words that summoned the gateway to her own time and place.

A wary silence followed Vasha's disappearance, as the tavern's patrons waited to see what might next transpire. Liriel recalled the spectacular brawl and returned the hostile glares without flinching. "Trust me, it could have been worse."

And that, she decided much later that evening, was an excellent summary for the day's adventure. Her encounter with Vasha could have turned deadly in a thousand different ways. True, Liriel had not gained the ability to travel through time, but she had acquired a new book of rune lore. She'd also received a valuable reminder of the wisdom of clinging to her drow ways.

Whatever benefits the direct approach might have, it was too damned predictable.

*Originally published in Realms of the Arcane
Edited by Brian M. Thomsen and J. Robert King*

SECRETS OF BLOOD, SPIRITS OF THE SEA

One of the things I enjoy most about writing short stories is the opportunity to try new things. This is a metastory—a story about a story, as told by a wemic loremaster to his elf captors. Who these elves are and why they're hunting wemics is never revealed. For all we know, they might have very good reasons. But the wemic doesn't think so, and he rebukes them by relating a legend about the creation of the sahuagin race.

It's a grim tale, and the events it describes might not actually have taken place—by which, of course, I mean that these events may not be FORGOTTEN REALMS *"canon." But as Professor Indiana Jones once told his archaeology class, there's a difference between "truth" and "fact."*

SECRETS OF BLOOD, SPIRITS OF THE SEA

You, there! You, the elf with ink-stained fingers and eyes the color of rain. Come closer. I could not harm you even if I wished to do so. Your nets are strong.

You are chieftain of this hunting party, are you not? Yes, so I thought. It is even so with my people. Loretellers and spirit-talkers are leaders among the wemic.

This surprises you, elf? We lion-folk are not the savages of common-told tales. Oh, hunters we are, and warriors, too—make no mistake about that—but wemics know much of music and magic, tales and legends.

Do not doubt me: I am Shonasso Kin Taree, second O (or "grandson," as you two-legged folk reckon kinship) of the great Kanjir, and I am loreteller of the wemic tribe Taree. Loose me from this net, elf, and I will tell you a tale long hidden, a story of dire magic and of fearsome creatures that no living wemic on this savannah has ever seen, except in night-visions sent as evil portents.

Yes, I thought this offer might interest you! Of all the two-legged folk, elves have the sharpest curiosity. I see you have parchment and quill at the ready. Before we begin, tell your kindred to put up their spears. You have my word that I will bring neither claw nor blade against any of you until the telling is done. And then, I will fight only if forced to defend myself against your displeasure.

You would never attack a bard whose tale displeased you? Hmmph! As my grandsire would say, "Leave that tale untold 'til the deed is done." But since you're so eager to give pledge, promise me this: Swear to write down my words just as I speak them, and to put the scroll in a place where many might read this tale and remember.

Good. I have your oath and you have mine. And now you shall have the story, as it was told to me.

In a time long past, when elves and dragons battled for supremacy in a world still young, there lived a dark-elven wizard whose powers were unmatched, except perhaps by his enormous pride.

Ka'Narlist was archmage of Atorrnash, a once-mighty city whose secrets have slept for centuries in the deep jungles of a faraway land—secrets that are whispered still beneath a hundred seas.

The dark elf's lair was a great fortress of black stone that stood high and proud atop a seaside cliff. From his keep, Ka'Narlist could look out over the Bay of the Banshee, a vast spear of seawater that thrust deep into southern Faerûn. Far below his castle, the sea thundered and sang and shrieked—mournful, ceaseless music that darkened the wizard's thoughts by day and haunted his reverie by night.

Put away your maps, elf. That bay is long gone—lost when the One Land was sundered and scattered by best-forgotten magic. Do not be surprised that I know of such things. Our legends are as ancient as your own, and more honest.

Now, shall we continue?

As the years passed, Ka'Narlist's eyes began to linger upon the stormy bay. He spent long hours pondering what might lie beneath the vast waters, both in the bay he saw and in the trackless seas beyond. Though scholar he was, he did not wish merely to know: he intended to possess.

Such ambitions were not unusual among his people. The Ilythiiri, the dark elves of the south, were fierce, warlike people who plundered and conquered and enslaved a thousand tribes. Not even their fair-skinned elven kindred were safe from their raids! Ka'Narlist had earned his wealth in such raids, and he also brought back slaves from many lands to labor in his keep, and to feed his pride. One of these captives was Mbugua, a shaman of the wemic. Of him we will speak again.

Despite all their power, the Ilythiiri were seldom content. Ka'Narlist possessed enormous wealth, magical spells beyond the comprehension of your mightiest mages, and the fearful respect of his tribe. Even so, as he gazed out over the watery realm that no dark elf could truly claim to rule, he came to think of his honors as he did the rocky shore: even the mightiest of stones is worn down into sand by the pounding sea that is time. He came to envy the timeless powers of the gods. He aspired to claim such powers as his own.

Since Ka'Narlist was a scholar, he knew legends that spoke of entire races brought into being to serve the purposes of their makers. If Gruumsh One-Eye had his orcs and the Earth Mother her leviathan, surely a wizard of his stature could fashion a race of his own—creatures of his own making that would sing praises to him, that would enhance his power and increase his dominion.

There was no question in the wizard's mind as to what that dominion should be: Ka'Narlist wanted control of the sea depths. After much thought, he decided to create a seagoing people, a fierce race driven to brutally conquer their watery domain—in Ka'Narlist's name, of course. So that his "children" could never rise against him, he decided not to gift them with magical powers. Speed, stealth, voracious hunger, and treacherous cunning would be their weapons.

It was a simple matter to decide what must be done; the doing was far more difficult. But not, on the whole, unpleasant. At least, not unpleasant to one such as Ka'Narlist...

☙ ☙ ☙ ☙ ☙

"Hand me the hooked knife," Ka'Narlist murmured absently. His attention was utterly fixed upon tormenting the unfortunate kodingobold strapped onto his study table; he did not bother to raise his crimson eyes to the wemic who stood attentively at his elbow.

Mbugua had the tool ready before the words were spoken—he had aided his master too many times not to understand what was needed—and he slapped the smooth handle onto the wizard's outstretched palm.

The wemic would have preferred to turn the blade, to drive it deep between two fragile elven ribs or to slice off a couple of black fingers. Long and painful experience had shown him the folly of such action. Whenever Mbugua had attacked the Ilythiirian wizard, the intended wound had appeared not on the elf, but upon the wemic's own person.

Many times had proud Mbugua sought his freedom; many times had he woken on his pallet with a pounding head and dim memories of the horrible rituals that had restored his maimed body. Once, only once, had he managed to deal a mortal blow, and thus had escaped Ka'Narlist into death. But the wizard's dreadful god, Ghaunadaur, had wrested the wemic from his afterlife and brought him back to this wretched captivity. Even after many years, memories of this horrific experience tore Mbugua screaming from his sleep. The evil that was Ghaunadaur, the power that was Ka'Narlist—the two had become one in Mbugua's mind.

Since the day of his too-brief death, Mbugua had, to all appearances, served his master without question or complaint. He did all things well, even attending Ka'Narlist on tasks such as this—tasks that could turn the stomach of a hunter, and that made the noble wemic's every instinct shout that it would be a holy act to run a spear through a being who could calmly, systematically inflict such pain on a living creature.

Not that Mbugua had any use for kodingobolds. They were nasty, odorous, rat-tailed creatures—ugly things with four-footed, doglike bodies that were topped with scrawny humanoid torsos and sly, bug-eyed faces. Gray of skin and of soul, they seemed to possess neither conscience nor ambition. Kodingobolds lived solely on whatever they could steal. They were cowards who fought only if they greatly outmassed and outnumbered their prey. And they had a particularly fondness for the flesh of young wemics. In years past, many an adventurous and wandering wemic cub had fallen prey to the disorderly packs of kodingobolds that ranged the savannah. Mbugua's own tribe had nearly exterminated the murderous, thieving little creatures, and the wemic shaman did not mourn their loss. Even so, the look he cast at the shrieking, writhing kodingobold bordered on sympathy.

He himself had suffered similar experimentation, albeit with considerably more fortitude. Mbugua had been one of the first to pay the price for Ka'Narlist's latest ambition. The wemic's body had been probed and sliced and sampled until at long last the wizard was satisfied he had his sought-for answer. It was the blood, Ka'Narlist claimed—the secrets of life were in the blood.

Mbugua was a shaman, and his people and his magic said otherwise, but what words could argue against the wizard's terrible success? Ka'Narlist had used his wemic slave's blood as an ingredient in some dark magic; the eventual result was the birth of two new creatures—a tawny beast who boasted Mbugua's proud black mane and powerful four-footed body, and a humanlike infant with a wemic's dusky golden skin and catlike eyes.

Ka'Narlist's joy had matched Mbugua's horror. To the wizard, this represented the successful "separation" of the wemic into his apparently component parts: human and lion. To the wemic, this was an atrocity beyond comprehension. The elated Ka'Narlist did not notice the outrage and the grim purpose on his slave's leonine face. If he had, he could not have failed to realize that Mbugua had sworn a blood oath against him.

And yet, such knowledge would have mattered not at all. Ka'Narlist was secure in his pride and his power. The dire pledges of a wemic slave meant nothing to him. His own godlike work and the creatures it would eventually spawn: this, and only this, mattered to Ka'Narlist.

And so through the years, while the lion-things begotten from Mbugua's stolen blood increased into a pride, and the near-human lad became but one of many such servants laboring in the wizard's household, Ka'Narlist captured or purchased rare creatures to study. The dark wizard searched for the blood secrets that made each race unique—indeed, the secrets of life itself. Though the castle's halls and stables and dungeons were full of strange beings born of his magical experiments, the wizard was not yet content.

"You have made many other kobolds, and you have released enough dingo-creatures into the hills to endanger your tribe's flocks and herds," Mbugua pointed out, lifting his voice to be heard above the kodingobold's agonized shrieking. "What more can you gain from this pathetic creature?"

For a moment, the wizard's knife ceased its grim work. "Not every experiment went as planned," Ka'Narlist murmured in an abstracted tone. "I must have reasonable assurance of success before I begin the final stage."

The final stage.

To the wemic, these words represented the ultimate obscenity. Among his people, children were treasured by the entire tribe, and the arrival of each healthy cub was an occasion for feasting and merriment. What Ka'Narlist proposed to do was unthinkable: the dark elf intended to create horrific children from his own blood, children that would be slaves at best, coldly discarded if they did not fulfill the promise offered by Ka'Narlist's "reasonable assurances of success."

A sudden molten shriek ripped through Mbugua's grim reverie. The kodingobold's struggles, which had increased steadily as Ka'Narlist's ministrations systematically spread white-hot pain into every bone and sinew, abruptly ceased. The little creature went rigid, its body arched back, as taut as a hunting bow. Mbugua saw that the end was near, and reached for the next-needed tool.

A low, eerie keening filled the room, a sound that would ever remind Mbugua of a gathering storm. Oddly defiant and swiftly growing in power, it was not a cry that one would expect to emerge from throat of a frail and cowardly kodingobold. But Mbugua the shaman heard this cry for what it was: even in the meanest of creatures, the force of life was strong. Every defense that nature had placed into the kodingobold's body was fighting the approach of death with a berserker's frenzy. Its life-force was as intense as midday sun focused into a single beam of light—powerful and primal as it made ready to spring free into the spirit world. In this final moment of mortal life, the kodingobold was more than a miserable outcast of the wild dog-folk: he embodied the very essence of his race.

Mbugua handed his master the bleeding bowl.

With a practiced hand, Ka'Narlist flicked a knife across the rigid, corded veins of the creature's throat, held the bowl and caught the pulsing blood without spilling so much as a drop. And all the while, he chanted words of dark power that he had learned (or so he claimed) at the feet of his dreadful god.

When at last the kodingobold lay silent and still, the wizard gave a single nod of satisfaction. "Dispose of the carcass, then attend me in my spell-chamber."

"As you command, Master."

Ka'Narlist heard the note of hesitation in his slave's voice. For a moment, he was puzzled: the once-rebellious Mbugua was now the most docile and reliable of all the wizard's servitors. Then the memories came, and with them, understanding. Ka'Narlist turned a supercilious smile upon the wemic.

"Ah. You wish to sing the creature's spirit away first, I take it?"

"If my master permits it," Mbugua said in a stiff voice. Among his people, a shaman owned the respect of his tribe. The Ilythiirian wizard's disdain for spirit-magic smote the wemic's pride and kindled his wrath.

"Tell me," Ka'Narlist began, in the sort of voice one might use to tease information from a silly, sulky child, "what do you think might happen if you didn't indulge in these little games and rituals? Would we be tripping over vengeful spirits on every stairwell?"

Mbugua met the dark elf's mocking gaze. "Would you truly wish to find out?"

The wizard's smile flickered, then fled. He turned away, flicking the fingers of one hand in a gesture of dismissal. "Do what you will with the carrion. It matters not."

When Ka'Narlist's faint footsteps had faded into silence, Mbugua unstrapped the dead kodingobold from the table and slung the body over his shoulders. The wemic made his way down the winding stairs that led from the wizard's spell tower to the great hall below.

A mind-staggering variety of creatures thronged the vast room, going about their appointed tasks with an alacrity born of fear. A flock of winged elves, their fingertips sparkling with minor magics, fluttered high overhead as they labored on the multitude of long, narrow windows that ringed the hall, each a priceless work of art fashioned from multicolored gems. Several four-armed ogrish kitchen slaves bustled through on their way to the dungeons, carrying the evening meal to those unfortunate creatures who awaited Ka'Narlist's attentions. A score of miniature red dragons, each no bigger than a plump meerkat, darted about, lighting candles and oil lamps with small gouts of their flaming breath. A horde of goblin slaves busily scrubbed the intricate mosaic floor. They might have been a common enough sight, but for the rare streak of whimsy that prompted Ka'Narlist to breed goblins with gaily colored hides: sunny yellow, topaz blue, bright clear pink. To Mbugua's eye, the hall looked like a meadow filled with hideous, two-legged flowers.

As the wemic stalked through the great hall on silent, massive paws, all others fell back to make way. There was none in the hall who lacked personal experience with the wizard's dark work, and they held Ka'Narlist's leonine assistant in almost as much dread as the wizard himself.

The massive front door was flanked by a pair of minotaur guards, huge beasts armed with wicked scimitars and unnaturally long horns. Before Mbugua could growl a command, the bull-men leapt into action. They raised the portcullis and then threw their combined weight against the wooden bolt barring the outer door. The bar gave way with a groan, and the doors swung outward.

Mbugua padded out into the courtyard, gratefully filling his lungs with the cool evening air. The wizard's lair was always filled with smoke from the braziers, fetid steam from a dozen vile magical concoctions, and the ever-present scent of death.

The wemic made his way down a steep path to the rock-strewn coast below. There was a small cove, ringed with high-standing stones. He could do what he willed here, for the cove could not be seen from the castle windows and courtyard. The wizard's servants feared Mbugua too much to follow him here; the wizard himself was too prideful to imagine that a mere slave might do anything of harm or interest. Mbugua's captivity and loyalty were maintained by powerful magical bonds: Ka'Narlist trusted in his own magic.

It was that very trust, that pride, and that magic that Mbugua would turn against the dark elf. These were the only weapons he knew strong enough to defeat the wizard.

The wemic dropped the kodingobold's body onto the hard-packed soil. He stooped and picked up a small, perfectly round black object that was hidden in plain sight among the many stones. Then, closing his eyes, he reached his arms high and began the slow, rhythmic breathing that cleared his mind and prepared him to see and hear the things only a shaman could know.

In moments, Mbugua sensed the kodingobold's spirit, an unseen presence lingering like a furtive shadow. The wemic began to dance, at first padding slowly around the slain kodingobold, then in darting turns and leaps like a lion cub at play. His human arms wove a mystic pattern in counterpoint to the rhythm of his paws, magically describing the path the kodingobold's bewildered spirit must follow. He sang as well—a deep, surging chant that soared out over the twilit sea and melded with the magic of the dance.

The wemic shaman had performed many times, but this time, it was slightly, profoundly different. When at last Mbugua stood silent, his tawny form glistened with sweat as he gazed with mingled triumph and horror at the black pearl that lay in his hand, vibrating with a silent song only a shaman could hear. The gem was a magical weapon, a device created by Ka'Narlist that could swallow the magic of his enemies. Ka'Narlist kept a heaping basket of these hungry gems in his arsenal. The wemic had stolen two of them, and had adapted the fearful devices to his own purposes.

Within his hand, within the pearl, was the trapped spirit of the kodingobold.

"Forgive me," Mbugua murmured, his pride doing battle against the apology his honor demanded. Yet he did not regret what he had done. Ka'Narlist had his work, and Mbugua had his own.

The wemic reclaimed the other "hidden" pearl from the shore and began the ritual anew—but this time, his song was infinitely darker and more seductive. This time, Mbugua intended to cast magic that would lure the spirit of a living being into his snares.

Your kindred are avid listeners, elf. See how they lean in, attending to my tale! They seem troubled by the wemic's plot. I have heard that elves do not disturb the afterlives of even their enemies. This says much to commend you, if it is true. I have also heard that elves show honor to bards, yet none among you has offered water or wine to sooth my throat and to speed the tale.

Ah, thank you. You are a most gracious host. Yes, I feel quite refreshed now. Yes, I would be pleased to continue.

"You have not sought me out in many moons," Satarah observed. Her calm, musical voice gave no hint to the question in her words, and her golden face was calm as she handed her "father" a steaming mug of tea.

But Mbugua's ears were made sharp by guilt, and he heard the unspoken reproof. "The wizard grows ever more obsessed with his work. I have had little time to call my own."

"And since you are here, you must have some purpose," the girl stated plainly. "I do not see you otherwise."

The wemic sighed. "I have done what I could, Satarah. I named you for my own mother. I tried to teach you the ways of the pride. But it is difficult. This . . . this is not the life I would have chosen for you."

"Nor this body."

The wemic could not dispute her words, or fault her for the bitterness with which she spoke. Satarah was one of the "children" created from his blood, and as such he owed her the love that was any child's due. But it was difficult. It was difficult even to look upon her.

Satarah was beautiful—not even the wemic could deny that—but she was not one of the lion-folk. She had two long legs rather than four, shapely human feet rather than paws, and a slender, curvy body. Even Satarah's face was more elfish than wemic, with delicate features and no hint of the blunt cat nose that so often appeared on the children begotten of Mbugua's stolen blood. The few lingering hints of her wemic heritage only made her more exotic: her silky black hair was as thick and abundant as Mbugua's mane, her skin had a golden, sun-dusted hue, and her large, almond-shaped eyes were a catlike shade of amber. Yes, she was very beautiful, and nearly ripe for mating. Neither fact would long escape her master's attention.

"Why have you come?" Satarah repeated softly.

The wemic met her eyes. "Has Ka'Narlist taken you to his bed yet?"

Satarah's gaze kindled. "Is the wizard still alive? Am *I* yet alive? Answer those questions, and you have answered your own!"

Her fierce tone and blazing eyes smote Mbugua's heart and firmed his purpose. The bonds of blood were strong indeed: Satarah might not look like his child, but he saw something of himself in her indomitable pride. This one, regardless of the conditions of her life, would ever be free.

"You cannot strike the wizard without bringing harm to yourself," he advised her.

The girl grimaced. "This I have already learned." She lifted the heavy mass of her hair and showed him the multitude of long, livid streaks that scored her neck and shoulders.

Mbugua recognized the mark of fingernails, and noted with a touch of pride that Satarah used her hands in battle as a wemic maiden might employ her forepaws. It was a shame that such wounds had not remained upon Ka'Narlist, who so deserved to bear them!

"If he has sought you out once," the wemic noted grimly, "he will do so again."

"And when he does, I will fight again!" she growled. "I quenched his ardor in blood, and will do so again! I will have my honor or my death. It matters not which."

Mbugua started to bid her otherwise, but something in Satarah's eyes made him hold his tongue. He could not—he *would* not—instruct this fierce girl to tamely submit herself to the wizard. But he took the necklace he had made—a dainty clam shell decorated with his wemic clan symbol and hung on a string of freshwater pearls—and handed it to her.

Satarah took the bauble with glad, greedy fingers. For a moment the girl's face was bright with the pleasure of receiving a pretty gift from her father's hands, and the elven wizard was utterly forgotten. Then her eyes—eyes

The Best of the Realms • 137

that saw nearly as much as a shaman's—settled upon Mbugua's uneasy face.

"What has this to do with the wizard?" she demanded, getting to the heart of the matter.

Mbugua decided to answer in kind. "There is an enspelled pearl within the clam shell. Wear it when Ka'Narlist sends for you. It will steal a portion of his spirit."

The girl nodded thoughtfully. There was no hint of fear in her eyes as she contemplated this attack upon her powerful master. "But how can this be done, that he will not notice?"

"Look at the sky," Mbugua advised her. "Does its sapphire hue dim when you take a single breath? Are the stars drawn closer when the winds sweep down from the north? The sky cannot be diminished so. Thus it is with the spirit: it is a thing without beginning or end. The single breath of it that is drawn into the pearl will not disturb the wizard."

A rare smile broke over Satarah's face, and she quickly slipped the necklace over her head. "This I will do, and gladly. I only regret that it will bring the wizard no pain!"

"There is one more thing I need of you," Mbugua said hesitantly, "but first I must tell you more about Ka'Narlist's work than you will want to hear." When the girl nodded her encouragement, he told her of the wizard's determination to create a race of seagoing creatures from his own blood, a vicious race that would conquer and control the seas.

"Soon he will beget his first blood-child," Mbugua concluded. "I want my blood to mingle with Ka'Narlist's in that monster's body. I would bind the creature to me with the blood-bonds of the wemic clan, and turn him against the wizard. This is not something I do lightly, and for it, I will need your help. Your blood."

Satarah regarded him narrowly, hearing his reasoning but suspecting it. "Why not use your own?"

"Is Ka'Narlist such a fool, that he would not notice if

his creature was born with four legs and fur?" Mbugua retorted. "You carry the blood of the wemic clan, but your outward form is more like that of an elf. It is still a risk, but a smaller one."

The girl shrugged. "I care not for the risk, but I don't see why the wizard's creature would work against him."

Again Mbugua heard the unspoken question behind her words. He dared not tell her the second half of his plan—his determination to imbue the creature with Ka'Narlist's own rapacious spirit, with the wizard's driving ambition for conquest. Mbugua's fondest, darkest hope was that the creature would set its sights upon Ka'Narlist's impressive wealth, and devise a way to own it. It would not be the first time that a son ousted his father, nor would it be the last. Moreover, the creature would not have Ka'Narlist's magic, and could in turn be overthrown. Mbugua dared not tell Satarah any of this for fear the wizard might somehow get it from her. He would tell her what he could, and pray that she was daughter enough to understand.

"Why would this creature *not* seek vengeance," Mbugua said, "seeing that the wizard enslaves many of his wemic kindred? The ties of blood-bond are powerful in the clan. Do you not know this to be so?"

Satarah's fingers clutched her father's gift, traced the rune that he had etched unto the clamshell—the rune that proclaimed her, a woeful thing begotten of a foul wizard's magic, a member of a proud wemic clan. Her eyes were bright and fierce as they sought Mbugua's.

"The bonds of blood are strong. I will do all that you ask."

The wemic cupped her cheek in his massive hand, and sadness smote him deeply as he realized it was the first caress he had ever offered to his elflike child.

Satarah gripped her father's tawny hand with both of her own. Then she stepped back and squared her shoulders as if preparing herself for the battle ahead.

The Best of the Realms • 139

Is that wineskin empty? Loretelling is thirsty work. Listening also has a way of drying the throat, and you and your kindred listen well. A finer audience I have seldom seen!

A trick? How so? Surely a band of elven hunter-warriors is match for a single wemic loreteller, whether you drink or no. Such suspicions do not speak well for you, elf. As my grandsire would say, "A thief never forgets to bolt his own door."

And have I not given my oath that I will not fight until the tale is told?

Oh, very good, elf! You turn my own taunt back against me—a nimble riposte! Yes, I have also pledged to give you the entire story, and so I shall.

That very night, the inhabitants of the wizard's castle shivered as they listened to the wemic shaman's song, carried to them by a mournful wind.

It was not an unfamiliar sound. They knew full well what it meant: yet another inhabitant of Ka'Narlist Keep had died. The knowledge that their turn could come at any time chilled them as they listened to the wemic's rhythmic chant. But tonight, the shaman's voice seemed somehow different—infinitely sadder and throbbing with suppressed wrath.

Far below the listening castle, Mbugua sang the spirit of Satarah on its way to the proud afterlife awaiting wemic warriors.

But first, he'd taken from her body two things: a vial of the blood that flowed freely from her many wounds, and a black pearl vibrating with a spirit so malevolent, so ambitious and vile that it could only be Ka'Narlist's. Of this, the wemic shaman was certain, as certain as he was that the true daughter of his blood and his spirit lay dead before him.

Success was his. Later, perhaps, Mbugua would be grimly pleased. Now there was only grief, deeper and more profound than he had expected to feel.

When the ritual was completed, when Satarah was well and truly gone, the wemic roared his rage and his anguish out over the uncaring sea.

And far above the windswept shore, the inhabitants of Ka'Narlist's castle shivered at the terrible sound. They had many reasons to fear the wizard; the fact that he himself did not fear the wemic was high among them.

☉ ☉ ☉ ☉ ☉

In the birthing chamber, a female sea elf's moans mingled with the resonant chanting of the wemic shaman. Mbugua crouched beside the shallow pool where the elf woman labored, humming and chanting softly as he sang the child within her toward the light.

The sea elf tensed as yet another massive contraction rippled across her rounded belly. Her body arched, her mouth opened in a shriek of pure anguish. Mbugua reached into the water and caught the babe as it slipped from her body.

At once, the wemic knew that he had succeeded in shaping Ka'Narlist's magical begetting. The infant was not at all what the wizard had intended. It was a boy-child, perfectly formed, and utterly sea-elven, from his softly pointed ears to the fine webbing between the fingers of his tiny, flailing fists. But Mbugua's shaman senses, finely tuned to the new life in his hands, felt the blood-bonds of his own clan tying him to the child. The wemic shaman continued to sing, this time a song of welcome, as he tended the child and the exhausted sea elf who had birthed it.

The female's eyes followed Mbugua's every move, and slowly the despair in them changed to wonder—and the dawning of a mother's intense love. But Mbugua shook his head when she reached hungry arms out for the beautiful newborn. Although her blood had had a part in the infant's begetting, though she had carried and brought it forth according to the ways of nature, though the child might appear to be nothing more or less than a perfect sea elf, the babe was none of hers. Already Mbugua could sense the still-amorphous spirit of the child. This was truly Ka'Narlist's own.

At that moment, the wizard strode into the room and peered down at the infant in Mbugua's arms. His dark face twisted with rage and disappointment.

"Another failure," he muttered, and turned away. "Dispose of it."

"As you command, Master," Mbugua called respectfully after the departing wizard. With one massive forepaw he slapped aside the elf woman's desperate, grasping hands, and he padded from the chamber with the doomed infant in his arms. Other slaves would tend and console the female, for she would be needed again—the sea elf was a proven breeder who had produced three live children of her own. Ka'Narlist would waste little time on this slave's recovery: Mbugua was certain that before the crescent moon grew full, yet another of the dark elf's twisted offspring would be magically planted within her belly.

The wemic carried the newborn down to the edge of the sea, ignoring its thin, indignant cries. To his private cove he went, and his savage roars chilled those who listened in the castle far above.

They heard, but they did not understand.

In response to Mbugua's summons, a sea-elven woman emerged from the waves and waded ashore. She took the babe from the wemic's arms, then unwrapped the damp blanket that swaddled it so that she might examine the tiny fingers and toes.

"The babe is perfect," she said at last. "Are you certain of its nature?"

"As certain as I am of my own," Mbugua said flatly. "Raise him, as we agreed, and he will in time avenge your stolen kin. But trust him not! Ka'Narlist has bred violence and hatred into this one."

"I will remember, and watch," the elf agreed. "And I will tell him tales of the wizard's power and wealth, and let him know this would be his rightful portion, had his father not discarded him."

The wemic nodded. "One thing more: whenever you hear my voice raised in ritual song, bring the babe close to shore so that he might watch and learn. Let him see me sing away the spirits of Ka'Narlist's victims. Let him learn to hate his wizard father for the evil that he does. And when he has learned this lesson," Mbugua said softly, "then will I teach him to fight!"

☙ ☙ ☙ ☙ ☙

Nearly a year passed, and again Mbugua crouched beside the birthing pool to aid the same sea-elven woman. This time, the soft play of the cleansing fountain and the chanting of the shaman were the only sounds in the room. The elf woman lay limp, uncaring, as nature followed its ordained path and the child tore its way from her body.

This time, Ka'Narlist himself attended the birth. He watched with keen interest, and when his wemic slave raised the child from the pool, a smile of fierce elation lit his dark face.

"At last, success!" the wizard exulted.

But Mbugua could only stare at the horror in his hands. The infant was hideous, monstrous. It was also strong: already it could lift its head, and it struck out purposefully at the wemic with tiny claws that etched lines of blood along Mbugua's hands and wrists. Although elflike in such matters as number and placement of limbs, the creature was covered with dark green scales. Small black fins sprouted from its head and body. The head lacked both hair and ears, and the face was dominated by a pair of enormous black eyes and a long slit of mouth. It had yet to draw breath and cry; Mbugua found himself hoping it never would.

Muttering an oath, Ka'Narlist struck the infant from the stunned wemic's hands. The tiny monster splashed into the pool. Bubbles rose from the water, along with an eerie, high-pitched shriek that sent a shiver down Mbugua's spine. To the shaman's sensitive ears, the cry was a harbinger of death to many innocent sea folk.

"Cut the cord, put the babe to breast," Ka'Narlist scolded. "You are the midwife here, not I! See to it!"

Mbugua fished the infant from the pool, quickly tended its needs, and placed it in the elf woman's limp arms. Her dazed, empty eyes widened with sudden horror, and her apathy exploded into hysterical screams. Too late, the wemic understood why.

The infant's mouth was flung open wide, impossibly wide. It was lined with rows of tiny, triangular fangs like those of a shark. The babe clamped down, and Mbugua heard the dreadful sound of teeth grating upon bone. He caught a glimpse of the sea elf's ribs before the flow of her lifeblood turned the waters of the birthing pool a deep crimson.

Ka'Narlist frowned and flicked his fingers: the dying elf woman's shrieks stopped abruptly. The wizard nodded thoughtfully as he watched the babe chew and swallow its first meal.

"How better to train them to hunt sea elves than to give them a taste of sea-elven blood with their first breath?" he mused.

He turned to Mbugua. "Fetch all the captive sea-elven females, then go to the slave markets and buy all that are available. We will need as many hatching hosts as we can acquire, since it would seem that they can be used only once."

The wizard smiled, seemingly amused by the stunned expression on the wemic's face. "Come, now—away with your tiresome scruples! This is a great day. When the sea is mine to command, you may boast that you witnessed the birth of the sahuagin race!"

◉ ◉ ◉ ◉ ◉

The years passed, and the vast walled pools and water-filled dungeons on Ka'Narlist's estate soon teemed with sahuagin.

Even Mbugua had to admit they were amazing creatures. They reached maturity within a year, and, unlike most of the wizard's other creations, they could reproduce. This they did with astonishing fecundity. After three years, Ka'Narlist ceased to magically breed the sahuagin, leaving them to their own devices. Within ten years, Ka'Narlist had a tribe.

The sahuagin learned nearly as quickly as they bred. They could swim from the moment of their birth and could walk in their second moon of life. As soon as they could grasp a weapon, they were taught to fight on land and in the water. Within twenty years, Ka'Narlist had an army.

Throughout these years, Mbugua spent much of his time at the pools and the training pens, watching as Ilythiirian raiders—themselves slaves to the wizard—trained the sahuagin in the fighting arts of the dark elves.

The creatures proved to be fierce fighters, neither giving nor asking quarter in their battles against each other, and showing ruthless delight in slaying the sea-elven fighters who from time to time were tossed into their pools. But never—never once—did any of them turn tooth or claw or blade upon one of their dark-elven masters. From the moment of birth, each sahuagin was trained to regard the dark elves as gods, and Ka'Narlist as chief among them. He was, quite simply, their Creator. None of the sahuagin ever set eyes upon Ka'Narlist, but they were taught to fear, obey and revere him.

At last the day came to release the sahuagin into the sea. They were brought for the first time into the castle's great hall, to be awed by a wondrous display of music and light and magic—things that none of them had seen at close hand, things that seemed to them to be true manifestations of a mighty god. At the height of the ceremony, Ka'Narlist himself appeared, hovering above the assembly, his form magically enhanced to enormous size and limned with eerie, dancing light.

"The moment of your destiny has arrived," the wizard announced in a voice that shook the hall's windows. "The sahuagin will become a great people. You will conquer the seas, plunder its treasures, and know enormous wealth and power! This is your right and your destiny, as the created children of Ka'Narlist. In all you do, bring glory to the name of your lord and god!"

"Ka'Narlist!" the sahuagin host responded in a rapturous, thunderous roar.

The wizard smiled benevolently and extended his hands. Black pearls dripped from them and rained into the grasping claws of his dark children.

"You know what these are, and have been trained in their use. For each sea elf you slay, you will return one of these pearls—with the elf's magic captured inside. Magic is meant only for the gods. Regard the death of each blasphemous sea elf as an act of worship, and the pearls as proof of your loyalty to me! For have I not given you life, a kingdom to rule, and weapons with which to conquer it?"

The sahuagin nodded avidly, for their lord's reasoning was most agreeable to them. Also, they had learned to their pain that what the great Ka'Narlist could give, he could also take away! Those sahuagin who harbored the slightest hint of rebellion or heresy had died horribly, mysteriously, in full sight of their scaly kindred. Clearly, it was folly to oppose their dark lord, and an honor to serve one so powerful.

Ka'Narlist spoke a few more words, then at last released the sahuagin to seek the sea. They tore from the hall and swarmed down the cliff, all the while hooting and shrieking oaths against their sea-elven foes.

When all was quiet, the wizard floated to the marble floor and turned a smile upon his wemic slave. Of all Ka'Narlist's servitors, only Mbugua was granted the honor of attending this ceremony. Indeed, the wizard kept his aging wemic at his side almost constantly—a witness to his glories and an audience for tales of his yet-unfulfilled ambitions.

"The world below the sea is but the start," the wizard proclaimed. "Soon all the world will know the name of Ka'Narlist! I will be not a mere wizard, but a god!"

"Notoriety does not make a god. If it did, then the courtesan Xorniba would be queen of all gods, rather than merely an expensive human whore," Mbugua observed with a candor that was becoming his habit.

And why not? His life-task had been done, and done well. It would be completed by one far better suited than he. The wemic no longer cared whether the wizard took lethal offense at such remarks.

But Ka'Narlist merely smiled. "Notoriety does not make a god, but magic?"

The wizard held up one of the black pearls. "The magic of the sea-elven wizards is nearly as potent as my own. Think upon this: what will I become when I possess a hundred of these? A thousand? When the stolen magic of a thousand thousand sea elves is woven into a single net of magic and power?" Again Ka'Narlist paused for an exultant smile. "With power such as that, the gods will come to me. Do not doubt: I will become a god indeed."

☯ ☯ ☯ ☯ ☯

Mbugua did not doubt.

Once, many years ago, the dark god Ghaunadaur had done Ka'Narlist's bidding and wrested the wemic from his afterlife. The shaman had sensed then the strange partnership forming between wizard and god. If Ka'Narlist truly succeeded in stealing the magic of the sea elves, he might well possess magic enough to purchase his way into the pantheon of his dark gods. It was not hard to believe: they were much akin, Ghaunadaur and Ka'Narlist. And Mbugua would witness it all. He was bound to the wizard by unbreakable ropes of magic: if Ka'Narlist attained godhood, immortality, it would amuse him to retain Mbugua's spirit in captivity throughout countless ages to come.

The wemic hastened to his cove, more frightened than he had been since the long-ago day of his capture. He had long known about Ka'Narlist's pearls, but he thought them to be nothing more than another vessel to hold the magical wealth the wizard hoarded in such abundance. It had never occurred to Mbugua that Ka'Narlist intended to systematically plunder sea-elven magic. Such loss would gravely weaken the sea folk's defenses against the sahuagin horde, perhaps bring about their utter ruin.

The prospects were appalling: the destruction of a wondrous elven people, the rise of the sahuagin to the rulership of the seas, the possibility that the evil that was Ka'Narlist might become immortal. At all costs, the dark elf's creatures must be stopped.

At the edge of the shore, Mbugua roared out the signal that would bring his sea-elven son from the waves.

Malenti, the shaman had named him, after a legendary wemic fighter. So far, Malenti showed every promise of living up to his name. He had learned all that Mbugua had to teach him, and with astonishing speed: all the fighting styles known to the wemic, all the tactics taught to the sahuagin, even the ambush strategies perfected by the now-extinct kodingobolds. To accomplish what he must, Malenti would need them all.

The sea elf came quickly to Mbugua's call, striding out onto the land to exchange a warrior's salute with the wemic. For once, Mbugua did not ponder the strangeness of the webbed hand that clasped his wrist: he measured with gratitude the strength in the elf's grip, and noted the battle-honed muscles that rippled beneath the green, mottled skin.

"The sahuagin are already ravaging the sea," Malenti said without preamble. "They have slain a score of the merfolk, and laid siege to the sea-elven city just offshore. They have sworn to slay every elf who dwells within."

"You must stop them," implored Mbugua. "And if you cannot, at least stop them from returning to Ka'Narlist with their black pearls!" Quickly, he outlined the wizard's dire ambition.

Too late, it occurred to him that such knowledge might be dangerous in the hands of one as ambitious as Malenti.

"I have no use for stolen magic," Malenti said calmly, as if he divined the wemic's thoughts, "but you are right in saying that these pearls must be kept from Ka'Narlist. If he becomes as powerful as he would like to be, how will I oust him and claim his kingdom as my own?"

These callous words sent through Mbugua a shiver that started at the top of his spine and darted down the length of his leonine back. It was true that this was the very path he'd hoped Malenti's ambition might take; however, the ease with which the young sea elf spoke of his father's death was chilling.

Malenti had already turned away. His hand was upon his dagger as he splashed into the sea, as if he could not wait to shed sahuagin blood.

And thus it was, for many years to come. The sahuagin hordes returned to Ka'Narlist's keep with the dark of each moon, as they were pledged to do. But they brought with them not piles of dark pearls, but tales of fierce battles and ambush, and of a mighty sea-elven leader who had raised the sea folk against them.

Malenti, he was called. Malenti, the Sahuagin Scourge.

As Mbugua listened to the stories told of his sea-elven son, he struggled to keep his swelling pride from his face. Ka'Narlist, however, was not so stoic.

"A thousand spears and my highest favor to the sahuagin who brings me this Malenti!" vowed the furious wizard as the latest moon-dark ceremony drew to a close. "Bring him in alive, and I will match the reward with a thousand tridents!"

For such a treasure, any sahuagin would cheerfully slay his nearest kin. The monsters took to the sea with renewed ferocity, each determined to win the promised reward and the regard of their lord.

Even so, nearly three years passed before the sahuagin finally captured their nemesis. They dragged Malenti to Ka'Narlist Keep, entangled in nets and bleeding from a score of small malicious wounds, into the great hall to await the judgment of their lord.

Despite the seeming gravity of the situation, Mbugua's heart was light as he made his way into the hall in response to the wizard's summons. By all reports, Malenti had amassed an enormous army of sea folk. Surely the army was gathered at shore's edge even now, awaiting only Malenti's command to strike. Time and again had the sea elves overcome the sahuagin fighters: the wemic was confident that they would do so again, and that, at long last, Ka'Narlist's brutal reign of magic and misery would end.

When the hall was full and the clacking speech of the excited sahuagin had subsided into a few scattered clicks, the wizard made his appearance. In a magically enhanced voice, he recited the charges against Malenti, then granted him the right to speak before sentence was carried out.

"Take away the nets," Malenti demanded boldly. "When I stand before you, when I look into your face, then will I speak."

With a cruel smile, the wizard lifted his hands. Lines of flame leapt from his fingers and singed away the entangling nets, doing no small damage to the prisoner in the process.

Bereft of much of his hair, his skin much reddened and blistered, and his blackened garments hanging in tatters, Malenti nonetheless rose proudly to his feet and faced down the powerful wizard.

"At last we meet . . . Father," he said in a ringing voice that carried to every corner of the great hall. He paused, obviously enjoying the stunned expression on Ka'Narlist's face and the hushed expectation of the sahuagin throng.

"Oh yes, I am the first of your sahuagin children, the one you discarded when you found my appearance unpleasing. I am Malenti, the Sahuagin Scourge. The *sahuagin* scourge," he emphasized, "for such I am indeed. Though I did not have the advantages of training and weaponry that you lavished upon these others, I have done what I could." He paused, lifting his arms as if to invite the wizard's inspection

The wemic tensed, certain that the signal to attack was soon to come. Moments passed, and it did not. It occurred to Mbugua that the wizard was studying Malenti closely, and that the wizard did not seemed at all displeased by what he saw.

The sea elf shrugged off the remnants of his charred shirt, revealing a hauberk of incredibly delicate chain mail into which were woven thousands of small black pearls. Mbugua's shaman senses caught the fragile, silent song of captured magic; with horror he realized that each pearl contained the stolen magic of a sea elf.

But Malenti cannot use the magic, Mbugua thought,

suddenly frightened that his protégé might attack—and fail. He has not the gift for it, nor has he been trained! What did he presume to do?

As if he heard the question, Malenti turned to gaze directly into the wemic's golden eyes. "You taught me well," he said mockingly. "And now I turn your own truth back against you: the deepest secrets of life are not in the blood, but in the spirit. Blood-bonds are powerful indeed, but spirit easily wins over blood!"

Ka'Narlist's eyes kindled with crimson flame as he realized Mbugua's part in this. He rounded on the treacherous wemic. "You were to destroy that first sahuagin!"

"You will come to rejoice that he did not," Malenti retorted. He deftly pulled the net of magic over his head and brandished it. "These are the pearls I claimed from your servants over the years, as well as many hundreds more that I gathered myself. I am sahuagin," he said again, his eyes daring those assembled before him to dispute that fact. "I hate the sea elves as much as any of you. But they trusted me, and they died all the more easily for it."

The elflike sahuagin lifted the web of pearls high. "This is my tribute to the great Ka'Narlist, the first tribute of many! Release me to the sea, and I will continue to slay sea elves for as long as I live." He shook the hauberk so that the black pearls glistened.

Ka'Narlist smiled faintly, knowingly, as he regarded the son of his spirit. "And what do you desire for yourself, in exchange for this tribute you offer?"

"Only that which is my due: a high position of power among the sahuagin armies, a large share of the wealth of the seas, and the utter destruction of the sea elves! I already know what you desire, and it is in my best interest to see you achieve it." He added softly, so that his words carried only to the dark-elven wizard and the stunned wemic who sat at his side, "I would like to be known as the firstborn son of a god!"

"The bargain is made," Ka'Narlist began, but Malenti cut him off with an upraised hand.

"I want one thing more: the life of the wemic who betrayed you. Oh, I do not wish merely to slay him! As the proud Mbugua has taught me, it is the spirit that whispers the secrets of life! Imprison his in one of these pearls, and I will wear it until the day I die. And forever after, let his spirit roar his songs and his stories out over the waves, that what has been done in this place will be remembered for as long as people listen to the voices of the sea!"

With a heavy heart, Mbugua heard his sentence proclaimed by his blood-son, and confirmed by the dark elf he had hoped to overthrow. As Ka'Narlist chanted words of magic and the treacherous Malenti drew his dagger across Mbugua's throat, the wemic prayed with silent fervor that someone, someday, would understand that a wemic's voice was trapped amid the sounds of the waves and the winds, and would find a way to sing his spirit away to its final rest.

※ ※ ※ ※ ※

Thus did the sahuagin come into being. And thus it was, from that day to this, that the sahuagin from time to time bear young that resemble sea elves in all things but their rapacious nature. These are called "malenti," after their forefather. Sometimes such young are reared and trained to live among the sea elves as sahuagin spies; more commonly they are slain at birth. The sahuagin have learned that this is prudent—the malenti are considered dangerous even by their vicious kindred, for in them, the spirit of Ka'Narlist lives on.

As for Mbugua, some say that his spirit was released to its reward many long centuries past. And yet it is also said that on a stormy night, one can still hear a wemic's roar of despair among the many voices of the sea.

And so, my elven captor, you have the story, as it was passed to me by my grandsire, who had it from his.

Why would the lion-folk tell such a tale, you ask? Perhaps because the elves will not. Yes, there is danger in speaking of such magic. It is true that for every wise wemic who hears the warning in this tale, there will be a fool who sees in it the glittering lure of a dragon's hoard. So regard it as myth, if such pleases you. And indeed, it may well be this story was not built upon the solid stone of fact.

But remember this, elf, and write it upon your scroll: oftentimes there is far more truth to be found in legend than in history.

Originally Published in Dragon #246, April 1998
Edited by Dave Gross

THE GREAT HUNT

Readers frequently observe that Elaith seldom displays the magical abilities that his game stats allow him. There's a reason for that. He's a sneaky bugger, and it seems likely to me that he'd downplay his magical ability and use his spells as another sort of hidden weapon. In this story, however, Elaith pulls out some fairly high level magic when he and Arilyn Moonblade have a run-in with a band of Malar worshipers.

THE GREAT HUNT

Twilight lingered long in the northern woodlands, and it seemed to the small band of hunters that the sun was loath to set on a day of such glorious carnage.

But night could not be denied, and with the darkness came a temporary end to the hunt. The three hunters cast a final longing glance toward a trail they could no longer see, and then settled down to make camp and await the moonrise.

Their campfire kindled, and a questing wisp of smoke rose toward the forest canopy in a meandering path, as if seeking the company of other smoke from other fires. There would be many campfires in this forest this night, as the Talons of Malar sang their boastful songs and celebrated the first day of their sacred hunt.

The youngest of these Talons, these hunters, was a half-orc lad only this day blooded. His name was Drom, and like every faithful follower of Malar the Beastlord, he had been summoned to the Great Hunt. The half-orc's blood still sang with the glory and frenzy of the slaughter.

He crouched by the fire to regard by its flickering lights his first trophies. To his horror, Drom felt himself obliged to swallow hard and look away. For some reason, the three torn and bloody elven ears lying in his palm raised his gorge as the battle itself had not.

Grimlish, an orc of immense size and hideous, green-hued visage, grunted in approval at the trophies. It was because of Grimlish that Drom had taken the ears. Grimlish was a strong hunter who held great honor in the tribe. What Grimlish was, Drom aspired to become. The orc wore around his neck a long leather thong, decorated with many grisly bits of tanned leather, dyed bright red but unmistakable in their origin.

Drom wanted a necklace like that, and he was eager to earn it. From his belt he took a small wineskin, filled not with wine but with a potent mixture of tanning acid and crushed berries. He slipped his three trophies into the skin, and considered the day's work a good start.

The big orc sat down beside the fire and undid the chin strap of his helmet. That helmet was another thing that Drom envied, another thing he hoped one day to emulate. It was constructed of metal-banded leather, and decorated by a rack of elk antlers, each point sharpened to a razor's edge and dipped daily in fresh blood. It was a marvelous helm, worn in homage to an avatar form the god Malar sometimes took upon himself when he wished to roam these forests.

Yet even as the thought formed, Drom knew he could never wear such a helmet. Grimlish stood seven feet tall and was immensely strong. His shoulders were nearly as broad as the haft of a spear, and his neck was massive enough to support the antlers, strong enough to wield them in battle.

Drom was no weakling, and despite his youth he boasted great height and prodigious strength. But he was more human than orc. His face was beardless, but the yellow down on his chin gave promise of a northman's beard. Only his size, and the enlarged canines that thrust upward from his lower lip, gave proof of his orcish heritage.

Drom slid a glance over at the orc, who was busy with his own trophies. "A good hunt," he ventured.

"Five," the orc boasted, holding up the proof of his kill. "And two more before the sun returns."

The half-orc nodded. Today the Talons of Malar had routed a community of elves and slaughtered most of them in pitched battle. Once the moon rose, the hunting would be different. The hoard had broken up into small bands now, the better to run stragglers to ground.

There were three Talons in this band, all of them from the renegade Snow Wolf tribe. Their third member, a human known only as Badger, was a man of late middle years. His chest and arms were knotted with muscle and covered with tattoos, as was his clean-shaved head. Badger approached the business of killing with a glee and ferocity that awed and sometimes frightened the other members of the tribe. And that, Drom allowed, was saying a great deal. After all, they were all followers of the Great Wolf, and as fierce as any of their four-legged brothers.

Drom had been born into the Snow Wolf tribe, a small band of northmen fanatic in their worship of their totem animal. Over the years, they had mingled with like-minded orcs who hunted the same expanse of tundra, as well as the occasional renegade who slid into the pack. Badger was such a man—an outcast among his kind, surviving because he was cannier and more fierce than most. Despite the man's small stature and advancing years, he was a fearsome sight. One side of his lower lip had been pierced to accommodate a gold ornament shaped like an orc's tusk. On his opposite cheek was branded the symbol of Malar—a beast's paw, with talons dripping blood. Grim trophies hung about his waist from a well-laden weapons belt: small skulls, the teeth of great predators, and a silver wolf's tail.

They all wore the wolf, in one form or another. Drom wore a skin about his neck like a cloak, and Grimlish had attached a tail to the back of his helm. These were not trophies, but tributes. They followed Malar, but they still venerated the wolves, and wore skins in honor of these canny hunters.

Drom, in particular, looked to the wolf for inspiration and guidance. From his earliest years, the wolf had haunted his dreams, filling his waking thoughts. The wolf pelt on his shoulder had the comforting warmth of a brother's hand. Indeed, the wolf who'd yielded the pelt had been more of a brother to Drom than any two-legged male of his village.

Drom had been a mere child when he first set eyes upon the silver she-wolf, heavy with young. Following the wary female to her den had been no easy matter, but Drom had finally found it: a hollow under a small, rocky hillock. For weeks he'd watched the den, waiting for the pups to venture out into the wider world. Drom had watched, enthralled, as the three pups played and tussled and explored. He had lifted his hand to his mouth to stifle delighted laughter at the sound of their first, infant howls. He had watched them grow into hunters, learned from them, and picked the fiercest as his own. And he had done what any male of his tribe must do: he had challenged and bested his brother wolf.

Drom lifted one hand to stroke the silvery fur that draped his shoulders. He was certain the wolf's spirit bore him no ill will. It was the way of the pack: honor was due to worthy foe or well-earned prey. Did not the wolves sing after a difficult hunt, in praise of both hunter and hunted?

As if in echo of his thoughts, a long, eerie cry rose into the night, gathering power as it rose and fell.

The giant orc grunted in approval. "The Singing Death. A good omen. We will hunt well."

"We will hunt *women*," Badger said in disgust. But as he spoke, he drew a long knife from his belt and regarded the blood upon it with deep hunger.

Drom understood. The elf female was not yet dead, and it galled the old hunter to sit calmly at the fire while her blood dried on his blade. Though Badger spoke of her with derision, Drom had never seen a female fight so fiercely, or so well. In his mind, the fact that Badger had gotten close enough to the female to mark her as his prey was a shining testament to the old one's skill.

"Many hunters sought the blood of that one. The ravens feed on them tonight," Drom pointed out.

Badger scoffed, misunderstanding the intended compliment. "Perhaps you wish to die an old man?"

This was the deepest insult one Talon of Malar could offer another. But though Drom was young, he was too wise to challenge the human.

"If I can reach your years, and equal your kills, I will consider myself a true hunter," he said calmly.

Badger looked surprised, then pleased. "Maybe the male elf will be yours to kill."

Coming from the human, this was high praise. "I will hunt well," Drom promised.

The three of them settled down around the fire, to tell stories of past glories and to await the coming of the moon.

✥ ✥ ✥ ✥ ✥

The attack on the elven village had been sudden, brutal. From all sides they'd come, closing in like a pack of wolves intent upon bringing down a lone stag. In a single moment, the time it might take an elf to pull on his boots or kiss his lady, the gaiety of a spring market faire had been transmuted into a bloody, shrieking nightmare.

None of the elves had doubted for an instant that they were fighting for their lives. This had been no mere raid, no band of brigands meaning to despoil the village of treasure. The symbol of Malar, the beast's paw with bloody claws, had been much in evidence, proclaiming the intent of the orcs and northmen who swarmed the village and the fate that awaited the elves—and the merchant caravan that had wandered unwitting into the path of a Great Hunt.

But with the caravan were many well-seasoned warriors, their swords hired by the promise of gold and their loyalty ensured by the fearsome reputation of their employer. Elaith Craulnober, a moon elf merchant lord, fought alongside his mercenaries, and fought better than most of them.

More than a score of the orc dogs and human mongrels fell to his blades. Elaith killed them with brutal efficiently, though he would have preferred to deal a slower death—or better yet, leave them sorely wounded, maimed past any hope of hunting and cursed with a long, inglorious life.

But Elaith had no leisure for such games. The elves were gravely outnumbered, and though they fought bravely, the slaughter was swift and terrible. Within moments of the attack, the moon elf knew that the battle was lost. He'd commanded the elves in the old tongue, demanding that they take to the trees, scatter and flee.

All had obeyed him, save one. A half-elf female stayed, standing back-to-back with one of the hired swords, a northwoman of immense girth and fierce skill. Together the women had guarded the base of a giant cedar, holding off a circle of Malar's hunters and buying time for several wounded elves to climb to safety.

In retrospect, Elaith realized that he should have expected nothing different. In matters of honor and courage, Arilyn had few peers. There was no one he'd rather have at his back, and no one to whom he owed a deeper loyalty.

And so he had come to her aid. He'd pulled a knife from his boot and hurled it. The gleaming weapon spun end over end, destined to bury itself between the shoulder blades of the orc warrior bearing down on Arilyn. Elaith had not waited to see the orc fall.

He'd drawn swords and charged the circle, cutting his way toward the half-elf. When he'd gotten nearly through, he'd dropped into a crouch and deftly cut the hamstrings of the fighters on either side of her. The falling bodies had provided a momentary cover, and he'd used it to slam his swords into their sheaths and sprint toward Arilyn. Not slowing, he'd dodged an orc's battle axe, ducked under the half-elf's defensive parry, and slammed a fist into her jaw. He'd come up still running, with a stunned Arilyn slung over his shoulder and the spell components for a Dust Cloud in his hand.

The last thing he'd seen upon abandoning his company was the spear lunging toward the mercenary who'd stood with Arilyn. The northwoman was too much the warrior to scream, but she'd grunted like a slaughtered sow when the spear punched through her ribs.

Arilyn had jolted at the sound, and Elaith braced himself against her outrage, which was typically expressed in a blistering diatribe delivered in Elvish and leavened with dock-side profanity. But she had held her tongue and had enough sense not to fight him, and so they had both escaped with their lives.

But now, while the night was yet dark and the moon elf deemed the moment safe for a brief rest, Elaith saw the true reason for Arilyn's uncharacteristic docility. He had been a heartbeat too slow, a single pace too late. The half-elf had been wounded. She was bleeding profusely from a gash that opened her arm from shoulder nearly to elbow. There was more blood on her forehead, trickling down from a glancing head wound some orc's weapon had dealt her when she'd been helpless in Elaith's arms. A livid bruise was already forming on one side of her face. The moon elf eased her down, cursing himself, the gods in general, and Malar in particular.

Arilyn set aside the sword she held—it would take a far greater wound that that she'd taken this day to induce her to drop it—and allowed Elaith to lower her to a fallen log. She glared up at him, her blue and gold eyes fierce in her too-pale face.

"Forgive me for striking you, Princess. Your safety was my first concern, and I could think of no other way to dissuade you from continuing the fight."

She impatiently waved this away. "You left your hirelings to die."

The elf lifted one shoulder in a dismissive shrug. "They are human."

"I am half human," Arilyn retorted.

"You are also half dead," Elaith pointed out. Though the remark was said in dark humor, there was more truth in it than he liked to speak. He put a hand on the stubborn warrior's shoulder to keep her from rising, and then knelt to tend her. He took a knife from a wrist strap and carefully cut away the blood-soaked fabric of her shirt.

As Elaith examined the wound, the invisible fist that gripped his heart began to relax. "It is not as bad as I feared. None of the main blood routes are severed, and there appears to be no serious damage to the muscles. I will have to clean and stitch it, though."

Arilyn nodded, then waved away the bit of thick leather he handed her to bite upon. She set her jaw and looked away as he worked, her eyes scanning the forest.

"The stream there. We can follow it for a while,

then run, then take to the trees and double back to the stream. Do that repeatedly, and vary the pattern twice or thrice, and veer off to another stream when the flow converges, and even the Malarites will be hard pressed to follow our trail."

The plan was solid, and under better circumstances it may well have worked. "But how long could you hold such a pace?"

Arilyn turned and met his eyes. "As long as I have to."

Elaith did not doubt that she would try. "And if we are overtaken, you would stand and fight?"

She shrugged, as if asking him to get to the point.

The moon elf sighed. Arilyn might be only half elven by blood, she was as stubborn and heartstrong as the elven princess who'd birthed her. Because of Arilyn's heritage, Elaith owed her an elf lord's allegiance, as well as the loyalty of near kin. But there were times, and this was one of them, when he wanted to throttle her. Hers was the sort of traditionally elven thinking that, in Elaith's opinion, had led to the decline of the race, and would undoubtedly lead to her death and his.

It was time for new tactics.

Elaith's sharp eyes scanned the forest. Downstream, a doe dipped her muzzle into the dark water.

A slow, cunning smile curved the elf's lips. "To the stream, then, and quickly," he agreed. "The hunt will begin in earnest with the coming of moonrise."

☙ ☙ ☙ ☙ ☙

The howling intensified, filling the forest around them with eerie music. Grimlish rose and gathered up his horned helm and his gear. The others followed suit. The moon would soon rise: the wolfsong heralded its coming as surely as a rooster's call foretold the dawn.

Suddenly Badger froze. He swore softly and with great

delight as he reached for his longest knife. Drom followed his gaze. There, in the shadows of a young pine, was a large silver wolf. Its amber eyes regarded them with keen interest.

Forgetting his order in this particular pack, Drom reached out and stayed the old hunter's hand. "It will not attack."

Even as he spoke, Drom's conviction wavered. Wolves were unpredictable, and their ways were too complex and mysterious for most people to fathom. To farmfolk, timid sheep that they were, the wolf was a ravening monster. Rangers, druids, and other like-minded fools took an extreme view: they romanticized the wolf as a noble soul, uncorrupted by the greed and whim that plagued humankind, unselfishly strengthening the bloodline of its prey by culling the weak, the old, the infirm. Drom scorned both of these views, not because they were false—there was some truth to both of them—but because neither captured the true spirit of the wolf, or the Wolf People who took inspiration from the Singing Death. In the year just four winters past, the caribou calves had simply disappeared, though the cows had been heavy in the spring and there was no late, killing snow. The spore of the wolves told the tale: for weeks they ate caribou and little else. Yet even so, surely they had killed more calves than they could possibly eat. Though Drom and his village had suffered that following winter for lack of food, this told the young half-orc that even the grimly practical tundra wolves were not immune to the pure glory of the hunt, the joy of the kill.

In short, who could know what mysterious purpose lurked behind this wolf's amber eyes?

Badger threw off the half-orc's restraining hand. "Attack? Of course it won't attack. Wolves are too smart. It is one, and we are three. It will run. But if we could catch it, it would be a fine kill."

"We have other prey," Grimlish pointed out. "Let us be off."

The two hunters fell into pace behind the big orc. The trail was almost ridiculously easy to follow, for the female left a trickle of blood spoor. Drom envisioned the elf with a mixture of anticipation and awe. Now *that* would be a fine kill!

She was tall, with a wild tangle of black hair and eyes that blazed blue fire. Many of the Talons of Malar had fallen to her sword. Even when it must have been clear that all was lost, that death was certain, she had stood her ground. She might be fighting still, had not a male elf with silver hair and a hawk's wild eyes intervened. The male had cast a spell—a cloud of light and stinging dust that had sent the Talons reeling back. It had given the two elves time to escape, but it had not obscured their trail.

The trail of blood dwindled, but still the Talons followel. A smear of blood on a newly-leafed branch, an occasional deep indentation in the moss when the male's boots had trod. Usually, elves left little sign of their passing, but the male was still carrying the wounded female.

As the hunters walked, the large wolf followed, its silver-tipped fur reflecting the moonlight. Badger grew increasingly restive, but Grimlish would not permit the man to attack.

"The wolf is an omen," the big orc insisted. "Perhaps even a spirit guide."

Badger spat. "The wolf is a wolf. Who's to say it's not testing us?"

There was some wisdom in the human's words. Wolves often tested their prey, tracking them for long hours and making experimental forays, withdrawing if they deemed the task too dangerous. For a wolf, perhaps one of every fifty hunts begun ended in a kill.

"We are three, the wolf is one. Perhaps it is *you* who wishes to die an old man," Grimlish said coldly. The look of disdain he sent the human settled the matter, and reduced Badger to sullen silence.

They followed the trail deeper into the forest, to a fallen tree not far from a swift-running stream. The elves had stopped here, probably to staunch the tell-tale flow. There were no footprints leading away, which meant that the male was once against walking lightly. But the female was weakened now, and staggering. There were smears of blood on branches and vines, the marks a wounded elf might leave if pain made her careless.

She had not gone far. A hundred paces, no more, and she had fallen heavily into the underbrush—small, broken twigs shouted the story. There was more blood.

"Her wound opened," Drom murmured.

But Badger was not so sure. "Alone, the male might survive. To stay with the female means certain death. But is he cunning enough to know this, and ruthless enough to act upon this knowledge?"

"It would seem not," Grimlish said. The orc knelt nearby, brushing away some of the half-decayed autumn leaves to get to the spring-soft mud beneath. Pressed into it was a print of an elven boot. The male had shouldered his burden once again.

The trail led to a stream—a simple-minded ploy, one that had even inexperienced Drom snorting in derision. A few paces downstream, they found the trail's end. Beside the stream bed stood an ancient oak, its roots partially exposed by the eroding flow. Some of the soil had been hastily dug, then pressed back in.

Badger spat. "An elf cairn. We lost the female."

Drom was not so sure. He circled around the stream in search of the trail. It was there, but faint—the still-damp outline of an elven boot on an otherwise dry rock. "The sign continues here. Only one elf. But it could be that the other took to the trees. Perhaps the cairn is a trick. Perhaps they both live, and they plan to flank us, one to draw us into battle and one to attack by surprise. It is not the usual way of elves, but it would be a worthy plan."

He was about to say more, but the approach of their silvery shadow stunned him into silence. Cautiously, ears back and belly to the ground, the wolf crept closer—so close that any of the three Talons could reach it with a kick. For the first time Drom noted the creature's prominent ribs, its submissive posture. The wolf was alone and hungry. Its mien was that of a supplicant, asking the more powerful members of the pack for permission to feed.

Drom backed away and gestured for the others to follow. The wolf, understanding that it would not be challenged for the meal it scented, began to dig at the roots.

"One elf," Grimlish concluded, turning away to follow the trail.

They tracked the male for hours. He was clever, moving from stream to land to tree and back, in a complex pattern that had the hunters circling back more than once. So they continued through the night, until the moon set and the first light of dawn began to creep through the forest.

The wolf rejoined them with the coming of light, its silvery muzzle still stained with the blood of its meal. Sated and content, he padded along behind them, as if he were fully a member of their pack and eager to share in the next kill. This seemed to amuse Badger, who said no more about taking its pelt.

To his surprise, Drom found that he himself was not so easily won. All his life he had admired the wolf, numbering foremost among its virtues the ability to adapt. He believed he understood the animal as well as any man or orc could, but *this* wolf's amber eyes held secrets Drom could not begin to fathom.

But then the trail ended, and there was no more time for such thoughts. The three Talons stared in astonishment at their quarry.

A lone elf stood in a forest clearing, ready for battle. But it was the female, not the silver-haired male. Her wounded arm had been tended and bound, and there was a fading scar on her forehead that had not been there the day before—evidence of powerful healing magic at work. She drew her sword and whistled it through the air, with a deft and dangerous skill that proclaimed louder than words her ability to stand and fight.

Badger swore as he drew his blade, the same long knife that had marked her as his prey. Dropping into a crouch, he began to circle, just beyond reach of her sword. He stalked and tested, lunging in from time to time to measure her reach, to observe the force and power of her attacks. The other Talons bided their time, letting the human tire the elfwoman. The wolf, also, stood watch, sitting on its haunches.

But Grimlish soon tired of this sport. He leveled his spear and charged. The elfwoman spun, bringing her sword down hard on the haft of the weapon. The force of her blow drove the spear's point downward, and it plunged deep into the forest floor. Grimlish could not halt his charge. The spear bent like a bow in his hands. He released it, an instant before it would have flung him up and over the elfwoman. The weapon sprang upright, quivering like a sapling in a gale. Grimlish fell back, but not before the female's sword scored a deep gash across his chest.

Badger darted in for the kill. With astonishing speed, the elf pivoted and kicked out. Her booted foot caught the man just below the ribs and bent him double. Before he could recover, she swept her sword into a powerful upward arc. Badger's bald, tatooed head went spinning off into the forest, and his headless body slumped to the sodden earth.

But in her triumph, the elfwoman ensured her defeat. The powerful blow opened her wound, and the bandage on her arm turned as deep a crimson as the tanned ears on Grimlish's trophy necklace. The wounded orc, scenting another victory, drew a pair of long knives and closed in, hissing at Drom to stand back and leave this kill to him.

Suddenly the orc jerked, his massive back arching and his arms thrown out wide. The morning light glinted from the jeweled hilt of the knife buried deep between his shoulder blades. The female stepped forward and drew her sword cleanly across Grimlish's throat.

Suddenly Drom understood the reason for his nagging uncertainty. He and his fellow hunters had been tricked.

The trail of blood to the cairn was false, an illusion they might have seen through but for the actions of the wolf. Something had weighted down the male's step, something had been buried beneath that tree, but it was no elf.

"A doe," said a voice behind him, an elven voice musical in tone and rich with dark humor. Before the half-orc could move, a strong hair seized his yellow braid, and the keen edge of a knife pressed hard against his throat.

Drom knew that his death would be swift and well deserved. He had cloaked himself with the pelt of a wolf to signal his respect for the animal and his desire to emulate him. Yet the elf had done him one better. In cloaking himself with the illusion of the wolf, the magic-wielding elf had proven himself the better hunter.

"Elaith, wait," the female protested, clutching her wounded arm and eyeing the clever ambush with disapproval. "He is just a boy."

"A *boy?* He cut down the village elder and sliced off his left ear. If this half-breed orc is old enough to kill, he is old enough to *be* killed," the male said coldly.

Still she hesitated. "But from behind? It is not the way of an elf."

"It is the way of a wolf," Drom countered, his voice steady. "I am bested, and I am content to die."

The female's eyes flicked to Drom's face, then over his shoulder to the elf who held him captive. A canny, knowing look glinted in her blue eyes.

"He wants to die," she said softly. "The others won't have him back."

There was a long pause. The male did not loosen his hold on Drom's hair, or move the knife from his throat. The half-orc could almost feel his captor's frustration and indecision.

Then the knife lifted, moved to the side. With a quick slash, the elf traced a wound in Drom's weapon arm that matched the one Badger had dealt the female—but deeper, rifting the muscle in a way that would never truly mend. Drom did not cry out, not then, and not even when the male's blade bit through his left boot, just above his ankle. Unable to stand, never again able to hunt, Drom slumped to the ground.

The female's eyes filled with fury. "Do you have any idea what you've done to him? It would have been kinder to kill him outright!"

The elf called Elaith circled around, his wolf-gold eyes bright as he surveyed the ruined hunter. "Yes, I suppose so," he said mildly. With that, he turned and disappeared into the forest.

The female hesitated, then she reached into a bag at her belt and stooped beside Drom. She placed on the ground a healing potion and a small roll of cloth—a bandage, with a small bone needle thrust into it. With this, he would mend himself, and perhaps survive.

But why would he want to?

"The wisest wolves, the canniest hunters, find new ways," she said. Her voice was low and intense, and something in it drew Drom's gaze to hers. "If they truly wish to, they can find new and better packs."

For a long moment, half-orc and half-elf, hunter and hunted, regarded each other with understanding and honor.

Then she was gone, moving lightly after the wolf-clever male.

An agonized howl burst from the young hunter, born of the pain of his injuries, and the loss of the only life he'd ever known. The eerie cry echoed deep into the forest and lingered long in the mist-heavy air. And when at last the sound faded away, Drom found that the stillness within was a strangely beautiful thing.

Acting on an impulse he did not quite understand, Drom reached into his bag and drew out the little flask of tanning fluid. He flung his trophies into the underbrush. Something there caught his eye, and he dragged himself over for a closer look.

There, where the half elf had disappeared into the forest, was a bent twig. And not far beyond, another. She had left a trail for him, a clear trail that even a lame and wounded boy might follow. A trail to *her*.

New ways, a new pack. Was it possible?

A smile touched the corners of Drom's lips as he reached for the needle and the bandage. Perhaps not, but it would be a worthy hunt.

*Originally published in Realms of Mystery
Edited by Philip Athans, June 1998*

SPEAKING WITH THE DEAD

Let me tell you, it's not easy to set a mystery in a world where secrets yield to spells and corpses tend to sit up and point cold, gray fingers at their killers. Clerics can summon the spirits of the dead and compel them to answer three questions, and one of the immutable cosmic laws is that the dead cannot lie.

When the body of a gnome innkeeper is discovered with Elaith Craulnober's dagger through the heart, the gnome's wife, a priestess, has a brief but very public chat with her husband's spirit. The results don't look good for Elaith, and the task of proving his "innocence," at least in this particular matter, falls to Danilo Thann.

SPEAKING WITH THE DEAD

The sun began to disappear behind the tall, dense pines of the Cloak Wood, and the colors of an autumn sunset—deep, smoky purples and rose-tinted gold—stained the sky over the Coast Way.

Every member of the south-bound caravan quickened his pace. While splendidly mounted merchants urged their steeds on and drovers cracked whips over the backs of the stolid dray horses hitched to the wagons, the mercenary guards loosened their weapons and peered intently into the lengthening shadows. The trade route was dangerous at any time, but doubly so at night. But truth be told, most of the caravan members lived in greater fear of their own captain than of any chance-met monster or band of brigands. Elaith

Craulnober was not an elf to be trifled with, and he had bid them make the fortress by nightfall.

"Last hill! Fortress straight ahead!" shouted one of the scouts. The news rippled through the company in a murmur of relief.

From his position near the rear of the caravan, Danilo Thann leaned forward to whisper words of encouragement into his tired horse's back-turned ears. The ears were a bad sign, for the horse could be as balky as a cart mule. Once they crested the last hill, all would be well. The sight of a potential stable would spur the horse on as little else could, for he was a comfort-loving beast. He was also a beauty, with a sleek, glossy coat the color of ripe wheat. Danilo had turned down several offers from merchants who coveted the showy beast, and had shrugged off a good deal of jesting from the other guards. Dan felt a special affinity for this horse. The "pretty pony," as the sneering mercenaries called him, had more going for him than met the eye. He was beyond doubt the most intelligent steed Danilo had ever encountered, and utterly fearless in battle. His mincing gait could change in a heartbeat to a battle charge. In Dan's opinion, the horse would have been a worthy paladin's mount, if not for its pleasure-loving nature and its implacable stubborn streak—both of which were traits Dan understood well.

He patted his horse's neck and turned to his companion of nearly four years, a tall, rangy figure who was wrapped in a dark cloak such as a peasant might wear, and riding a raw-boned, gray-dappled mare. The rider's height and seat and well-worn boots suggested a young man of humble means, well accustomed to the road. This, Dan knew, was a carefully cultivated illusion. This illusion was a needed thing, perhaps, but he was growing tired of it.

Danilo reached out and tugged back the hood of his partner's cloak. The dying light fell upon a delicate elven face, framed by a chin-length tumble of black curls and dominated by large blue eyes, almond-shaped and flecked with gold. These marvelous eyes narrowed dangerously as they settled on him.

"What in the Nine bloody Hells was that about?" Arilyn demanded as she jerked her hood back into place.

"It seems days since I've had a good look at you, and what's the harm? We're almost at the Friendly Arm," Danilo said. His smile broadened suggestively. "The name suggests possibilities, does it not?"

The half-elf sniffed. "A bard from a noble merchant clan can travel wherever he pleases, drawing attention but not suspicion. But I am known in these parts as a Harper agent."

Danilo rather enjoyed the reproof, spoken as it was in a musical alto. He dismissed her concerns with a quick, casual flip of one bejeweled hand. "When we passed through Baldur's Gate, certain precautions were in order. But I hear the gnomes who hold this fortress are admirable little fellows—easygoing folk who set a fine table and mind their own affairs. And the Friendly Arm is perhaps the only truly neutral spot within a tenday's ride. Nothing much ever happens within the fortress walls, so why should we not relax and enjoy ourselves?"

"We have business to attend," she reminded him.

"I'm honored that you take your responsibilities to the caravan so seriously," said a new voice, one slightly lower and even more musical than Arilyn's, rich with dark, wry humor. The companions turned to face a silver-haired elf, just as he reined his cantering horse into step with Arilyn's mare. Neither of them had heard the newcomer's approach.

Enchanted horseshoes, no doubt, Danilo mused. Elaith Craulnober was known to have a fondness for magical items, and a wicked delight in keeping those around him off guard. The elf also valued information. Though Elaith would probably have given Arilyn anything she asked of him, Danilo suspected the elf had another motive for allowing a representative of the Thann merchant clan to ride along with his caravan. Elaith knew that both Danilo and Arilyn were Harpers, and that members of this secret organization usually had duties far more pressing than acting as caravan guards. No doubt he wondered what these might be, and how he might profit from this knowledge.

Arilyn mirrored the elf's faint smile. "I take all my responsibilities seriously. *Too* seriously, if Danilo is to be believed."

In response to that, Elaith lifted one brow and murmured an Elvish phrase, a highly uncomplimentary remark that defied precise translation into the Common trade tongue. His jaw dropped in astonishment when both Arilyn and Danilo burst into laughter. After a moment, he smiled ruefully and shrugged. "So, bard, you understand High Elvish. I suppose that shouldn't have surprised me."

"And had you known, would you have chosen your words with more tact?" Danilo asked, grinning.

Elaith shrugged again. "Probably not."

The three of them rode in silence for several minutes. Something that for lack of a better term could be called friendship had grown between the elf and the Harpers, but Danilo never lost sight of the fact that theirs was a tenuous alliance. They were too different for it to be otherwise. Elaith Craulnober was a moon elf adventurer, landowner, and merchant. He had far-flung interests, few of which were entirely legal, and a well-earned reputation for cruelty, treachery, and deadly prowess in battle. Arilyn was half-elven, the daughter of Elaith's lost elven love. She was as focused upon duty as a paladin, and Danilo suspected that she would not allow a shared history and a common heritage to stay her hand should Elaith step beyond the bounds of law and honor. Danilo was, on the whole, a bit more flexible about such things. He had traveled with Elaith when circumstances had enforced a partnership between them, and they had developed a cautious, mutual respect. But Danilo did not trust the elf. There were too many dangerous secrets between them, too many deadly insults exchanged, too many treacheries barely avoided.

At that moment, they crested the hill and the fortress came suddenly into sight. Nestled in a broad valley just to the east of the trade route, it was a sturdy and defensible holdfast of solid granite. A tall, thick curtain wall enclosed an austere castle and a bailey big enough to house perhaps a score of other buildings. This holdfast, once a wizard's keep, was now a wayside inn held and operated by a clan of gnomes.

The massive portcullis rose with a whirring of gears— a sure sign of a gnomish devise, noted Danilo. Most of the holdfast's inhabitants were simple folk occupied with the maintenance of the castle, but in recent years a few gnomes from the island of Lantan had settled at the Friendly Arm, bringing with them the worship of Gond the Wonderbringer and a corresponding fondness for mechanical devices that were often entertaining and occasionally useful.

The chain raising the portcullis slipped, and the pointed iron bars plunged downward. One of the men approaching the gate shrieked and lunged from his horse. He hit the dirt and rolled aside just as the portcullis came to an abrupt stop, mere inches from its highest point. This brought much laughter and many rough jests from the other members of the caravan, but Danilo noticed that they all rode through the gate with more alacrity than usual.

Inside the fortress wall, chaos reigned. The holdfast was home to perhaps three- or four-score gnomes, hill-loving folk small enough to walk comfortably under the belly of Danilo's tall horse. Most of these gnomes seemed to be

The Best of the Realms • 181

out and about, busily loading goods into the warehouses, tending horses in a long, low stable, directing the wagons into covered sheds, or bustling in and out of the many small buildings that filled the Friendly Arm's grass-covered bailey.

Danilo took the opportunity to observe this unusual clan closely. They looked a bit like dwarves, although somewhat shorter and considerably less broad than the mountain-dwelling folk. The male gnomes wore their beards short and neatly trimmed, and the females' faces, unlike those of dwarf women, were smooth and rosy-cheeked. All the gnomes had small blue eyes, pointed ears, extremely long noses, and skin that echoed all the browns of the forest, from the gray-brown of the dusk-wood tree to the deeply weathered hue of old cedar. They favored forest shades in their clothing as well, and the lot of them were dressed in browns and greens, with an adventurous few adding a hint of autumn color.

They were certainly industrious folk. Nearly every pace of the courtyard was occupied by horse or wagon, but the gnomes directed the seeming chaos with the ease of long practice. A northbound caravan had arrived shortly before Elaith's, and the southerners were still busily securing their goods for the night. Merchants shouted instructions to their servants in a half dozen southern dialects. A few swarthy guards loitered about, leaning against the walls and sizing up the newcomers with an eye toward the evening's entertainment. In Danilo's experience, it was always so. The road was long, and travelers were ever on the lookout for a new tale or tune, some competition at darts or dice or weapons, or a bit of dalliance. Most of the guards from both caravans had already gone into the castle's great-hall-turned-tavern, if the din coming from the open doors was any indication.

"Shall we join the festivities?" Danilo asked his companion. He handed the reins of his horse to a gnomish lad—along with a handful of coppers—and then slipped an arm around Arilyn's waist.

She side-stepped his casual embrace and sent him a warning look from beneath her hood. "I am supposed to be your servant, remember?" she warned him. "You learn what you can in the great hall while I talk to the stable hands."

The young bard sighed in frustration, but he had no argument to counter Arilyn's logic. He nodded and turned aside, only to step right into the unsteady path of a stocky, dark-haired man. There was no time to dodge: they collided with a heavy thud.

The dark, smoky scent of some unfamiliar liqueur rolled off the man in waves. Danilo caught him by the shoulders to steady him, then pushed him out at arm's length—after all, one could never be too careful. The man was unfamiliar to him: a southerner, certainly, with a beak of a nose under what appeared to be a single long eyebrow, a vast mustache, and skin nearly as brown as a gnome's. He appeared harmless enough. He carried no apparent weapons, and his rich clothing suggested a bored merchant whose only thought was to wash away the dust of a long road with an abundance of strong spirits.

"Are you quite all right?" Danilo inquired politely. "Shall I summon your manservant to help you to your room?"

The man mumbled something unintelligible and wrenched himself free. Dan watched him stagger off, then glanced back for a final look at Arilyn and did an astonished double take. She had fallen back into the shadows between two small buildings and dropped to one knee. There was a throwing knife in her gloved hand, held by the tip and ready to hurl.

"I know that man," she said as she tucked the knife back into her boot. "Worse yet, he knows me. He was in the assassin's guild with me, in Zazesspur."

Danilo swore fervently and joined Arilyn in the

shadows. Together they squeezed back into a narrow, gnome-sized alley. "Well, at least this confirms that we are on the right path," he said in a low, grim tone. "I suppose it could be mere happenstance that a hired sword from Zazesspur shows up at this particular time, but it's my observation that true coincidence is a rare thing—except in Selgauntan opera, of course. . ."

Arilyn nodded absently. "I'll find out who sent him."

Danilo swallowed the protest that was his first instinct. Arilyn had spent many months posing as an assassin in Tethyr. The competition among those ranks was fierce and deadly at the best of times, and she had not left the guild under good terms. But she was right: they needed to know what prompted an assassin's presence in this neutral holdfast. Even if the assassin's purpose was not the same as the Harpers', no one would risk violating the peace of the Friendly Arm unless the need was dire, or the potential gain great. To do so would bar the doors of the fortress against the wrongdoers for a gnome's centuries-long memory. This was a severe penalty in these troubled lands, which for so many years could claim few truly neutral places.

Still, change was in the air. The seemingly endless civil war within Tethyr was winding to a close. Zaranda Star had been acclaimed queen in the city of Zazesspur, and was on the way to solidifying her hold on the entire country. To this end, she was preparing for a marriage of convenience to the last known heir to the royal House of Tethyr. There were factions, however, whose interests were better served by chaos and who had no desire to see peace come to their land. When the Harpers learned that there was a potential challenger to Zaranda's throne, a distant relative of the soon-to-be-king and thus a potential bride, they foresaw trouble. Danilo and Arilyn had been sent to find the young woman and bring her to safety in the Northlands before someone else made her a pawn in a renewed struggle, someone who might send an assassin to retrieve—or do away with—the unsuspecting girl.

Yes, concluded Dan glumly, Arilyn had no choice but to face the assassin.

"Be careful," he murmured. Before she could protest, he framed her face in his hands and tipped back her head for a long and thorough kiss.

"You know better than to distract me before battle." Her tone tried for severity, but did not quite succeed.

Danilo chuckled. "I shall take that as a compliment."

He turned and strode into the castle, his manner far more insouciant than his mood. But this was his role to play, and he would attend to his part no less faithfully than did Arilyn.

Since this was his first visit to the Friendly Arm, he looked around with interest. The great hall had been set up as a tavern. Long tables and sturdy wooden chairs were scattered about, some of them gnome-sized, others intended for the comfort of taller travelers. A wild boar roasted on a spit in the enormous hearth, and kettles of steaming, herb-scented vegetable stews kept warm in the embers along either side. The air was thick with the fragrance of fresh bread and good, sour ale. Several young women moved briskly about the room carrying trays and tankards.

Prompted more by habit than inclination, Danilo slid an appraising eye over the nearest barmaid. She was young, not much past twenty, and blessed with an abundance of black hair and truly impressive curves. The former was left gloriously unbound, and the later were displayed by a tightly-laced scarlet bodice over a chemise pulled down to expose her shoulders. Her skirts ended several flirtatious inches above her ankles, and her black eyes scanned the room. They lit up with an avaricious gleam when they settled upon the richly-dressed newcomer.

The barmaid eased her way through the crowd to

Danilo's side. A passing merchant jostled her at a highly opportune moment, sending her bumping into the Harper. She made a laughing apology, then tilted her head and slanted a look at him through lowered lashes. "And what can I get *you*, my lord?"

"Killed, most likely," he said, thinking of the response this flirtation would earn from the half-elf who was prowling the shadows beyond the brightly-lit hall. "Or severely wounded, at the very least."

The barmaid's dumbfounded expression brought a smile to his lips. "Wine, if you please," he amended. "A bottle of your best Halruaan red, and several goblets."

As she wandered off to relay this order to another barmaid, Danilo scanned the tables for the captains of the northbound caravan. Before he could make his way over, he found his path barred by a stout, stern-faced, white-bearded gnome whose crimson jerkin was nearly matched in hue by an exceedingly red and bulbous nose.

"Bentley Mirrorshade," the gnome announced.

Danilo nodded. "Ah, yes—the proprietor of this fine establishment. Allow me to intro—"

"I know who you are," Bentley interrupted in a gruff tone. "Word gets around. There'll be no fighting and no spellcasting. Leave your weapons at the door. Sophie here will peace bind your left thumb to your belt."

Danilo winced. "It appears I will never live down that incident in the Stalwart Club."

"Never heard about that one." The gnome nodded to the barmaid who had greeted Danilo earlier. She fished a thin strip of leather from her pocket and deftly secured the bard's hand. As she worked, Danilo scanned the room and noticed that he was not the only one subjected to such precautions: all known mages were peace bound, and everyone was required to leave weapons at the door.

Danilo made his way to the merchant captains' table. After the introductions were made, he poured out the first of several bottles of well-aged wine, and listened as the conversation flowed. Although the merchants talked a great deal, they said little that informed his cause.

As the night wore on, Danilo found his eyes returning with increasing frequency to the door. His fellow travelers trickled in as their duties were completed and the caravan and its goods secured. Elaith was one of the latecomers. Danilo noted with interest that the elf was subjected to peace binding. Few people knew of the moon elf's considerable magical abilities. Dan had heard that Bentley Mirrorshade was a highly gifted mage, specializing in the illusionist's art. Obviously, he didn't miss much. Still, Dan suspected that Elaith managed to retain a good many of his hidden weapons.

The evening passed and the hall began to empty as the gnomes and their guests sought their beds. As soon as he reasonably could, Danilo left the hall in search of his partner.

He found Arilyn in the stable, currying her mare. She looked up when he came into the stall. Her face was pale and grim beneath its hood, and gave clear testament to her evening's work. Fighting came easily to the half-elf—Danilo had never seen anyone who could handle a sword as well—but killing did not. Even so, Danilo sensed at once that something else weighed heavily on her mind.

"Tell me," he prompted.

"I had to wait until Yoseff was alone," Arilyn said in a low, furious tone. "He had a meeting. With Elaith Craulnober."

Danilo hissed a curse from between clenched teeth. "Why am I not surprised? Did you hear what was said?"

"No, nothing. Elaith must have cast a spell of silence, or some such thing."

"Now what?" mused Dan, running one hand through his hair in a gesture of pure frustration. He had investigated Elaith's purpose in this trip, which was allegedly to acquire exotic goods from faraway Maztica in the markets of Amn. The elf would make a fine profit selling these wares to the merchants of Waterdeep, but he had also arranged to acquire goods that were restricted or forbidden outright: feather magic, enspelled gems, possibly even slaves. Danilo had considered this the extent of Elaith's planned mischief; apparently, he had been wrong.

"And the assassin? What had he to say for himself?"

"Yoseff was never one for conversation," Arilyn said shortly. "But he carried a few things that might help us."

She reached into the bag that hung from her belt and took several glittering objects from it. The first to catch Danilo's eye was a finely wrought gold locket on a heavy gold chain. A very nice amethyst—brilliant cut, thumb-sized, and deep purple in hue—was set into the front of the locket and a wisp of fine, black hair was nestled within.

"An amulet of seeking," he surmised, fingering the soft curl. "Hair so soft could only have belonged to an elf or a baby. I'm guessing the latter. So we not only have a fair idea who the assassin came to find, but also who sent him—may all the gods damn the woman who would so use her own child!"

Before he could elaborate, a female voice, raised in a keening wail, cut through the night. It was a chilling sound, an age-old, wordless song of mourning. It spoke of death more clearly than any cleric's eulogy, and far more poignantly.

Arilyn bolted from the stable with Danilo close behind her. They dashed through the nearly empty hall, toward the babble of gnomish voices in a side chamber. A thick-chested gnome barred their way, an odd-looking fellow with hair and skin of nearly matching shades of slate gray. Danilo recognized him from descriptions as Garith Hunterstock, Bentley's second-in-command. Though the gnomish commander was determined to keep them out, the Harpers were tall enough to see over the heads of the crowd.

In the room beyond, Bentley Mirrorshade lay in a spreading pool of blood. The hilt of a jeweled dagger rose from his chest.

"No one in, no one out," the gnome guard decreed. He raised his voice and began to bellow orders. "Lower the portcullis and bar the gates! Archers, to the walls! Shoot down anyone who tries to leave the fortress before the murderer is found."

◈ ◈ ◈ ◈ ◈

Later that night, Danilo and his "servant" attended a grim gathering in the castle's hall. The body of Bentley Mirrorshade lay in state upon a black-draped table. Lit torches lined the walls, casting a somber, golden light.

The crowd parted to allow a green-robed gnome woman to pass. Respectful silence filled the room as Gellana Mirrorshade, the high priestess of Garl Glittergold and the widow of Bentley Mirrorshade, made her way to her husband's bier. She carried herself with admirable dignity. Her pale brown face was set in rigid lines, but her eyes were steady and dry.

The priestess spoke into the silence. "You are gathered here to see justice done. It is no small thing to speak with the dead, but evil deeds must not go unpunished."

Gellana began the words and gestures of a complicated ritual. Danilo watched closely; nothing about the spell was familiar to him. He had studied magic since his twelfth year with no less a teacher than the archmage Khelben Arunsun, but the magic of a wizard and that of a priest were very different things. Apparently, the priestess was skilled and devout, for a translucent image of Bentley Mirrorshade slowly took form in the air above the pall.

"The dead must speak truth," Gellana said softly, "and in life or in death, Bentley Mirrorshade would tell no direct lie. Tell us, my husband, who is responsible for this death."

The specter's eyes swept the assemblage. His stubby, translucent finger lifted, swept to the left, and leveled at Elaith Craulnober with a sharp, accusing stab.

For the first time in their acquaintance, Danilo saw the elf's composure utterly forsake him. Elaith's face went slack and ashen, and his amber-hued eyes widened in stunned disbelief.

"What nonsense is this?" the elf protested as soon as he could gather enough of his wits to fuel speech. "I am innocent of this thing!"

"Silence!" Gellana demanded. She held a jeweled dagger up for the ghostly gnome's inspection. "Was this the weapon used?"

The spectral head rose and fell once, slowly, in a nod of confirmation. Despite the gravity of the occasion, Danilo could not help but observe that the gnome's spirit had a remarkable flair for drama.

"And whose dagger is this?" persisted Gellana.

"It belongs to the elf," proclaimed the spirit. "It is Elaith Craulnober's dagger."

Gellana Mirrorshade's eyes were hard as they swept the gathering. "Have you heard enough? May I release my husband, and in his name order the death of this treacherous elf?"

A murmur arose, gathering power and fury. The accused elf stood alone in an angry circle of gnomes, buffeted by a storm of accusation and demands for immediate retribution. Elaith's eyes went flat and cool, and his chin lifted with elven hauteur as he faced his death.

That gesture, that purely elven mixture of pride and courage and disdain, was to be his salvation. Danilo had always been a fool for all things elven, and this moment proved no exception. He sighed and quickly cast a cantrip that would add power and persuasion to his voice.

"Wait," he demanded.

The single word thrummed through the great hall like a clarion blast, and the gnomes fell suddenly silent. Garith Hunterstock froze, his sword poised to cut the elf down. Danilo reached out and gently eased the gnome's blade away from Elaith Craulnober's throat.

"The elf claims innocence," he said. "We should at least consider the possibility that he speaks truth."

"Bentley Mirrorshade himself accused the elf!" shouted a high-pitched gnomish voice from the crowd.

"The dead do not lie!" another small voice added.

"That is true enough," Dan agreed in a conciliatory tone, "but perhaps there is some other explanation that will serve both truths."

Inspiration struck, and he glanced at Arilyn. She stood near the back of the room, nearly indistinguishable from the shadows. "Earlier this evening, Elaith Craulnober was seen meeting with a known thief and assassin. Perhaps this man stole the dagger, and used it to kill the gnome?"

"That is not possible," Arilyn said flatly. "The assassin was dead before Bentley Mirrorshade's murder."

"Dead?" Garith Hunterstock said, turning a fierce glare in her direction. "By whose hand?"

The half-elf returned his gaze steadily. "He attacked me; I defended myself. You will find his body behind the smokehouse."

"And who might you be?" demanded the gnome.

Arilyn slipped down her cowl and stepped into the firelight. Before she could speak, a young gnome clad in forest green let out a startled exclamation. "I know her! She's the Harper who fought alongside the elves of Tethyr's forest. If she says the stiff behind the smokehouse needed killing, that's good enough for me. And if she speaks for yonder elf, I say that's reason enough to think things over real careful."

Dozens of expectant faces turned in Arilyn's direction. Danilo saw the flicker of regret in her eyes as she met Elaith's stare, and he knew what her answer would be.

"I cannot speak for him," she said. "On the other hand, it never hurts to think things over. Lord Thann has apparently appointed himself Elaith Craulnober's advocate. Give them time—two days, perhaps—to prove the elf's claim of innocence. I know of Bentley Mirrorshade, and nothing I've heard suggests that he would want anyone denied a fair hearing."

A soft, angry mutter greeted her words, but no one could think of a way to refute them. Garith Hunterstock ordered the elf taken away and imprisoned. The others left, too, slipping away in silence to leave Gellana Mirrorshade alone with her dead.

☙ ☙ ☙ ☙ ☙

As the sun edged over the eastern battlements of the fortress, Danilo made his way down the tightly spiraling stairs that led to the dungeon. It was a dank, gloomy place, lit only by an occasional sputtering torch thrust into a rusted sconce.

Since Elaith was the only prisoner, his cell was not hard to find. Danilo followed the faint light to the far corner of the dungeon. The elf's cell was small, the ceiling too low for him to stand upright. The only furniture was a straw pallet. Elaith wore only his leggings and shirt, and his thumbs were entrapped in opposite ends of a metal tube, a gnomish device of some sort designed to make spellcasting impossible. He had been stripped of weapons, armor, and magical items. These lay heaped in an impressive pile, well beyond reach of the cell.

Danilo eyed the glittering hoard. "Did you actually wear all that steel? It's a wonder you could walk without clanking."

The elf's furious, amber-eyed glare reminded Danilo of a trapped hawk. "Come to gloat?"

"Perhaps later," he said. "At the moment, though, I would rather hear what you have to say."

"And you would believe me?"

"I would listen. That seems a reasonable place to start."

The elf was silent for a long moment. "I did not kill the gnome."

"You know, of course, how difficult it is for the dead to lie," Danilo pointed out. "The spirit of Bentley Mirrorshade named you as his killer. The weapon that dealt the killing stroke is yours. The proof against you is formidable."

"Nevertheless, I am innocent," Elaith maintained. A sudden, fierce gleam lit his eyes. "I am innocent, and you must prove me so."

Dan lifted one eyebrow. "Since I have a full two days, shouldn't I warm up with an easier task? Pilfering Elminster's favorite pipe maybe, or bluffing an illithid at cards, or persuading Arilyn to dance upon a tavern table?"

"I did not say the task would be easy, but when you signed on to travel with my caravan you promised your support and aid to the expedition."

"Insofar as its purpose was lawful and just," Danilo specified.

"What better way to fulfill this pledge than to clear an innocent person, unjustly accused? And why would you speak for me in the tavern, if you had no intention of following through?"

The Harper shrugged. "Excellent points. Very well, then, let's assume for argument's sake that I will take on this task. Consider my dilemma; even under the best of circumstances, 'innocent' is not the first word that comes to mind when your name is mentioned."

"Perhaps the gnome priestess erred."

"An unlikely possibility, but one I have already considered. Gellana Mirrorshade permitted me to test the murder weapon myself," the Harper said. "I cast the needed spell not once, but three times. Each time the result was the same. The dagger is indisputably yours, and it was indeed responsible for the killing stroke. Now, I understand that most people would hardly consider my command of magic sufficient to such a task—"

"Save your breath," Elaith said curtly. "I have seen what you can do. Your command of magic exceeds my own. If it suits you to play the fool at court and muck about with minstrelsy in taverns rather than proclaiming yourself a wizard, that is your affair."

"Enough said, then. Let's consider the murder weapon. Was the dagger ever out of your keeping? Did you entrust it to another? Lose it in a game of dice? Anything?"

Elaith shook his head. "I didn't even notice it was missing." With a grim smile, he nodded to the pile of weapons outside his cell. "I carry several, you see."

The Harper folded his arms. "The situation is bleak, make no mistake about it. But it might interest you to learn that I, too, seem to be without an item or two. It would appear there is a very talented pickpocket at work here. I was jostled by the assassin Arilyn dispatched, and you were seen meeting with. And speaking of which, is there anything you would like to tell me about that?"

"No."

"Not a surprising response, but I had to ask," Danilo commented. "As I was saying, this assassin would be my first suspect. It is possible that he had a partner."

"It is possible, and a good place to start," the elf allowed. "Then you will do it? You will honor your pledge?"

"Don't get your hopes too high. Arilyn bought us some time, but not much."

Elaith's gaze faltered. "She believes that I am responsible for the gnome's death."

The Harper didn't deny it. Arilyn had had a great deal to say about Danilo's defense of the rogue elf. Dan's ears still burned from the heat of their argument. "My lady is occasionally more elven than she realizes."

This earned a small, wry smile from Elaith. "If she could not be supportive, at least she has been fair. More than fair. I don't suppose my other employees have followed her example."

"The caravan guards have already drawn their pay from the quartermaster, and plan to scatter once the gates of the city are opened. Forgive me, but the prevailing attitude seems to be that this is a long overdue justice."

The elf was silent for a long moment. "I am not unaware of the irony in my situation," he said finally, "but I maintain that I am innocent of this murder. Go now, and prove it!"

☙ ☙ ☙ ☙ ☙

That morning, over a breakfast of bread, cheese, and newly-pressed cider, Danilo related the conversation to Arilyn. "And I have but two days to accomplish this miracle," he lamented in conclusion. "You couldn't have asked for a tenday?"

The half-elf sighed and stabbed a piece of cheese with her table knife. "I doubt it would help. You know Elaith as well as anyone, and you know he could have killed that gnome. He nearly killed you once."

"Three times, actually, but why quibble?"

Arilyn sighed cast her eyes toward the ceiling. "Why do you persist in this?"

"My promise to help Elaith, and the task that brought us here," he said quietly.

His partner nodded, accepting this reasoning. "What do you propose to do?"

"You're not going to like this," Danilo cautioned, "but we could ask the priestess to speak to the spirit of the dead assassin. We need to know who he was working for, and who he was working with."

Arilyn's lips thinned. "You know elves do not believe in disturbing the dead."

"But gnomes do. Gellana Mirrorshade can hardly deny us this, considering that she called back her own husband's spirit. And what other course could we take?"

"Nearly any would be preferable," the half-elf grumbled, but Danilo read the surrender in her eyes and tone. He tossed several silver coins on the table to pay for the meal and followed Arilyn out of the tavern. One of the dark-haired barmaids sashayed over to clear the table and pocket the coins. The barmaids were hardworking girls, Danilo noted, recognizing several faces familiar from the night before.

Retrieving the assassin's body was an easy matter. The gnomes had simply tossed it into the midden wagon along with the remnants of the wild boar they had roasted for their guests the night before, some chicken bones, and an over-ripe haunch of venison. The gnomes regularly removed any leftovers to the forest to feed the animals who lived there, and to return their bounty to the land. They gave the dead assassin no less respect, and no more.

Danilo wrinkled his nose as he shouldered the dead man. "I can see why Gellana didn't want to do the ritual on site. That venison should have been buried long ago."

"The same could be said of Yoseff," retorted Arilyn, "but that's another matter. Don't you think it odd that Gellana Mirrorshade told us to bring his body to the temple?"

Her partner immediately seized her meaning. "Come to think of it, yes," he agreed as he fell into step beside her. "Gellana Mirrorshade summons her own husband's spirit in a tavern. Why would she afford greater honor to a human assassin? Perhaps she feared that the curious tall folk who gathered at last night's summoning would ill fit the Shrine of the Short."

Arilyn's lips twitched. "The gnomes call it the Temple of Wisdom. But perhaps the size of the temple explains the matter."

It did not. The Temple of Wisdom was undoubtedly a gnomish work—a curious, asymmetric building fashioned of forest-hued stone and marble and filled with odd statues and embellished with gems—but the vaulted ceilings made concession for human supplicants. In fact, the shrine was large enough to accommodate all those who had witnessed the solemn ritual in the tavern the night before. This puzzled Danilo. He watched the gnomish priestess carefully as she spoke the words of the spell.

A dank gray mist gathered in the hall and coalesced into the shape of the man who has jostled Danilo the night before.

"Word your questions carefully," Gellana advised, "for the dead will tell you no more than they must."

Danilo nodded and turned to the specter. "Who were you sent to find?"

"She was named Isabeau Thione; I know not what she is called now."

Arilyn and Danilo exchanged a look of mingled triumph and concern. This was indeed the woman they had been sent to find, and their competitors were also close on her trail.

"Who sent you?" Danilo asked. "If you do not know names, describe the person or people."

"There were two: a fat man who smiles too much, and a small woman. She had the look of the old nobility of Tethyr; fine features, dark eyes, and a curve to her nose. She wore purple, in the old style."

Danilo recognized Lucia Thione, an agent for the Knights of the Shield, recently exiled from Waterdeep for treachery against the secret lords who ruled that city. She had never come to trial; hers was a private justice. She was given over to Lord Hhune, her rival. The man had apparently kept her alive for his own purposes. And Lady Thione, ever a survivor, had apparently found a way to earn her keep. Twenty years before, she had birthed a daughter in secrecy and given her away into fosterage. Apparently she now planned to reclaim the girl and present her as a more suitable bride to the royal heir than Zaranda Star, a common-born mercenary with a purchased title. Danilo foresaw two possible results: the girl would be accepted and crowned queen, thereby increasing Lucia Thione's influence and status in Tethyr, or she would be rejected, but in the process providing a focal point to rally the anti-Zaranda sentiment and foment rebellion.

"Thione and Hhune," Danilo commented in an aside to Arilyn. "The Harpers erred when they made that match."

She nodded and turned with obvious reluctance to the spirit of the man she had killed. "What was the purpose of your meeting with Elaith Craulnober?"

The spirit sneered. "The elf's purpose was the same as mine, the same as your own! Oh, yes, he knew you sought the Thione heiress. He agreed to take you with him for that reason. He is using Harper hounds to sniff out his quarry."

Arilyn turned away. "I have heard enough," she said shortly. "Send him back."

The priestess murmured a few words, and the figure of the assassin faded away. Danilo thanked her, and led his grim-faced partner out of the temple.

"We need to talk to Elaith," he said.

"*You* talk to him. Yoseff was all I can stomach for one day."

"At least come and listen," he cajoled. "You might hear something that I miss. The answer lies right before us—I am certain of that!"

"Finally, you're making sense," the half-elf said. "Elaith is guilty of murder and more. He planned to find that girl sell her to the highest bidder. He used us to that end. What more answer do you need?"

When they reached the dungeon, Danilo repeated most of these sentiments to Elaith while Arilyn looked on in stony silence. "None of this endears us to your cause, you know," he concluded. "Frankly, I'm disposed to let the matter stand."

"I have your pledge," Elaith insisted. "You must press on."

Danilo sighed and rubbed his hands over his face. "What more can I do?"

"Find the girl," the elf insisted. "Find her, and learn who else seeks her. Who else would wish to see me condemned to death?"

"Had I more time, I would write you a list," Danilo said dryly. He took the amethyst locket from his bag and held it up. "This is an amulet of seeking, taken from your erstwhile friend Yoseff."

"We won't find her here," Arilyn said, speaking for the first time. "Bentley Mirrorshade kept the peace for over twenty years. He could never have done that if he got caught up in the endless local fighting, so he swore never to admit anyone to the stronghold who claimed to be of the Tethyrian royal family. We can assume that the girl was never at the Friendly Arm."

"Can we, indeed?" mused Danilo. "Now that I think on it, wouldn't Bentley's vow provide a perfect cover for the girl's presence?"

"Bentley is known as an honorable gnome," the half-elf countered. "What purpose would he have in breaking his sworn word?"

"Saving the life of an infant seems purpose enough. For that matter, he could have kept to the letter of his word: he swore not to admit anyone who *claimed* ties to the royal family. An infant could hardly make such a claim. If indeed Lady Thione's child was brought here, it is possible that the gnome did not know at the time who the child was."

"But he learned," Arilyn surmised. "He probably died to protect that knowledge."

"It is worth pursuing," Dan agreed. He nodded a farewell to Elaith, and he and Arilyn walked toward the stairs.

"Did you notice the barmaids at the inn? Any one of them could be the woman we seek—they are all about the right age, and by the look of them, any one of them could be kin to Lucia Thione."

Arilyn considered this. "Their presence in the gnomish stronghold is difficult to explain otherwise. Do you want to take a closer look at them?"

Her partner responded with a smirk. Arilyn bit back a chuckle and tried to glare. "I'll come looking for you in an hour."

"Make it two," Danilo murmured. "In such cases, it pays to be thorough."

He made his way back into the tavern and tried to strike up a conversation with the gnome barkeep. All the inhabitants of the fortress were stunned by their leader's murder, and none of the small folk were inclined to share information with the human who had defended the accused elf. But Dan pieced together a series of grudging, one-word answers and eventually learned that there were a total of eight barmaids, six of whom were on duty.

Since Danilo was more interested in a woman who was not on duty, he left the castle and went to the barmaid's house, a stone structure built right against one of the curtain walls. Danilo knocked softly on the wooden door. When there was no answer, he tried the door and found it unlocked.

There was but one large room, simply furnished with straw pallets softened by down-filled mattresses. Two women lay sleeping. Danilo recognized one of them as Sophie, the girl who had administered the peace bonds the night before. A shadow of suspicion edged into his mind.

He stooped by her bed and softly called her name. When still she slept, he tapped her shoulder, then shook her. Nothing woke her.

Danilo rose and took a couple of odd items from the bag at his waist, then cast a spell that would dispel any magic in the room. The result was only half what he expected.

"Sophie" was not a woman at all, but a pile of laundry. The other barmaid was not a woman either but an iron golem, a magically-animated construction enspelled to look enough like Sophie to be her cousin. One apparently solid stone wall was breached by a wooden door that was closed but not barred.

The Harper crept closer for a better look. The golem was curled up in mock slumber, but when it stood it would be nearly twice the height of a tall man. The body, shaped roughly like that of a human woman, probably outweighed Danilo's horse three or four times over. No wonder so few gnomes held the fortress, Dan realized. An iron golem could stop a war-horse's charge without getting knocked back on its heels, crush an ogre's skull with one fist, and shrug off blows from all but the most powerful magical weapons.

Still, this golem was in need of repair. There was a considerable amount of rust along some of the joints, requiring filing and oils at the very least, and possibly the ministrations of a blacksmith. Danilo guessed that the golem could still do considerable damage in its current condition. He backed out of the room, grateful that the stone floor, which had no doubt been built to support the construct's great weight, did not creak.

He bumped into Arilyn at the door. "The barkeep thought I might find you here," she said.

"Keep your voice down," he implored, nodding toward the golem.

But his spell had faded, and the figure that rose from the pallet appeared to be nothing more than an angry girl.

The Best of the Realms • 201

The illusion-draped construct rushed forward, fist raised for a blow.

Arilyn stepped forward, her forearm raise to block the attack. There was no time for explanation, so Danilo did the only thing he could; he leaped at Arilyn and knocked her out of the golem's path. Her angry retort was swallowed by the sound of an iron fist smashing into the wall. Jagged fissures raced along the stone, carving a spider-like portrait on the wall.

The half-elf's eyes widened. "Iron golem," Danilo said tersely. "Rust on the elbow joints."

Arilyn nodded in understanding. In one swift movement, she rolled to her feet and drew her sword. Danilo reached for his, then remembered that only magic-rich swords could have any impact. After a moment's hesitation, he reached for a thin, ornamental blade he wore on his right hip—a singing sword with a ringing baritone voice and an extremely bawdy repertoire.

"Softly," he admonished the sword as he tugged it free of its sheath. "There might be more of these things waiting tables in the castle." Obligingly, the sword launched into a whispered rendition of "Sune and the Satyr."

Arilyn shot him an exasperated, sidelong glance, and then turned her attention to the golem. The woman-shaped construct turned slowly to face the half-elf, spewing a cloud of roiling gray smoke from its mouth. The golem balled one fist into a deceptively dainty weapon. Arilyn sidestepped the attack, holding her breath and squeezing her eyes shut against the stinging gas. She brought her sword up high and delivered a powerful two-handed blow that would have cleaved an orc's skull in two. A harsh clang resounded through the room, and Arilyn's sword vibrated visibly in her hands. There was not so much as a scratch on the illusionary barmaid, and as the gas cleared, the golem wrapped its arms around one of the beams that supported the building and began to rock.

As dust and straw showered down from the thatch roof, Danilo remembered his glimpse of the golem, recalled how the iron plates of the arms were arranged. He lunged forward and thrust his weapon into the arm. The magic sword slid between the plates and out the other side. The blade bit deeply into the wooden beam the golem was holding, pinning one arm fast.

Arilyn stepped in and swung again, hitting the golem's other arm at the crook of the elbow. She felt the give of rusted metal and struck again, and then again. The limb fell to the stone floor with a clatter, the illusion dispelled. Its iron fingers flexed and groped. Arilyn tried to kick the arm aside and swore when her boot met unyielding iron. She sidestepped the twitching limb and struck again and again, chopping at the construct like a deranged woodsman determined to fell a tree one limb at a time. With each piece she knocked or pried loose the construct's struggle weakened.

But not soon enough. The golem, now plainly visible for what it was, managed to work its impaled arm free. Danilo's singing sword went skidding across the floor.

At once the half-elf struck, thrusting her own blade back into the same place. She leaned into the sword to hold it in place and shot a look over her shoulder at Danilo. "Melt it," she commanded. "It's the only way to be sure."

Danilo hesitated, quickly considering his options. Fire would only restore the golem. Lighting, then. He lifted both hands and deftly summoned the force, holding it between his hands in a crackling ball as he shouted for Arilyn to stand clear.

Magic flowed from his fingertips in an arc of blue-white lightning. The construct wilted like a candle left out in the sun; the moonblade remained impeded in the wooded post, unharmed by the magical assault.

Danilo went to Arilyn and brushed a stray curl off her damp forehead. When he gathered her close, her arms went around him instinctively.

"Casting an illusion on an iron golem—very clever," he murmured. "Bentley Mirrorshade was a powerful illusionist, and a clever gnome."

Arilyn lifted her head from his shoulder. "And?"

"One of the main tenants of the illusionist's craft is to make people overlook the obvious. What is the most obvious question, and the one question no one thought to ask?"

The half-elf pondered this. A small, wry smile lifted the corner of her lips when the answer came to her, and she eased out of Danilo's arms. "Give me the amulet of seeking," she said. "I'll go after the girl."

☉ ☉ ☉ ☉ ☉

Within the hour, Danilo again stood in the Temple of Wisdom. The body of Bentley Mirrorshade had made it there at last, and it was laid out in the enclosed courtyard in the center of the temple, upon a bier of stacked wood well-soaked with fragrant oil. It was no coincidence, thought Danilo, that the gnomes were preparing so hasty a funeral. After this ritual was completed, nothing he could do would save Elaith.

He explained his intentions to Gellana Mirrorshade. The gnomish priestess was not happy with his request, but she had pledged her aid to his quest for justice. She sent Garith Hunterstock to the dungeon to retrieve Elaith.

"The accused has a right to tell his story," Danilo said, "but he does not wish to do so before so many witnesses. The elf is weaponless and bound; I can confidently ensure the priestess's safety."

Gellana shrugged and spoke a few gnomish words to her fellow clerics. All left the temple. When the only sound was the steady dripping of the large Neveren water clock that stood like a monument in the courtyard, Danilo bid the priestess to summon Bentley Mirrorshade. When the ghostly gnome stood before them, Danilo turned to Elaith.

"You were late to the tavern last night. Did you have dinner?"

The elf looked at Danilo as if he had lost his mind. "I ordered, but did not eat. The gnome's murder was discovered before my meal arrived, and the tavern closed."

"Ah. And what did you order?"

"Medallions of veal, I believe, with capers and cream. Why?"

Danilo ignored the question. "You were also subjected to a peace bond, of the sort given to mages. Is your magical skill widely known?"

"It is not," the elf replied. "I find that the best weapon is often the one you keep hidden."

"Well said. So it would appear the gnomes knew more of you than is commonly told. Who tied your thumb in a peace bond?"

The elf shrugged. "A human wench, overblown and under-clad. Dark hair. I did not ask her name."

"That sounds like Sophie. Is peace bonding her task?" Danilo asked Gellana. The gnomish priestess responded with a cautious nod. The Harper held up a small sack of green-dyed leather. "Is it also her task to relieve guests of their valuables? This coin purse is mine. I lost it in the tavern and found it this morning in Sophie's chest. But Sophie herself, I could not find. A marvel, considering that the fortress is sealed."

Gellana scowled. "You had me summon my husband to listen to this nonsense? If you have questions for Bentley Mirrorshade, ask them!"

Danilo nodded agreeably and turned to the specter. "Is Bentley Mirrorshade dead?"

"What kind of question is that?" snapped Gellana.

"A very good one, I should think," the Harper replied. "It is the one question that no one thought to ask. When presented with a body, everyone's instinct was to look for the killer. But Bentley Mirrorshade is an illusionist of some skill, and considerable sophistry. Looking back, it strikes me that your questions at the summoning, dear lady, were rather oddly worded. You referred to the spirit by name, but never the body. The elf was responsible for 'the death,' and his weapon struck the killing blow—that is all that was said. Elaith would be responsible indeed, if the death in question was that of the veal calf he ordered for his dinner."

Danilo held out his hands, his palms open and empty. "Shall I cast the needed spell?" he asked the priestess. "One that can dispel the effects of others' spells?"

"Don't bother," said a gruff voice from the vicinity of the clock. A door on the pedestal cabinet flew open, and Bentley Mirrorshade, very much alive, strode toward his bier. He snatched the illusionary specter from the air and crumpled it as a frustrated scribe might treat a sheet of blotched parchment. On the bier, as Danilo expected, lay the body of a brindle calf.

The gnome illusionist folded his stubby arms and glared up at the Harper. "All right, then, you got me. What now?"

"That depends upon you." Dan said. "Tell me, why did you stage your own death?"

Bentley rolled his shoulders in a shrug. "Had a responsibility to the girl. She's trouble, and no mistake about that, but she don't deserve the likes of this elf sniffing around. I got no use for those who would use the girl to stir up rebellion, and even less for those who would hunt her down to enrich themselves." He glared at the elf.

"And by leaving behind your own illusionary corpse, you created a diversion that allowed the girl to escape unnoticed, and that condemned Elaith Craulnober to death. Masterfully done," Danilo complimented him. "But how did you intend to explain your eventual return from the grave? I have my suspicions, mind you, but I'd like to hear you tell the tale."

The gnome had the grace to look sheepish. "I've been known to go off fishing now and again. Gives me time alone, time to think. I thought to come back when this was over, act surprised by this rogue's fate. And you're right in what you're thinking, Harper; I thought to pin the blame for the illusion on you. You're known for pranks, and for spells gone awry."

Danilo took note of the remarkable change which came over Elaith during this confession. Understanding, then profound relief, then chilling anger played over his elven features. Danilo sent him a warning look.

"I must say, this leaves me with something of a dilemma," the Harper said. "Elaith has been found to be without guilt in this case, but to make public your scheme would upset the balance in the Friendly Arm, and would alert others who seek the Thione heiress."

"True enough," the gnome agreed. "What's your thinking, then?"

Danilo sighed. "I see no real choice. I shall take the blame for the illusion, as you intended. If asked, I can cite old and very real enmities between myself and Elaith." He turned to the elf. "In return for this, I expect your word that you will not hinder Arilyn and me in our task. We intend to take Isabeau Thione—better known as Sophie the pickpocket—to safety in the north."

Bentley snorted. "You're gonna take the word of such a one as this?"

"In your position, I would not be too quick to cast aspersions on the honesty of another," Elaith said, his voice bubbling with barely controlled wrath. "I am what I am, but the Harper knows that my word, once given, is as good as that of any elf alive, and better than that of any gnome. And so you may believe me when I swear that if ever I meet you beyond these walls, I will kill you in the slowest and most painful manner known to me."

The gnome shrugged. "Fair enough. But mind you, take

care who you're calling a liar. I never said a single thing wasn't Garl's honest truth. An illusion ain't never a lie—people just got a bad habit of believing what they see."

Danilo took Elaith's arm and led the furious elf from the temple. "I will keep my oath to you, bard," the elf hissed from between clenched teeth, "but there is another I long to break! Like any other elf I believe disturbing the dead is a terrible thing. But I would give fifty years off my life to continue this discussion—with that wretched gnome's *real* spirit!"

The Harper shrugged. "We are neither of us quite what we seem, are we? Why, then, should you expect anything else to be what it seems?"

Elaith glared at him. After a moment a smile, slow and rueful, softened the elf's face. "If a moon elf of noble family commands half the illegal trade in Waterdeep, and if a foolish minstrel from that same city displays insight that an elven sage might envy, why should we make foolish assumptions about speaking with the dead?"

He extended his hand. A simple gesture, but for once, the Harper felt no need to seek for hidden meanings or illusionary truths. He knew the elf for what he was, but there were some absolutes that Danilo took when and where he found them. Friendship was one of them.

Without hesitation, he clasped Elaith's wrist in a comrade's salute.

Originally publishing in Dragon #259, May 1999
Edited by Dave Gross

STOLEN DREAMS

Everyone knows some variation of the story about the six blind men and the elephant. Even as a kid, I understood that this tale was universally applicable. No one, no matter how good his eyesight or how fair and balanced his view, ever sees the whole picture. Two different points of view can yield two very different tales without contradicting each other. I decided to experiment with this notion and retell the events of "Speaking With the Dead" from the perspective of Sophie, a human barmaid who was left with the gnomes as an infant and raised without knowledge of her name or heritage.

STOLEN DREAMS

The bustle of an arriving caravan filled the courtyard of the Friendly Arms tavern. Inside the tavern's great hall, a tiny brown woman—short even by the standards of the gnomes who ran the fortified travelers' rest—scrambled onto one of the smooth-planked tables and clapped her small hands for attention.

"Caravan from Waterdeep coming through! Step lively, now." Her voice boomed through the vast room, surprising in its depth and resonance. In response, a small army of gnomes began to scurry about in frenzied last-moment preparation, like roaches scattering before the light of an unexpected lantern.

Or so they seemed to Sophie. She'd lived

among these small folk for all of her twenty-odd years, and never had she been so heartily sick of them as she was this night. Although she was only a serving wench, she dreamed of grander folk, better places, and opportunities only the wide world could offer. Some odd quirk of fate had left her a foundling babe, and a second, darker turn had landed her on the doorstep of gnomes who insisted that she stay until she worked off the cost of her early keep.

The other girls—there were seven of them—had similar tales. Indentured servants all, they occasionally bemoaned their ill luck but seemed content to accept their fate. Not Sophie. Let other fools toss their coins into the alms pots at Tymora's temples and pray for Lady Fortune's favor. Sophie had noticed that the harder she worked, the better her luck seemed to be. Tonight she would work very hard indeed.

She wiped her hands on her apron and tugged at the hem of her tightly-laced bodice, pulling the crimson garment as low as she dared. It was easier to steal from the travelers who frequented the Friendly Arms once their attention was fixed upon something interesting.

"You're selling ale and stew," observed a gruff voice behind her, "but you're advertising other wares. We don't sell that here, girl, so stop teasing the customers."

Sophie hissed a sigh from between gritted teeth and turned to glare down at the gnome who called himself her guardian and employer. Her jailer, more like it!

Bentley Mirrorshade was stout and brown-skinned and much weathered by the passing of years and the use of magic. To Sophie's eyes, he had little in common with the magic-users who passed through on their way to better places. Not for him the embroidered spell bags, the studied grace of gesture, and the trained resonance of tone. No fine robes draped his squat form, and no potions of longevity smoothed the wrinkles that seamed and whorled his face like the patterns in wood. Indeed, except for the rosy hue of his bulbous nose and the slightly darker crimson of his jerkin, he might well have been carved from wood.

"My fingers tingle," she informed him. "I can't smell the stew over the scent of money. Listen to the din out there! Look at the fine weapons the merchant's guards carry. Tonight is the night, I feel it!"

The gnome sighed. He had long ago become resigned to the larcenous streak in Sophie's nature and had worked out a compromise that served both his reputation and her sanity. But he could not resist wagging a stubby brown finger in admonition.

"Remember the Mirrorshade Cipher, wench."

Sophie rolled her eyes and held her hands out to her sides, palms up, pantomiming a scale see-sawing in a fruitless quest for balance.

"The treasure worth keeping, the risk worth taking," she recited in a mocking singsong. "But what risk could there be this night? Waterdeep merchants are fat and smug and lazy."

"There are wizards in Waterdeep," the gnome reminded her. "Play your games if you must, don't get caught lifting some silly trifle. That sort of thing ruins an inn's name, and what would you be without the Friendly Arms?"

Sophie tossed her head. "Free," she retorted.

Bentley Mirrorshade sent her a look that was both dour and long-suffering. He fell silent as a small group of the travelers came into the hall, and his small, shrewd blue eyes scrutinized each one in turn.

As she waited the gnome's verdict, Sophie reached into her pocket for a handful of long, thin leather thongs. One of her favorite tasks was peace-binding the left thumb of visiting mages to their belts. On the surface of things, it was a foolish convention—most spells could be cast one-handed—but it had its purposes. For one thing, it left the visiting magic-users smug, certain their gnomish hosts were ignorant of magic and awed by those who practiced it. Bentley Mirrorshade was in truth a highly skilled illusionist, but he was not above using simple, mundane ploys to distract the eye and create a desired effect. Peace-binding also gave Sophie a decided edge. The pressure of the thong, the awkward position of the hand—this was enough to nudge the senses off balance. Men thus distracted were less likely to notice a sudden lightening of their purses.

"This caravan carries more magic-users than a bugbear has ticks," the gnome observed. "Peace-bind that fat man wearing purple, and the woman in leather armor. And those two over there, the young skinny ones tripping over their robes. And be looking for a tall elf with silver hair. When he comes in, bind him tight, but otherwise leave him be." A new swirl of wind drew the gnome's gaze back to the door, and he sucked in a sharp, startled breath.

"Danilo Thann," he said flatly. "Better wizard than he wants you to think. Bind him well, or there'll be trouble later, sure as kobolds are ugly."

Sophie's eyes lit up with pure avarice. The newcomer handing his coat to the doorkeeper was the most promising pigeon she'd seen in a month of tendays. A young man, tall and fair, splendidly attired and wearing more jewels than any sensible traveler would dare display. He wore two fine swords, which he handed to the gnomes who collected weapons at the door. Sophie slid a measuring eye over him. A nobleman, judging from the heraldic crest embroidered onto one shoulder of his tabard and the easy, innate arrogance of his stance and manner. The green leather bag at his belt was too big to lift without risk, but the coin purse hanging over his left hip, the small silver knife tucked into his boot, his emerald pendant—these were as good as hers.

Sophie pushed past the gnome, ignoring his protests

as she eased her way through the growing crowd. With practiced calculation, she stepped into the path of a thick-bodied merchant. They collided, and she bounced off him and all but fell into the young nobleman's arms.

She pulled away with a laughing apology, running her hands through her abundant dark hair as if to smooth it into place. It was an artful move, one she'd practiced and perfected, designed to lift her bosom to impressive heights and draw an admirer's eyes slowly up to her equally remarkable face.

"And what can I get *you*, my lord?" she said meaningfully.

The nobleman took note of her performance, but did not seem inclined to applaud. "Killed, most likely," he said mildly. "Or severely wounded at the very least."

Her puzzled look earned her nothing but a smile and a request for expensive wine. A cold fish, this one! Sophie took off in a huff with his coin purse tucked into her pocket. When Bentley sent her back a few moments later to peace-bind the nobleman, she tied the thong more tightly than necessity demanded.

The night wore on without further incident. Sophie collected coins, bangles, even a few travel cups and personal table knives. The cups and knives would be easily returned to their owners when the night's sport was through, explained as a wench's error in clearing the tables. The other things would be more difficult, but only slightly so. Sophie was as adept at returning the stolen items as she was in acquiring them. And return them she would. So far, she had collected nothing worth keeping. According to Bentley, never had she done so.

It was beginning to dawn on Sophie that, as far as Bentley Mirrorshade was concerned, she would never find a treasure whose value outweighed the risk. They were playing a game that only one could win, and the winner was the gnome who made the rules. If she desired to be completely honest, Sophie would have to admit that she'd realized the truth of Bentley's ploy long ago. She had pretended otherwise, for the game amused her and gave her an opportunity to hone her skills. More importantly, it allowed her to hope that someday she could win free of this place.

A false hope, of course—one of Bentley's small illusions, no more convincing than the little farce of peace-binding.

Her disgruntlement grew as the night wore on. Other than the coin purse she'd lifted from the young nobleman, most of her "treasure" was of little worth. Most of the knives were lead or bone, the bracers and bangles either brass or copper and devoid of either valuable carving or precious stone. But this caravan was from Waterdeep! Where were the gems, the gold and silver?

A glint of lamplight on silver—at last!—drew her eye to the door. There stood a tall, slender moon elf, frowning slightly as he unburdened himself of weapons. Surely this was the elf of whom Bentley had spoken. A small, delighted smile curved Sophie's lips as her appraising eyes settled upon the elf's belt. Though he had given up a half dozen weapons, he was permitted carry such tools as were used at table, as well as small items deemed too valuable to entrust to another. The elf retained several such items, including a dagger fashioned of silvery metal the same hue as the elf's hair—a color so pale it was nearly white. That marked it as elven steel, priceless even without the elaborate carving and lavish jewels that graced the hilt.

Revelation jolted through Sophie. This was it! This had to be the treasure whose worth out-measured the risk of stealing it! The elf carried so many fine things that he would not miss that single small knife. Surely Bentley would acknowledge this, and concede that the game they played had at last been won! She could buy free of this place tonight!

Exultation swept through her, quickly chased by a sense of betrayal and then cold, furious rage. Bentley *knew* this elf carried treasures. Of course he did, and that was why he warned her clear of him.

Bentley Mirrorshade, whatever his other faults might be, was a gnome of his word. Once the priceless dagger was hers, the gnome would have no choice but to honor the bargain they'd made years ago, and that would mean the loss of his most popular tavern wench.

Sophie tamped down her wrath and forced an inviting smile onto her face. She elbowed one of her fellow wenches aside and undulated over to the silver-haired elf.

"And what can I get *you*, my lord?" she purred as her fingers reached toward freedom.

❖ ❖ ❖ ❖ ❖

Bentley Mirrorshade stared with horror at the glittering hoard laid out before him. Several long moments passed before he lifted his eyes to Sophie's face. The depth of emotion in them set her back on her heels, for she could not begin to fathom the mingled sorrow and fear in the gnome's small blue eyes. She had expected either the anger or the resignation of a gambler who knew himself beaten.

"What have you done, girl?" he said in a faint voice.

Sophie tossed her dark head. "I've bought my way free, that's what I've done! You can't claim that dagger isn't worth the risk of taking it."

A strange, ironic little smile twisted the gnome's lips. "Depends upon how much value you give your life. That dagger belongs to Elaith Craulnober. He's a rogue elf, and not a forgiving sort. They say not a man or woman crosses him and lives."

"So? 'They' say many things, few of them true."

Bentley gave her a long, somber look. "Do you remember Hannilee Whistlewren?"

It took Sophie a moment to attach the name to the remembered image of a small, rosily smiling face. "The halfling wench. She worked as a laundress for a moon or two, then left with the caravan bound for Lurien."

"That's the tale we put about. Maybe you also remember the fouled well."

That she recalled instantly. For months she and the other girls had had to carry heavy buckets from the spring just outside the fortress walls. Suddenly the gnome's meaning grew clear. "The halfling was killed and tossed into the well?"

"Pieces of her came up in the bucket," Bentley agreed grimly. "Small pieces."

Some of the gnome's fear began to edge into Sophie's heart. "Elaith Craulnober?"

"That'd be my guess. Last thing Hannilee did, far as we could figure, was bring fresh linens to the elf's room. Maybe her fingers were a mite sticky. Never could find cause to accuse him, but the tale sings in tune with many another I've heard."

Sophie's bright hopes faded. "I'll return the dagger at once. He'll never know."

"No." Bentley spoke quietly, but emphatically. "I'll deal with this. It could mean your life if you were caught with the dagger—"

He broke off abruptly, as if considering some new and promising thought. "Your life," he mused, "or *mine*."

It did not take Sophie long to weigh these options. "Have it your way." She began to gather up the other treasures. It would take her most of the evening to return them to their unwitting owners.

But by the time she'd tied the third coin bag back in place, Sophie began to reconsider the gnome's offer. It was not like Bentley to be so solemn; usually the gnome was all grit and bluster. Perhaps her first instinct had hit the mark after all—perhaps she had finally found the item valuable enough to offset the risk involved.

There was one sure way to find out, and it wasn't from the

treacherous, slave-driving gnome. Not directly, at least.

Sophie deftly lifted the keys from Bentley's pocket and slipped away from the tavern to the low-ceiling chamber that served as his workroom. The lying little troll was as adept at creating magical illusions as he was at shaping the truth into whatever form suited his purposes. Somewhere among the jumble of pots and vials and powers would be something useful.

A few moments later, Sophie strode awkwardly toward the stables, trying to school the swish from her hips and add length to her stride. Thanks to a bottle of vile-tasting potion, she wore the form of a burly, bearded mercenary who served as Elaith Craulnober's second in command. In such guise, it would not do to be seen mincing about like a Calisham harem boy.

She found a tall, thin lad in the first stall, busily grooming a dappled mare. "May the gods save me from tripping over these gnomes, because they're too stupid to get out of the way," she said, wincing at the bluff, deep sound that emerged from her throat.

The boy's only response was an indifferent shrug, but Sophie pressed on. "One of them tried to buy Craulnober's dagger for five hundred gold. The elf turned him down, of course. What's the thing worth, do you think?"

The gloved hand stilled, and the lad lifted his gaze to Sophie's face. "Lord Craulnober's business is his own. Not mine, and I daresay not yours."

The voice was low, the face deeply shadowed by the hood of the rough cape, but Sophie saw what was there to see. This was no lad. A female, and judging from the size and tilt and color of those eyes—blue as sapphires, and flecked with gold—she was probably not entirely human. A prickle of mingled fear and distaste shimmered through her. She quickly covered her reaction with a boisterous laugh and a comrade's slap on the shoulder.

"Well said, lad! You passed the test, and I'll be telling

the elf so later this eve. He's got his eye on you for better things, you know."

"Cap'n?"

A whip-thin man with a scarred cheek had edged closer during this exchange. The tentative, inquiring note in his voice suggested that Sophie had blundered. She'd gambled that this elfwoman's true identity was secret from the rest of the caravan. Apparently she'd lost that wager. She gave the newcomer a sheepish grin and a shrug.

"It took three tankards to wash the taste of road dust from my mouth." She raised one hand to her temples. "Scarce can remember my own name, much less hers. The elf wench isn't much for gossip, is she?"

"No cap'n," the man agreed.

"And here I could use some company. Let me buy you a meal and drink, and you can remind me why we're here."

The man's eyes widened and then shone with pleasure at what was apparently an unaccustomed honor.

It took Sophie the better part of an hour and several of the coins she'd taken from the fair-haired nobleman, but finally the scrawny mercenary was getting around to the part of the story worth hearing. Worth the risk of stealing a shapeshifting potion, worth the risk of wearing a borrowed form, worth risking the possibility that her friend Belle might not keep the *real* captain busy until Sophie's task was done.

Worth *any* risk.

Sophie gestured for another round and edged the full tankard closer to her informer. The thin man was weaving now, wearing the beatific smile of one who totters on the brink between sentience and sleep.

"This wench we're looking for," she prompted. "How are we to know her?"

The mercenary turned a stare of bleary-eyed puzzlement upon her, but he obediently repeated what he thought his "captain" should know. "Got a mark on her thigh." He dipped an unsteady finger into the trencher and used a bit of gravy to draw three lines on the table. "We're to work our way through the wenches, careful like, until we find her."

Sophie stared at the familiar mark. "A birthmark."

He snorted. "Something like. The mother cut that onto her baby's thigh so she'd know the brat if ever she had cause to look for her. A piece of work, that woman."

That woman. *Her mother.* For a moment, Sophie conjured a wistful image of a pleasant home, the comfort of being the pampered daughter of a human household, not the servant of a gnome clan. The mark cut into her flesh was nothing—a bit of unremembered pain. It was the potential that interested Sophie.

"What cause does she have to be looking for the wench now?'

"Cause enough! Things down Tethyr way got turned boots over britches. Time was, everyone with a drop of royal blood was butchered like a hog."

Royal blood! Hers?

The man started to tilt slowly to one side. Sophie grabbed a handful of hair and hauled him upright. "And now?" she prompted.

"Some folks still see things thataway. Some don't." He paused for an enormous yawn. "Craulnober took bids from both sides. We get the wench and sell her to whoever comes up with the best price."

Sophie had heard enough. She released her informer and fled the great hall. Behind her the thin man snored contentedly, his scarred cheek pillowed on a half loaf of bread. She hurried behind the tavern. Once alone, she took a second vial from her sleeve and drained it, then leaned both hands on the wall for support as the waves of magic swept through her, reversing the illusion and returning her to herself.

No, not herself. At least, not Sophie the tavern wench. Not that, never again. If the mercenary's tale was true,

Sophie no longer existed—had *never* existed! And if this was the secret Bentley Mirrorshade hoarded, his theft was far greater than anything she had managed in her years of honing her thieving skills. He had stolen her heritage from her, her birthright, her dreams!

She found the gnome in the kitchen, standing over a vast kettle and tasting soup from a large wooden spoon. "Is it true?" she demanded.

Bentley held her gaze for a moment. He put down the spoon and turned toward the back door, gesturing for her to follow. He did not ask her what she meant. To Sophie, that was as good as an admission. With difficulty she held her tongue until they reached the back alley.

"How could you do this?" she said in a low furious voice. "You stole my freedom, my future. My *name!*"

The gnome heaved a sigh. "Sophie—"

"Not Sophie! Never that again!" She threw back her shoulders. "I am the daughter of Lucia Thione, a noblewoman of Tethyr with ties to the exiled royal family. Did my mother give me a name?"

"Isabeau," the gnome said faintly. "It's a lovely name she gave you. More than that, she gave you life, not once, but twice. She left you here in safe fosterage in a time when such bloodlines meant death. In some circles, it still does. The high bidder gets you, and your fate is not something the elf bothers himself over."

This agreed with the tale Sophie—no, Isabeau, she reminded herself—had already heard. Fury and terror battled for supremacy in her heart.

"You planned to collect that high bid yourself, I suppose. No wonder you warned me away from the elf!"

"Mind your tongue, wench! I made an oath to keep you safe, and that I've done for twenty years. I'd-a done it another twenty if you weren't too mule-headed to listen." Bentley's ire passed quickly, and he sighed again. "There are maybe three or four treasures worth keeping and never mind the risk. A baby's life is one. But there's no safety for you here. You'll have to leave."

All her life she had waited for this moment. Why did it seem less a triumph than a banishment? "You'd send me away, just like that?"

He sent her a reproachful look. "What do you take me for? I'm not turning you out to fend for yourself. You're to leave the fortress and hide at my fishing camp. When it's safe, I'll send for you and get you set up in a new place, with a new name."

"But not *my* name," she said bitterly. "I just learned it, and I have to give it up?"

The gnome folded his arms. "You'll be keeping your skin. Don't look upon that lightly. There's too many in Tethyr that would be happy to nail it to the wall. If you listen to me, maybe Elaith Craulnober won't have a chance to peel it off you with that there dagger."

A shiver passed through her. "Tell me what I have to do."

☙ ☙ ☙ ☙ ☙

The rest of the night passed swiftly. Excitement and fear carried Sophie along, quickening her steps as she hurried along the faint path that cut through the forest. Never had she been this far from the fortress, and the sheer novelty of it thrilled her. By the time the sun rose, however, the thrill was long gone. Dew moistened the ferns and brush, dampening her skirts until they clung to her legs and left her shaking with chill. By the time she reached the tiny cabin, she was ready to do precisely what the gnome had told her to do: rest and wait until he could send for her.

That docile mood lasted for perhaps an hour, while she built a fire from the pile of wood outside the hut and boiled water for tea. Her anger grew as warmth and strength returned to her limbs.

How dare Bentley Mirrorshade use her as a servant! All those years of waiting tables, enduring the limp jests and questing hands of the tavern's patrons. She was a lady, not a common wench! The men she admitted to her bed should have been lords, not the motley assortment of lovers she had taken over the years. None of them had been worth her time. None! Well, perhaps the minstrel who had lingered at the Friendly Arms through the waning and waxing of two moons, sharing her bed and tutoring her in the finer arts of thievery. He was worthwhile—not just for the training, but also for the collection of picks and knives she had stolen from him on the day of his departure.

The thought of this coup still brought a smile to her lips. But her smile quickly faded as she considered her loss. Her hidden heritage was the most egregious of thefts! Her dreams of wealth, position, society—all stolen by a parcel of gnomes.

Not once, but twice stolen. Bentley had sent her away to save her life. But the risk of being Isabeau Thione was nothing compared to the gain. Sophie gathered up her travel pack and stormed out of the cabin. She slammed the door shut, and kicked it for good measure.

"I will find a way to reclaim my heritage," she vowed. "And my first act as Lady Thione will be to avenge my stolen dreams! Bentley Mirrorshade will pay for what he has done to me. I'll kill the little wretch!"

"Too late," said a low, musical voice behind her.

Sophie whirled, her eyes wide and one hand clutching at her throat. A tall, thin figure slipped into the small clearing. It was the elfwoman from the stables, and she moved toward Sophie with the unmistakable grace of a warrior.

The woman took an involuntary step back, and bumped into the cabin. Her gaze darted about the clearing for escape, and saw none. The only possible weapon was the pile of deadfall wood piled up for kindling. But Sophie would fight with tooth and nail, if it came to that, to keep her day-old freedom.

She threw back her head and glared a challenge at her visitor. "You're working for that elf. He sent you after me. Well, I'm not coming with you."

"Wrong, and wrong twice again." The elfwoman lowered her hood, revealing a tumble of black curls and a delicate face dominated by large, gold-flecked blue eyes. "My name is Arilyn Moonblade. I work for the Harpers, who have an interest in Tethyr's future and, therefore, in yours."

Sophie's eyes narrowed. "I don't believe you. You elves always stand together."

"I am half-elven," Arilyn said evenly, "and at the moment, Elaith Craulnober is in no position to offer any threat to you."

"Lies!" Sophie dived to one side and came up with a stout limb in her hands. Lofting it like a club, she ran at the half-elf.

Annoyance flickered over her opponent's face. The half-elf dropped one hand to the hilt of her sword, but otherwise stood her ground.

More fool she. Sophie brought her club down with skull-splitting force and deadly intent.

The stick thudded dully into the packed earth of the clearing floor. Sophie found herself off balance and bent low by the force of her blow. Before she could regain her balance, the half-elf kicked her in the rump.

Sophie hit the ground facedown and hard, but she didn't lose her grip on her club. Agile as a cat, she rolled onto her back and surged to her feet, swinging as she went.

Arilyn sidestepped another blow and caught Sophie's flailing wrist. The woman struggled and cursed and slapped wildly with her free hand until the half-elf captured that one, as well. Nearly frantic now, Sophie kicked the half-elf in the shin, hard, and aimed another kick at her knee.

The Best of the Realms • 225

But again the warrior was too quick for her. Arilyn accepted the first blow and saw the second, disabling one coming. A quick twist of her body took her beyond reach of Sophie's vicious kick. She kept turning, holding Sophie's wrists and forcing her to turn as well. When they were back to back, Arilyn bent over suddenly.

The world spun as Sophie flipped over. She hit the ground, stumbled, and dropped to her knees. Overmatched she surely was, but she refused to concede. Dark, furious resolve filled her and she rose unsteadily to her feet. With one hand she hiked up her skirt, and with the other she snatched the knife she kept sheathed to her thigh. Holding it high and shrieking like a fiend, she rushed at the half-elf.

Lighting flashed, or so it seemed. The half-elf drew her sword, so fast that the hiss of drawn steel blended with the clash of weapons. Sophie jolted to a stop, stunned by the impact of the blow. The two females stood nearly toe to toe, and Sophie saw her own resolve mirrored in those elven eyes.

"What do you want?" she panted out.

"I told you. I'm supposed to take you to safety."

Sophie wretched her knife free and danced back. "Not this time. I've tried to leave the fortress before, and I've been delivered back to the gnomes by people who need the Friendly Arms and Bentley Mirrorshade's sufferance. Never again."

As she spoke, she hooked her toe under her fallen club. With a quick kick she tossed it into the air. To her enormous surprise, she caught it. Clutching it in a two-handed grasp, she began to circle her opponent.

The half-elf turned with her, sword held in guard position. But there was exasperation on her face—the expression of a tutor enduring a student's tantrum.

Something snapped in Sophie's heart. She threw herself at the half-elf, shrieking and kicking and flailing. She was beyond reason, beyond anything but a fury fueled by years of frustration and the desperation to regain her stolen dreams.

Her frenzy ended quickly, suddenly, in an explosion of pain that filled her mind with sizzles of crimson fire and then blinding white light. When the light receded and vision returned, Sophie realized that she was sitting on the ground. Her jaw ached and throbbed. She raised one hand and wiggled it experimentally, then she cast a baleful look up at her tormenter.

The half-elf glared at her. "Don't move. It would have been a lot easier to kill you than to keep you alive. You're not worth that much trouble twice."

Sophie acknowledged that this was simple statement of fact. She was alive at the half-elf's sufferance, of that she had little doubt.

But for what purpose? The gnome's warning came back to Sophie: many were the factions in her native Tethyr who sought out those with even a drop of royal blood. Few of them wished her well.

"Who are you working for, if not the elf?" she ventured.

"I told you. The Harpers want you alive. Elaith Craulnober is in no position to take action against you. At the moment he's in the dungeons under the Friendly Arms, being held for the murder of Bentley Mirrorshade."

"I don't believe it!"

The half-elf folded her arms and gave Sophie a long, speculative look. "I saw the body."

So Bentley had been right about the dagger; the risk of keeping it had been too great. But that realization brought no remorse to Sophie's heart, and no gratitude. The gnome had stolen her life and had forfeited with his own. There was a certain justice in his fate, and Sophie celebrated it with a short, bitter laugh.

This seemed to anger the half-elf. "The gnome was your guardian. You owe him your life many times over. This is the regard you show him?"

The woman shrugged. "Have you never heard of the Mirrorshade Cipher?"

"You can tell me about it on the way." The half-elf took a step toward her.

Sophie shrunk back. "I'm not returning to the Friendly Arms. I won't!"

"You don't have to. I'm supposed to see you safely to Waterdeep."

She considered the gnome's warnings, and the words of the scarred mercenary. There was danger in Tethyr. Waterdeep would be safer, certainly, but would it be much of an improvement?

"And what awaits me there?" she said bitterly. "Another tavern, more years of working off my debt to you and your Harpers?"

Arilyn hissed out an impatient sigh. "You will be introduced into society as the daughter of Lady Lucia Thione. You will have possession of your mother's estate and fortune. And as long as you stay out of trouble, you need have nothing more to do with the Harpers. It's the best offer you're likely to get. I advise you to take it without further argument. There are limits to my patience."

Sophie stared up at the half-elf for a long moment, searching for any sign of deception. Arilyn's face spoke of distaste for the task, but determination to see her duty through. A smile began to dawn on Sophie's face. No. *Isabeau's* face.

She held out her hand and lifted her chin to an imperious angle. "Help me rise," she said haughtily.

This seemed to amuse the half-elf. She nodded approvingly. "Good idea. It'll take a lot of practice to make a noblewoman out of you. Might as well start now."

Isabeau rose to her feet unaided and brushed off her skirts with as much dignity as she could muster. "Let's be off," she ordered.

The half-elf shrugged and led the way into the trees,

where a pair of horses waited. They rode in silence until the sun was high. Isabeau passed the time counting her new fortune, picturing herself living in splendor, thinking about the noblemen she would dazzle with her charm and beauty. She would start with the man who had ignored her the night before. He had scorned the offer of a tavern wench, but surely he would not resist Lady Isabeau Thione! Already her life at the Friendly Arms seemed a distant thing, a rapidly fading dream.

"Well, what is it?'

The words popped Isabeau's glittering fancy and jerked her rudely into the present moment. She focused with difficulty on the half-elf's face.

"The Mirrorshade Cipher," Arilyn prompted.

"The treasure worth keeping, the risk worth taking. Bentley Mirrorshade said those words often enough. He lived by them, and it's only fitting that he died of them."

"I'm not following," Arilyn said, in a tone that indicated she didn't expect to like the explanation.

"It's simple enough, wench." Ah, but it felt good to say such words, rather than to hear them! "I am Lady Isabeau Thione. I have title, wealth, a house of my own. A position in Waterdeep society. This is the treasure that Bentley kept from me. So great a treasure entails great risk. He took that risk, and the loss is his. It is right and fitting."

The half-elf studied her for a moment, then she shook her head. "You should do well in Waterdeep," she said coldly.

"I intend to," Isabeau said with a smile. "I intend to do very well indeed."

Originally published in Realms of the Deep
Edited by Philip Athans, March 2000

FIRE IS FIRE

This is another tale that explores new territory, in that it was the first time I ever wrote a first-person story. Actually, this one is told in dueling first-person viewpoints: a young wizard and a sahuagin invader whose paths converge during the siege of Waterdeep. It's one of the darker stories, and probably my favorite in this collection.

FIRE IS FIRE

30 Ches, the Year of the Gauntlet (1369 DR)

What did you do when the Sea Devils attacked, Grandsire?

Oh, how I savored that question! I could hear it in my mind even as I ran toward the battle. The words were as real to me as the stench of smoke that writhed in the sky above the West Gate, and they rang as loudly in my mind's ear as the boom and crash of wooden beams giving way under wizard fire. No matter that the question would be many, many years in coming. A wizard's apprentice learns that all things must first be conjured in the mind.

As I ran, I conjured apace. Wouldn't the little lad's face be expectant, his eyes bright with the pride that comes of a hero's bloodline? Wouldn't the bards leave off their strumming and gather near, eager to hear once again the tale of the great wizard—that would be me—who'd fought at Khelben Arunsun's side?

That's what it would come down to, of course. That would be the first question to come to everyone's lips: What did Khelben Arunsun do during the battle? How many monsters fell to the Blackstaff's might? What spells were employed?

I must admit, I myself was most anxious to know the end of this tale.

"Above you, Sydon!"

Panic infused my companion's voice, lifting it into the range normally reserved for frightened maidens and small, yapping dogs. Without breaking pace, I followed the line indicated by Hughmont's pointing finger.

The threat was naught but a goodwife at the upper window of the building ahead. She was about to empty a basin of night water out into the back street—a minor hazard of city life that did not abate even during times of conflict. Hughmont was at best a nervous sort. Clearly, he was not at his best, but he was my training partner nonetheless, so I snagged his arm and spun him out of the way. He tripped over a pile of wooden crates and sprawled, but if his landing was hard at least it brought him beyond reach of the fetid splash.

A word from me sent the tumbled crates jostling into line like soldiers who'd overslept reveille. They hustled into formation, then leaped and stacked until a four-step staircase was born. I whispered the trigger word of a cantrip as I raced up the stairs, then I leaped into the air, flinging out my arms as I floated free. My exuberant laughter rang through the clamor of the city's rising panic, and why should it not? What a day this was, and what a tale it would make!

Hughmont hauled himself upright and trotted doggedly westward, coming abreast of me just as my boots touched cobblestone. The look he sent me was sour enough to curdle new cream.

"You'd best not waste spells on fripperies and foolishness. You'll be needing all you've got, and more."

"Spoken like the archmage himself!" I scoffed lightly. "That bit of excitement is more danger than you'll face at the West Gate, I'll warrant."

Hugh's only response was to cast another worried glance toward the harbor. Smoke rose into the sky over southern Waterdeep, visible even in the darkness, and it carried with it the unsavory scent of charred meat and burning sailcloth. "How many ships fuel that blaze?" he wondered aloud. "The harbor itself must be aboil!"

"A dismal caldron to be sure, but no doubt many sahuagin flavored the chowder," I retorted.

Not even Hughmont could dispute this excellent logic, and we hurried along in mutual silence—his no doubt filled with dire contemplation, but mine as joyfully expectant as a child on midwinterfest morn.

I will confess that I am vastly fond of magic. My lord father paid good coin to secure me a position at Blackstaff Tower, and I have learned much under the tutelage of the archmage and his lady consort, the wondrous Laeral Silverhand. But not until this night did I fully understand how impatient I'd become with Lord Arunsun's cautions and lectures and endless small diplomacies. By all reports, the archmage hoarded enough power in his staff alone to drop the entire city of Luskan into the sea, yet I knew few men who could bear witness to any significant casting. The spells Khelben Arunsun used in the daily course of things were nothing more than any competent but uninspired mage might command. Mystra forgive me, I was beginning to view the archmage's famed power in the same light as I might a courtesan of reputed beauty and unassailable virtue: of what practical use was either one?

Then we rounded the last corner before West Wall

Street, and the sight before me swept away any disgruntled thoughts. The Walking Statue was at long last making good on its name!

Each footfall shook the ground as the behemoth strode down the northernmost slope of Mount Waterdeep. My spirits soared. No one but Khelben could create a stone golem ninety feet tall, fashioned of solid granite with an expression as stolidly impassive as that of the archmage himself.

But the statue faltered at Jultoon Street, stopping in the back courtyard of a low-lying carriage house as if made uncertain by the swirling chaos of the panicked crowd. After a moment the great statue crouched, arms flung back and knees bent for the spring. People fled shrieking as the golem launched itself into the air. It cleared house and street and landed with a thunderous crack on the far side of Jultoon. Shattered cobblestone flew like grapeshot, and more than a few people fell to the ground, bloody and screaming, or worse, silent.

A flash of blue light darted from the gate tower, and the Walking Statue jolted to a stop. The golem glanced up at the tower and shuffled its massive feet like an enormous, chastened urchin. In apparent response to an order only it could perceive, the statue turned toward the sea. Its stone eyes gazed fixedly upon the cliffs below.

"I wonder what it sees," murmured Hughmont.

I had no such thoughts, nor eyes for anything but the source of that arcane lighting. It came from the West Gate, a massive wooden barricade that soared fully three stories high, surrounded on three sides by a stone lintel fancifully carved into the face of an enormous, snarling stone dragon. Atop this gate was a walkway with crenellations and towers contrived to look like a crown upon the dragon king's head. Wizards lined the walkway, flaming like torches with magical fire. Brightest of all burned my master, the great archmage.

I broke into a run, no longer caring whether Hughmont kept pace or not. My only thought was to take my place with the other battle wizards, and in the tales that would be written of this night.

☙ ☙ ☙ ☙ ☙

These shores stank of magic. I could smell it even before I broke clear of the water. The scent of it was bitter, and the taste so metallic and harsh that my tongue clove to the roof of my mouth. I did not remark on this to any of my sahuagin brothers. Though I called the source of my discomfort "magic," they might name my response by another, even more despised word: *fear*. To me, the two were one.

I broke the surface. My inner eyelids slid closed, but not before a bright light burst against the endless dome of sky. Half blinded, I waded toward the shore.

Hundreds of sahuagin were on the sand, and scores of them already lay in smoking piles. We expected this. We had trained for it. Ignore the dead, storm the gate, breach the walls.

Good words, bravely spoken. They had sounded plausible when spoken under the waves, but what was not easier underwater? I felt heavy on land, dangerously slow and awkward. Even as the thought formed, my foot claws caught on a fallen sahuagin's harness and I tripped and fell to my knees.

It was a most fortunate error, for just then a bolt of magic fire sizzled over my head and seared along my back fin. I threw back my head and shrieked in agony, and none of my dying brothers seemed to think the less of me. Perhaps no one noticed. In the thin air sound lingered close and then dissipated into silence. How, then, could there be so much noise? If a hundred sharks and twice a hundred sahuagin entered blood frenzy amidst a pod of shrieking whales, the clamor might rival the din of this battle.

The Best of the Realms • 237

It took all the strength in my four arms to push myself to my feet. I stumbled toward the place where the baron, our warleader, stood tall with his trident defiantly planted as if to lay claim to this shore. Two paces more, and I saw the truth of the matter. A large, smoking hole had opened and emptied the baron's chest, and through this window I could see the writhing bodies of three more of my dying clan. One of them clutched at my leg as I passed. His mouth moved, and the sound that came forth was thin and weak without water to carry it.

"Meat is meat," he pleaded, obviously fearing that his body would be left unused on this shore, his spirit trapped in his uneaten body.

I was hungry after the relentless journey to this city—desperately so—but the stench of burning flesh stole any thought of feeding. Meat is meat, but even good sahuagin flesh is rendered inedible by the touch of fire.

I kicked aside his clinging hand and looked around for my patrol. None had survived. All around me lay carrion that had been sahuagin. Their once proud fins were tattered and their beautiful scales were already turning dull and soft. Meat is meat, but there were not enough sahuagin in the north seas to eat this feast. Our leaders had promised a great conquest, but there was nothing to be gained from this, not even the strength to be had from the bodies of our fallen kin.

Anger rose in me like a dark tide. Orders were orders, but instinct prompted me to turn back to the sea, to flee to the relative safety of the waves. As my eyes focused upon the black waters, what I saw drew another shriek from me. This time, the sound was triumphant.

The pounding waves stopped short of the sand, piling upon each other and building up into a massive creature born of the cold sea and magic new to Sekolah's priestesses. A water elemental, they called it. Like a great watery sahuagin it rose, and as it waded to shore each pace of its legs sent waves surging onto the black and crimson sand.

The sahuagin yet in the water took heart from this. Some of them rode the waves to shore and hit the sand running. They, too, died in fire and smoke.

The water elemental came steadily on. Blue light—endless, punishing, hellish light—poured from the flaming wizards. A searing hiss filled the air as the elemental began to melt into steam. The magic that bound it faltered, and the watery body fell apart with a great splash. It sank back into the waves, and where it had stood the waters churned with heat.

For a moment I was again tempted by retreat, but there was no safety in the sea, not when steam rose from it. So I lifted one of my hands to shield my eyes from the blinding light, and I studied the gate tower.

There were many, many wizards—far more than our barons had led us to expect. In the very center stood a dark-bearded human, tall by the measure of humankind and strongly built even to my eyes. If he were a sahuagin, he would be a leader, and so he seemed to be among the humans. All the wizards threw fire, and the dark circles on the smoking sand were all about the same size—ten feet or so, the length of a sahuagin prince from head fin to tail tip. All fire killed, but the fire thrown by the tall wizard turned sahuagin into fetid steam, and melted the sand beneath them into oil-slicked glass.

I turned tail and padded northward toward those wizards who merely killed. Great piles of stinking, smoking corpses were beginning to rise. Soon they would reach the top of the wall, and those who survived would swarm over the pile and into the city beyond. That part of the plan, at least, was going as expected.

As planned, no sahuagin approached the great gate. No corpses added their weight to the wall of wood. As I began to climb the mountain of carrion, I prayed to almighty Sekolah that none of the humans would fathom the reason for this.

Just then a new wizard took his place along the wall and hurried northward toward the spot I planned to breach. Judging from his size he was young. He was as small and thin as a hatchling and lacked hair that so disfigured the other humans. I was close enough now to see his face, his eyes. Despite the strangeness of his appearance, his eagerness was apparent to me. This one regarded battle with the joy of a hungry shark. A worthy foe, if any human could be so named.

Ignoring the searing pain of my burned fins, I readied myself for battle.

※ ※ ※ ※ ※

I raced up the winding stairs and onto the ramparts, smoothing my hand over my head to tame the curly red locks before I remembered that my head was newly shaved—I had grown tired of the taunts that had dogged me since childhood. A bald pate, which I contemplated decorating with tattoos as did the infamous Red Wizards, was more befitting a man of magic.

But the sight before me drove such trivial thoughts from my mind, freezing me in place as surely and as suddenly as an ice dragon's breath.

The sea roiled, the sand steamed, and enormous green-scaled creatures advanced relentlessly through a scene of incredible horror.

"Sydon, to me!"

Khelben Arunsun's terse command snapped my attention back to the task at hand. I edged along behind the spell-casting wizards to the archmage's side.

Before he could speak, the largest elemental I have ever seen burst from the waves like a breaching whale. Up, up it rose, until it was taller by half than even the great Walking Statue. Its shape was vaguely human in such matters as the number and placement of limbs, but never have I seen so terrifying a creature. Its wide, shark-toothed mouth was big enough to swallow a frigate. Translucent, watery fins unfurled along its arms, back, and head like great sails.

"Sweet Mystra," I breathed in awe. "Wondrous mystery, that mortals can wield such power!"

"Save it for your journal," Khelben snapped. "Hugh, mind the gate."

Hughmont hurried to the center of the dragon head rampart. He was not an accomplished mage, and his fire spells were as limited as festival fireworks—all flash and sparkle, but little substance. Even so, I had to admit that the effects he achieved were quite good. His first spell burst in the sky with rose-colored light—a titanic meadow flower budding, blooming, and casting off sparkling seed, all in the blink of an eye. It was most impressive. A few of the sea devils hesitated, and I took the opportunity to pick several of them off with small fireballs.

A spear hissed through the air. Instinctively I ducked, though it would not have hit me regardless, nor the man next to me. The man next to *him* was less fortunate. He jolted as the spear took him through the chest. The blow spun him around, and he lost his footing and toppled over the guard wall. He was falling still when the sea devils began tearing at him with ravenous hands.

Khelben pointed his staff at the grim tableau and shouted a phrase I'd never heard used in any magical context—though it was no doubt often heard during tavern brawls. Before I recovered from this surprise, a second, greater wonder rocked me back on my heels. The dead man's wizardly robes turned crimson—no longer were they spun of silk, but fire. The flames did not seem to touch the fallen wizard, but they seared the creatures that dared lay hand on him. The sea devils blackened and almost melted, like hideous candles tossed into a smithy's forge.

The archmage seized my arm and pointed to the

burning robe. "Cast *fire arrows* on that," he commanded, then he turned his attention to the next attack.

This was my moment, my spell—a new spell I had painstakingly committed to memory but had never had occasion to cast. I dipped into my spell bag for a handful of sand and flint pebbles, spat into it, and blew the mixture toward the sea. Excitement raced through my veins and mingled with the gathering magic—so potent a brew!—as I rushed through the chant and gestures.

The fire that enrobed the unfortunate mage exploded into a myriad of gleaming arrows, each as orange as an autumn moon and many times as bright. These flaming darts streaked out it all directions. Sea devils shrieked and writhed and died. It was quite wonderful to behold. This, then, was how my grandson's tale would start, with a partnership between the great archmage and me, a devastating double attack.

Before I could fully celebrate this victory, an enormous tentacle rose from the waves and slapped down on the beach. My eyes widened as my disbelieving mind tried to guess the measure of the creature heralded by that writhing limb.

Such mental feats were not required of me. Before I could expel the air gathered by my gasp of astonishment, another tentacle followed, then a third and a fourth. With heart-numbing speed the entire creature worked its way from the water. I had never seen such a thing, but I knew what it must be: a kraken, a titanic, squid-like creature reputed to possess more cunning than a gem merchant and thrice the intelligence.

The creature humped and slithered its way toward the gate. Khelben thrust his staff into my hands and began a series of rapid, fluid gestures I did not recognize and could not begin to duplicate. Silver motes sparkled in the air before us, then shot out in either direction and formed into a long, slim, solid column.

I could not keep the grin from my face. This was the Silver Lance—one of Lady Laeral's fanciful spells.

Khelben reached out and closed his fist on empty air. He drew back his hand and pantomimed a toss. The enormous weapon followed each movement, as if it were in fact grasped by the great wizard's hand. He proved to be a credible marksman, for the lance hurtled forward with great force and all but disappeared into one of the kraken's bulbous eyes.

The creature let out a silent scream that tore through my mind in a white-hot swath of pain. Dimly I heard the shrieks of my fellow wizards, saw them fall to their knees with their hands clasped to their ears. Dimly I realized that I, too, had fallen.

Not so the archmage. Khelben snatched the Blackstaff from my slack hand and whistled it through the air as if writing runes. I could see the pattern twice—once, as my eyes perceived it, then again in the cool dark easing of the pain that gripped my mind.

The silent scream stopped, and the pain was gone. *Where* it had gone was apparent. The kraken thrashed wildly in an agony I understood all too well. Somehow Khelben had gathered the force of that foul mind spell and turned it back upon the creature.

The kraken seemed confused by its great pain. It began to drag itself along the sand in a hasty retreat to the sea, yet one of its flailing tentacles probed about as if seeking something important. The tentacle suddenly reared up high, then slammed straight toward the gate. I caught a glimpse of thousands of suction cups, most at least the size of a dinner plate and some larger than a northman's battle targe, and then a great length of that sinuous limb slammed against the wooden door and held firm. The kraken did not seem to notice this impediment to its own escape. It sank into the sea, still holding its grip on the door. Wood shrieked as the gate bulged outward.

I took this as happenstance, but my master was more versed in the ways of battle. His brow knit in consternation as he divined the invaders' strategy.

"Brilliant," muttered Lord Arunsun. "The gate is thick and well barred—no ram or fuselage could shatter it. But perhaps it can be pulled outward."

He gestured toward the Walking Statue. The golem vaulted over the city wall, and its feet sank deep into a pile of sea devil corpses. Lady Mystra grant that someday the sound of that landing will fade from my ears!

With a noise distressingly like a thousand boots pulling free of mud, the golem extricated itself and strode to the shore. Huge stone fingers dug into the kraken's stretched and straining tentacle. The golem set its feet wide and began to pull, trying to rip the tentacle free of the gate, or, perhaps, free of the kraken. Terrible popping sounds filled the air as one by one the suction cups tore free of the wooden door. Then the flesh of the tentacle itself began to tear, and enormous bubbles churned the water in explosive bursts as the submerged and possibly dying kraken struggled to complete its task. The gate bulged and pulsed in time with the creature's frantic efforts. I did not know which would yield first: the gate or the kraken.

A splintering crash thrummed out, blanketing the sounds of battle much as a dragon's roar might diminish birdsong. Great, jagged fissures snaked up the massive wooden planks of the gate. The statue redoubled its efforts. Stone arms corded as the golem strove to either break the creature's hold or rend it in twain.

Finally the kraken could bear no more. The tentacle came loose suddenly, abandoning the gate to wrap snakelike around the golem's stone face. The Walking Statue struggled mightily and dug in its heels, but it was slowly dragged into the water, leaving deep furrows behind in the sand. The water roiled and heaved as their battle raged. Great stone arms tangled with thrashing kraken limbs for many long moments before both sank beneath the silent waves.

Lord Arunsun did not look pleased by this victory. "We are winning," I ventured.

"When there is so much death no one wins," he muttered. "Too much corruption in the harbor. This sort of victory could destroy the city."

A terrible scream sliced through the air. Somehow I knew the voice, though I had never heard it raised in such fear and pain. I spun toward the sound. Finella Chandler, a lovely wench who was nearly my equal in the art of creating fire, had apparently grown too tired to control her own magic. A fireball had exploded in her hand, and she flamed like a candle. She rolled wildly down the slope of the inner wall and ran shrieking through the streets, too maddened by pain to realize that her best hope was among her fellow wizards.

A second shriek, equally impassioned, rang out from a young fellow I knew only as Tomas. He was a shy lad, and I had not known that he loved Finella. There was no doubting it now. The youth spent his magic hurling quenching spells after his dying love, but her frantic haste and his made a poor match. I shuddered as I watched Finella's last light fade from sight.

Khelben gave me an ungentle push. "To the north! The sahuagin have nearly broken through."

For a moment I stood amazed. This possibility had not once occurred to me. I had no idea how I would fight sea devils in the streets of Waterdeep. The gods had gifted me with a nimble mind and a talent for the Art, but I was not a large man and I was unskilled in weapons. My fire spells would not serve in the city. Old timbers and thatched roofs blazed like seasoned kindling, and as Finella had learned to her sorrow, fires were far easier to start than to quench.

New urgency quickened my steps, and with new seriousness I reviewed the spells remaining to me. I prayed they would suffice. The sea devils had to be stopped now, here.

I ran past Hughmont and seized his arm. "Come with me," I said. "Frighten them with your sparkles and purchase me time."

He came along, but his hand went to his sword belt rather than his spell bag. I was alone in the possession of magic, and I spent my spells freely as we pushed northward. I tried not to contemplate what I might do when my magical store was emptied.

When we reached my assigned post two dire things occurred in one breath. Just as exhaustion dwindled my last fireball into harmless smoke, two enormous, webbed, green-black hands slapped onto the rim of the guard wall directly before me.

Six fingers, I thought numbly. The sea devils have six fingers. The malformed hands flexed, and the creature hoisted itself up to eye level.

I forgot everything else as I stared into the blackness of those hideous eyes. They were empty, merciless, and darker than a moonless night.

So this is what death looks like, I mused, then all thought melted as mindless screams tore from my throat.

◈ ◈ ◈ ◈ ◈

The hairless wizard began the ululating chant of a spell. It was a fearsome noise—more ringingly powerful than I would have thought possible without water to carry it. For a moment fear froze me.

A moment of weakness, no more, but the wizards were quick to exploit it. A second wizard, this one pale as a fish's underbelly, ran forward with upraised sword. This was a battle I could understand.

My first impulse was to spring onto the parapet, but I remembered that none of the humans seemed to carry my particular mutation. They all had but a single pair of arms. I held my place until the fighting wizard was almost upon me, but with my unseen hands I reached for two small weapons hooked to my harness.

He came in hard, confident. I lifted a knife to catch his descending blade. The appearance of a third arm startled him and stole some of the force from his attack. It was an easy thing to throw his sword arm high, so simple to slash in with a small, curved sickle and open his belly.

The sweet, heavy, enticing scent of blood washed over me in waves. I heaved myself up and lunged for the proffered meal. Strictly speaking, this was still an enemy and not food, but that was easily resolved. I thrust one hand deep into the human's body and tore loose a handful of entrails. Life left him instantly, and I tossed the food into my mouth.

"Meat is meat," I grunted between gulps. Wizard or seal pup, in the end all flesh was food.

Blessed silence fell as the hairless wizard ceased his keening chant. He began to back slowly away. His eyes bulged and ripples undulated through his chest and throat. A moment passed before I recognized this strange spellcasting for what it was: sickness, horror, *fear*. In that moment, my personal battle was as good as won.

Nor was I alone. Other sahuagin had breached the walls and were fighting hand-to-hand with the humans on the wall. Some wizards still hurled weapons of magic and flame, but most of them seemed to have emptied their quivers.

Triumph turned my fear into a shameful memory. I gulped air and forced it into my air bladder to fuel speech. "Where is your magic fire, little wizard? It is gone, and soon you will be meat."

The wizard—now nothing but a human—turned and fled like a startled minnow. For a moment I hesitated, frozen with surprise that any warrior would turn tail in so craven a fashion. This was what their magic-wielders came down to in the end. They were as weak and as soft as any other human. This pathetic coward was the monster I had feared?

The irony of it bubbled up into laughter. Great, gulping, hissing laughter rolled up across my belly in waves and shook my shoulders. I chuckled still as I followed the cowardly not-wizard as he half ran, half fell down a winding flight of stairs.

Despite my mirth, my purpose was set. I would eat that which I had feared, and thus regain my honor.

☉ ☉ ☉ ☉ ☉

Sweet Mystra, what a sound! Next to that hideous laughter, everything else about the battle cacophony was as sweet music. I ran from that sound, ran from the death in the sea devil's soulless black eyes, and from the memory of brave Hughmont's heart impaled upon a sea devil's fangs.

In the end, all who fought and fell at West Gate would find the same end, the same grim and lowly fate. Be he shopkeeper or nobleman wizard, human or sahuagin, in the end there was little difference.

Behind me the sounds of booming thunder rolled across the sands. I sensed the flash of arcane lighting, the distinctive shriek of a fire elemental, but I no longer cared what magical wonders Khelben Arunsun might conjure. I no longer *thought*. I was animal, meat still living, and I was following animal instinct and running from death.

Death followed me through the city, running as swiftly as the sea devil behind me. The cataclysm of defensive spells had sparked more than one blaze. To my right a corduroy street caught fire, and flames licked swiftly down the row of tightly-packed logs. On the other side of the street a mansion blazed. There would be nothing of it come morning but a blackened shell, and the charred bones of the aged noblewoman who leaned out of the upper floor window, her face frantic and her hands stretched out imploringly. These things I saw, and more—more horrors than I could fit into a hundred grim tales. I noted them with the sort of wordless, mindless awareness that a rabbit might use to guide its path through a thicket as it flees the fox. Screams filled the city streets, and the scent of death, and the crackle of fire.

Fire.

For some reason, a measure of reason returned to me as my benumbed mind took note of the rising flames. I remembered all I knew of sea devils, and how it was said that they feared fire and magic above all things. That was why I had been chosen for the West Gate, why I had been summoned to the walls to fight beside the archmage. I possessed a number of fire spells. There was still one remaining to me, encased in a magic ring I always wore but had in my fear forgotten.

The building beside me already blazed—I could not harm it more. I tore up a set of stairs that led to a roof garden, and I could feel the heat through my boots as I ran. The sea devil followed me, its breath coming in labored, panting little hisses.

When I reached the roof I whirled to face the sahuagin. It came at me, mindlessly kicking aside blackened stone pots draped with heat-withered flowers. All four of its massive green hands curved into grasping claws. Its jaws were parted, and blood-tinged drool dripped from its expectant fangs.

I would not run. Hughmont—the man whom I had regarded so smugly and falsely—had stood and fought when he had no magic at all remaining. I tore the small ring from my finger and hurled it at the sea devil.

A circle of green fire burst from the ring, surrounding the creature and casting a hellish sheen over its scales. From now until the day I die, I will always picture the creatures of the Abyss bathed in verdant light. The sea devil let out a fearful, sibilant cry and dropped, rolling frantically in an attempt to put out the arcane flames.

I looked about for a weapon to finish the task. There was a fire pit on the roof, and beside it several long iron skewers for roasting gobbets of meat.

Never had I attacked a living creature with weapons of steel or iron. That is another tale that will remain untold, but by the third skewer the task seemed easier. With the fourth I was nearly frantic in my haste to kill. The sahuagin still lived, but the green fire encasing it was dying.

Suddenly I was aware of a rumbling beneath my feet, of a dull roar growing louder. The roof began to sink and I instinctively leaped away—

Right into the sahuagin's waiting arms.

The sea devil rolled again, first tumbling me over it and then crushing me beneath it as it went, but never letting go. Frantic as the sahuagin was to escape the fire, it clearly intended that I should end my days as Hughmont had.

Though the creature was quick, the crumbling building outpaced its escape. The roof gave way and fell with an enormous crash to the floor far below. I felt the sudden blaze of heat, the sickening fall . . . and the painful jerk as we came to a stop.

Two of the sea devil's hands clasped me tightly, but the other two clung to the edge of the gaping hole. The creature's vast muscles flexed—in a moment it would haul us both away from the blaze.

It was over. No magic remained to me. I was no longer a wizard—I was meat.

My hands fell in limp surrender to my sides, and one of them brushed hard metal. It was the sickle blade that had torn Hughmont.

I grasped it, and it did not feel as strange in my hands as I'd expected. The sahuagin saw the blade too late. I thought I saw a flicker of something like respect in its black eyes as I twisted in its grasp and slashed with all my strength at the hands that grasped the ledge. I had no more fire spells, but it mattered not.

"Fire is fire," I screamed as we plunged together into the waiting flames.

Somehow, I survived that fall, those flames. The terrible pain of the days and months that followed is also something that will never be told to my admiring descendents. The man Sydon survived, but the great wizard I meant to be died in that fire. Even my passion for magic is gone.

No, that is not strictly true. Not gone, but tempered. A healing potion fanned the tiny spark of life in me, and gave a measure of movement back to my charred hands. Khelben Arunsun visited me often in my convalescence, and I learned more of the truth behind the great archmage in those quiet talks than I witnessed upon the flaming ramparts of the West Gate. With his encouragement, now I work at the making of potions and simples—magic meant to undo the ravages of magic. While there are wizards, where there is war, there will always be need for such men as I. Fire is fire, and it burns all that it touches.

Grandsire, please—what did you do when the sea devils attacked?

Someday I might have sons, and their sons will ask me for the story. Their eyes will be bright with expectation of heroic deeds and wondrous feats of magic. They will be children of this land, born of blood and magic, and such tales are their birthright.

But Lady Mystra, I know not what I should tell them.

Originally published in Dragon #282, April 2002
Edited by Dave Gross

POSSESSIONS

This is the first and, as yet, the only ghost story I've written. It tells a little about the background of Farah Noor, a minor character in the Counselors & Kings trilogy. Again, this tale offers a familiar scene through another pair of eyes, as Noor witnesses events related in the novel The Floodgate—*events that led to Kiva's madness and her hatred of Halruaa's wizards.*

It is such a dark tale that some people have had difficulty equating it with the mild-mannered soccer mom I appear to be. When Dave Gross, the editor of Dragon at the time, asked for a tidbit of personal information to include in a two-sentence author bio, I mentioning that I'd just been asked to fill in for the PTA president of the local elementary school. While this factoid was true enough, the suggestion was entirely tongue-in-cheek. But Dave gleefully seized this notion, and it took some persuading to convince him to let it go. Apparently I'm not the only one who's really fond of irony.

POSSESSIONS

Noor could hear someone chanting. The sound was distant, dreamlike, as if filtered through deep mist. Yet the power in the chant was undeniable; each word pushed at the darkness that had inexplicably engulfed her.

She struggled toward awareness, like a dreamer who knows herself a player in some unpleasant drama of her own making. Finally she shook off slumber, only to find herself floating over a slender, raven-haired girl who lay, face down and arms outstretched, before a shining alter.

A sharp stab of fear sent Noor reeling back, flailing at the empty air and kicking wildly in a vain attempt to gain a footing. She hit the wall behind her, hard enough to bounce away. None of this shattered the oddly lingering dream. Disoriented and deeply puzzled, Noor gazed about in search of clues to her present state.

The girl on the floor was young and willowy, with hair the glorious shining ebony common to Ghalagar nobles. She was clad in scarlet and black—a necromancer's colors, colors Noor had recently taken to wearing despite her father's objections. So this girl, this supplicant, must be her. Noor accepted that. But why was she floating here, looking down at her own body?

Her gaze swept the room. The walls and alcoves and altar were fashioned of a rare blue-veined marble that resembled fine opals. Silver chalices stood on marble pedestals, and an elusive hint of incense filled the room like moonlight. A tall priest stood over Noor's body, chanting as he waved a wand that leaked shining blue smoke. He was robed in white vestments, and the silver circlet on his brow marked him as a high priest. Noor expected no less, for this was the chapel on her family's ancestral lands.

Understanding came to her in a sudden, bright flood. The chanting was a prayer, requesting a vision from Mystra, Lady of Magic. Family custom demanded a mystic journey, a threshold that must be passed before a wizardly apprenticeship. This detachment from herself, this strange, floating experience, must be part of her vision.

It was odd, though, that she remembered so little of what had come before. Odd, too, that she and the priest were alone. The Ghalagar clan always gathered to see fledgling wizards on their way.

Noor studied her prostrate form. She was dressed for rough roads, and her feet were shod with boots rather than her customary jeweled slippers. Most of the rings on her outstretched hands looked unfamiliar to her, but that was not so surprising. Gifts from her indulgent father and numerous suitors were so plentiful that she had chests full of jewels never yet worn. She did, however, recognize the large black and red circlet on her left thumb. Carved from obsidian and set with a giant ruby, it was a deathwizard ring.

So *that* was why her father had not come!

Anger, black and bitter, welled up in Noor's heart. She embraced it, for it was less painful than the sting of rejection. Granted, necromancy was the least regarded of Halruaa's nine Arts, but she could not understand her father's aversion to her chosen path. Wealth, lineage, and beauty were already hers: Noor aspired to power. Toying with the hearts and pride and honor of her suitors was a fine diversion, but as a necromancer, she could possess their very souls, and hold life and death in her jeweled hands!

The chanting grew louder as it gathered magic from the Weave that sustained and connected all. Noor's heart pounded in cadence with the quickening power. She threw back her head and laughed with anticipation, not caring that her astral form made no sound.

She could not have been heard, regardless. The priest's chant had risen in power until it engulfed the room, until it became too large for a human voice to contain. The chant tore free of the priest and bore down on her like a hundred thundering hooves.

The magical onslaught swept her away. For a moment Noor was a leaf in a monsoon gale—utterly, terrifyingly adrift. Then unseen hands caught her, and pulled her with a single wrenching tug back into her prostrate body.

Noor came to with a gasp. She pushed herself up onto her hands and knees, feeling dizzy and unaccountably heavy.

The priest knelt before her. Gentle fingers cupped her chin and raised her face to his. "Lady Noor?" he inquired.

Dark eyes, kind and concerned, searched her face. The priest used her given name, and his touch held the familiarity of long acquaintance, but his face was that of a stranger.

Panic fluttered through Noor, filling her belly like the baiting wings of caged birds. She turned her head sharply aside to remove her chin from the priest's grasp and rose unsteadily to her feet.

"Lady Ghalagar," she corrected in cold, regal tones—a voice that one of her suitors had likened to an ice sculpture honed by generations of wealth and privilege. "I am ready for my journey."

A small, sad smile ghosted across the priest's face. "Yes, I can see that you are. Welcome back. Your boat has been prepared and provisioned."

She darted a quizzical look at him. "Boat?"

"Your journey will take you to the Confluence," he explained. "It is a place of great power, where the warp and weft of Mystra's Weave—"

Noor cut him off with a single imperious gesture. "Who are you, to instruct me on my family's history? I know my destination, priest. I also know that the paths to the Confluence have been dry throughout my lifetime and yours."

He averted his eyes. "The River Ghalagar overflowed its banks."

This news set her back on her heels. The river that rioted down from the Lhairghal peaks was a slow and sedate thing by the time it reached her family estates. It brooded its way through ancient woodlands and emerald-green horse pastures with an air of middle-aged resignation, finally to disappear into the Swamp of Ghalagar. Never in her life had the river overflowed! How could such a thing happen, and she not remember?

Noor quickly moved past the shock of this revelation to consider the implications. If she needed a boat to reach the Confluence, it was entirely possible that swamp creatures had made their way through the floodwaters to that magical place.

Her lips curved in a feline smile. The swamp was a

cauldron into which life disappeared, and simmered, and rose again in unexpected ways. Few travelers were equal to the swamp. Noor could think of no better place to test her fledgling powers.

Suddenly the priest's concern took on new meaning. Noor's chin went up, and her cheeks burned with insulted pride. "You think I will fail," she stated coldly. "You consider the challenges ahead beyond my skills and courage."

She thrust out her hand so that the ruby in the Deathwizard ring caught the torchlight and glowed like a malevolent eye. "I earned the right to wear this ring, and to wield the powers it holds!"

Noor glared at him, silently daring him to curse her, as her father had done. Deathwizard rings were rare and precious. The price was always high, always paid in blood. This ring had cost Noor her virtue, her father's favor, and the lives of three good men. Even so, she counted it a bargain.

The priest's gaze faltered before her furious challenge, and he bowed his head. "This is your threshold, Lady Noor. The decision to pass through or turn aside belongs to you, and no other."

She gave a curt nod and strode purposefully from the chapel. The door swung open as she approached, creaking, as she had never remembered it doing, as if its magic were somehow tainted by the priest's reluctance. Then Noor's gaze fell on the garden, and all other thoughts fled. She stopped so abruptly that she had to seize the doorframe for support.

The chapel garden had been all but swallowed by the floods. Trees that had provided fruit and shade were hunched over like broken old men, and the courtyard's bright mosaic paving had been reduced to an indecipherable jumble of cracked and faded tiles. Once a broad sweep of marble stairs had led to sunken gardens that were the pride of her family and the envy of their neighbors. Now, the steps disappeared into murky water, and their marble was cracked and begrimed with green scum. A servant stood in knee deep water, holding the rope that secured a low, shallow skiff.

Noor's gaze slid over the small craft. The prow rose in a graceful curve, but the boat itself was broad and low-sided and nearly as flat as a barge. It skimmed like a water bug, barely dimpling the surface. She let out a small sigh of relief. At least one thing was as it should be! Such boats were commonly used during monsoon season to travel through swamplands and flooded fields, moved by spells so simple that nearly any Halruaan child could cast them.

She allowed the servant to hand her into the boat. After settling down, she fixed in mind her desired destination and began the easy, singsong chant of the spell. The boat glided steadily toward the Confluence. Noor held her head high, determined to ignore the blighted landscape and focus on the task ahead.

Her resolve soon faltered. She turned this way and that, gazing in open horror at the changes wrought by storms she could not remember. Ancient, barren trees loomed overhead, moss draping the skeletal branches like a moldy shroud. The air became heavier, fetid. Large bubbles simmered free of the murky water, and the deep, grumbling calls of swamp creatures came from all around her.

A giant dragonfly darted past, so close that wings of rainbow gossamer brushed Noor's face. She shied violently away, shoving her fist into her mouth to muffle her startled scream. Showing fear could be deadly, for the dragonfly's touch was far from accidental. The creatures fed upon carrion and soon-to-be carrion. It had "tasted" her, and decided that she was not yet near enough to death to be of interest. Or perhaps it had recently feasted on the storm-provided bounty.

Noor closed her eyes, trying not to imagine the bloated

bodies of drowned horses. Her father's breeding farms lay near the chapel. She did not wish to see what had become of those sleek, fleet animals, or watch the dragonflies gather in feeding frenzy. She had seen such a thing once. They had gathered as thick as flies, their brilliant colors shimmering like obscene flowers in a breeze as they reduced a rothé cow to bone.

A frustrated sigh escaped her. The monsoons that fueled such flooding must have been fierce, yet she could remember nothing. No doubt the ritual left her confused. Her memory would surely return once the threshold journey was complete. If it did not, she would have that wretched priest flayed alive, and his hide tanned for boot leather!

Suddenly the boat lurched to the port side. Noor slapped her hands against the low sides to keep from tumbling off her seat. But the boat continued to tip, the starboard side moving slowly, heavily up. Noor threw herself onto the boat's floor and braced her feet against the port wall. The boat rose until it stood upright on its side, then continued its path until it leaned ominously over the dark, hungry water. Finally the boat stopped, quivering like two strong wrestlers locked in combat, too evenly matched to prevail and too stubborn to cede victory.

Noor clung desperately to the seat to keep from falling. "You'll never capsize me!" she shrieked at her unseen foe. "My father's magic protects the boat!"

"And you, as well?" inquired a dry, mocking voice. "I don't think so, little deathwizard."

Shock numbed her, silenced her. Noor had spoken out of fear and bravado, never expecting a response!

"Speak up, girl! A well-bred lady does not stand about gaping like a carp."

A second wave of dread shivered through Noor. She had heard these words before, many times, scolding and prodding her throughout her childhood and toward "proper behavior." The voice had been leeched of tone or pitch, but there was no mistaking the crisp, exaggerated precision of the words. Well-bred ladies were, above all, *articulate*.

"Grandmother?" she whispered.

"Give me the ring, little deathwizard, and go home."

"No!" The word tore from Noor in a rising scream, fueled by terror and fury and denial.

The boat slammed back down. Fetid water splashed over Noor, and the jarring impact sang down her spine like a banshee's wail. She gritted her teeth against the pain and rolled aside.

Just in time. A skeletal hand lurched over the side and drove down hard. Bony fingers screeched against wood as the hand groped about for its prey.

Noor scuttled back, crab-walking away from her attacker. But oddly enough, curiosity outweighed fear. If this undead thing had indeed been her grandmother, why could it speak? Her grandmother had been an imposing matriarch, but not much of a wizard. The spells that transformed a dying wizard into an undead lich were far, far beyond the woman's meager skills.

"Who gave you this power?" Noor demanded.

A second hand grasped the edge of the boat. Bony fingers flexed, and then a skull rose above the side of the boat. The famous Ghalagar hair was gone, replaced by lank strands of seaweed. Empty eyes regarded Noor above sharp, aristocratic bones.

"Deathwizard," the skeletal moaned. There was an eternity of sorrow in that word, yet the jawbones still moved in a manner than ensured ladylike annunciation. And then, they shattered into a thousand pieces as crimson lightning flashed from the ring on Noor's hand.

Noor stared at the wisp of fetid smoke, all that remained of the skeletal wizard. She glanced down at her left hand. Still clenched in a fist, it was thrust out, twisted so her thumb pointed toward the attacker. Crimson fire still smoldered in the deathwizard ring.

"Worth the price," she whispered, adding the destruction of her undead ancestor to the cost of the ring. She took a long, steadying breath, and then renewed the spells that sent the boat gliding over the dark water.

The mist steadily deepened as Noor neared the Confluence, closing around her until she could not see past the prow. She was therefore startled when her boat grated against stone and ground to a halt.

At that moment a strangely cold wind blew though the swamp. The mist parted to reveal a tall black tower, a wizard's tower, built upon the very point of the Confluence.

After a moment of stunned silence, Noor rose to her feet, shaking with wrath. This was her land, her inheritance! She climbed out of the boat, too angry to puzzle over the fact that she stepped out onto dry land.

A pair of fierce gargoyles guarded the door, gray stone demons with elven ears and heads crowned with writhing snakes. Unimpressed, Noor looped the mooring rope around a menacing stone hand. Balling her fist, she pounded on the tower door.

It swung open immediately to reveal a comely young man clad in the crimson robes of a necromancer's apprentice. A practical color, by Noor's estimation, for only a few damp spots and a faint coppery smell betrayed the blood that stained his garments. The lad gave her a friendly, open smile and a courteous greeting, and offered to take her to the master. Disarmed and curious, Noor followed him.

The room through which they passed was round and vast—much larger than the exterior of the tower had suggested possible—and it bustled with activity. A dozen red-robed apprentices hurried about, carrying sharp implements or shallow bowls brimful of blood. Cages stood about in no apparent order, filled with strange creatures unlike any Noor had ever seen.

That *no one* had seen before, she realized. She looked about with real interest as she followed her escort through the teeming chaos. Along one wall was tethered a line of centaur-like creatures, human torsos rising from the bodies of strange and mighty beasts. A small wind buffeted her as they passed a young griffin that bated its wings tentatively, its eagle-like beak moving as it muttered to itself in a plaintive, very human voice.

An excited smile burst over Noor's face. She had heard of such things—combining forms, transferring the life force of one creature into another body. This was necromancy at its most exciting!

"What is he doing?" Noor asked, nodding toward another crimson-clad youth. The young man stood on a stool, using a long wooden paddle to stir the contents of an enormous cauldron. Apprentices came and went, pouring thick red sludge into the pot.

"Cats," the apprentice said cheerfully, pointing to the sludge. "The jungles are teeming with them. We're rebuilding a man with a cat's muscles. Measure for measure, cats are ten times as strong as men, and far more quick and agile."

As Noor watched, a human skeleton rose from the thick and fetid soup. Chains linked its wrists to handles on either side of the cauldron. The skeleton fought against its bonds, writhing and struggling as if to shed the alien flesh that slowly gathered upon its bones.

"Reverse decomposition," Noor said slowly. She had heard of such a spell. It was exceedingly difficult, and obviously painful. But when the process was complete, what a servant the necromancer would possess!

She considered her grandmother's final word in this new light. Perhaps that final, whispered "deathwizard" was not a taunt, but an answer to Noor's question. Most likely her grandmother's remains possessed speech and memory not because of any magic the woman had once claimed, but through the power of the wizard who had raised her!

The apprentice gestured to a tall, black-robed man who stood with his back toward them, reading from a massive book that floated before him. "The master," the lad said simply. He bowed to Noor and left her.

She took a deep breath, trying to reclaim some of her indignation. "Lord wizard," she called out as she stalked toward him.

He turned, and something in his gaze stopped Noor in mid stride. His was a striking face, graced with fine features and framed with an abundance of glossy black hair. He might have been handsome, but for black eyes as soulless as a shark's.

Nevertheless, Noor met his gaze. "You are trespassing upon Ghalagar lands, my family home. This tower was raised in defiance of our ancestral claims, and against Halruaan law. What have you to say to this?"

"I am Akhlaur," the wizard responded, as if that explained all.

As indeed it did.

Noor's heart thudded to a painful stop, then took off at a gallop like a bee-stung mare. The room tilted and spun wildly as she dropped to one knee before the greatest necromancer of their time.

"I am Noor, first daughter of Hanish Ghalagar. Your presence here lends my family grace, my lord, and I bid you welcome in my father's name."

A wicked glint sparkled through the wizard's eyes, proclaiming her words as the lie they truly were. Building a tower on another wizard's lands, especially in these dark and contentious times, was a challenge the Ghalagar family could not ignore. There was no way this could end but in war, and they both knew it.

Even as the thought formed, another path opened—one so bright and full of promise that Noor gasped with the wonder of it.

The Best of the Realms • 265

"My lord Akhlaur, it is my family's custom that every youth and maiden must pass a threshold. We journey to this place of power, seeking a vision from Mystra."

Akhlaur lips curved with dark amusement. "And I am the vision the Lady granted? Apparently she possesses a fine sense of irony!"

Noor rose to her feet quickly, before her courage failed. "We make this journey before taking vows of apprenticeship, to test our true path." She held up her hand, and showed him the deathwizard ring. "It is my desire to learn the necromancer's Art. I am the Ghalagar heiress. If you accept me as apprentice, none will challenge your right to this place."

"Do you think I need such an alliance?" Akhlaur asked, more in curiosity than anger.

She dipped into a hasty curtsy. "Of course not, my lord. The advantage would be entirely mine."

The necromancer glanced at her hand. "You have a deathwizard ring," he stated. Without hesitation Noor stripped it off and handed it to him.

Akhlaur turned the ring over, studying the workmanship. "A princely gift. What did you do to acquire this ring?"

Noor told him.

The wizard seemed neither shocked nor impressed by Noor's candid recitation. Indeed, he seemed waiting for something more. Noor gestured toward the bustling activity. "You accept many apprentices, Lord Akhlaur. Take me, and I swear I will serve you as well and faithfully as any other."

He studied her for a long time, measuring her with his unfathomable black eyes. "We will see."

Abruptly he turned and strode through the vast chamber. After a startled moment, Noor followed. They passed through a back door and walked between rows of long, low buildings that looked rather like her father's stables. The floodwaters had receded here, and the ground was dry and firm. Herbs scented the air, and flowers nodded in a gentle breeze. She knew some of them: purple monkshood, maidentowers in shades of rose and soft coral, and delicate blue and white skitterbreeze. Deadly poisons all, despite their beauty.

The wizard paused before a stone building. "This is where my elves live," he announced, "and this, also, is where most of them die. If you've a soft heart or a weak stomach, speak now. I've no patience for tears and tantrums."

Though the building had no windows, though the door was stout and solid oak, Noor could hear the terrible screams that echoed through the building. "I am ready," she said in a voice that, even to her own critical ears, sounded admirably cool.

They passed through a stout wooden door into the shallow of hell. Noor kept her eyes focused on the necromancer's back, ignoring as best she could the wretched cells that lined both sides of the long corridor.

Akhlaur led her to a small, stone cell, and to the source of the agonized cries. On a small cot lay a female wild elf, hardly more than a girl, pinioned by wrists and ankles with iron chains. She writhed in the most horrific travail Noor had ever witnessed. Her coppery skin was beaded with sweat, and her belly, not yet rounded with full term, churned and buckled as if something were trying to fight its way out through her skin.

"I have not yet succeeded in bringing one of these to term," Akhlaur observed. "The creature is stronger than its female host, but it is not yet ready to be born, and will die as soon as it breaks free."

Noor swallowed the bile that rose in her throat. "What creature, my lord?"

"You have heard of the laraken?"

She nodded. They were creatures of legend, voracious monsters that haunted swamps and fed upon magic carried by unwary travelers. They were said to resemble floating yellow globes framed by a pair of fleshy tentacles. No living man had actually encountered one and returned with a trophy, but stories of sightings were told in the taverns, and children frightened each other by whispering the bloody tales.

"I summoned the laraken, and used them as building blocks for a more interesting and powerful monster," Akhlaur said matter-of-factly. "And I believe I have found a way past this particular inconvenience." He illustrated this comment with a casual wave of one hand toward the dying elf woman.

Noor followed him down to the end of the corridor. In the last cell, an elf maid crouched in the corner, clad only in her own long, jade-green hair.

"Look at me, Kiva," the necromancer commanded, speaking in a tone other men might use to summon a hound.

Compelling magic thrummed through Akhlaur's voice. The elf's chin lifted, slowly and heavily, as if the force of her will was almost equal to the great necromancer's compulsion. The silent battle raged for several moments before its inevitable conclusion. The elf's head snapped back, and her gaze locked with Akhlaur's. Golden eyes burned in a small, angular face. The hatred in them was neither human nor sane.

The scalding heat of the elf's fury hit Noor like a physical blow. Instinctively she took a step back.

But Akhlaur's smile was almost proud. "This one has spirit! Even so, she would never survive the growth of the laraken spawn had I not forged a death-bond with her. I doubt there'll be much left of her after the laraken's birth, but while I live, she cannot truly die."

Noor let out a long, tremulous sigh. This was horrible, yet it was wonderful! This was precisely the sort of power she longed to possess!

"A death-bond," she repeated wistfully. "That spell is not known to me."

The necromancer's gaze shifted from the captive elf to the ambitious noblewoman. "It could be," he said softly.

Something in his tone froze Noor's blood and prompted the calm, reasoned voices inhabiting the back of her mind to scream out warnings. Yet when Akhlaur reached out to her, she placed her hand in his. Nor did she pull away when he plucked a small, curved knife from the empty air and lowered it purposefully to her palm. As he began to chant, Noor closed her eyes and thought about the power that would be hers.

☙ ☙ ☙ ☙ ☙

Twilight deepened the shadows of Noor's ancestral woodland as she followed on Akhlaur's heel, as she had done a hundred times. In her hands she carried an enormous crimson gem, shaped like a many-pointed star and glowing with life.

The forest was strangely silent, but for the furtive, shuffling sounds of the hunting laraken. The monster foraged ahead like a hound scenting a trail. And as Noor walked, the crimson gem grew brighter and brighter.

Noor steeled herself to confront the source of this gathering power. As she rounded the massive trunk of a bilboa tree, sunlight glinted off a perfect crystal form—an elf-shaped statue as transparent as water, and colder than death.

No matter how many times she witnessed this transformation—and she had seen it many times—it still chilled her that creatures could be snatched from life so quickly and completely that their absence left visible holes in the Weave. Yet she could not deny that this was precisely what Akhlaur had done. The laraken fed upon magic, draining it from every source it encountered, and passing this bounty along to its master. The life forces of countless elves had passed into the gem. Elsewhere in Halruaa, other dark servants and powerful artifacts added stolen magic to Akhlaur's storehouse of power. Soon, none would be able stand against him. The necromancer was on the verge of conquering all of Halruaa, and Noor's dream of power was coming near to fulfillment.

Even so, Noor was tempted to throw the glittering gem to the forest floor, just to see if it could break. And perhaps, to see if the souls imprisoned within could be freed by such a mundane act.

She quickly brushed aside the impulse. Wild thoughts occurred to her from time to time; even as a child riding with her father, she occasionally wondered what might occur if she urged her horse to leap over a ravine. All people had foolish, fleeting notions. Only madmen acted upon them.

"It is enough for today," Akhlaur announced, gazing with satisfaction upon the glowing gem. "We will return to the tower."

Noor glanced into the dusk-shadowed trees. "And the laraken?"

"Leave it," the necromancer said negligently. "Let it hunt and feed as it will."

"We are a good ways from the tower," she reminded him.

"What of it? If I require the laraken, you can summon it with a few words."

Noor nodded. The relationship between Akhlaur and the laraken was even more complex than the death bond that linked her to the necromancer. Magic flowed from the laraken to the wizard, but never once had she seen Akhlaur cast a spell upon the laraken. She suspected that he could not, though she had never once given in to the temptation to ask. Challenging Akhlaur was yet another example of the sort of impulse to which only madmen yielded.

She watched as her master deftly summoned a magic portal, a shimmering oval that caught the last long, golden rays of the sun. She took his hand when he offered it, and they stepped together over the bright threshold.

They emerged a few paces from the tower, to find the wizard's holdfast as silent as a crypt. Even the raucous birdsong from the surrounding forest was hushed.

Akhlaur's eyes darted to the crimson gem and narrowed with speculation. For a long moment he listened to voices that Noor could not hear.

"So he has found me at last," he murmured. Without explanation he strode into the tower.

Noor followed, and stopped dead on the threshold. By all appearances, a storm had swept through the tower. The floor was covered with a thick sheet of ice. Several of Akhlaur's apprentices lay dead in frost-shrouded mounds, others stood trapped in ankle-deep ice. Stone guardians lay in piles of rubble. Magical treasures strewed the floor in scattered, broken bits. At least a score of wizards waited in somber formation, wands held like ready swords or hands filled with bright globes that coursed with the snap and shudder of contained power. Noor's gaze slid over them, and then snapped back to a stooped, white-haired man. She moved closer, peering at the aged wizard.

"Father?" she murmurred, not quite believing her eyes. Less than three years had passed since she entered Akhlaur's service, and when she had left home, Hanish Ghalagar had been a man in his vigorous prime. Her father had often warned that powerful magic exacted a stern price, and the proof of this claim was etched into his own face.

"The change your see in me is but a small thing to that I perceive in you." Hanish did not speak aloud; subtle magic carried the words from his mind to his daughter's ears, but there was no missing the deep sorrow and regret they carried.

Even now, he was ashamed of her! Noor's chin lifted. "Why have you come, *Father?*" she said loudly, with a precise articulation that her grandmother might have envied. "To free me, or kill me?"

Her tone was flippant; her question was not. Hanish Ghalagar was a powerful wizard, as were the men and women with him. Yet her master took little note of the exchange between Ghalagar patriarch and his estranged daughter, and seemed not at all concerned by the strength and numbers of the invading party.

"Well met, Zalathorm," Akhlaur said with a hint of amusement.

One of the wizards broke from the group and strode forward. He was nearly a head shorter than Akhlaur. His hair and beard were a soft brown, a pallid color by Halruaan standards. There was nothing in his face or garb to suggest power, and his hands were empty of weapons or magic. But Noor knew the name—she had heard stories of the wizard who was slowly bringing peace and order out of the killing chaos Akhlaur had created in his rise to power.

"I wondered when you'd get around to visiting," Akhlaur went on. His gaze slid dismissively over the battle-ready wizards, lingering for a moment on Hanish Ghalagar. "*These* are the best allies you could muster? Let me transform them into mindless undead. It could only improve them."

Noor's eyes darted to her father. His face darkened with familiar temper, and he lifted his wand to avenge this insult. Before Noor could shout a warning—whether to her father or her master, she could not say—light burst from Hanish's wand.

It veered away from Akhlaur and streaked toward Noor like lightning to a lodestone, flowing into the crimson gem. Her black hair rose and writhed about her face as her father's magic coursed into the gem. Hamish's wand quickly spent itself, blackened, and withered to ash. Yet still the magic came, flowing until the hand holding the wand was little more than skin-wrapped bone. When at last the lightning ceased, a desiccated shell wrapped in the rich robes of Hanish Ghalagar fell lifeless to the floor.

Noor stared, too stunned to grieve, barely noticing that the crimson gem rise from her hands and float over to Zalathorm. The wizard deftly caught the artifact.

"You cannot harm me with that," Akhlaur said, still with a hint of amusement in his voice.

"Nor you me," Zalathorm returned grimly. "With this gem, we entrusted our lives to each other's keeping."

The necromancer lifted raven-wing brows in mock surprise. "Why, Zalathorm! Take care, or I shall suspect you of harboring doubts about our friendship!"

"Doubts? I don't know which is the greater perversion: the use you have made of this gem, or the monster you made of the man I once called friend."

Akhlaur glanced at his apprentice. There was nothing in his eyes that acknowledged Hanish Ghalagar's death, or noted the bitter tears streaking Noor's face. "Tiresome, isn't he?" he said with a sneer, tipping his head in Zalathorm's direction. "But what can one expect from someone whose family motto is 'Too stupid to die?'"

In response, Zalathorm lifted the gem with one hand and began to trace a spell with his free hand. Every wizard in the room mirrored his gestures.

Suddenly the tower disappeared in an explosion of white light and shrieking power. Noor's senses, keenly attuned to the Confluence, felt the rending tear as the tower was wrenched free of its moorings.

She fell to her knees, blinded by the sudden flash and shaken to the depths of her soul by the enormity of this casting. Powerful magic was common in Halruaa as rain in summer, but moving an entire tower, a wizard's tower— *Akhlaur's* tower!—was an astonishing feat!

But to what purpose?

The white light faded. Noor blinked away the sparks that danced and swam in her vision and struggled to focus upon her master. He crouched in guard position, like a master swordsman, his weapons a skull-headed scepter and an ebony wand. Noor knew the spells stored in these weapons, and understood that Akhlaur could hold off magical attacks for a very long time. Her gaze slid to the necromancer's face. A puzzled moment past before she understood his wild eyes, his twisted expression.

Akhlaur was afraid.

His darting gaze fell upon Noor's face. "The laraken!" he howled, brandishing his specter at the wizards who began to circle him like hunting wolves. "Summon the laraken!"

So that was why the wizards had moved the tower! Away from the laraken, they had hope of engaging the necromancer in spell battle without adding their magic to his! Indeed, they had somehow stripped the tower of its defensive magic. No spells poured from the powerful artifacts in Akhlaur's hands.

Noor's hands began to move in the gestures of summoning. But her eyes drifted to the withered shell that had been her father, and then to the gleaming gem that now held his magic.

And, perhaps, more than his magic. Akhlaur's elves had added their life force to the gem's power. Noor could not say with certainty what afterlife awaited a human wizard slain and swallowed by the necromancer's greed.

An image flooded her mind, a vivid memory of her father leaning low over the raven-black neck of his favorite horse, racing over the emerald fields and laughing with joy. He had taught her to ride before she could walk, to love the freedom of a wild gallop over the vast lands that were her birthright. For a necromancer's power, Noor had betrayed both her father and her heritage. Yet Hanish had sacrificed his magic and his life to wrest her from Akhlaur's hand. Perhaps he had only come to reclaim the family land. She would never know. She supposed it shouldn't matter—after all, she had made her decision, and he his.

Her hands faltered. The unfinished spell crackled through her fingers as her uncertain gaze swept the room. Several of the wizards had leveled their wands at her, ready to loose killing spells. But all of them looked to Zalathorm, who held up a restraining hand and studied Noor with eyes that were both sympathetic and measuring.

"Your father," he said softly, "was a hard man, but a good one. He believed that magic carries a stern price. He came here to pay his daughter's debts."

Noor's eyes darted to the glowing gem in Zalathorm's hands. For a moment she knew a terrible affinity to the trapped souls. Because of the death bond she shared with Akhlaur, she could never truly die, not while he lived.

"You will free them?" she asked in a ragged voice. He inclined his head in solemn agreement.

A ghost of a smile touched her lips. Noor began anew the gestures of the summoning spell, altering it slightly. She began to chant, intoning words of power she had learned at the necromancer's side.

The spell was an ancient casting, one that Akhlaur had employed in the creation of the laraken. Power crackled through the tower as the Weave shifted, opening a gate into another, very different place. A roar like that of an angry sea filled the air, and rising above it, a keening, vengeful shriek.

Magic exploded through the tower for a second time. The circle of wizards fell back, uttering cries of horror as they beheld the creature that appeared in their midst, stepping from a shimmering oval.

Noor held her ground. She had seen such creatures before, captured and tormented by the necromancer. This one had taken part of the laraken's creation, no more willingly and nearly as painfully as the elfwoman who had birthed the monster.

The creature was twice the height of a man and as heavily muscled as a dwarf, and its fearsome body was covered with green-black scales. Eels writhed around its head like the snakes of a medusa, framing a hideous, asymmetric face. The water demon—for such it was—shielded its glowing red eyes with taloned hands. Its gaze fell upon the necromancer. Hatred burned in its eyes like hellfire.

"Akhlaur," the demon said in a grating, watery voice, pronouncing the word like a foul curse. It sprung, massive hands curved into rending talons.

The necromancer dropped his useless weapons and seized the creature's wrists. With preternatural strength he grappled with the demon, chanting defensive spells. Magic crackled like black lightning around the struggling pair. The writhing eels on the demon's head shrieked and flailed about in agony as they burned and withered. One by one, they fell limp to creature's massive shoulders. Fetid steam rose from the demon's body, and green-black scales lifted from its flesh like worn shingles. Too furious to understand its own death, the water demon moved Akhlaur inexorably back toward the gate.

The necromancer's hate-filled eyes sought Noor's face. He captured her gaze and jerked the demon's hand, pantomiming a slashing motion.

Noor's head snapped back, and four burning lines opened her throat. She felt a terrible sundering, as if her spirit was being ripped from her flesh, and then she felt nothing at all.

The next thing Noor knew was a sense of darkness fading into thick gray mist. Even before her vision cleared, Noor knew that she was back at the Confluence—she could feel its power. Akhlaur's tower had also returned to its rightful spot, but it was ghostly, insubstantial. Through its misty form, Noor could see a mossy obelisk, nearly half submerged in swamp water.

Puzzled, she looked around. Water was everywhere, as it had been when she first arrived at the tower. Gone were the elves' prisons, the stables, the gardens full of flowering poisons.

Noor stood in the barge that had brought her here, and she was not alone. A young woman, garbed in red and black travel clothes and wearing a fortune in Ghalagar jewels, stood less than arm's length away, staring at her with horror-glazed eyes.

For a long moment Noor gazed at a face very like her own: delicate features, dark eyes enormous in a pretty face gone far too pale. Noor reached out to the girl, half expecting her to mirror the gesture. But the girl shrunk back, flinging out one hand as if to ward off a blow. She uttered a choked little cry as Noor's fingers grazed her small hand, and the deathwizard ring upon it.

Pain, unexpected and searing, flashed through Noor. She snatched her hand away. What matter of creature was this? Her flesh was hard as stone, and burning hot!

The fleeting contact seemed to have the opposite effect upon the girl. Her face, already pale, blanched a whiter shade. She tore the obsidian ring from her finger, revealing a livid blue band beneath—skin as dead and frozen as the feet of fools who got caught in storms on the Lhairghal peaks. The girl's terrified eyes darted to Noor, and then to ghostly tower, which was swiftly fading away.

"It was a dream," she said in a faint, choked voice. "None of it was real!"

"Of course it is," Noor responded tartly, out of patience with mystery in general and this shrinking wench in particular. "You would deny the most powerful necromancer of our time?"

"Our time?" The girl's laughter was brittle, with a hysterical edge. "Akhlaur is long dead!"

A faint, nameless apprehension stirred in Noor's heart. "That is impossible. I am bound to Lord Akhlaur by a death bond. His death will be mine, and while he lives, I cannot truly die."

For some reason this only seemed to deepen the girl's horror. Then something else dawned in her eyes. Noor would have called it pity, but that was not an emotion people dared turn in *her* direction!

The girl collected herself with visible effort and pointed to obelisk. "This monument was raised two hundred years ago, in memory of a dark time and heroic ancestors."

Noor bristled. "Whose ancestors? This is Ghalagar land!"

The girl was silent for a long moment. "The swamp waters are rising. Powerful magic, you see, carries a stern price."

"So I've heard tell," Noor said coldly.

"Family legend claims that when the obelisk is fully submerged, Halruaa will cease to be. Legend also claims that a spirit lingers here, weeping. Her tears, whether they be penitence or pique, mingle with the rising waters."

"What is that to me?" Noor said heatedly. "You speak of legends, and family, yet this had been Ghalagar land since the dawn of Halruaa!"

"It *was* Ghalagar land. The family name was changed, so that we would always remember the price of magic. I never understood why until now."

"Changed? To what?"

The girl took a deep breath and met Noor's eyes. "Noor."

For a long moment Noor stood speechless. She could make no sense of this odd pronouncement, or of much else that had happened since she stepped into this barge.

Then it occurred to her that she was not in the barge, but standing just above the surface of the water, just as she had floated above this girl at the onset of the ritual.

So that was it, then. The battle in Akhlaur's tower had jolted her from her body—which, inexplicably, was independent enough to resist the reunion. Fortunately, Noor had a necromancer's skill now, and a deathwizard ring. With such power in her possession, she would soon resolve the matter. She reached for the ring, but the girl shrunk away.

"You and I are one," Noor reminded her. She lunged forward, arms outstretched to embrace and engulf her material form. "We are both Noor."

The girl shrunk back, shaking her head in frantic denial. *"Farrah,"* she gasped out. "My name is *Farrah* Noor, and no magic is worth such a price!"

So saying, she hurled the deathwizard ring into the mist and dropped down to huddle into the prow of the boat. Her blue lips moved in silent chant as she sped through the words to the enchantment. The boat began to move away from the Confluence.

Noor watched the skiff float away, skimming over the waters and leaving no sign of its passing. She noticed, without thinking it particularly odd, that her own feet did not even dimple the waters upon which she stood.

The skiff disappeared into the mists. Noor tried to follow, but the water held her fast. She struggled like one in a nightmare, unable to move, unable to flee.

Time passed. Noor could not say how much, nor did it seem particularly important to know. Exhausted by her struggle, she sank down at the base of the obelisk. Beneath her the water felt as firm as a dark, murky mirror.

But not completely dark, she noted. There, far below, was the ruby gleam of the deathwizard ring, glowing as it had when she had used it to fend off the undead Ghalagar matriarch. Noor's spirits lifted at the thought of possessing this treasure. As she studied the water, it seemed to her that the ring took on a richer hue, and that the light grew and splintered off into glowing fragments. Her excitement grew as the shards of light deepened and focused, revealing not one ring, but several!

She let out a little crow of triumph. It was a rare necromancer who owned more than one such ring! They would be among her dearest possessions. They would bring her great power.

Noor reached for the rings, but the water would not part for her seeking hands. She tried again and again, but the surface of the water was an impenetrable as glass.

As Noor slumped, defeated, against the half-drowned obelisk, memory stirred. This was vaguely familiar. Young wizards had come before, and would again. After all, it was the family custom. And some of them would hurl their deathwizard dreams into the mist.

They would come again, but she so hated waiting! It was cold in the swamp, painfully cold. She huddled at the base of the obelisk, wrapped her arms tightly around her shivering form. Despairing tears slid down her transparent cheeks, mingling with the slowly rising waters.

*Originally published in Realms of Shadow
Edited by Philip Athans, April 2002*

A LITTLE KNOWLEDGE

The Counselors & Kings trilogy visits the land of Halruaa and introduces the jordaini, a class of magic-dead warrior scholars who serve as advisors to Halruaa's wizard lords. The jordaini are not only trained for this job, they're bred for it. And that, of course, is fraught with all the issues that arise when genetic engineering is discussed.

It took two hundred and thirty-seven tries to successfully clone a sheep. What on earth—or for that matter, what on Toril—should be done with the failed attempts at creating a particular kind of human?

This story deals with two deeply flawed humans; a "defective" jordaini who, by law, should have been destroyed at birth, and a sorcerer who is tormented by the ability to see all possible outcomes of any situation.

A LITTLE KNOWLEDGE

19 Marpenoth, the Year of Wild Magic (1372 DR)

Long rays of morning sun slanted through Halruaa's ancient trees, reaching out like tentative fingers to waken the rain-sodden village. But Ashtarahh was already long awake and bustling with activity.

The summer monsoon season was over. The village diviner decreed that yesterday's storm would be the last. Already the rice fields and brissberry bogs were alive with harvesters, moving barelegged through ankle deep water as they sped their task with morning-glad songs.

Mist clung to the fields and swirled around the small buildings, pinned between land and sky by the hot, dense air and the swiftly climbing sun. No one wondered how the moisture-laden skies could absorb yesterday's rains; the answer was in the lush Halruaan landscape, and in particular the tall, thin trees lining the forest's edge, swaying dreamily to music only they could hear.

The vangi trees came with the first rains, sprouting up overnight like verdant mushrooms. They grew with incredible speed—two or three handspans a day. By the end of the monsoons, they were ready for harvest. Several children, agile as monkeys, shimmied up the segmented trunks to pluck the fist-sized purple fruit at the top. These they tossed into the canvas sheet held taut and ready by the four glum-faced, land-bound boys who'd drawn short straws. Several young men stood ready with machetes. Once the fruit was taken, the trees would be cut, dressed into lengths, and dragged to the road. The village streets were cobbled and the forest roads deeply sheltered, but the path leading through the fields was slow to harden after the rains. Each year fresh rows of vangi trees were pressed into the muck, forming a bumpy but mostly dry path for market traffic.

This path ended between two shops: the blacksmith and the wheelwright. Smoke rose in billows from the forge, and two apprentices busily rolled new wheels into waiting racks. A trip down the vangi corduroy road was a bone-rattling gauntlet, and more than one of the expected market carts would not survive it unscathed. But visiting merchants and artisans shrugged off splintered wheels, unshod oxen, and broken axles as the cost of doing business in Ashtarahh.

The late summer market was especially busy. Market stalls and tents rapidly took shape under the hands of carpenters and minor wizards. The owners of more permanent shops folded back the protective canvases, wielded brooms, and set out their wares. The clack of looms and the tart aroma of ripe cheeses filled the air. Bright glass vials of brissberry cordial stood in lines, looking like enormous ruby necklaces. Lengths of fine white linen gleamed in the morning sun, and skeins of brightly dyed yarn hung in arched windows in deliberate imitation of rainbows. But the most famous of Ashtarahh's crafts were its cunningly woven tapestries. These hung at every third stall, transforming the market into a veritable gallery.

Villagers who were not otherwise engaged strolled along the cobbles, admiring the woven art. Most of the tapestries depicted scenes from Halruaan history and legend. Skyships were commonly depicted, as were the magical creatures common to Halruaa: the brilliantly colored, many-legged crocodilians known as behirs, the winged starsnakes, even the dreaded laraken. Some of the tapestries depicted famous and infamous wizards. Small magical effects enlivened some of these scenes, sending bursts of light arcing between spell-battling foes. A large weaving of a quite-literally blazing phoenix—the new standard of King Zalathorm—drew admiring attention. The biggest crowd, however, was the group stealthily converging upon the southwest corner of the square, where Ursault the All-Seeing sat with his crooked, cast-off loom.

Ursault was a thin, unassuming man of indeterminate age. His long, rather stringy locks had gone gray, and his face was unmemorable but for his pale eyes—a hazel more gray than green, an oddity in a land of dark-eyed, black-haired people. The title "All-Seeing" held gentle mockery, though it was rumored that it had once been spoken with respect. Once, it was said, Ursault had been a powerful diviner, one who saw many possible paths with equal clarity. But the vast and various potential of the future was a burden too large to carry, and Ursault had retreated to this sleepy village, content to weave his confused visions into tapestries no one wanted, and only he could understand.

A band of boys wove through the stalls as they crept toward the wizard, their grins wide and white in small dirty faces. Several of them scooped mud from between the cobbles and readied the first wave of attack.

The wizard looked up and smiled in gentle welcome. No knowledge of the coming mischief was written in his pale eyes, but a small, ominous gray cloud appeared directly over the head of the band's leader, a stocky little urchin who answered to Dammet.

The unwitting boy hauled back for the throw. Instantly the cloud exploded into a tiny, belated monsoon, drenching the boy and sending his comrades skittering away, hooting with delighted laughter. Liquid mud dribbled between Dammet's fingers as his weapon dissipated.

A second boy darted back and hurled his mud ball with a deft, side-armed toss. Ursault moved one hand in a vague little gesture and the mud changed in midair to a crystalline white. He caught the snowball and tossed it back to the urchin. The boy yelped with surprise and tossed the ball from hand to hand, marveling at the unfamiliar sting of cold.

"Taste it," Ursault suggested.

Uncertainty flooded the small face, but the mixture of encouragement and taunting from his friends decided the matter. He took a tentative lick, and his eyes rounded with delight.

"Mazganut cream," the boy announced grandly.

He dodged several grasping hands and darted off, his prize clutched possessively. Two of the boys started to give chase, but abandoned the notion after their first few steps. There was a bigger game to be played, and their faces were smug with anticipation.

Dammet pushed a smaller boy forward—an ungainly lad with an intense but unfocused stare. Dammet flipped a lock of wet black hair off his face and draped an arm around the boy's tensely-hunched shoulders.

"Here's my man Tad," he announced. He leaned down to scoop up more mud, which he slapped into the boy's hand. "You might say he's skittish. If he kept his mind stuck to one idea for more'n a heartbeat, the shock of it would likely kill him. And he can't throw worth goat dung. There ain't no way you could know where this mud ball's gonna hit."

Indeed, the wizard's face furrowed as he contemplated the possibilities. An expression of near panic seeped into his pale eyes.

"Maybe not, but you can figure out where *I'll* hit sure enough," announced a rumbling voice. A short, stout man stepped out from behind the stall's tumble-down wall, brandishing a vangi switch. "Now *git*."

The boys *got*, scampering off with scant regard for their less agile champion. Tad stumbled after them, howling protests against his abandonment.

Ursault glanced at his rescuer. Though the wizard was seated upon a low stool, he was eye to eye with the newcomer, a man whose barrel-chested torso was supported by uncommonly short, bandy legs. He was about the height of a dwarf, but was most definitely not of that race. His face was as beardless as a boy's though he was well into adulthood. There was no hint of any other race about him to explain his stature—he lacked the small frame and hairy feet of Luiren's halflings, and the bulbous nose and blue eyes common to gnomes. Yet some wag had called him a Gnarfling—an unlikely combination of all three races—and the name had stuck.

Something that for lack of a better name could be called friendship had grown between the two village misfits. Gnarfling was the only person who regularly sought out Ursault's company, and who actually seemed to enjoy the old wizard's tales. He leaned in and regarded the tangle of thread on the wizard's loom.

"What do you make of this?"

"Melody Sibar's peacock chicks," Ursault said, pointing to a matted blob of gray thread. "They'll hatch today. Or perhaps tomorrow. At least, those that intend to hatch at all."

"That ought to cover it."

Gnarfling uncorked a flask, which they passed back and forth a couple of times. He belched companionably and settled down, preparing to enjoy the morning's storytelling. His look of contentment faded when he noted a stout woman bustling purposefully toward them.

"Landbound skyship a'coming under full sail," he muttered.

The description was not far off. Vilma was Dammet's mother, a cheery, chatty woman who frequently—and justifiably—looked a bit flustered and windblown. Wisps of black hair escaped her single braid and her round face was rosy-cheeked from her morning's work. Like her son, she was always busy, never still. But unlike many of the villagers, she made time to chat with Ursault now and again, mostly because he was one of the few people in Ashtarahh who tolerated Dammet's pranks.

With a grateful sigh, the woman shouldered off the straps that held a basket of newly-harvested brissberries. The fruit was heavy, covered with a thick rind and a nutlike shell, and extracting the juice was a long process. She unhooked a small cleaver from her belt—a needed tool for the task ahead—and began to smooth a whet stone over it.

"What's coming to this little corner of Zalathorm's realm, lord wizard?"

"A white dog," Ursault said mildly.

"Fearful doings," she said with a grin.

He nodded somberly. "That dog will be the death of more than half the people in a neighboring village."

A small brindle pup ambled by, not far from the wizard's stall. Vilma gave a good-natured chuckle. "That's Dammet's mongrel pup, and the closest thing we got to a white dog hereabouts. Not much of a threat there."

"Not for several seasons, no, but then the dog will wander far from the village and mate with a renegade wolfwere. Their offspring will have pure white fur and look more dog than wolf. In human form, she will be a comely maid."

Vilma responded with a thin smile. "My man Tomas will enjoy this tale, that's for sure and certain! His eye for a pretty girl will be the death of him." She shook her cleaver, an unconsciously lethal gesture.

"True enough, but his death will not come at your hands," Ursault replied.

The woman's smile faded, and fear crept into her eyes. When a wizard—even a mad wizard—spoke of death, it was time to start kindling the funeral pyres.

"Of course, if your boy Dammet remembers to tie the brindle dog when the harvest moon blooms full, the white maid will never be. A lot of trouble that will save." Ursault cocked his head, as if listening to unseen voices. "But on the other hand, a lot of trouble that will cause. This same wolfwere maid could bring doom to the floating city. A lot of trouble that will save. On the other hand—" He broke off with a grunt, momentarily silenced by a sharp, warning nudge from Gnarfling's elbow.

The woman's smile returned, edged with both relief and pity. "Floating cities now, is it? Here in Halruaa?"

Ursault shrugged. "Sometimes yes, and sometimes no."

"That ought to cover it," Gnarfling said meaningfully.

Vilma's gaze darted toward the short man and moved quickly away. Her tolerance did not quite embrace the odd little man. Everyone in Ashtarahh knew most everything about everyone else, and found comfort in this universal lack of privacy. But not even the most imaginative gossip among them could invent a story that could in satisfactory fashion explain Gnarfling, or define his purpose in coming to Ashtarahh. Vilma had a limited imagination and a healthy suspicion of anything than lay beyond its bounds. She gave Ursault a tentative smile, then hauled up her basket and took off at a brisk pace.

Gnarfling reached for his flask and gestured with it toward the loom. "What else you see in there?"

A forlorn expression touched the wizard's face. "Everything," he said softly, his voice sad and infinitely weary. "Everything."

The small man cleared his throat, uneasy with his friend's pain. "Well, how about you start a new weaving, and let's see where it goes."

Ursault obligingly drew a small knife and cut the tangle from his loom. He made a complicated arcane gesture, and a new set of vertical threads appeared on the crooked frame. For a long moment he studied the warp threads, as if examining and discarding many possibilities. Finally he took up a shuttle and began to layer in the weft.

His hands flashed with a wizard's exquisite dexterity, adding a thread here and a new color there. Before long a pattern began to emerge. Glowing, silvery threads connected in a fine web. The fabric between this web, however, remained a dark and indeterminate color, deep as moon-cast shadows. Gnarfling frowned in puzzlement as he noted that Ursault was threading in some mud-splattered crimson. Even this bright color disappeared into the shadowy gloom.

"What do you make of that?" he demanded.

"That's the Weave," Ursault replied, naming the web of magic that surrounded and sustained all of Halruaa and, for all Gnarfling knew, the rest of the world as well. "At least, it's Ashtarahh's place in the Weave."

Gnarfling leaned in and squinted. Sure enough, he could make out the faint outline of the village, as it might appear to a soaring hawk, carved out of the tightly packed web that represented the jungle. Fainter, thinner silver threads connected the fields and buildings, and tiny glowing dots seemed to mill about the open area—an uncanny representation of the market square and the people who readied it.

This was the first discernable picture Gnarfling had ever seen on Ursault's loom. For some reason that worried him. So did the intense expression on the wizard's face as he tossed colors haphazardly into the pattern, only to have them swallowed by the strange, shadowy void that separated and defined the silvery Weave.

In short order a small tapestry hung on the loom. Ursault studied the weaving intently, and Gnarfling studied Ursault.

"You see something, don't you?"

"Everything," the wizard responded again in wondering tones. "Everything."

The response was familiar, but there was a new note in his voice, something that sent tiny fingers of cold dancing down Gnarfling's spine.

After a moment, Ursault moved one hand in a flowing circular pattern. The unseen colors shifted, and a man's face took form in a gap between the glowing silver threads, a face depicted with precision and clarity that the best of Ashtarahh's weavers could not match.

The man was young and exceedingly lean. His high, sharp cheekbones leaned precariously over the deep hollows below, and the thin black mustache on his upper lip looked as tremulous and impermanent as a perching moth. His face was exceedingly pale for a Halruaan, and a sharp contrast to the feverish brightness of his black eyes.

"Trouble coming," muttered Gnarfling. He was well acquainted with trouble and plenty familiar with wizards—which, to his way of thinking, were two words for the same thing. "When?"

In response, Ursault merely shifted his gaze from the loom to the market square.

The square was filling rapidly. Visiting merchants strolled along the paths, eyeing the tapestries and sampling bits of cheese. The trundle of carts over the corduroy filled the air with a pleasant rumble. Already two of these carts had been hauled off the path to languish by the wheelwright's shop, listing heavily over shattered wheels. A young man stood by one of them, arguing with the apprentices and punctuating his complaints with overly dramatic gestures.

Gnarfling's eyes went straight to a thin young man, narrowing as they took in the too familiar theatrics. The newcomer didn't have the look of a merchant or artisan. He was tall and thin, not much past twenty summers, and obviously possessed more money than sense. He traveled alone in an expensive covered cart drawn by matched horses. His emaciated form was draped with fine robes of purple-trimmed black, and jewels flashed on his gesticulating hands. All of these things fairly screamed "wizard."

Even without the trappings, there was an intensity about the newcomer that suggested magic, yet Gnarfling could sense no hint of Mystra's Art about the young man. His nose for such things was as keen as any hound's, and, more to the point, as keen as any *magehound's*. These instincts, and the permanent disguise offered by his stunted form, had kept him alive for over thirty winters.

Why then, he wondered, was he so uneasy?

"He's looking for you," Ursault said, as mildly and as matter-of-factly as if his companion had spoken aloud, "that's why."

The small man shot to his feet as if he'd just sat on a hedgehog. The sudden movement seemed to draw the newcomer's eyes. Recognition flared in his strangely burning gaze, and for a moment Gnarfling stared into the youth's face like a hare mesmerized by a hawk.

Then, suddenly, the young man was standing directly in front of Ursault's stall.

Gnarfling blinked once in surprise, and a few times more to adjust his vision. He instinctively sniffed for the scent of magic, but all he smelled on the newcomer was the cumulative effect of several days on the road: the faint odor of wet cashmere, the musty stench of dirty clothes, and a perfume that smelled of dangerous herbs and pending lightning—a scent no doubt meant to mask the other, more mundane smells.

"I am Landish the Adept," the young man announced grandly.

Gnarfling collected himself and folded his stubby arms. "Good for you. Me, I got no business with the outlandish or the inept. You want I should ask around, and see if someone else might?"

Pure fury simmered in the man's intense gaze, a rage out of scale with the small insult. "Are you certain you have no business with me?" he said meaningfully. "Absolutely certain? Tell me, *jordain*, what am I?"

A small sizzle of panic raced through Gnarfling, quickly mastered. Surely this revelation was nothing new to Ursault the All-Seeing, and no one else was close enough to hear the damning secret.

"What are you?" he echoed scornfully. "The back end of an ox, so far as I can tell."

The man's eyes narrowed. "'Outlandish and inept,'" he repeated. "A strange choice of words for someone who purports to be an itinerate field hand."

Gnarfling stared for a moment, then his shoulders rose and fell in a profound sigh.

"You're a magehound," he said in disgust. "Well, even a slow and stupid hound sometimes blunders into a vhoricock's nest."

"A jordaini proverb," Landish said smugly, clearly enjoying himself. "You should guard your words more carefully."

"Don't see what harm it could do at this point. A magehound," Gnarfling repeated in disgust.

No," stated Ursault.

There was a conviction in that single word that dismissed all other possibilities. Gnarfling sent a puzzled look at the wizard, and was astonished at the simmering wrath in the old man's usually vague, mild eyes.

"Mirabella," Ursault said grimly.

The small man's heart seemed to leap in his chest like a breaching dolphin. Mirabella was the woman who'd saved an outcast jordaini babe, one whose stunted form was deemed unsuitable for the rigorous physical training given Halruaa's warrior-sages. But there was nothing wrong with his mind, and the soft-hearted midwife charged with his destruction knew enough of jordaini ways to give him a bit of the training, enough to keep him alert and alive—until now, at least.

Landish's gaze snapped to the wizard's face and for a moment he looked deeply troubled. His face cleared.

"Ah. A diviner, I suppose. You see the results of my work, if not the actual workings."

"Your *work?* What'd you do with Mirabella?" roared Gnarfling.

He threw himself into a charge, his stubby hands leaping like twin hounds for the man's skinny throat.

Then he stopped, stunned by the white, leprous growth that had appeared on his short digits. As he stared, the small finger on his left hand listed to one side, then broke off entirely and fell to the muddy ground.

"*That,*" Landish said succinctly. "She won't be missed. Just as you won't be missed."

"Mirabella is not yet dead," Ursault said as he rose to his feet. "She may not die. The old speckled hen, the one destined for the soup pot, is going to lay her first egg since the last new moon. If she lays it in the hencoop, Mirabella will die. If the hen ventures into the gardens, a tamed hunting kestrel will see her and swoop. This will draw the eye of a passing hunting party. They will follow their hawk and find Mirabella. The hunter has a terrible fear of the plague. If he is the first to see the woman, he will flee in panic and the others will follow, never knowing what he saw. But if his horse throws a shoe—there is a loose nail and the shoe could be lost any time today or tomorrow—his greenmage daughter will be the first to find Mirabella. She can mix the herbs and pray the spells that will cure the woman. The herbs grow near Mirabella's cottage. She may find them, provided that—"

"Enough!" howled Landish, his dark eyes enormous in his too-pale face. "What madness is this?"

"He's mad, that's for sure and certain," Gnarlish said, jerking a leprous thumb toward Ursault, "but that don't stop him from being right. His way of telling the future is like throwing a really big fireball—the target can be found somewhere in the big, smoking black hole. If there's anyone left to look for it."

Ursault turned the loom around, revealing the weaving and the scenes depicted in it. Landish's face was still there, and so was a small, snug cottage, complete with speckled hens and an elderly woman sprawled, facedown and still, in the courtyard. A soft moan escaped Gnarfling.

"You named yourself an Adept," Ursault said to Landish, "and so you are. You are a Shadow Adept, though this is not known to your master, the necromancer Hsard Imulteer. You intend to ambush and destroy your master, but fear that your growing powers will give you away before you are strong enough to prevail. Desiring to test your shields, you prayed to dark Shar, the goddess of shadows and secrets, and she led you to a hidden jordain. You wished to see if a jordain could perceive your true nature, and you believed that my friend here presented a small risk. Obviously he is gifted at perceiving magic in others, or how would he evade the magehounds for these many years? If he had been able to perceive you for what you are, what harm could come of it? He could not accuse you without also giving himself away."

The young man's face paled to a papery gray. "This is

not possible. No one could know these things!"

"They don't call him Ursault the All-Seeing for naught," Gnarfling pointed out.

Landish began to pace. "Yes, I have heard that name," he muttered in a distracted tone. "A wizard who sees so many possibilities he cannot discern the truth. Paralyzed, driven mad, finally fleeing into a hermit's life. Seeing all, knowing all—the possibilities are staggering!"

Gnarfling began to see where this was headed. He'd met wizards before who believed they were the exception to every rule, magical and otherwise.

The Shadow Adept stopped before Ursault and fixed his intense black gaze on the older wizard's face. "You can see all possible futures—including those influenced by practitioners of the Shadow Weave. This is a great gift, my friend!"

"Gift, or curse?" said Ursault softly. "It is difficult to say."

Landish shook his head vigorously. "Halruaa is famed for wizardry, but few know of the Shadow Weave. We who are blessed by Shar can move in secret."

"But as you gain power, your ability to perceive the workings of Mystra diminish," Ursault concluded. "You may be hidden from wizards, but their ways, in nearly equal measure, are hidden from you."

"You grasp the salient point," the young Adept said, nodding approvingly. "Clearly, you do not want this gift and—forgive me—you have not proven strong enough to handle it. It has become a burden, one I would gladly lift from you."

"A little knowledge," cautioned Ursault, "is a wonderful thing."

Landish let out a sardonic chuckle and dismissed this notion with a wave of one skinny hand. "Come, let us make a bargain. I will give you the herbs needed to cure your short friend and the old dame who raised him."

"No deal," said Gnarfling sternly. "Ursault already knows what herbs are needed. He can find them himself, no help from you."

"Of course he can find them, and of course he can cure you and the old woman—'if this, and if that,' " mocked the Adept. "And let us not forget 'unless this and the other.' Count your fingers—how many remain? Are you willing to trust your life and the woman's to a mad old wizard, and the whims of fate?"

"Same question, back at you." The small man folded his arms. "That mad old wizard could just kill you and have done with it."

"No," said Landish smugly, "he couldn't."

The wizard considered this claim for a moment, then agreed with a grim nod.

"You see? This discussion is a mere formality. I could simply take this man's powers from him. He knows this, and he knows how. It would be easier for me, and far more pleasant all around, if he yields them willingly."

"Mageduel," Ursault suggested. "Take the three of us to Mirabella's glen, and you and I will do battle for the title of All-Seeing."

"Done!" the Adept said gleefully.

He stepped behind the wizard's stall and conjured an oval portal, gleaming with dark, purple-black light. He made a mock-courtly gesture for the others to precede him.

Gnarfling charged through the portal and hit the ground running. He bolted toward his foster mother, dropped to his knees, and gently turned her over with hands that felt strangely numb. He recoiled in grief and horror at the ravaged mess the Adept's spell had made of her face. He lifted one hand to stroke the old woman's hair away from her eyes, and grimaced at the sight of his own hand. He didn't look much better off.

He looked to the center of the courtyard. The wizards faced each other, an expression of intense concentration on each face as they attuned themselves to each other and to their competing Weaves.

A sly smile crossed Gnarfling's face as he perceived the wizard's stratagem: an Adept of the Shadow Weave would have little power in a mageduel arena.

Indeed, a dazed expression crossed the Adept's face as he ventured into the older wizard's convoluted mind. His feverish eyes started to dart about, as if tracing the paths of a hundred startled ground squirrels.

Landish pulled himself together with visible effort and said, "As you yourself observed, I am apprentice to a powerful necromancer. There is still enough of Mystra's art remaining to me to vanquish you, old man. Surely you foresee this."

"It is a possibility," Ursault admitted, "but only one of many."

The younger man sniffed. "A cube, fifty paces on all sides. I could manage more, but the smaller the arena, the swifter my victory."

"As you wish." Ursault smiled faintly. "And in defiance of the rules, you may take your spellfilcher gem into the arena with you."

He did not point out that the man was intending to do precisely that, but the meaning was there all the same. Landish's face flushed at this gentle rebuke, but he spun around and began to stalk off his portion of the arena. Ursault did the same. A translucent, faintly glowing red cube began to take shape around them, growing on all sides as they moved farther apart.

"Just let him rob you and be done with it," muttered Gnarling. "That'll serve him right and fair."

Landish began to mumble the words of a spell. A brilliant golden flame erupted from the ground before him. Bright droplets turned into insects—deadly magical fire gnats whose touch could raise blisters and whose bite could set living flesh aflame.

A faint blue mist surrounded the older wizard as the glowing insects swarmed in. Each one met the aura with a faint, sharp sizzle and flared out of existence.

Tremors shook the ground as invisible fingers of necromantic magic reached deep into the soil. The clearing stirred, and small puffs of dirt and sod exploded upward as long-dead bones fought their way into the light. The older wizard countered with a quick gesture, then he clapped his hands sharply together. A thunderous rumble echoed through the clearing and the old bones shattered to dust.

On the battle raged, and each spell Landish cast was anticipated and countered. The young man's thin, wolfish face contorted with rage, and he hurled his remaining spells one after another, so quickly that spell and counterspell seemed to follow each other as quickly as two sword masters' thrusts and parries.

So intent was Gnarfling on the battle that he did not at first notice the glowing gem on the Adept's hand. A large amethyst, brilliant purple, was taking on light and power with each of Ursault's counterspells.

"The spellfilcher gem," he muttered, cursing Landish as a cheat and coward.

The light intensified until it filled the arena and spilled out into the clearing. Finally Ursault collapsed, falling to one knee and drawing in long, ragged breaths. As Landish has promised, the process of taking his magic from him had not been easy or painless.

The Adept stood triumphant in the eerie light. The hand bearing the glowing gem was fisted and held high, and his eyes shone with the bright, multifaceted dream that was his future.

Gnarfling eased Mirabella from his arms and went over to haul the old wizard slowly, painfully to his feet.

"You shoulda thrown the fight," he grumbled.

"And willingly pass this curse to another, even such a man as this?" Ursault shook his head.

"You knew he was going to win, though."

"It was a possibility. One of many."

With Gnarfling's help, the wizard made his way over to Mirabella. After a moment he shook his head. "She needs more help than I can give her."

The short man sat back on his heels and considered the tangled tale Ursault had told earlier. "If that and if this," he mused.

He leaped to his feet, went to the hencoop and kicked it resoundingly. Half a dozen hens exploded from it, squawking in protest. One old biddy scurried into the field.

Landish's howl of protest cut through the clearing like a machete. Even before he looked up, Gnarfling knew what he would see.

The small form of a kestrel circled against the clouds. Within moments the hawk went into a diving stoop, tempted by the plump, slow-moving meal below.

The rumble of horses' hooves turned thunderous as the hunting party burst from the forest and onto the old corduroy path. Gnarfling blinked in surprise at the size of the entourage: at least six wizards, plus squires and a plain-faced young woman in simple tunic and trews. That would be the greenmage.

Her gaze fell upon the old woman, and she let out a small cry. A bolt of lightning sizzled toward her—and was stopped just short of a strike by an answering bolt flaring from one of the mounted wizards. The hunters spurred their horses toward Landish. They dismounted and began to circle the young adept.

"You didn't mention the other wizards," Gnarfling said.

Ursault smiled faintly. "Knowledge is not quite the same as wisdom. It is not necessary, or wise, to speak of everything you know."

But Landish had not yet acquired this wisdom. He advanced swiftly, his hand fisted and his spellfilcher ring held out to capture the first spell flung at him.

"The first of many," Ursault observed. He sighed in resignation.

"What's going to happen?" Gnarfling asked. He suddenly seemed to hear his own words, and grimaced. "Sorry. Old habit."

"The only thing that could happen," the wizard replied. "The ability to *recognize* several possible futures does not grant a corresponding ability to *avoid* them.

Gnarfling responded with a nod and an evil grin. When several powerful wizards were concerned, one possible future apiece seemed more than enough to ensure the Adept's thorough and messy demise.

The battle that followed was swift, but violent enough to meet Gnarfling's expectations. When all that remained of Landish the Adept was a smoking, greasy circle on the blasted clearing, the greenmage came up and took Gnarfling's hands between hers.

"The same blight," she murmured, her brows pulled down in a deep frown. "It is a necromantic spell, but not one I have seen before."

"Are you not Suzza Indoulur, niece to Lord Basel of Halar?" asked Ursault.

Her eyes widened, and she responded with a nod.

"Your name is spoken as a capable greenmage, but did I not also hear that you are studying for the priesthood of Azuth?"

"News travels swiftly through this forest," she said cautiously.

"The herbal potions and prayer spells of Constandia of Azuth against the leprous blight may prove efficacious," suggested Ursault. "Even a novice priestess might be granted such a spell. I believe I saw some wild priestcap flowers just off the path. Shall I gather some for you?"

She considered this, nodded, then set to work. In short order Mirabella was sitting comfortably, sipping a steaming herbal brew as the greenmage gently smoothed priestcap ointment over the old woman's face. Gnarfling was grinning like a gargoyle and flexing his ten pink fingers, which were longer and more dexterous than they'd been before Landish's spell and Suzza's healing ministrations.

"I can make more ointment for your legs, if you like," the greenmage offered. Her gaze fell on his stunned face, and she added hurriedly, "I mean no offense. I just thought you might like your legs to match the rest of you. Everything else seems just fine. That is, a man as handsome of face and form . . . What I meant to say was . . ." She trailed off a second time, her lips folded tightly together and her face blooming a vivid pink.

Her confusion suggested other possibilities, even more wondrous than the prospect of looking as other men. "Might not hurt to even things out a mite," he said casually. "Kind of you to offer."

The greenmage sent him a tentative smile and set to work with a wooden bowl and pestle. She scooped the ointment into a small pot and pointed to a curving mark carved into the pottery.

"This is my family sigil. Trace it with one finger and repeat the words I will give you, and it will bring you to our estates near Halar. I would like to see you again to make sure the cure is progressing."

"And if it doesn't?" asked Gnarfling, gesturing to his stubby limbs.

The greenmage's soft smile didn't falter. "Even then."

She spoke a short, strange word and had Gnarfling repeat it. When she was satisfied with his pronunciation, she rose in one swift, surprisingly graceful move and strode to the impatient band of wizards. Her father's squire handed her the kestrel, and she tied the little hawk's jesses to her saddle pommel. They rode off without a backward glance, their horses clattering over the rough corduroy path.

Gnarfling watched them go, and for the first time, his future seemed bright with possibilities. He turned to his wizard companion.

Force of habit prompted him to ask, "What now?"

Ursault's smile held a world of contentment. "Isn't it wonderful? I have no idea."

Originally published in Dragon #335,
August 2005
Edited by Erik Mona

GAMES OF CHANCE

Elaith Craulnober is one of my favorite characters, but the truth of the matter is that he's not "my" character at all—or at least, he didn't start out that way. His first in-print appearance was a brief paragraph in the first edition game product Waterdeep and the North, *written by* Forgotten Realms *creator Ed Greenwood. The entry caught my eye when I was researching Realmslore for* Elfshadow, *my first book, and for some reason the rogue moon elf captured my imagination. I included him in that first novel. Only later did I learn that Elaith was more than just a bit player invented for a game product—he'd been part of Ed's personal campaign for years.*

Ed has been very gracious about this, and fortunately we seem to be on much the same page when it comes to this character. He has repeatedly said that he's happy with the directions Elaith has taken and content to let me run with the character.

Still, I've always felt a little guilty about having shanghaied another writer's character. Early on, I learned that writing in a shared world works a whole lot better if you don't define "sharing" as "everything in the lore is up for grabs, no matter who created it."

But having stolen Elaith, I felt obligated to give him interesting things to do. He took an active role in the events of City of Splendors: A Waterdeep Novel, *and he'll be even more prominent in* Reclamation, *the upcoming Songs & Swords book. This short story gives a glimpse into one of Elaith's many business affairs—a glitzy casino in Waterdeep. It also revisits his daughter, Azariah, and her determination to inherit the Craulnober moonblade. Please note that Elaith's thoughts concerning moonblades reflect his personal bias and the level of information available to him; as such, they do not necessarily reflect the whole truth, or the "canon lore" concerning these magic swords.*

Over the years, many readers have wondered if there's any significance in the similarity between Elaith's name and mine. Circumstances being what they are—Ed created the character long before he knew me from Lolth—it is clearly a matter of coincidence. But when I'm in a fanciful mood, I'm not quite so sure of that. I might not have created Elaith, I might not look or act or think as he does, but I understand him far too well for my peace of mind.

GAMES OF CHANCE

There were a thousand ways to cheat, and until tonight, Elaith Craulnober had thought he knew them all.

The moon elf watched, amber eyes narrowed in speculation, as Oltennius Gondblessed worked his way through Tymora's Fancy, a high-coin gambling establishment Elaith had recently built upon the ruins of a North Ward tallhouse. Oltennius was newly come to Waterdeep, and little was known of the man other than his name and the rather obvious intelligence that he hailed from Lantan.

Oltennius's appearance was typical for a native of that Sword Coast island: gingery hair, large, slightly protruding eyes of an odd pale green, and skin the hue of bleached parchment that was wearing thin and starting to yellow. He was short and vaguely egg-shaped, and his garments, which had been cut to fit a slimmer, taller man, boasted rich fabrics but were rather worse for wear. The seat of his black velvet breeches was smooth and shiny, and many of the threads quilting the yellow silk vest had worked their way free of the stitchery pattern to waft in the scented breezes that cooled the crowded room. Oltennius wore no gems, but he kept close at hand a simple wooden snuffbox, which he consulted at close and regular intervals.

The threadbare southerner stood out among the glittering Waterdhavian pleasure seekers, and as such was the target of many arch glances and none-too-softly whispered jests. He seemed as unaware of these insults as he was his own shabby finery, for he was entirely focused upon winning.

And win he did. So far this evening, Oltennius Gondblessed had bested the Eagleshield brothers at dice, won three different card games, twice predicted which rune would mark the end of the Year's Turning Wheel, and guessed which of the white mice or tiny, gem-colored lizards would finish first at the miniature racetrack. For every race.

Elaith sniffed. "Gondblessed," indeed! Not even Tymora, goddess of good fortune, smiled upon her faithful with such consistent and profitable result.

He glanced across the room to where a gray-skinned illithid stood amid the shadows of a small, fragrant jungle of exotic flowing plants, its long facial tentacles idly toying with the branches. The creature turned blank white eyes to its employer and answered the unspoken question. *No, Lord Craulnober, the Lantanna has no psionic ability, nor any magic that I can perceive.*

The elf grimaced. What, then? How had Oltennius Gondblessed succeeded at the game so many Waterdhavians had played and lost?

"Give it back, I say!" demanded a loud and indignant male voice. "Do you have any idea who I am?"

Elaith glanced toward the front entrance, where a familiar scene was playing out.

A well dressed, black-bearded young man was brandishing an empty scabbard at the hostess of Tymora's Fancy, a delicate moon elf maiden who also served as the establishment's brawl-stopper. Rapidly fading motes of light swirled around the man like tiny, schooling fish. The hostess caught Elaith's gaze and rolled her eyes skyward before turning back to the irate patron.

"Either you're Lord Melshimber or you're a very talented doppleganger," she said sweetly. "The house rules have not changed since you were here last night, my lord: no spells, no magical items, no exceptions."

The bearded man shook the scabbard again. "Have you any idea how valuable this sword is?"

"*Was*," the hostess reminded him. "As you were warned in the forehall—as *all* are warned every night—Tymora's Fancy offers a fair and level field of play. To that end, all clandestine magical items are disintegrated."

It was a lie, of course. Elaith's warding spells whisked away the magical trinkets Waterdhavians tried to smuggle in, depositing them in a locked box in his back office.

Lord Melshimber accepted his loss with a shrug and sent a sheepish grin in the direction of his two smirking companions. It has become a popular game among Waterdeep's idle wealthy, this quest to bypass Elaith Craulnober's wards and get the better of the infamous Serpent. Elaith didn't mind, as this had swiftly made Tymora's Fancy one of the city's most popular and profitable gaming festhalls.

He turned his attention back to Oltennius Gondblessed, who had a large sum riding on the duel taking place at Clockwork Castle. Blood-battles between living creatures were illegal in Waterdeep, so Elaith had purchased several miniature clockwork knights in full plate armor. Two of these foot-high warriors bashed away at each other with tiny swords while a ring of spectators cheered and wagered.

An ancient gnome stood by, a priest of Gond Wonderworker in full clerical regalia, hired to certify the equal chances of the clockwork opponents—and to repair them, afterward. Something very like maternal concern was etched into the lines of the gnome's dried-apple face, and he stood wringing his hands in dismay as his metal charges battered each other for the pleasure of wealthy humans.

Elaith drifted over, curious about the greeting that had passed between Oltennius Gondblessed and the gnome cleric earlier that evening. The gnome honored the Lantanna with a deep, elaborate bow. Oltennius had responded in kind, dropping to one knee to take up the hem of the gnome's clerical tabard and kiss the runes embroidered there. To Elaith's eye, the two of them looked like a pair of low rent street thespians enacting an elaborate court greeting between some long-ago prince and high cleric. At the moment, however, both were absorbed in the small drama occurring in the miniature arena.

The little knight in brazen armor was winning, and his golden sword flashed repeatedly as he drove the silver-plated knight back to the stone wall, step by staggering step. The silver knight's helmet had been knocked askew, revealing the gear-works within. On came the brazen warrior, slashing away at this vulnerable spot. Victory—and perhaps demolition—seemed assured.

Elaith caught the look of mute appeal the gnome sent Oltennius Gondblessed. The southern opened his snuffbox and inhaled deeply, an act that visibly strained the seams of his fraying yellow vest.

Before Oltennius could shut the snuffbox lid, the silver knight dropping into a crouch, and then into a surprisingly nimble spin. One outthrust metal leg swept at the advancing warrior's ankles, connecting with a tinny clatter.

Clockwork arms milled wildly as the brazen knight strove to regain balance. But the silver warrior was on his feet, barreling in to shoulder-smash his unsteady opponent. The brazen knight crashed to the floor and did not rise, for the victor's sword was at his metal throat.

Elaith cast a simple spell, a simple cantrip that required little more than a flick of his fingers. Immediately a soft blue glow surrounded the arena—a widely recognized sign of magic at work.

At least half the spectators groaned, even before the arena master announced, "No winners. Magic-tainted match."

But the grumbles of protest were short-lived, and the hall quieted as people pressed in to see who had finally managed to get slip magic past the moon elf's safeguards. They watched in puzzlement as the blue glow faded from the arena, lingering only around the clerics and hired wizards.

Elaith made another small, subtle hand gesture, and the southerner's snuffbox lit up like an azure candle.

Indignation flooded Oltennius's face, but he had the sense to keep silent as two of Elaith's guards, tall men wearing deeply hooded black capes, escorted him to the back office. The elf followed, noting with a sardonic smile the renewed tumult of sound filling the festhall. The good people of Waterdeep were placing loud and grimly imaginative wagers on the Lantanna's fate.

☙ ☙ ☙ ☙ ☙

Oltennius Gondblessed allowed the two men to march him into a richly appointed study. As soon as the door shut behind him, he shook off the guards' hands, drew himself up, and faced down the silver-haired moon elf.

"I broke none of your city laws or your festhall rules," he said, speaking with a dignity befitting the scion of a long, distinguished line. "There is no magic in this box. Your spell might have been silent, *good sir*, but it told a lie nonetheless!"

"Of course it did," Elaith Craulnober readily admitted, either missing or choosing to ignore the typically ironic Lantanna insult. "If the snuffbox had been magical, it would already be in my possession."

This second admission of wrongdoing set Oltennius back on his heels. Lantannas valued honesty, and an accusation of falsehood was a deadly insult. The only worse charge, short of murder, was theft, and this singular elf had just casually admitted to both!

"May I see the snuffbox?" Elaith asked.

Oltennius hesitated long enough to earn a rib-bruising nudge from a guard's elbow. "Have a care," he cautioned as he handed it over. "It is exceedingly delicate."

The elf flipped open the lid and gave close study to the contents. "I have never seen such tiny or intricate gear-works. Impressive, but not particularly fragrant. Might I then inquire why you felt compelled to sniff it so frequently?"

Oltennius sidestepped the guard's prompting jab and folded his arms in silent defiance.

After a moment, the elf set the box carefully on the floor, straightened, and casually rested one boot on the lid. One silvery brow arched in unmistakable emphasis.

Panic leaped up like bright flame from somewhere deep in Oltennius's gut. "Don't!" he shrieked. "I will tell you all, only give me the box! It represents my life's sole work, and that of my father before me, and his mother before *him*, and so on, back to a time before the raising of the Dale Stone!"

The elf studied him in silence, no doubt wondering what sort of work might absorb the full attention of Gond-fearing artisans for over thirteen centuries.

As well he might.

"My ancestor, the first Gondblessed, was so named for his astonishing skill," Oltennius said, almost babbling in his haste. "He undertook a great challenge: an understanding of magic enabling one to detect, alter, and eventually to produce magical effects through mechanical means."

"Impossible," snapped the guard with sharp elbows. He brushed down the hood of his cape, revealing a narrow, angular face covered by tiny silvery scales.

A half-dragon! Oltennius snapped his gaping jaw shut and averted his goggle-eyed gaze, drawing in a long, unsteady breath as he gathered his wits. For some reason, the sight of this fearful minion brought to mind all the improbable stories he'd heard of Elaith Craulnober, and made them seem suddenly, disturbingly credible.

"The human is lying, or he is mad," the half-dragon stated.

"No doubt you're right, Tincheron, but as we've nothing more entertaining to do at present, we might as well hear him out."

Oltennius swallowed the lump in his throat and hastened to obey. "Gondblessed Manor, my ancestral home, stands on fertile lands. The income from our tenants has long provided a comfortable living for my family."

"And how much of that land remains to you?" the elf asked, his eyes skimming Oltennius's ancient, ill-fitting garb.

"Little," he admitted, "and attacks from sea creatures last year wreaked havoc among my remaining tenants. This device offered me a chance to rebuild my fortunes."

"By cheating at games of chance?"

"By altering *magic*," he corrected firmly, and launched into a long and highly detailed explanation of the mechanisms involved.

The elf held up one hand to cut him off. "Enough," he

said flatly, and there was something in his voice that chilled Oltennius far more than the sight of a man-shaped dragon. "This is madman's prattle, nothing more."

Oltennius tried another path. "Can lighting change to fire?"

"Certainly, if it strikes dry brush or a thatch roof," Elaith said impatiently.

"So one type of power can be transmuted into another, if the conditions are right. Is it possible to know that lightning has struck, even if your eyes don't perceive it nor your ears hear the thunder?"

"Of course. There are subtle changes in the air."

"Deviations on a constant!" Oltennius exclaimed. "The Weave is a constant source of power. Are we agreed upon that?"

The elf conceded with a curt nod.

"Just as your senses can perceive lightning, fluctuations in the Weave—magical items and spells, if you will—can be perceived by a device of sufficient sensitivity."

"Impossible," the half-dragon repeated.

"Why so?" argued Oltennius. "A simple spell can detect the presence of magic."

"Let us say, for argument's sake, that it's possible to detect magic with a gear-works device. What then?"

"When magic is present, the device can absorb some of that power and change it to another form. Compare it to *spellfire*, if you will."

"So it perceives and alters magic. To what end?"

"Whatever I choose," Oltennius said proudly. "It is my belief that the mind works in a manner very similar to lightning, but with thousands upon thousands of tiny flashes, flaring rapidly and constantly. A device of sufficient complexity can mimic, at least in part, these events. To put it in simplistic magical terms, I can 'speak' to this transmuting device like a wizard to his familiar, mind to mind, and tell it how to alter the magic it perceives."

Elaith considered him for a long, silent moment. "How many people know of this new magic?"

The man huffed in exasperation. "It's not *magic*. Only few gnomes of great age and high clerical rank know of the Gondblessed quest. I am the only living person to know its workings."

The elf glanced at half-dragon, who promptly pulled up his hood and glided back into the festhall.

The probable meaning of this crept over Oltennius like a winter frost. He clutched the box to his chest. "It is worthless to you! Kill me, and you have nothing but . . . but . . ."

"An ugly corpse to dispose of?" Elaith suggested. "That's hardly an appealing prospect. Tell me: If you were provided with sufficient materials and funds, a pleasant place to work and nothing to distract you, could you make one of these devices for me?"

"You . . . you would be my patron?" faltered Oltennius.

"A very generous one," the elf assured him.

Pride warred with practicality, but the battle was brief and the victory never in question.

Oltennius dropped awkwardly to one knee and gave the traditional pledge. "My hands, your house," he said stiffly. "May my work glorify Gond Wonderbringer and benefit my patron."

☙ ☙ ☙ ☙ ☙

The third bell after midnight sounded before Elaith had opportunity to open his safe box. It held the usual assortment of oddities—trinkets and trifles from far corners of Faerûn. Elaith tossed them aside to get to the weapon he'd stolen from young Lord Melshimber. That, at least, had real value. The scabbard Melshimber had been waving around was of elfish design, and even the simplest elven blade was a joy to wield.

The weapon was a long sword, very old but well kept. Elaith lifted it and took a few practice cuts, pleased with the weapon's exceptional balance. The new leather wrappings on the hilt were clumsy, but those were easily removed—

Elaith froze, and the leather wrappings fell to the floor unheeded as he stared at the smooth, milky gem set into the sword's hilt. A mixture of wonder and sorrow suffused him as he realized that, for the second time in his life, he held a dormant moonblade.

He turned the blade over and studied the seven runes marking the shining length. He stroked them with tentative fingers, noting that they did not mar the smoothness of the blade; they were not carved into the metal, but seemed to gleam forth from the heart of the sword. He had not taken time to closely examine the Craulnober blade, so stunned had he been by the sword's rejection.

The elf set the moonblade carefully aside. Come morning, he would make arrangements for it to be sent to Evermeet. The swords that had a part in choosing the royal family were not for such as Elaith Craulnober.

Nor for likes of Camaroon Melshimber.

A wave of rage, pure and primal, swiftly followed this thought. The elf tossed aside his best sword and thrust the moonblade into its sheath. Snatching up his cloak, he stalked out into the cold autumn night.

It didn't take him long to find the Melshimber manor, and less time to bypass the magical wards on the ornate iron fence. Determining which bedchamber housed the drunken, snoring lordling needed only the sort of spell Elaith had learned in the royal nursery. His rage still burned white-hot when he dragged Camaroon Melshimber from his bed and flung him against the wall.

The elf drew the moonblade and leveled it at with deadly intent. He might not be worthy to wield a living blade, but elven law and tradition were clear on this matter. Anyone who knowingly used a dormant moonblade as a common sword, or in any other way deliberately dishonored it, was to be slain with that weapon in fair combat.

"Arm yourself," he snarled at the groggy, sputtering man.

Incredibly, a sly grin curved the young lord's lips, and he lifted one hand to preen his short black beard.

"Aha!" he crowed. "I *knew* you were keeping the trifles we brought in!"

Trifles!

"And this knowledge," Elaith inquired coldly, "is worth dying to possess?"

Young Melshimber's smirk faltered, then twisted into his usual arrogant expression. Even now, he considered himself untouchable.

Elaith drew his second sword and tossed it at the man, who reflexively grabbed for it. Elven steel flashed, and an expression of profound astonishment crossed the human's face as blood poured from his slashed throat. His mouth worked for a moment, but only a few choked, gurgling sounds emerged.

The elf waited until Melshimber was quite dead, then he carefully cleaned both weapons and tucked them into his belt. The next cut required a special black knife, one Elaith kept tucked into his left boot for just such occasions. He worked quickly, chanting softly as he carved a necromancer's rune into the man's forehead, an ugly mark that would prevent priest or wizard from inquiring into this man's death.

The sky was fading to smoky sapphire as Elaith left the Melshimber mansion. He had no fear of discovery; a tunnel led from the estate's buttery to a well house three streets over. Knowledge of these hidden byways was one of Elaith's most valuable treasures.

He quickly made his way south to one of the most lavish and secure of his Waterdeep properties, a gated estate in the Castle Ward, not far from Piergeiron's Palace. Therein was his greatest treasure of all: his daughter Azariah, his sole hope for the Craulnober clan's restored strength and reputation.

She was being raised on Evermeet as a ward of the royal court, but the recent attack on the island kingdom had left her shaken and grieving. Queen Amlaruil had urged Elaith to take his daughter for the winter to give her some time and distance.

Elaith found the child at her studies, sitting demurely at her tutor's side, an open book on her lap. Azariah was pretty child, tall for her age and as leggy as a young colt. She resembled her sun elf mother, a mistress whom Elaith had enjoyed and forgotten. But Azariah was his legal heir, and heir also to the Craulnober moonblade.

The sentient sword had rejected him once, choosing dormancy over an unworthy wielder. By the grace of the gods and the consent of his Craulnober ancestors, the moonblade had been awakened, but Elaith had no illusions about its destiny. It would never be his, nor should it be.

Nor did he expect Azariah to wield it. Never, not once in the long and brutal history of the moonblades, had a gold elf successfully claimed a sword. But a living moonblade brought honor the Craulnober house, and it would be an attractive dowry. In time, Azariah would wed a moon elf of high family, and if her children bred true, the most worthy among them would inherit the sword

"Here it is!" the child said triumphantly, stabbing the page with one slender finger. "The law was written by Evermeet's Council of Elders, during the second year of Lady Mylaerla Durothil's rule as High Councilor."

Elaith's eyebrows rose. This was a pastime more befitting a magistrar than a girl of eleven winters.

"An interesting choice, Delaritha," he said dryly, addressing the elven bard he'd employed to continue his daughter's harp studies. "I look forward to hearing that law set to music."

318 • Elaine Cunningham

Two pairs of feminine eyes flashed to his face, holding identical wary expressions.

"Lady Azariah wishes to know more of her family moonblade," the bard explained.

"It is hers to hold in trust for her children. What more is there to know?"

The child rose to her feet, her face pale but determined. "When I come of age, I will claim the moonblade."

Elaith stared at her, too stunned to hide his astonishment. "What nonsense is this?"

"It is the law. It is my right," she whispered.

A strange and unwelcome insight struck him: little Azariah was not just his daughter, but her own person, with dreams and plans of her own. But so soon? Surely he could expect her to remain a malleable child for another decade or two?

"Have you learned nothing of the laws of nature?" he demanded. "Elves are not half this and half that. You are your mother's daughter, a gold elf. No gold elf has ever drawn a moonblade and lived."

"What of the Starym blade?" the child persisted.

Elaith sent the bard a look that should have slain her on the spot. "Have you been teaching her this nonsense, or is there someone *else* who should set her affairs in order before nightfall?"

The girl stepped between her father and her tutor—an oddly protective gesture for one so tiny—and dipped into a respectful curtsey. "The fault is mine. During the sea voyage I wished to learn more of the mainland. Another passenger lent me several chapbooks, most of them travel books written by a human named—"

"Volo," Elaith concluded flatly. "A wandering rogue who tells the truth only occasionally, and usually by accident. It's well that you remember that."

"I will," Azariah promised. "But is it not true that a half-elf inherited a blade? And she only fifteen winters at the time?"

The girl's small, pointed chin lifted proudly, and Elaith read in her face the words to come.

"Before you say anything about the worth of a half-breed compared to an elf of noble blood," he said softly, "you should know the moonfighter's mother was Amnestria of Evermeet, who was dear to me beyond measure. Her daughter, though half-elven, is a princess of the blood, and I will hear no word spoken against her."

"Yes, my lord," the girl said dutifully.

"Then let us have no more of this foolishness," he said sternly. "The matter is finished."

The color drained from Azariah's face. She stood her ground, though, and placed one hand on the elven lore book as if to gain strength from its ancient laws.

"With respect, my lord," she whispered, "the moonblade is mine to claim, and none can deny me."

"She's right, you know," announced an amused voice behind them.

Elaith whirled, angry that someone had managed to slip up behind him. Tincheron leaned against the door post, a smirk sitting oddly on his reptilian face.

The half-dragon was his oldest friend and distant kin, but Elaith was in no mind to told inconvenient truths. "Haven't I troubles enough, without you adding to them?" he snapped.

The humor faded from Tincheron's face. "Azariah's ambition troubles you? But I thought . . . "

"*Did* you?" Elaith inquired acidly.

The half-dragon reached into the hall and dragged Oltennius Gondblessed into the doorway. "I had assumed," Tincheron said quietly, "that you were testing your daughter's resolve. That you had this very contingency in mind when you offered the Lantanna your patronage."

Understanding flooded Elaith, and his eyes widened in sudden appreciation of this new and wondrous possibility.

"Lady Azariah, may I present to you one Oltennius

Gondblessed," Elaith said softly. "You will be working together for many mooncycles to come."

◈ ◈ ◈ ◈ ◈

To his credit, Oltennius applied himself to his new task with great enthusiasm, working throughout the long winter to adjust his device to the magic of the Craulnober moonblade. Unlike many humans, he did not waste breath bemoaning the "unfairness" of the elven swords. Elaith was glad of this, for he had heard *that* tale told too many times. If some sages had their way, any "worthy soul" would be carrying a moonblade, be he sun elf or sea elf, or for that matter, a half-orc courtesan with a heart of gold and tusks to match.

By the time Fleetswake rolled around and the worst of the winter snows had past, Oltennius declared his device ready for testing.

This, Elaith had not foreseen.

"Testing?" he demanded. "How, exactly, do you propose to do that?"

"The sword must be drawn. If its magic cannot be altered, we'll know."

The elf's eyebrows rose. "Yes, it's rather difficult to miss the lesson presented by a blackened, smoking corpse. But let us return to this notion of testing. Have you given any thought to what will happen if the magic *can* be altered?"

It was Oltennius's turn to be puzzled. "Wasn't that the entire point?"

"Of course," Elaith said impatiently, "but obviously Azariah cannot be allowed to take this risk. Another must take the test, but what if he who first attempts to *draw* the sword *claims* it?"

The Lantanna considered this for a several moments. "Well, that is a bit of a conundrum, isn't it?"

The soft whisper of metal on wood drew Elaith's

attention to the worktable where the Craulnober blade rested, carefully sheathed. What he saw there froze him for one heart-stopping moment.

Azariah had crept into the room, and she was slowly turning the metal scabbard so that she might take the hilt. The girl had heard them talking, and in her child's mind, one solution seemed clear: if her moonblade was ready to be drawn, it was ready for her.

She would die, that was a certainly. Even if the Lantanna's art proved effective—or even if Azariah herself might eventually prove worthy of a Moonblade—she was a child, and a child was far too fragile a vessel for such power. And since there were two living Craulnobers, the sword would slay an unfit wielder before it went dormant in the hands of the last in the clan.

All of this flashed through Elaith's mind in one fleeting, horror-struck instant. Then he let out a roar and exploded into action. He dived across the table, knocking the sword away from the child's grasping hands.

The sheath clattered to the floor and the naked sword spun on the table, blade slicing toward the wide-eyed child. Without thinking, Elaith seized the hilt.

Azure light surrounded him, and he stared in astonishment at the sword in his hand—the *living* sword—glowing with faint silvery light, marked with strange sigils that combined Espruar script with something that looked like draconic runes.

Numbly, Elaith conceded that this made sense. Some of the Craulnobers had been dragon riders—for that matter, he and Tincheron shared a common ancestor.

"Mine," implored Azariah, holding out her hands for the sword.

Anger rose in Elaith unbidden, darker and more powerful than any he had ever known. Foolish child! Even now, she had not the slightest understanding of the power she hoped to grasp!

He turned to give her a well-deserved scolding and found himself facing a tiny statue. Azariah stood wild-eyed and frozen, staring at him like a rabbit caught in a raptor's gaze.

Before Elaith could make sense of this, the clattering approaching of servants and guards, coming in swift response to their master's shout, suddenly stopped.

The elf turned toward the open door. In the hall beyond, a score of armed men stood like statues, as pale and terror-frozen as the child.

One of the figures shook himself and crept into the room, his scaly face both awestruck and wary. "Elaith? Cousin? Put the sword down before you kill them all," Tincheron said softly. "They're struck with a dragonfear, and a bad one at that."

But Elaith did not want to put aside the blade. It fit his hand so well, as if fashioned solely for his grasp. The dragonfear, too, was familiar—a natural extension of the rage that was his constant companion, hidden though it usually was by the fragile sheath of power, wealth, and dry wit.

The elf slowly turned toward the immobile Oltennius, whose plump face was frozen in an expression of that mingled terror and triumph. Oltennius Gondblessed had succeeded—and Elaith had failed once again.

With great difficulty, the elf sheathed his anger and dismissed the dragonfear it had summoned. When the Lantanna shook off the effects of the spell, Elaith drew his second sword and handed it to the human.

"Arm yourself," he said quietly, "and face the justice dealt to all those who dishonor the moonblade."

The deed was done quickly. Elaith pried the box—the achievement of a thousand years of ceaseless effort—from Oltennius Gondblessed's dead hand and hurled it against the far wall. The device shattered, showering the floor with splinters of wood and fragments of metal and wire.

Moonblade still in hand, Elaith turned toward Evermeet

and waited to die. Of course he would die, for who had dishonored this sword more than he? He had sought to twist ancient elven magic to suit his own pride. Volo's tall tales, Melshimber's presumption—such things were but a mooncast shadow of his misdeeds.

Yes, even now the device's mysterious effect was fading. Elaith could feel the gathering power in the sword, the killing heat starting to sear his hands.

A strong, scaly hand settled on his shoulder, and Tincheron held out the metal scabbard. His golden eyes held entreaty. "Lord Craulnober," he said simply, but those words held a world of meaning: honor, responsibility, *family*.

Despair slipped away to some hidden place in Elaith's heart, where it would no doubt regroup with rage to plot their next return. Elaith slid the moonblade back into its sheath, where it would await its rightful wielder.

The half-dragon gently set the sheathed blade aside and gazed regretfully at the shattered device. "Was that truly a needed thing? What of the Craulnober moonblade, and the Lady Azariah?"

What indeed? Who could say, but the gods who had decreed this particular deadly game?

Elaith gave the child a reassuring smile. "When she comes of age," he said quietly, "she will take her chances."

Published for the first time in this volume.

TRIBUTE

When we were writing the novel City of Splendors, *Ed Greenwood and I discussed revisiting Waterdeep's past, not in the usual flashback, but through "hero tales" told by Taeros Hawkwinter. Throughout the story, Taeros, a younger son of Waterdeep's merchant nobility, was secretly working on* Deep Waters, *a collection of stories recounting the legends and heroes of Waterdeep, which he intended as a gift for Azoun V, the infant king of Cormyr.*

But time and word count restrictions proved to be mortal foes of this notion. Although reference is made to Deep Waters *in the novel, none of Taeros's tales are included. Here's the story he wrote while waiting for his friends to arrive at their new Dock Ward retreat. It recounts a legend often told of a famous Waterdhavian landmark.*

TRIBUTE

In a time long past, many generations before men and elves raised a stone in the Dalelands to begin anew the reckoning of years, small bands of barbarians made themselves a home beside a deep water harbor. It was a good place, with fine hunting to be had in the surrounding meadows and forests. So many fish filled the seas that the water could hardly hold them all. Indeed, during each full moon of summer, small silver runchion wriggled ashore to lay eggs in the sand. Gathering these swift and slippery fish was considered great sport, an occasion for merriment and song. No one enjoyed these moonlit hunts more than Sima, one of two daughters born to the village cooper.

Sima was a merry lass, round as a berry and brown as a wren. But her sister, Erlean, was tall and fair, with hair the color of red wheat, and it was Erlean who caught the eye of Brog the chieftain. Bitter were his tears when the lot for the dragon's tribute was cast, and a stone redder than red wheat fell nearest the altar of sacrifice.

In those days, the lands from sea to sea were ruled by dragons, and each summer they came to claim tribute: one maiden, slain upon an altar stone, and carried off to tempt the palate of some distant dragon king. Each year the chieftain cast a handful of stones at the altar: river pebbles of red and white, coal-black stone, lumps of golden amber in every shade from palest blond to brown. The will of the gods decided which stone came to rest closest to the altar. The maiden whose hair was closest in color to that unlucky stone became the summer sacrifice.

Not a single maid in the village, save for Erlean, could boast of hair the color of red wheat.

So fierce was the love of Brog the chieftain for Erlean that he would not give her up. With dark words and soft promises he won the village cooper to his cause. The day of the first full moon of summer, the night when runchions ran, Brog proclaimed a feast. It was an easy thing for the cooper to add to the mead herbs that would send the villagers into early slumber. All drank but Brog and the cooper, and when Sima slept, they rubbed berry juice into her hair until it was redder than red wheat, and they bound her to the altar stone.

The villagers awakened in full moonlight to the thunder of wings as two red dragons came for the tribute: a warrior wyrm known as Hysta'kiamarh and his mate, a priestess whose name was nothing a human tongue could shape. Fearsome they were, and great was Sima's fear when she found herself upon the altar in her sister's place.

"I am betrayed!" she shrieked. "I am not the chosen sacrifice! Another should die, and not me!"

The warrior wyrm looked down at her, and his great fanged mouth curved into a sly and terrible smile. "I have always found a little treachery in a human to be a fine spice. Name your betrayers, loud morsel, and you shall go free."

"Swear it," Sima insisted. "Swear the most solemn oath you know that the one who caused me to be bound here will die in my place!"

"By the four winds, by the very breath of Tiamut, so shall it be," intoned Hysta'kiamarh.

Once his oath was given, the dragon extended a claw and sliced the ropes binding Sima's hands. She lifted her arm and leveled an accusing finger, sweeping it in a deadly path across the moonlit crowd of gathered Deepwater folk. Fear was written on every familiar face, but it burned brightest in the eyes of those who had betrayed her.

Sima saw what was in the eyes of her father and her chieftan, and for a moment she paused, trembling. Then her hand swept high to point at the largest red dragon.

"It was you, great Hysta'kiamarh," she cried out; "you who demanded this tribute, you who put me on this altar! Human hands tied the knots, but the cords binding all of us are in your grasp. By the ancient bonds of word and wind, it is Hysta'kiamrh who must die in Sima's place!"

Angry steam poured from the dragon's nostrils at these words, and flames leaped and burned within Hysta'kiamarh's yellow eyes. Hissing his rage at the girl's impudence, he raised his talons for the killing stroke.

At once a terrible wind roared up from the sea. A monstrous cloud, dark and dragon-shaped, raced toward the cowering villagers like a killing storm. It swept past Deepwater, only to wheel around in the sky and circle back with deadly intent.

The forsworn dragon tore his eyes from the fearsome sight long enough to send an inquiring glare at his companion.

His mate inclined her horned head in a solemn nod. "The Breath of Tiamut," the priestess confirmed. "As you swore, so shall it be. By word and wind, your life for the maiden's."

And as she spoke, the dragon-shaped cloud swooped down and engulfed Hysta'kiamarh. Cloud and dragon then shot into upward toward the watching moon. They disappeared together, high above Deepwater, in a crash that split the sky like the loudest thunder ever heard. A rain of dragon scales clattered down to the hard-trodden mud of Deepwater, sending the villagers into panicked flight.

But the curious moonlight soon worked its way back down through the swirling dust, and the villagers came close behind. All beheld a wondrous sight: the dragon scales had fallen to form an elaborate knot-work circle around the stone altar, upon which stood Sima, unbound and unharmed. The dragon cleric bowed to her as if to a chieftain's daughter.

"The bargain is fulfilled, the tribute is ended," the dragon said, her great voice rolling across sea and shore. "What the warriors of Deepwater could not achieve through strength of arms, one girl has won through her cleverness and loyalty." Then the she-dragon leaped into the sky, and was gone.

The villagers stood amazed, then as one they fell on their knees before the maiden who had saved them.

Sima climbed down from the altar to take her father by one hand and Brog, her sister's betrothed, by another. Raising them up, she gaily said, "The moon is full, and the runchions will soon return to the sea. Just because the dragons cannot eat, there is no reason why *we* should not!"

Merrily the people of Deepwater made their way down to the sands. They chased the fleeing little fish with much sport and laughter, until the moon went to its daytime slumber to the sound of happy songs, and the good scent of runchion stew.

To this very day, the dragon scale mosaic can be seen in Virgin's Square, harder than any stone. Thanks to Sima, never again did the dragons of the North demand a blood tribute from the people of Waterdeep.

Published for the first time in this volume.

ANSWERED PRAYERS

Probably the most frequent question in emails from readers is, "Will there be another Liriel story?" Windwalker *concluded the story I wanted to tell in the Starlight & Shadows trilogy and brought certain themes and threads to the intended conclusions, but many readers still want to know What Happens Next. This story is for them.*

It takes place nearly ten years after the final battle in Windwalker, *and it gets readers pretty much caught up with what's been going on in Liriel's life: the adventures, the companions, the accomplishments—and the temptations. There will always be temptations, because whatever happens in Liriel's life, whatever else she might become, she will always be a drow.*

ANSWERED PRAYERS

The port city of Hlammach had no shortage of taverns, but not many of them would willingly serve a drow. Liriel Baenre and her two companions had spent the better part of the evening working their way down Tavern Row before finding a table at a noisy dockside shanty.

It was a *good* table, right by the front window and, Liriel noted cynically, in full view of the passing sailors. Many did not pass at all, but stopped to stare at the unusual feminine trio on display: an ebony-skinned drow, a golden star elf, and a tall, lithe beauty who, except for the feral light in her amber eyes, appeared to be a moon elf.

Liriel had to admit this was a worthy ploy on the proprietor's part. She and her friends were window dressing—exotic bait for passing clients. Elves of any sort were not common in Impiltur, and three strikingly different elf women were certain to catch the eye. Several human wenches sprawled invitingly on a nearby couch, ready to offer alternatives when patrons learned the elves were not for sale.

A burst of raucous laughter rose from a nearby table, where a trio of drunken merchants obligingly displayed *their* wares to a saucy-looking light-skirt.

Sharlarra Vendreth rolled her eyes. "A thief, a cleric of Mystra, and a champion of Eilistraee walk into a brothel. Stop me if you've heard this one."

"Not *that* old jest," Liriel said dryly. She glanced at the third elf. "You haven't touched your ale, Thorn, after all your complaints about being thirsty enough to drink seawater."

The raven-haired warrior tasted her ale, grimaced, and put the mug down. *"Bilge* water is more like. And by the Dark Maiden, Sharlarra, keep your voice down! I know *wolves* whose howls don't carry as well."

"Thorn has a point," Liriel told the star elf. "As far as the good folk of Impiltur are concerned, you're not a thief, you're a *swordpoint*. Best keep it that way."

Sharlarra plucked at the sea-blue tabard that proclaimed her status: a hired blade working for the Impiltur military. One slim finger traced the three interlocking rings, the symbol of the Council of Lords that ruled the country in Queen Sambryl's name. The device was stitched in extravagant silver threads, the better to honor the three gods—Tyr, Torm, and Ilmater—most revered in Impiltur.

"We're *all* hired swords," the star elf observed. "In fact, if not for the high praise Jhanyndil of Rashemen heaped upon *you*, the council wouldn't have approved *any* of us. So why are Thorn and I the only ones wearing the three rings?"

Liriel pushed up the sleeve of her shirt and pointedly

334 • Elaine Cunningham

displayed her black forearm. *"Drow?* Remember that little detail? When the good folk of Hlammach see two swordpoints walking a dark elf down the street, they assume you and Thorn have a bad situation under control. But if all three of us were wearing the council's colors—"

"They'd probably think the tabards were stolen," Sharlarra concluded. "That didn't occur to me."

Such thoughts *always* occurred to Liriel. Even now, long years gone from her native Menzoberranzan, she still thought as a drow: no path ran straight, no question was simple, no plan held a single purpose. In her homeland, "devious" was high praise. She'd been raised on deceit and betrayal, trained to see layers within layers. A drow who did *not* see many possibilities in any situation was unlikely to survive long.

With such training, suspicion came easily. Friendship was much harder. Until she'd left the Underdark, the closest Liriel had come to having a true friend was her alliance with an insane, two-headed deep dragon. Since then, she'd been fortunate indeed. For several years now, she'd been running from adventure to adventure with Thorn and Sharlarra. And before that—

"Finally, here comes our food." Thorn nodded toward the serving wench, who was currently struggling her way through a gauntlet of grasping hands, a well-laden tray held high overhead and a bright, determined smile firmly fixed on her face.

The servant set out surprisingly appetizing fare: thick seafood stew served in hollowed-out round loaves, a platter of pungent cheeses, and bowls of sugared berries.

Thorn regarded her streaming trencher with approval. "I smell a joint of mutton roasting. Bring me a thick slice of that, as well."

The wench blew a curly brown lock off her face and shook her head. "Cook just put it on the fire. It'll be some while before it's ready."

Thorn turned a cool, amber stare toward the servant. "Is the fleece still attached to the mutton?"

The girl blinked. "N-no. Of course not."

"Then it's ready."

Liriel chuckled at the expression on the servant's face, and the speed with which she beat a retreat to the kitchen. Thorn's appetite was prodigious and not entirely civilized. Small wonder, considering that she spent much of her time running about on four legs.

And speaking of appetites, Sharlarra was not far behind, albeit in other matters. The star elf was surveying the other patrons with interest, boldly meeting their accessing stares with a friendly, open smile—not quite invitation, but not far from it, either.

Liriel didn't fault Sharlarra for her fun-loving nature, for she understood it well. Her years in the Underdark had been brightened by many a handsome drow playmate. Mutual prejudice made alliance with a surface elf unlikely, but from time to time, a human man caught her eye. Even so, there had been no one for her since Fyodor of Rashemen. Sometimes she wondered if there ever *could* be.

Her hand went to the symbol of Mystra hanging over her heart. Shortly after Fyodor's death, Liriel had found her true calling. Magic had always been her passion, but she felt the call of a cleric's path, as well. When she learned of Mystra, Lady of Magic and Mysteries, everything fell into place. Liriel's dedication to the goddess of magic had been as single-minded and her ambition as great as any priestess of Lolth. She pursued the goddess's favor and sought power with a focus and fervor that would have had her grandmother, the dreaded Matron Baenre, nodding in approval. But only recently had Liriel recognized the reason driving her rapid rise in Mystra's service:

Powerful clerics could resurrect the dead.

Thorn broke the drow's reverie by swatting Sharlarra

on the shoulder. "No courtship behavior, not here," she warned her. "We eat, we leave. That was the agreement."

"Too late." The star elf tipped her golden head toward the man swaggering over to their table.

Sharlarra's would-be suitor was a large man, too young for his girth. He had the slightly melted look some big-muscled adventurers get when days of hard riding give way to long nights devoted to dice and drink. Even so, his confident smirk bespoke a comfortable opinion of himself, and his garments and gear were flamboyant in the extreme. Huge roc plumes dyed a vivid purple swept down from the brim of an indigo blue hat. His tunic and breeches encompassed the color spectrum with multiple stripes in blues, greens, yellows, and oranges—a progression that ended with the brilliant red of his dragonhide boots. He was, in short, a walking rainbow, the sort of silly fop most people dismissed with a smirk and a shrug.

Liriel took this in with a glance before her eyes went to the man's weapons. They were decorative, yes, but the sword on his hip was well maintained and the grip showed the wear of frequent use. He had other weapons, too; daggers and knives which he probably thought were cleverly hidden, including a pair of daggers tucked into his oversized boot cuffs. His coin purse was heavy, and the red riding whip tucked into his belt matched the harness on the fine black stallion waiting in the attached stable. Liriel glanced at the table he'd just left, noting the half dozen men seated there. They, unlike the walking rainbow, made no pretense of being anything but what they were: well-seasoned fighters. And hunters, too, judging from the full quivers under their seats and the longbows propped against the wall. All of them wore belts of bright red dragon hide—a livery of sorts, proclaiming their hired allegiance.

Wonderful, Liriel thought glumly. The fool could fight, and he had men to back him up.

And then he surprised her by ignoring Sharlarra and walking directly over to Thorn.

"I know what you are," he said bluntly. "You might be able to hoodwink everyone else, but I know a lythari when I see one."

Thorn shrugged. "Then you are not quite the fool you appear."

"This is a most fortuitous meeting, if not without irony," he went on, ignoring her insult. "I am hunting exotic wolf pelts for my trophy hall, and rumors of werewolves in the Gray Forest brought me to Impiltur. But none would take me into those woods, so I settled for hunting of a different sort in a dockside brothel. And here we both are."

The lythari woman looked him up and down. Her lip curled. "Are you even *allowed* to mate?"

He fell back a step, brow furrowed in puzzlement. "Allowed? Whatever are you talking about?"

Thorn shook her head in disgust and turned back to her companions. "I keep forgetting that humans don't follow pack law. Among my people, the right to breed is earned."

"Or bought?" he wheedled, holding up a large gold coin.

Thorn sniffed. "No self-respecting bitch would lift her tail for the likes of you, not for all the coins in Impiltur."

The man's pleasant expression never faltered. "Then it's back to blood sport. No matter—it's all hunting, and all the same to me. At the moment, I alone know your true nature. But at a word from me, six hunters start competing for the bounty your wolf's hide will bring them."

"A word from me," Liriel said in equally pleasant tones, "and six hunters will be hit by a fireball big enough to leave nothing but a stinking grease spot on the tavern floor."

Finally the man's façade slipped, and he cast a slyly malevolent glance in Liriel's direction. "If you cast killing magic, drow, you will never leave the city alive. But of course, you know this full well."

And so she did. Her acceptance in Impiltur was a tenuous thing, despite the valuable services she provided. Her familiarity with the deep ways made her an asset to the bands of Warswords who patrolled the tunnels under the Earthspurs. The recent discovery of a temple of Laduguer, the evil god of the duegar, raised the possibility of trade with gray dwarf settlements. Liriel's ability to speak Undercommon was in great demand among enterprising merchants. Even so, the officials of Impiltur made it clear that she would be closely scrutinized. She would be permitted to use healing spells and other beneficial clerical magic, but no "drowlike" behavior would be tolerated.

And that, Liriel noted, was a conundrum. If ever a man merited the full attention of her darker nature, it was this smirking fool.

Well, a drow had other weapons than magic and steel, and not the least of them was reputation. Drow females learned certain skills along with word-weaning: how to wrap knife-bladed sarcasm in silky words, how to project malice and evil as naturally as oil lamps cast light, how to promise death without drawing a weapon.

Liriel willed a malevolent gleam into her eyes and curved her lips into a cold, cruel smile. "You seem well versed in Impiltur law," she said in a clear, ringing voice. "You don't look like much of a hunter, but the council might hire you as a clerk or scribe."

The man's smirk faded away. "I'll have you know that these boots are a trophy."

"A red dragon. Impressive," Liriel purred. "Tell me, did you kill the roc, as well? Or did one obligingly molt a few feathers in your general direction?"

By now the tavern had grown dangerously quiet, and the wary expressions on the patrons' faces indicated that their pleasantly dark fantasies concerning Liriel had given way to even darker thoughts—stories they'd heard told of the drow.

The proprietor hurried over to the table, all but wringing his hands in dismay. "I want no trouble here."

"Who does?" Thorn replied coolly. She glanced at Liriel, taking in the slim black fingers curved around the clerical emblem. She tapped Liriel's boot with her foot. The drow responded with a thin, wicked smile. Thorn sealed their unspoken agreement with a nod and turned back to the tavern keeper.

"I paid for this meal, and I intend to finish it. After, this man and I can settle our differences outside."

The fop's smirk returned, and his sword hand closed around the hilt of his weapon. "A duel is yet another kind of hunt. Your terms are quite acceptable. I await your pleasure." He gave the lythari a mocking little bow and walked back to his table.

Sharlarra's worried gaze went from Liriel to Thorn. "You're planning something. Do I want to know what it is?"

The lythari ignored her. "How long do you need to work your spell, drow?"

"No more than a quarter bell." Liriel glanced toward the moon. The fat crescent had already begun its descent, and appeared to be in danger of impaling itself upon the mast of a large ship. That was good fortune—the ship would serve as a reference point and help her chart time's passage. Thorn didn't need such aids, but Liriel had yet to master the art of measuring time by the movement of the moon and stars.

By the time Thorn polished off the last crumb of her bread bowl and devoured a slab of very rare mutton, the moon was almost touching the ship's boom. Liriel figured this delay was due to design as well as hunger; by the time Thorn had finished feeding, the streets were nearly deserted.

Finally Thorn rose to leave. The garishly clad hunter almost beat her to the door in his eagerness.

They strode to the middle of the street, faced each

other, and drew swords. The first clash echoed down the nearly empty street. Steel hissed as the blades slid free, then sang out again in three quick, ringing notes.

The opponents circled each other, testing with short feints, quick lunges and deft parries. They were much the same height, so neither had the advantage of reach. Thorn was faster, the human was stronger. The two appeared well matched, and certainly presented a vivid contrast. Thorn had removed her sea-blue tabard to signify that this fight was not of an official nature, so there remained little color about her. Thorn preferred to dress in unrelieved black, for that was the color of her pelt in wolf form. Long black hair framed her pale face, unbound but for the single streak of white—the mark of Eilistraee's favor—woven into a thin braid.

By now most of the patrons and quite a few of the wenches were crowded around the window, watching the battle on the street beyond. Sharlarra leaned close to Liriel. "Shouldn't we go out there?"

The drow shook her head and continued her silent prayer. She was right where she needed to be—surrounded by people who expected a drow to attack by sword or spell. They would see no gesture, hear no word.

Now, if only *Mystra* would hear . . .

The warmth of the Lady's presence stole into Liriel's heart, and she knew her prayer had been answered.

A faintly glowing red mist rose from the dirty cobbles. Similar tendrils of mist wafted from the tavern and out the open window, merging with the expanding red cloud.

The murmur of wagers and jests surrounding Liriel gave way to heavy silence. She rose and pushed her way over to the window to watch the answer to her prayer unfold.

The mist began to swirl as if in agitation. Then, almost too quickly for the eye to follow, it took on an unmistakable form. The rainbow-garbed fighter fell away from the still-misty shape of a young red dragon, and he stumbled over the rough cobbles on feet that were suddenly, inexplicably bare.

In the blink of an eye, the mist disappeared. The now-solid creature shook its horned head. A shudder passed down its massive form, making it look oddly like a dog shaking off water. Its eyes focused and took in the grim street, the sleeping harbor beyond. Then it roared, and the brothel patrons dived for cover under tables. Sharlarra sensibly followed suit, leaving Liriel standing alone at the open window.

Most of the revelers heard a dragon's roar and didn't think to inquire further, but Liriel, her mind still opened to the goddess, heard something more: a keening lament for whatever celestial world the creature had been forced to forsake.

For a moment memory burned bright, and Liriel experienced anew the peace and homecoming she'd glimpsed when she had eased Fyodor's spirit into the afterlife.

Tears filled her eyes, and shame her heart. How could she consider, even for a moment, disrupting such bliss?

The resurrected dragon readjusted to life with surprising speed. Its wings snapped open, lifting it from the ground for a short, quick strike. Fanged jaws snatched up the astonished hunter. The dragon wheeled, hopped onto the roof of the low, stone warehouse across the street, and leaped into the sky. It winged off, and for a moment the outline of a dragon and its still-living prey, bare feet kicking wildly, was silhouetted against the setting moon.

The six hunters made a sudden rush for the stables. They mounted their horses and took off in pursuit, loudly promising rescue or vengeance.

Sharlarra was the next to respond. She darted out of the tavern and down a narrow alley. Liriel and Thorn fell in behind, knowing from long experience the star elf's knack for evading pursuers.

They ran until they were certain there would be no pursuit. By then the pre-dawn bustle had begun, and the streets quickly filled with wagons carrying goods to market.

Morning in any city started much the same. Chimneys coughed smoke as hearth fires kindled. The smell of baking bread wafted from a large community oven. Tavern doors began to swing open, and street vendors trundled their carts along the cobblestone. Lirel turned resignedly to Thorn, expecting that the lythari would be ready for her morning meal.

She found her friend regarding her with somber compassion. "So you *can* do it."

The emphasis was pointed, holding a meaning Liriel could not quite grasp. She made a circular gesture with one hand, inviting further comment.

"Resurrection is a powerful spell, but it always seemed pointless to me. A sentient being restored to life is likely to seek justice by killing his murderer, who is avenged in turn. Death follows death, and so the cycle continues."

"If resurrected people truly wanted to seek justice," Liriel said softly, "they would leave their killers alone and slay instead the people who brought them back."

The lythari nodded. "That is not quite what I meant, but it is truth nonetheless."

Sharlarra, who had been listening to this exchange with uncharacteristic gravity, let out a soft murmur of enlightenment.

"So I guess you got the answer to your prayer," she observed. "And I'm not talking about resurrecting a dragon using dragonhide boots as the required body part. I love the way you think, by the way."

Liriel sent her a quizzical look. "So what *are* you talking about?"

"It might take me a while to figure out what's going on, but I catch up eventually. We won't be going to Rashemen to visit the resting place of a certain warrior any time soon."

"No." The drow's tone did not invite further discussion.

Sharlarra smile held both sympathy and admiration. "I try to avoid religion whenever possible, but it seems to me most people pray for things to happen without stopping to consider whether or not they *should* happen. Mystra knew what was in your heart, and answered both questions at once."

"Another truth," Thorn observed, sounding slightly surprised. "Have you any other wisdom to impart?"

The star elf responded with a wink and a smile. "Of course, but you might not see it as such. I think we should leave the city for a few days to do some hunting. I could use a good run, and besides, the taverns here overcook their meat something dreadful."

Thorn responded to the teasing with a derisive sniff, but her eyes brightened at the prospect. "You couldn't run down a sleeping rabbit."

A smile stole across Liriel's face as she listened to her friends' familiar banter. Theirs was a strange sisterhood, perhaps, but it eased the sadness that never quite seemed to go away.

As they walked, Liriel pondered what Sharlarra had said. What if the star elf's whimsical words held truth? What if the gods listened to unspoken prayers? Did they care to know what was hidden in the hearts of their followers? *Could* they know?

Improbable as it sounded, it would seem so. The life Liriel had known over the past ten years was beyond anything an Underdark drow could have imagined. How could she have prayed for friendship and love, when she understood neither? Perhaps Mystra knew what she most desired, and started to answer these prayers before they took form.

Liriel was profoundly grateful for this, but the thought

also left her uneasy. There was much darkness in her soul, and prayers that were best left unspoken and unanswered.

"Lady of Mystery," she whispered, "I will love you as well and serve you as faithfully as any priestess alive. In return, I only ask that you never forget, even for a moment, that I am a drow."

FIC
CUN

Cunningham,
Elaine,
1957-

The best of the
realms.

$7.99

70437

DATE	BORROWER'S NAME	

WHITE PLAINS HIGH SCHOOL
MEDIA CENTER

BAKER & TAYLOR